ABOUT TANIA JOYCE

Tania Joyce is an author of contemporary and new adult romance novels. Her stories thread romance, drama and passion into beautiful locations ranging from the dazzling lights and glitter of New York, to the rural countryside of the Hunter Valley.

She's widely traveled, has a diverse background in the corporate world and has a love for sparkles, shoes and shiraz.

Tania draws on her real-life experiences and combines them with her *very* vivid imagination to form the foundation of her novels. She likes to write about strong-minded, career-oriented heroes and heroines that go through drama-filled hell, have steamy encounters and risk everything as they endeavor to find their happily-ever-after.

Tania shuffles the hours in her day between work, family life and writing. One day she hopes to find balance!

Visit www.taniajoyce.com

I0593615

SCARRED STRINGS

The Flintlocks Rockstar Romance Series - Book 1
by
Tania Joyce

SCARRED STRINGS by Tania Joyce
Published by Gatwick Enterprises 2022
Brisbane, Australia.

Copyright © Tania Joyce 2022
All content and lyrics original works by Tania Joyce
The moral right of the author has been asserted.

All rights reserved. This publication (or any part of it) may not be reproduced or transmitted, copied, stored, distributed or otherwise made available by any person or entity (including Google, Amazon or similar organizations), in any form (electronic, digital, optical, mechanical) or by any means (photocopying, recording, scanning or otherwise) without prior written permission from the publisher.

SCARRED STRINGS
The Flintlocks Rockstar Romance Series – Book 1
EPUB format: ISBN: 978-0-6489905-6-7
Kindle format: ISBN: 978-0-6489905-5-0
Paperback: ISBN: 978-0-6489905-7-4

Cover Photography by: Eric McKinney / 6:12 Photography
Model: Santiago S.
Edited by: Creating Ink

For more information on the author please visit: www.taniajoyce.com

Keywords and Subjects
New adult romance, young adult romance, contemporary romance, rockstar romance, rock star romance, fake relationship, enemies to lovers romance, celebrity romance, Hollywood romance, movie star romance, rocker, band, musician, music romance.

This is a work of fiction. Names, characters, businesses, places, events and incidents are either the products of the author's imagination or used in a fictitious manner. Any resemblance to actual persons, living or dead, or actual events is purely coincidental.

A broken heart can heal with time and love.

Chapter 1

FLINT

It had been 104 days, nine hours, and fifty-five excruciating minutes since my brother died. His death was still raw—it was like it had happened yesterday. Just like the clock ticking on the wall, the pain in my shoulder and the seat belt burn mark slicing across my chest were constant reminders. *Every. Fucking. Second.*

I'd survived. But why?

I put my feet on my manager's desk in his home office. I crossed my ankles and leaned back in the leather chair. The inside of my head pounded like a booming bass drum stuck on a looping four-to-the-floor beat. The gentle rock and sway on the seat threatened to bring the nausea pooling in my gut into my throat. Downing a bottle of vodka last night had been self-inflicted stupidity. But it was the only thing that had numbed the ache and emptiness inside my chest. It had helped me to forget my pain. *Temporarily.* If waking on my sofa, cuddling an empty bottle of vodka against my ribcage was rock bottom . . . I was there.

I stole a cigarette out of the packet by Blake's laptop, put it between my lips, and lit it. I closed my eyes and inhaled deeply. The end of the cigarette sizzled and singed as I sucked. Smoke filled my lungs. The nicotine spun my head. The buzz curled through my veins. Then, I coughed. Spluttered. Gagged.

Ew! Yuck.

Smoking is disgusting. I may be fucked up . . . but I'm not that bad.

Sitting upright, I stubbed out the cigarette in the bin underneath the desk and discarded the butt. I hated smoking. I just needed something to distract my mind, occupy my hands, and stop myself from lifting another drink to my lips at eleven o'clock on a Wednesday morning.

I resumed my position, leaning back on the chair. Putting my boots up on the desk, I stared out the condo window at Downtown LA. Traffic blocked the streets. People dashed along the sidewalk. Everyone was living their lives. Why couldn't I?

I'm dead inside. Why didn't I die with my brother?

The black door to the office swung open and in walked my band and Blake, their faces grim and drawn.

"Where've you been?" I didn't move from Blake's chair. "You're late. Your housekeeper had to let me in."

"Flint Glover. Nice to see you too." Blake rested his butt on the corner of the desk. His Texan accent was strong and drawn out, reminding me of Matthew McConaughey's. "I've been talking to the guys for the past hour upstairs on the pool deck."

Without me? That wasn't a good sign.

"Thanks for meeting me at home," Blake said. "Sorry, the renos at work are taking longer than expected."

"S'okay," I mumbled, swiveling slowly on the chair.

Blake Poulton was one of the nice guys in the music business. He'd worked with my band—The Flintlocks—for six years, taking us from high school garage-based wannabes to on-the-charts musicians. We were nowhere near a *huge* household name but we were successful. We'd been planning to tour and write our third album when tragedy struck.

Everything had gone to shit . . . and by everything, I meant me.

"Flint, you look like crap." Cole Tanner, my drummer, flopped onto one of the steel-framed chairs in front of Blake's desk. "When did you last shower?"

I swiped my hand over my stubble . . . no . . . my scruffy beard. "Don't know. Two . . . maybe three days ago."

Slip—Sebastian Lipfield—our lead guitarist, pulled up another chair. "Dude, this has to stop. Now."

"Stop what?" I sniffed my freshly laundered T-shirt. *All good.* I'd put on deodorant to come out. I wasn't that feral.

"Consider this an intervention." Blake's deep voice pinned me to my seat.

A what? I stopped rocking and stared at Blake. "I don't need a fucking intervention."

"Yeah. You do." Blake moved a pile of folders on the desk and turned more toward me. "We know you've been struggling, but we have new pressing issues. Yesterday, I was called to a meeting at WestTyme Records. Your label has been considerate, accommodating, and compassionate about your loss. But they can't sell records for a band that isn't being talked about or being seen. They think you've given up on your music. So . . . they've given you a deadline. You have four months to get your shit together. You need to write your new album and hit the studio by the end of September, or they will release you from your contract."

I grimaced. Panic seized my heart. My temples throbbed with a constant pounding that resembled a Def Leppard concert. *This can't be happening. I can't lose our contract. I need more time.*

"Come on, Flint." Slip rested his elbows on his knees.

His long, wavy blond hair fell forward over his shoulders in straggly strands like he'd just been surfing. *Probably had.* His brown eyes pleaded. "Phil would want this. He'd want us to find someone new and continue to play."

Ice shot through my veins. "No one can replace Phil. He was my fucking brother."

"And he was our friend." Cole splayed his hand across his heart. His shaky tone carried as much anguish as I did in the marrow of my bones. "We came 'round yesterday, but you didn't answer. We wanted to spend the day with you. It was Phil's birthday, man. What happened? Were you up in the mountains again? Or just writing yourself off?"

"The latter," I muttered.

Cole ruffled his fingers through his short brown hair. Even after months of our band being on hold, he was toned as an elite athlete. No letting loose, eating and drinking whatever he liked in his downtime. He could grace the cover of men's health magazines . . . or model. *Fitness freak.*

His green eyes darkened. "Flint, this is serious. This is our career we're talking about. We want to make new music. We need to move on."

My vision blurred. How could I face music without Phil? He'd been the zing in our zany rock songs. The one full of life and laughs. I clenched my fists and dug my fingernails into my palms. I missed the feel of a guitar in my hands, but I hadn't been able to play one or sing a tune since the accident. My love of music had been killed in the car with Phil. "I'm not ready."

"Well. Find a way, bud." Blake crossed his arms. "There is no time limit on grief, but life has to go on. *You* have to move on. That's why we're here. You need to clean yourself up. Get sober. Stop popping pills or whatever shit you're doing to destroy yourself. Find a reason to live again."

Tears pricked the back of my eyes, but none would fall. I

was all cried out. "How the fuck am I supposed to do that?"

Cole stroked the tip of his chin. A smug smirk twisted the corner of his lips.

I wanted to wipe it off Cole's face with my fist.

He chuckled. "You're not gonna like the plan Blake's come up with. But we're supporting the idea."

I glared at Cole, then Slip, then Blake. I already didn't like whatever bullshit they'd come up with. "What idea?"

"I had lunch with a friend the other day and mentioned you, purely out of concern." Blake folded his hands on his lap. His tone deepened with an edge of warning. "You're not an addict—just fucked up over your loss. I get that. But keep up this behavior and you'll end up in rehab."

"Never." I wasn't that bad. Was I?

"Since you refuse to attend therapy, the two of us came up with an alternate solution that might appeal to you." Blake's gaze hardened. "One way I think that will help you move forward is to get out of your damn house and attend a few events and functions. You don't have to perform. But . . . go out. Be seen. Be part of the action. Being around other artists and people in the industry might help reignite your spark. Being in front of fans won't hurt either."

Shit. I lowered my chin and my long black bangs flopped forward, brushing against the tip of my nose. I'd barely left my house or Cole's parents' cabin up near Big Bear since the accident at the beginning of February. I'd avoided the city. Everywhere in LA reminded me of Phil. I slumped in my chair. "How can I go out when I feel like death?"

Seriousness threaded through Blake's blue eyes. "This friend I mentioned is a talent agent. Harlow represents some medium-to-high-profile movie and TV personalities. He has a new client that wants to—" He rolled his hand through the air. "How do I put it so I can be politically correct?"

"Blake?" A sly smile slid across Slip's lips. "You don't need to watch what you say around us."

"Okay. Good." He chuckled and relaxed his shoulders. "He has a young lady who needs re-imaging and rebranding. After years of being typecast as an American sweetheart, she wants to shed that skin and *spice up* her image for more mature roles. Her current TV contract ends soon. Harlow is confident that pairing you two together at key events will attract a certain amount of attention."

The breath rushed from my lungs. "You want me to *what?*" I couldn't believe my ears. "Fake date some chick?"

"Don't think of it as a fake date. Think of it as an insurance policy against your career," Blake said. "She needs media attention to secure the auditions she's after. *You* need to show the record execs you're toning down your behavior, sobering, and taking the necessary steps to get back in the game."

But I wasn't ready to go out, let alone date. It had taken every ounce of my strength to leave the house this morning. I rubbed my dry eyes with my fingertips. "I don't need you to set me up. I won't play your stupid games."

"It's not a game," Blake said. "It's business."

"Come on, Flint." Slip flicked his hand at me. "You need to face the world again. Do what you're good at. Thrive on some hype. You've got the looks of a badass rocker. You've got the reputation of being one, even though only a quarter of what's been printed about us is true. You turn heads walking down any street."

I grimaced. "Is that a compliment?"

"Duh! Yes." Cole grunted. "On top of your talent, it's why you're our front man. You're walking publicity, and right now, we need all the publicity we can get."

I puffed air through my nose. Not all of our media coverage had been positive, but even the bad stuff hadn't hurt our popularity. "So what are you suggesting exactly? That I become this chick's escort?"

"No . . . yes . . . shit, no." Blake grabbed one of his cigarettes. Lit it. Took a drag, then blew out a cloud of smoke. "This isn't for money. Think of it as a reciprocal benefit. You'll be helping each other out. It's fresh, edgy publicity for her. Therapy for you."

"I don't need fucking therapy." I didn't need a fucking therapist to tell me I missed my brother. I shot forward in the chair; my feet hit the floor with a *thud*. I swiveled to face them. Anger laced my voice. "I'm not ready to go out."

"Flint." Slip held his palms wide. "We need you to try something, anything, to come back to us. We know you're lost. And hurt. We've talked, drunk a shit load of booze, cried a ton of tears, but man, we need you to pick up that fucking guitar and write new tunes. We need to record an album and play in front of crowds again. We don't want to lose our contract. We've worked too goddamn hard to get where we are. Don't throw what we've achieved away."

My heart stumbled over itself, but I was quick to regain composure. "I won't be a pawn in some chick's fame game."

"That's not what this is about." Cole rubbed his hands down his thighs. "Don't you want to play again? Tour? We want to get bigger and better, not fold and disappear from the airwaves forever."

Cole had always kept our band focused on the music. He was the one who kept us grounded.

I'd grown up with Cole and Slip on the same suburban street in Pasadena. We may have gone to different schools—Slip and I had slummed it in public while Cole went to a privileged private—but our love of music had bought us together.

Cole's tone turned tenacious. "Flint, please? Go to a few events with this girl. Find your love of music again."

I closed my eyes. I couldn't deny I missed music and singing and performing. I missed my friends. And my family. Sucking in a shaky breath, the air burned my lungs. I'd lost too much. Now I was looking down the barrel of losing my best friends, my band. They were all I had left.

"You have three options, Flint." Blake flicked his cigarette ash into an empty pencil canister on his desk.

So that's the ashtray.

"Option one is to go to a few functions with this young gal and hopefully find your way back to music. Option two is to lose your record deal, fold the band. Option three is to stay on this destructive path that will lead you to rehab or potentially kill you. And that would be a fucking waste. You're talented. So snap the fuck out of it." He stubbed out the remains of his cigarette. "You have four months, Flint. Four months to sort your shit out. Do you want to stay in this hell and fuck up your future? Do you want to disappoint millions of fans? Piss off your label?" His tone was sharp but blunt and to the point. Blake never sugarcoated anything. That was why we got on so well. "What's it gonna be?"

The solemn shade of gray on Slip's face, and the tears looming in Cole's eyes, punched my heart. Their desperate concern had been the first thing in months to penetrate the icy vastness inside my chest. Since childhood, these guys had always been there for me. I couldn't let them down. I had to do this, if only for them.

Fuck. I scratched at my long, itchy stubble. I couldn't believe I was contemplating this. "Who's the chick?"

"Sutton Summers."

"Who?" I searched my brain. I didn't know the name.

"Sutton Summers." Blake picked up a tin of mints, popped it open, and tossed one in his mouth. "She's the lead on that show, *Take Two in Brentwood.* It's a bit like a female version of *Bel-Air,* only she's a sweet country girl from Nebraska."

Nope. I still drew a blank. "Don't know her. Never seen the show."

Cole pulled out his cell phone from the side pocket of his cargo shorts and tapped the screen. He turned the phone and showed me a picture. "This is her."

Leaning closer, I squinted, zoning in on the picture. Sutton posed in front of a sponsor board for some hospital fundraising event. At least she was attractive, in a cute, innocent, Carrie Underwood kind of way. But with her perfectly styled blonde hair, fake eyelashes, glamorous makeup, and designer gear, she had *high-maintenance* written all over her. "What the hell? She looks sixteen."

"Nope. She's twenty-three." Cole slipped his phone back into his shorts.

I buried my face in my hands, then raked my fingers through my thick hair. "You guys really want me to do this?" Had I really left them no choice? Was I that much of a screw-up?

Obviously yes.

Slip slumped back in his chair as if exhausted and out of options. "Yeah. We do. We care about you, man."

Could I do this?

I hadn't been on a date in years. The last time I'd dated was Lena, my girlfriend of close to two years. She hadn't handled my band's increasing popularity. Fame and gossip had created cracks in our relationship, but her move to Atlanta for her career had torn us apart. I'd been happy for her, supported her decision, and wanted her to be a success and follow her dreams. But that didn't mean it didn't break my fucking heart when she left.

Sutton wasn't my girlfriend. And she wasn't afraid of the limelight.

Well . . . she'd better not be.

And she'd better have thick skin.

The paparazzi were always hungry for gossip in this town. If I went out with her, I couldn't guarantee all the news about us would be good. Based on previous experience.

I massaged the throb in my temples. *Damn it.* Was this the way forward? Dating some chick I didn't know? "How long do I have to do this for?"

"Three, maybe four months tops."

"All summer?"

"Yep. That's enough time for her to raise her profile and enough time for you to clean up your act." Blake picked up the stapler off his desk and rolled it around in his hands. "The Hollywood Stars TV Awards are on next Saturday night. I can arrange for you to go with her. What do you say?"

"What? They're big awards. I can't rock up to a huge event with someone I don't know. Can I meet her beforehand?" *What was I doing?* "If I fucking hate her, which is highly likely, I'm not gonna go through with it."

"Fine." Blake put down the stapler, grabbed his cell phone, and scrolled through his calendar. "Harlow and I are going out to dinner this Friday night. We can arrange to meet and introduce you to each other at a nearby bar beforehand. How's that sound?"

"This is bullshit." Eyeing the three of them, I didn't know whether to laugh or cry. "You know that, right?"

Cole fidgeted with his signet ring. "Flint, we need you to try something new."

I lowered my chin. As I sucked in a deep breath, a shudder rippled through my ribs. I didn't want to end up more of a wreck. Seeing my best friends sitting across from me at their wits' end was one helluva wake-up call. I didn't need another.

I'd do anything for these guys.

I wanted to stop feeling like the hole in my chest would never heal.

I'd tried running. Meditation. Fixing a rock wall at the cabin. Drinking. But nothing had broken the chains that held me down. There was no way I would end up in rehab. No way I'd lose our contract. So that left me with only one option.

Blake waved his cell phone. "So, can I call Harlow with the news?"

Cole's leg jiggled. Slip gnawed on his lower lip. Their eyes begged me.

Shit.

Shaking my head, I let out a slow breath, then flicked my long hair out of my eyes.

What do you get if you cross a fuckup rock star and an over-ambitious American sweetheart?

Fuck knows! But I was sure it wouldn't be pretty.

"Guys, I'm sorry I've let you down. You're my brothers. I don't want to be a screwup anymore." If I had to haul my ass out of the gutter, I may as well try to have some fun in the process. I missed laughing and music and partying. "You two know me better than anyone. Do you think I can do this?"

Cole nodded. "We wouldn't have agreed to Blake's plan otherwise."

A sweet girl. A couple of events. A few smiles for the cameras. *Easy, right?*

How that was supposed to reignite my spark for music was beyond me. But I trusted these guys. I was in no fit mental state to argue.

Could I pull this off?

I had to. For my band.

I jabbed my finger at them. "I'm doing this for you and our music. I make no promises. But fine . . . I'll give it a shot. I'll fake date the shit out of this chick." I turned to Blake. "Call Harlow. I'm in. Make Friday happen."

Chapter 2

SUTTON

Raising my vodka martini to my lips, my hand shook. I took a dainty sip. The dash of lemon tingled on my tongue. But the drink wasn't strong enough to settle the nerves twisting and tumbling in my stomach. What Harlow, my agent, had proposed—fake dating some rock star for publicity—was ludicrous, but I needed something radical. I shouldn't have to go to these extremes to give my career a shake. But . . . this was Hollywood.

I swiveled on the bar stool and glanced around the overcrowded popular-for-celebrity-spotting Hollywood bar full of fellow actors, studio crew and friends having Friday after-work drinks. I couldn't see anyone who resembled Flint.

Why the hell had I agreed to do this?

"He'll be here." Harlow leaned against the counter and chuckled over the rim of his beer. "Blake assured me he'd get Flint here, even if he had to drag him."

I smoothed my hand over my pale pink cocktail dress, making sure the hemline across both legs was even. Why was I nervous? I'd met hundreds of guys. But after googling Flint for background information, my doubts flashed red. Most of the articles on him were old news. Months old. All were tales of wild parties, drunken escapades, and hot onstage performances that led to girls, girls, and more girls. But then, three months ago, he'd disappeared after the death of his brother. *Totally understandable.*

But was this a huge mistake? Me? Dating a rock star? This could ruin my career, not turn it around. "Why did you pick this guy again?"

"For attention, sweetheart." Harlow raised his voice so I could hear him over the loud music. "This guy turns heads. And supposedly, he's a talent not to be wasted and needs some ass kicking."

Oh God. What am I in for? I don't want to play nanny.

"Do I look okay?" Glancing into the mirror behind the bar, I checked my straightened blonde hair, my fine fake lashes, and flawless makeup. I was no supermodel, but I scrubbed up okay. I was just average. Average in height. Average in looks. Slim, but not skinny. For that reason, would Flint, who probably dated stunners and A-list stars, take one look at me, laugh, and bolt for the hills?

I took another mouthful of my drink—a big one this time.

Harlow grinned, showing off his perfectly straight, perfectly white teeth. With his dimpled cheeks and kind eyes, he could be mistaken for *Black Panther*'s Michael B. Jordan. "Little lady, you're the most angelic of angels. But here's to changing that. Trust me. I've gone through this process of re-imaging with several clients. This will work."

I gave him a thin smile. I didn't trust anyone in this town. Being betrayed by those closest to me, by those who should've loved me, protected me, and had my best interests at heart had left a bitter taste in my mouth. At twenty-three, I wasn't a naïve childhood star who had been taken advantage of anymore.

God help anyone who stood in my way.

I'd taken a chance on signing with Harlow. He had a reputation for turning careers around. That was what I needed. But his bold plan had me breaking out in hives. I'd done nothing like this before. "This better work, Harlow. My reputation is on the line."

"So is mine." The confidence gleaming in his eyes didn't falter as he sipped his beer.

I peered at my watch. 7:34p.m. Flint was more than thirty minutes late. I hated people not being on time. Time was money in this town, and I didn't have much of either. "This Flint guy better not stand me up."

Booming music drummed through the sound system. People bustled and moved around and behind me. They hugged their friends and returned to the bar again and again for drinks. The chatter elevated as more partygoers rocked into the venue.

Still no sign of Flint.

This was ridiculous. He wasn't coming. What a waste of time.

I'm out of here.

I grabbed my purse and turned on my stool to leave. But a sturdy man in a light gray suit broke through the crowd. He held his arms wide and beelined for Harlow. "We made it."

Harlow laughed and hugged him. "Blake. Finally."

"Sorry we're late." He thumbed behind him. "I had to drag this one out of bed . . . literally."

My breath hitched. *Oh, wow. Flint.* I straightened, drawing my shoulders back.

He was taller than I'd expected, easily six foot. With messy hair as black as midnight, short in the back but with long bangs that brushed against the tip of his nose, he had the most electric ice-blue eyes I'd ever seen. Dressed in black jeans and a slim-fit button-down shirt that stretched tight across his toned chest, he was much better-looking in real life than he'd seemed in the pictures on the Internet.

Holy smokin' cowboys . . . no . . . rock stars.

My heart drummed an erratic beat. Fever flushed my skin and between my legs clenched. *Steady there, girl.* Normally, I didn't care for facial hair, but all I wanted to do was run my fingers through Flint's short scruff to see how soft it was.

He half grinned . . . or was that a sneer?

Swaying on his feet, he swept his hair back to reveal finely chiseled cheekbones, then held out his hand. "Hey. I'm Flint."

Manners. Nice.

"Hi. I'm Sutton." I slipped my hand into his. His shake was firm, his skin soft. But when he didn't let go, my insides skipped like a kid in kindergarten.

"Sorry for being late." He released my hand, then tucked his into the back pockets of his jeans. "I lost track of time."

I arched an eyebrow. "Sleeping?"

"Something like that."

His gaze ran over me from head to toe. Heat crept up my neck and settled in my cheeks. The gentle strum of my pulse picked up in pace.

But I was quick to slam on the brakes.

Flint's expression remained carved in stone, sculpted and hard as Mt. Rushmore. There was no sexy glint in his eyes. No flirtatious lift of his chin or arch of his eyebrows. No Joey Tribbiani *how-you-doing* grin.

Fine. He wasn't into me. I wasn't surprised. Girls like me didn't get guys like Flint.

Refusing to deflate like a beach ball, I sat taller in my chair. Attraction had nothing to do with our plan. In fact, would a lack of it make this easier? Less complicated?

"Flint, nice to meet you." Harlow shook Flint's hand. "I'm glad you're here to meet Sutton and discuss the plan Blake and

I have devised. After tonight, if you agree to proceed, we'll line up a string of events and functions for you to attend. If not, we'll find someone else to meet our needs."

"He better fucking agree, or I'll toast his balls." Blake clutched and shook Flint's shoulder. Fair warning hovered in his tone.

"Yeah. Whatever." Flint's voice remained flat.

Damn. Where did Harlow find this guy? I wanted this gig to be fun. Flint was supposed to be a party animal, a rock god, the charismatic crowd pleaser. At this point in time, dating roadkill would be a livelier option.

Harlow downed the last mouthful of his beer, then placed the empty glass on the counter. "Blake and I will leave you two alone, so you can get to know each other."

Flint's frosty gaze melted, transforming into shimmering pools sparkling with mischief behind his curtain of black hair. "We'll be fine, won't we, Sutton?"

Okay. Wow. The way my name rumbled deep in his throat? *Super. Freaking. Sexy.* The wickedness in his gaze? *Hot.* Where had that come from?

Maybe he should stay as lifeless as a dead animal. I didn't need to do something stupid and fall for this guy, his moves, or pickup lines. I'd been burned enough. And this guy had *heartbreaker* written all over him. "Yes. We'll be fine."

"Have fun." Harlow kissed me on the cheek. "I'll call you tomorrow to see how things go."

"Okay. Bye. It was nice to meet you, Blake." I waved them farewell, then clutched my purse against my stomach to settle the jittery butterflies. Flint better not be a creep.

"All right, then." Flint shuffled toward the bar. Some drunken partygoer behind him fell backward, knocking Flint against my side.

Ow! But hit with a blast of hot air, I sucked in a deep breath.

His chest pressed against my arm. His citrusy cologne, with a hint of orange and something similar to the cinnamon slice my mom used to make, filled my senses. Closing my eyes, I tingled all over, but the ache in my heart strobed low and deep.

I missed my mom. *Every. Single. Day.*

"You all right?" His tone lacked any genuine concern for my wellbeing. "Shall we get this shit over with?"

"Yes." I rubbed my arm; it didn't hurt. Not even a scratch. Blinking several times, I found my composure. "That's why we're here."

He leaned against the counter and flicked his finger toward my martini glass. "What are you drinking?"

"A vodka martini with a twist of lemon, a dash of orange bitters, and three olives, please. Stirred, not shaken."

He puffed air through his nose. "Yeah . . . Not gonna happen." He waved down the bartender. "Can I grab a bottle of Grey Goose Vodka and two shot glasses, please?"

My mouth fell open. Did he just ignore my request? "Excuse me, but didn't you just offer to buy me a drink? Isn't it a bit early in the night for shots?"

"It's never too early for shots." He flicked a finger at my empty glass. "You don't need all that fancy shit. It's mainly vodka, anyway. Straight is best. Try it. You might be surprised."

He grabbed the bottle and the glasses and pointed toward a spare round booth on the other side of the venue. "Shall we?"

"Sure." The sooner this was over, the better. I jumped off the stool, followed him to the table, and slipped into the black leather seat beside him.

He poured the shots and slid one in front of me. Picking up his glass, he huffed, half grinned, and shook his head. "Here's to being setup."

He knocked back his drink.

Okay. I can do this. I picked up my glass. I took a deep breath, held it, then downed the shot.

Whoa! Straight vodka!

I coughed. Spluttered. Thumped my chest. My throat burned. My lungs ignited. But . . . the cold vodka tasted good.

"You okay?" His lips curled as he tried not to laugh.

"Uh-huh." Licking the fire from my burning lips, I placed my glass on a coaster. If someone lit a match, I'd combust. "Flint, if you don't want to go through with this plan, I'll find someone else."

"I'm here, aren't I?" He poured and downed another shot.

"Your manager assured my agent you're a decent guy. But my first impression is you're a train wreck. If getting drunk all the time is normal, this is over before we even start."

"No. It's not normal." Staring at the bottle, he let out a slow breath. Sadness darkened his eyes. "It's been a rough week. So before I head out with my friends after this, I'm gonna have a few shots. Don't stress. I won't down the entire bottle."

I arched my eyebrow, not convinced he wouldn't give it a crack.

He slumped back against the seat. "Sutton, I'm fucked up from here to Sunday in more ways than you could ever imagine. But I need to get my shit together. That's why I'm here." He poured fresh shots. "After tonight, that is."

I eyed the vodka. I wasn't sure how many more I could have of them before I'd fall to the floor. I wasn't a big drinker. One martini often lasted me more than an hour.

He swiveled toward me. Concern dug deep grooves into his brow. "Why the hell do you want to do this? With me? You're"— he waved his hand up and down at me—"attractive enough in that sweet, innocent, good-girl way. I'm sure thousands of guys would jump at the opportunity to be seen with you."

The intensity in his eyes, drilling into me, threatened to blow my act of self-assurance and poise. Everything about his overpowering presence and his stunning good looks intimidated me. I'd never been around musicians before, especially ones with wild reputations.

"I don't want just *anyone.*" Thankfully, the vodka had doused some of my nerves. "This is business. Harlow and I had set a criteria; we need someone who has experience in the spotlight, has a certain look and reputation. Is single. And *I* wanted someone who could do the job without becoming romantically involved. I'm not interested in dating. I'm focused on my career. Nothing else."

The corner of his mouth quirked. "If you're just after attention, why don't you go to some clubs and parties, get rotten drunk, and be photographed by TMZ like every other person our age in this business has done? That's bound to attract headlines."

TMZ was still an option. But I wanted to make the right choices. Smart choices. Even this plan could backfire if not executed correctly. "Trust me. I've considered many options to stop being typecast as a teenage prim-and-proper princess. But becoming a drunken mess isn't the right approach. To attract the attention of directors, producers, and casting agents, and land a more serious role, I need to project an element of maturity and show the world I've grown up."

He grunted. "Then I think you picked the wrong guy."

He certainly wasn't helping me to change that opinion.

He'd better improve, or I was out of there.

"Harlow thinks otherwise." I downed a shot and threw him a challenging glare. "So if you need this as much as I do, cut the crap and convince me why you're the right man for the job."

Chapter 3

SUTTON

For this publicity stunt to work, Flint needed to shape up or ship out. I wasn't looking for idle gossip. The sooner he understood that, the better. Harlow had chosen him for more reasons than his good looks, so we had to understand each other and set the ground rules. And *oh boy,* did I need them. I needed to get my hot rushes under control. Everything about his sexy hair, kissable lips, and gorgeous eyes made me want to do wicked things I'd never contemplated before. More than half the bar—the guys and the girls—were giving Flint that *how-about-it* look. But his inquisitive gaze remained on me, quickening my heartbeat. We needed those rules in place, and quick. "Flint, you need to tone down your image, whereas I need you to sex mine up a little, right?"

His eyes glinted in the flashing lights. He leaned in and lowered his voice. "I can definitely sex you up if you want?"

An inferno ignited in my cheeks. My gaze ran up his toned arms, across the arch of his chest, and over his face, settling on his lips. What would sex with someone that hot be like? Wild and ravenous? Fast and mind-blowing? Wicked and toe-curling?

Wait. Nope. Don't go there. "No. That's not what this is about."

He sank back into the soft seat. Propping his elbow on the table, he rested his head against his palm. "You don't need me or any other guy to help you get what you want."

"That may be true in most industries but not in Hollywood. This place is as shallow as Hal. I have played a princess or an American sweetheart on TV since I was six. That's all casting agents see. I need to change that."

His brow furrowed. "What's wrong with being a sweetheart?"

"Nothing, but it's time to expand my horizons." I was over playing a high school kid. "I want to break into new genres, take on more challenging roles, and be adventurous. To do that, I need to change. But I don't want to ruin my career in the process."

He cocked an eyebrow as he rubbed his fingertips across his scruffy chin. "So, you're aiming for naughty, but nice?"

"Yes." I giggled. I liked that take on what I wanted to achieve. It fit perfectly. But as I twisted my shot glass around on the table, doubt spiraled through my gut. "Flint, this is a crazy plan, but it has to work. I'm not an A-list actress. I'm on an average show with a just-above-average paygrade. As a single person, I don't get noticed. I'm not aiming for blockbuster roles, but if they come my way, great. But to land decent auditions or score closed casting calls, I need to be in the forefront of everyone's mind." With brutal honesty, I laid it all on the table. "Being seen with someone like you, a hot, sexy guy with a somewhat bad reputation on my arm, will raise eyebrows. The good girl dating the badass rock star is a shock factor guaranteed to attract attention. When a director, casting agent or producer sees my name in the headlines, they'll take notice."

A playful smile curled across his lips. "You think I'm hot and sexy?"

Oh, hell yeah. Was I salivating? But I kept myself in check and rolled my eyes instead. "You're very good looking. I'm sure you know that. But you can keep your pants on. You're not my type. Give me a pro athlete any day. I love my baseballers." *Like my ex.* But that relationship had died a slow, heartbreaking, painful death. Deep down, I didn't know what my type was anymore. But I was adamant it wouldn't be some arrogant, cocky rock star who oozed too much sex appeal.

"Really? A baseballer?" He edged closer. He hooked his arm behind me and rested it on the back of the seat. Our knees brushed together. Our thighs touched. Shocks of electricity zipped up and down my leg. Dipping his head, he loomed before me, pinning me to my seat with his icy-blue gaze. "Are you sure about that?"

My heartbeat quickened, fluttering against my ribs. His deep voice did strange things to my insides. Warmth hit my girly parts, which hadn't had any attention in more than eight months. He leaned even closer. Twisting, I leaned away from him just so I could breathe. "What are you doing?"

He jerked his head toward a few girls drinking at a nearby table, staring at us. "Attracting attention."

"Oh . . . right."

I could do this. Be near him. This was a test to see if we could pull off this charade. *Come on, Sutton. Act. You can flirt.* Lowering my gaze, I took a deep breath to steady myself, then looked up at him and pasted on my sweetest smile. "Yes. I'm absolutely sure."

"Nice try." He brushed the tip of my nose with this fingertip. "I'm still not buying your reason for doing this. There's got to be more to it."

I fidgeted and fumbled with a coaster. My B-grade celebrity

status had bombed into a solid C. My friends had moved on to more popular shows. I was a *has-been* . . . and close to financial ruin thanks to those I'd trusted. I'd been screwed over one too many times in this industry. For the first time, after lengthy court battles and cases, I was free and determined to make it in this business on my own. I was done with people running my life, telling me how to act and who to be. Engaging Harlow had been my choice, my decision. His expertise and innovative approach scared me and would push me out of my comfort zone. But I needed to do this . . . for me. If this didn't work, I could lose everything. My condo. My reputation. My career.

I met Flint's questioning gaze and set assurance in my tone. "My show wraps at the end of summer. That gives me just over three months to find a new job."

I'd asked the impossible of Harlow. Castings for shows or movies could take three to six months, if not longer. But I couldn't afford to be out of work. Not having an income terrified me. Working in this industry and keeping up appearances cost money . . . Dresses, accommodation, travel, maintaining hair, nails, and makeup cost a small fortune. I couldn't survive on residuals alone. A new role would give me the security I needed, and I'd move anywhere across the country for the part. "With many new shows filmed interstate, it is highly likely I'll have to move. That's why I don't want to risk becoming involved with anyone. This is a short-term gig. The less we get messed up in each other's lives, the better." I didn't need more heartbreak caused by long-distance.

"Too fucking right."

"So, why should I put my reputation on the line and take a chance on you? Is there more to your side of the story?" I softened my tone. "We've signed confidentiality agreements; you can tell me anything. Harlow told me you could lose your record deal. Is that right?

"Yep." Staring at his shot glass, he slid it back and forth on the table.

I hesitated for a moment. "Has this got something to do with the loss of your brother? That must have been hard for you."

"Yeah. It sucks." He stilled his glass. His shoulders sank two inches like his spine had lost its ability to hold him upright. "I haven't been able to play since Phil died."

The pain in his voice slammed against my ribs.

"I can't write songs. Most days, I wish I'd died in that car accident with him. But despite everything that has happened, and how shitty and lost and empty I feel, I love my band." The smallest spark flared in the depths of his eyes, but it disappeared in a blink. "Cole and Slip mean the world to me. I don't want to be dropped by our label. They want us to hit the studio in September. Somehow, I need to get back on track. Although I don't feel it in my heart and just breathing hurts without Phil around, I'm doing this for them. I need to find music again. Some normalcy. They think being social at civilized events will help. That being seen with you will improve my image and impress our label."

I jutted my chin toward the vodka. "Are you sure the drinking isn't a problem?"

"It's not. Except for the occasional blowout." He smirked, but it didn't last. He wiped his hand down his face. "This week was hard. It was my brother's birthday on Tuesday. I haven't handled that well. But I assure you, I can behave when I have to."

Here's hoping. "Do you do drugs?"

"No . . . well . . . the random molly. The occasional joint. But that's for fun."

I wouldn't know. I'd never had any. Not even pot. "Do you need some acting lessons on how to pretend that you're into me?"

He arched one eyebrow as his gaze fell to my waist. He scanned upward, lingered on my cleavage, and skimmed ever so slowly across my exposed collarbone, up my neck, along my lips, then met me square in the eye. "No. I'll just be me."

Wow! My breath quickened. He just eye-fucked the hell out of me. How did guys do that? "Okay." Too much air rushed through my voice.

Pull yourself together. This is business and he's acting.

I tucked my hair behind my ear, unsure of where to look—his eyes, his mouth, his arms . . . *hmm.* All were too nice and tempting to touch. I swallowed hard to clear my throat.

"Are you a virgin?" He tilted his head to the side as he searched my face for the truth.

I jerked my head back. "What's that got to do with anything?"

"It means, are you gonna break out in a hot sweat every time I look at you or touch you? Have you ever been in a relationship? Do you know what love and affection are so you can convince people *you* are into me?"

My head spun, processing his gazillion questions. "Have you ever been in love?"

"Yep. Don't need any of that shit right now."

"Neither do I. So have I had boyfriends? *Yes.* Am I a virgin? *No.* Have I had my heart broken? *Yes.* But I'm a darn good actress. I'll pull this off." Maybe not right at this moment, but I would. *Damn it.*

"Good. Better start acting then." His mouth pulled into a smug smile. Even that looked good on him. *Ergh!*

"Don't underestimate me." I circled my hand in front of his face. "You can keep this smart-assed cockiness to yourself."

He chuckled, his blue eyes shimmering in the bar's dim lighting. "Sutton. Relax. I'm just teasing."

How could I relax when he was in my face? "Well, don't. I need to know I can trust you to be respectful." I straightened my shoulders. "If we commit to this, we need to be seen as exclusive. So, over the next three months, if you have to be with someone, please be super discreet."

He leaned forward and lowered his voice. "Maybe I should just take you home when I feel the need."

I fidgeted with the single Swarovski crystal pendant on my necklace. *Was it hot in here?* I leaned sideways, away from him. "Me? Ah. No. Not going to happen."

"You sure about that? You're fidgeting. I'd say you're into me."

"Don't flatter yourself, playboy. I'm just apprehensive about what we're agreeing to do."

"You keep telling yourself that, sweetheart." He refilled his shot glass, then waved the bottle towards me, but I shook my head.

"No, thanks. I'm driving."

"Suit yourself." He downed the shot, slammed the glass onto the table, and wiped his mouth with the back of his hand.

He scanned me up and down again. Every time he did that, my skin hummed, and a wave of heat rushed through my veins. *Stupid body.* It had been way too long since I'd had a boyfriend— that was all. Maybe I should take my advice and hook up with someone discreetly. *God, no.* I wasn't that desperate.

"Please don't take this the wrong way." He flicked a finger at my dress. "But if you want to stand out, are you going to kill this innocent princess vibe you've got going on? Or are we working with . . . this."

I ran my hand over my skirt. What was wrong with my outfit? But I wilted like a willow. I did dress like Rachel Berry in the first season of *Glee*. He was right. I needed a bit of a makeover. "The stylist who used to dress me worked for my fa—my former manager. I want nothing to do with her."

"I have a friend who's in town next week. She's dressed me

and the guys for the odd event and shoot. She's worked with us since our first album. Want me to see if she can meet you?"

"Sure? Who is it?"

"Kara Collins."

I gaped. Did I hear him correctly? "You mean . . . *the* Kara Collins? As in, Everhide? As in, Hunter Collins's wife?"

"Um, yeah. We've been friends for years. Kara's great. Everhide's tour is passing through LA. I'll see if she can meet us."

My heart galloped. "Yeah. Sure." I kept my voice level and calm, but my insides screamed like a crazed fan. *Holy Shit! I love Everhide!* "That would be awesome. Thank you."

Oh my God. I'm going to meet Kara. Freaking amazing.

I grabbed the vodka and topped up our glasses. One more drink wouldn't hurt.

"Hold on there, princess." He did that smirky half-grin thing that pulled me up short. He leaned closer, leaving only a foot of distance between us. "For this fiasco, how convincing do you want to be?"

I inhaled deeply. *Hmm.* If delicious was a smell, it was Flint Glover. Citrus and cinnamon were my new favorite scents. My gaze fell to his lips. Rosy temptation hovered mere inches away. I swallowed the dry lump in my throat. "What do you mean?"

"If we do this, what are the rules of engagement? The boundaries? Kissing, touching, holding hands. All that shit. What is consensual?"

I placed my hands on my lap. My fingers shook as I fidgeted with my ring. "Um . . . I guess hand holding, hugging, and kissing on the cheek are okay. No lips. In front of the cameras, we need to pull off flirty touches, sweet hugs, and sexy glances." Fire blazed in my cheeks just thinking about him touching me or having to look into those hypnotic eyes of his for too long. "Is that all right? What about you? What is acceptable?"

"You can touch me anywhere you like. Anytime you like. I don't care."

Oh, wow. Okay. "Thanks. But I can control myself." Here's hoping.

He pointed to my hair. "May I?"

What did he want to do? Fix my hair? *Whatever.* I rolled my eyes and nodded.

With a gentle brush of his fingertips, he swept my long hair over my shoulder, then brushed his fingertip down along the line of my jaw. He caught the tip of my chin.

I couldn't look away, captivated by his gorgeous eyes. My heart thundered so loud in my chest I could hear it thudding over the music booming through the bar.

A mischievous smile played across his lips. "Want to practice fooling everyone?"

"No. You're drunk." My words came out too breathy.

"Not even close. But definitely buzzed. Is it okay if I kiss you?"

"Kiss me? Like . . . on the cheek, right? I said no lips.

He dipped his head from side to side. "I'm more of a go-with-the-flow-type guy."

Shit. I hadn't kissed a guy outside of my show in nearly six months. What did I do with my hands? Did I keep them on my lap? Touch his cheek? His leg? His chest? *Oh crap.*

"Sutton?" He caressed the back of my head, rubbing his fingers deeper into my hair. "Stop fidgeting."

"I'm not." I totally was.

He edged closer. His lips hovered two inches from mine. His long bangs slipped forward and tickled my face. "Yes, you are. Want me to stop?"

My heart raced and jumped. *Yes. No. Yes.* "No."

Out of the corner of my eye, I saw a table of guys watching. Some girls had their cell phones propped at us. Flashes flashed.

Oh my God. This was working.

Flint grinned, then pressed his soft lips against my cheek. He lingered there for a slow, head-spinning second.

Maybe it was two seconds. Maybe three.

My eyes fluttered shut. *Oh, wow!*

He trailed soft kisses toward my ear. "Was that acceptable?"

Oh, hell yes . . . I mean, no.

I caught my bottom lip between my teeth, steadied my breath, then pasted on an impish smile. *I can do this.* I would give the onlookers an Oscar-worthy performance of playing a corrupted innocent. "It's a pass." I flattened my hand against his chest. His heart raced as fast as mine. I hadn't expected that. *Hmph.* Had the kiss affected him? *Doubt it.* "Are you trying to cause trouble?"

Humor shimmered in his eyes. "I was testing the boundaries. You set the rules; I won't cross them. It doesn't mean I won't play on the edge of those limits. But if you ever want to change the game plan, you let me know."

Butterflies swirled up a storm in my stomach and screamed at me to do away with the rules, but I was quick to swat them away. "I won't be changing anything. Let's keep this professional. Your seductive charm won't work on me."

"I wasn't trying to seduce you." His vodka-laced breath teased my face. "If I was, I'd have your panties off by now and you'd be writhing on this sofa, screaming my name as I made you come."

Oh, boy. Would he use his tongue or his fingers?

Crap. Nope. I don't want to find out.

I poked his chest and drove him back. "Keep dreaming, lover boy. This is business. Both of our careers are at stake."

That shut him up. For two seconds.

"Fine." But warning hovered in his tone. His jaw tensed. "You can spin whatever bullshit you like to yourself, this crowd, to the media, and anyone else you want to, but don't ever lie to me."

"Okay. Same goes." I barely moved my head to nod. If I could erase the heat flushing my cheeks and the fire coiling between my legs, I'd be fine. Flint Glover was dangerous. But he was exactly what I needed to reignite my career. "Flint, I need this publicity stunt to work. In this fucked up town, I need to cause a buzz, some hype, and a little controversy to land a new job. I'm not sure how I can help you reconnect with music, but I'll do my best. I'll play my part to show your execs you've settled down. I'll do whatever I can to help you see life is worth living."

He let out a sharp breath. "You better be good, because I need a lot of convincing."

"We can do this." I threw him a sweet smile and nudged my elbow against his arm. "Do you think you can suffer attending a few shows with me? Be photographed and throw some of your charisma around in front of a camera or two?"

Nerves and excitement coiled through my veins. Going out with him would blow my mind, regardless of what anyone else thought. He was way out of my league.

He took a swig of vodka straight from the bottle. His Adam's apple lurched as he swallowed. He stared off into the distance, toward the bar. "Sutton, I don't know what the fuck I'm doing. I don't feel charismatic. I'm afraid this farce will be a big, fat waste of time. I'm terrified I won't be able to play music again or write another song without my brother. But I need to try something, anything, to get better for my band. So now we've met, you're not a total bitch, and we can hold a conversation, I'm not against the idea."

My heart squeezed at the desperation and grief in his voice. "Me either. We know the ground rules. We've got confidentiality agreements in place. What goes on between us stays between us. Let's take this one event at a time. If we don't get along or circumstances change, we'll call it quits. If I can help you in the smallest of ways, and vice versa, this will be worth it." I swiped up my full shot glass and held it toward him. "So, what do you say? Do we have a deal?"

This plan had to work. It had to. Or we were both totally screwed.

He chinked the bottle against my drink. "I literally have nothing else to lose. So why the fuck not?"

Chapter 4

FLINT

I dabbed the nick on my cheek. Blood dotted the tissue. Cleaning up my act hadn't started on the right foot. I'd cut myself shaving ... four fucking times. My jaw, the tip of my chin, and two spots on the side of my neck had paid the price. *Idiot.* I hated to admit it, but despite my injuries, having smooth skin again felt better. My throat no longer itched. After a couple more blots and wipes to remove the blood, I checked myself in the mirror. Finally ... no more bleeding.

The time blazed 11:02a.m. on my watch. *Shit.* Sutton would be here in half an hour. She'd insisted on driving to meet Kara, who'd agreed to dress us for the string of events our managers wanted us to attend. If Sutton wanted to play chauffeur, it was fine by me.

But as I stared at my reflection, the emptiness in my chest erupted in pain. It always came out of nowhere, without warning. One minute I was doing okay, and the next ... I wasn't. I keeled over and clutched onto the edge of the counter. I closed my eyes. *Phil? What the hell am I doing?*

I couldn't believe I'd agreed to be a part of a publicity stunt.

Every muscle at the back of my neck knotted and twisted tighter. My skin broke out in a feverish sweat. I wasn't ready to face the world. I hated that I'd been forced into a corner. I always dealt with everything, in my own time, in my own way. This whole plan was ridiculous.

But something about Sutton had struck me in the guts. What had me more intrigued than her don't-fuck-with-me attitude and innocent smile was how she'd tried to hide her nervousness. I had to kill her doubts about my drinking. That was easily done. I hadn't drunk since the weekend. I was done with writing myself off. But the tremor in her hand, the flush in her cheeks, the flinch when I'd touched her had presented an entirely different set of problems . . . mutual attraction.

Fuck!

I'd liked her sass. She'd projected confidence, but her eyes had revealed her anxiety. I'd always been attracted to the quiet, shy girls—not the overzealous ones who clawed their way through a crowd to get to me. Sutton had smelled like she'd bathed in cherry blossoms. Her dark brown eyes held more mystery than every season of *CSI*. Her gorgeous, curved lips bordered on perfection. Her tits and legs, hidden under her simple sexy dress, were a ten . . . and I hadn't even touched them or seen them fully exposed. Somehow, I had to snuff out the fire she'd ignited in my veins. I was too much of a hot mess to date anyone. I didn't need to burden her with my truckload of bullshit problems.

I wasn't ready to *feel*. Not anything or for anyone.

I'd keep this strictly professional.

For the past week, Blake and Harlow had filled our social calendars. So much for one event at a time. As I read every email and took every phone call and talked to April, my publicist, I'd run on autopilot, agreeing to do anything they'd suggested.

But I'd been fooling myself.

I couldn't do it. My head spun. My pulse throbbed inside my temples. The pressure inside my brain grew to the size of Canada. *Fuck!*

I had to call Sutton. It was best to put an end to this crapfest before it started.

I headed into my bedroom, pulled on a clean T-shirt and a fresh pair of jeans, and made my way down the hall. But halfway along, I stopped. Staring at the door to my music studio, I struggled to breathe. My heart crackled and crumbled.

As I released every ounce of air from my lungs, tears stung the back of my eyes. Placing my palms on the door, I rested my forehead against the cool surface.

Just breathe. In. Out. In. Out.

I'd take one second at a time. One hour at a time. One day at a time.

You can do this.

I swallowed the solid, dry lump in my throat and opened the door.

As I took a few steps inside, my knees wobbled.

I hadn't been in my studio since Phil died. Not once.

At the far end of the room, by the enormous window that looked out over the garden, Phil's bass guitar lay on one of the black sofas where he'd left it. His closed notebook sat on the coffee table with a sheet of my lyrics resting on top. We'd been working on a new song before heading to Slip's party. We'd never finished it. Now we never would. The empty tumbler Phil had drunk from sat beside his notebook; smudged fingerprints clouded the glass.

A shudder ripped through my gut. My eyes burned. I shouldn't be in here. I had to call Sutton. I snapped my eyes shut and turned toward the door. But my feet wouldn't take another step. The hairs on my arms and at the back of his neck prickled. Closing my eyes, I could still feel Phil's presence. Feel his vibrant energy. Hear his loud laugh. See the happiness in his eyes when we played and wrote music.

But . . . he was gone.

"Bro." I clutched at my chest. "I miss you every fucking day." I swayed on my feet, struggling not to collapse. "I don't want to hurt anymore. I need your help."

In a daze, I ambled over to the coffee table and glanced at my lyrics. They were about Rici, the first girl I'd been interested in since my ex, Lena, had left. I'd called dibs, but Phil had been so smitten by Rici at Slip's party, I'd backed off. It had sucked, watching them hook up. Why hadn't Phil told me he'd liked her too? The words on the page punctured my ribs.

> *It feels like forever since I walked down this road,*
> *Feels like forever since time seemed to slow.*
> *Dancing and kissing, I can't wait to see how this unfolds,*
> *Think we could be onto something, so babe, you should know.*
> *Yeah . . . tonight,*
> *Tonight.*
> *I'm gonna make you mine. All mine.*

My vision blurred. If I hadn't gotten so wasted that night, drowning my dented heart, would Phil still be alive? Rici had texted me several times post-funeral. I'd ignored every one. I didn't need to be reminded that they'd been together or hear '*sorry for your loss*' one more time. Had Phil brought this on himself? He was far from innocent. *But fuck.* I'd do anything to have him back.

I sank onto the sofa beside Phil's bass. "I hope you have a million angels looking after you in Heaven. But please, Phil, show me the way out of this hell I'm in?"

Blinking the dampness from my eyes, I glanced around the room. My electric guitars filled the rack against the far wall.

My two acoustics sat on stands beside my mic. A set of Cole's drums lay centered on a beige rug toward the side wall. Slip's spare guitars were stowed away in cases by the keyboards. Two of Phil's bass guitars rested against the mixer. Cables and cords snaked across the floor, leading to mics and amps and speakers. Everything was exactly where we'd left it.

The deathly, chilling quiet and the cool air seeped into my skin. It squeezed the breath from my lungs. Hurt my ribs. I used to spend days on end in here with the guys, playing, practicing, writing.

Now . . . nothing.

I ran my trembling fingers over the body of Phil's bass beside me. I plucked one string. The twang was as dead as my soul. "Do you think I should cancel going out with Sutton? Do you think pretending to be alive will help?" My voice, barely above a whisper, snagged in my throat. "You'd like her. You'd call dibs on her for sure. She's got that innocent look you liked in girls . . . that I like. But I'm afraid Sutton and I will look like Tinker Bell and Tommy Lee. No one will buy that shit."

Fuck. I can't do this.

I wasn't ready to face the crowds. The fans. The photographers.

I didn't care what reporters said about me, but Sutton didn't need any ridicule.

I rushed from the room, raced down the hallway, and grabbed my cell phone off the kitchen counter. I texted Sutton.

I'M CANCELING. NOT DOING THIS. SORRY.

I hit send. I hated letting people down. But my heart just wasn't in it.

In less than two seconds, my cell phone rang. I winced at her name lighting the screen. She wouldn't be happy. I hit answer and put the phone to my ear. "Guess you got my message."

"Hey? Are you okay?" Her voice was soft and compassionate—not what I'd expected. I'd expected screaming and cursing.

"Yeah. I'm sorry."

"I'm three minutes away. See you in a sec."

Shit.

By the time I'd downed a glass of water, I heard the car pull up in the driveway. Moments later, the doorbell rang.

I walked out to the foyer and opened the glass-paneled door.

Holy shit.

My dick certainly wasn't dead, twitching and pulsing to life. Sutton's long golden hair, styled like she was a '40s screen siren, shimmered in the late morning sunshine. Her navy tailored shorts and stiletto sandals made her sexy legs look extra-long. The low neckline of her pink blouse highlighted her decent cleavage.

Damn. I should've asked her to wear sweatpants and a hoodie to kill any temptation. So what if it was the first day of summer.

"Hey? What's going on?" She took a small, tentative step forward. "I thought you agreed . . . oh no, have you been crying?"

Lowering my chin, my hair fell across my eyes. I didn't like anyone seeing me being emotional. "Some days are rough."

Her gaze drifted over my bare arms, scanning my ink. With every inch she covered, heat shimmered in her eyes. Her lips parted. That made me grin. My button-down shirt had covered my tattoos when we'd met. I didn't have many markings. I had a butterfly on my inner bicep, thanks to a drunken night out with Lena. Four archer's arrows ran the length of my right forearm—one for each member of our band. And a flock of small blackbirds flying on the inside of my left arm were symbolic for feeling free, like I could fly, when I was playing music. But not anymore. I'd been shot out of the sky.

"Can I come in?" She fumbled with her car keys and cell phone. "Just for a few minutes?"

"It's not going to help, but sure." I opened the door wider and waved her through to the open-plan living area, checking out her ass as she passed me.

Her strappy high heels clicked on the polished concrete floor. She placed her belongings on my rustic dining table and strode over to the huge bi-fold doors that gave way to the view of my pool area and Hollywood Boulevard below.

"Wow. That is amazing. Being a rising rock star can't be half bad if you can afford a joint like this."

I stuffed my hands in my jeans pockets and ambled toward her. "We've done okay for ourselves." More than okay. There was nothing wrong with reaping some reward from our success, right? My four-bedroom, single-story home was nowhere near as extravagant as the other guys' places. But I had to have the view of the city, not the mountains.

"You live in this huge house by yourself?"

"Yeah." I leaned against the dining table. "I like space. I don't like being cramped."

"Why?" Smartness snuck into her tone. "Did your parents lock you in a closet when you were naughty as a kid?"

My heart hit the floor. I sucked in a deep breath to hide the pain. "No. Nothing like Harry Potter. My parents were great."

"Were?" She paled. "You mean . . . they've passed away too?"

"No." The haze of pollution hanging over the city hung like the heavy cloud looming in my chest. "They haven't talked to me since Phil died. Despite the fact that Phil had been driving that night, they blame me for the accident. I was the older brother. I should've been looking after him."

Her hand shot over her chest. "That's awful."

"Yeah, well. I guess they never cared for me as much as Phil." The truth hurt. I'd been fed lie after lie—that they loved me, cared about me, wanted me. Nothing was genuine anymore. And now, ironically, I was supposed to date a fucking actress whose job it was to lie. No wonder I wanted out.

She walked over to the wall and studied the photos of me and the guys playing at the Billboard Awards. We didn't win *Best New Band of the Year* three years ago, but it had been incredible to be nominated.

"You look nothing like your brother."

"No. I was adopted."

"Oh—" She spun around. Little worry lines creased her brow.

"Nah, it's fine." I'd never had issues with being adopted. I'd been raised in a loving, happy home. For twenty-four years, I'd believed my parents loved me the same as Phil. Turned out to be nothing but smoke and mirrors. Being disowned added another impenetrable layer of ice around my heart. "After my folks had trouble conceiving, they adopted me at birth. But two years later, they had Phil naturally. My parents were always open about it. I know my birth mom. She lives in Minnesota. She became pregnant on a one-night stand while backpacking through Scandinavia. My dad is a guy she hooked up with in Norway or some dude in Sweden. She's not sure. She's never been able to track them down. I get along well with her, and we catch up once a year. I'm not screwed up about being adopted . . . well . . . I wasn't."

Sutton held out her upturned palm. "Come. Sit with me for a minute."

Hmm. My fingers twitched, wanting to grab her, hold her, touch more of her body than her hand. What I should do was ask her to leave. Yet I'd messed up her day. She'd driven all the way from Santa Monica. At least I could give her a moment of my time. "You want a drink or something?"

"No. I'm fine." She sank onto the leather sofa.

I slid onto the seat beside her. Resting my elbows on my knees, I shook my head. "I'm sorry about today."

She swiveled toward me and placed her hands in her lap. "Flint, I know what it's like to lose someone. I lost my mom when I was thirteen. I know what it's like to have your love and trust in someone destroyed."

"Shit. I didn't know you'd lost your mom." In fact, I didn't know anything about her other than what she and Blake had told me. "How did she die?"

"Breast cancer. She was only thirty-seven. I've been through it—the grief, the sadness, the anger at the world. The burn for revenge and justice can eat you alive." She lowered her chin, but I hadn't missed the flash of sorrow in her eyes. With a shake of her shoulders, she straightened and pasted on a resilient smile. "But then, your heart heals. You get stronger. The pain and loss become bearable. Your survival instincts kick in."

I shot out a short breath. "I'm not there yet."

"Yeah. You are." She patted my knee. "You came to meet me. We've come up with a plan. You've shaved, which looks soooo much better."

I smirked. I liked her lusty tone. I liked her eyes raking over me. I liked her touching me.

She nudged my leg again. "You've taken a few baby steps. Some days will be harder than others. But I promise it will get easier. Our gig may not be perfect and may need to be adjusted along the way, but what if it helps you? Don't do this for your band, or your label or me—do this for you."

God. She sounded like Cole. No . . . worse. "It's . . . hard."

"I know." She clutched my hand and held it against my thigh.

Her warm touch permeated my skin. I didn't want to feel. But every one of my cells quivered beneath her fingers. The rest of my body wanted her attention. I didn't want this. I should move but couldn't.

Oblivious to the effect she had on me, she rubbed my leg. "I watched you on YouTube. You come alive when you play. You have an incredible voice. It'd be a shame to see that go to waste."

I turned my head toward her. "You watched our film clips?"

"Yes." Rosiness reddened her cheeks. "And a few of your live performances. You're good."

I huffed. "*Were* good."

"Flint." She shuffled an inch closer. "You *are* good. You can sit around here, continue to mope, drink, and feel sorry for yourself if that's what you want to do. It's your choice. I'll find someone else to help me. Or you can put on your big girl panties and get in the car so we can go meet Kara. We take this one day at a time."

"Sutton. I won't lie to my friends."

"Everyone lies a little, Flint." She sighed as if she'd clearly had enough of my crap. "Being photographed together and spinning a few lines during an interview or two won't hurt anyone. Other than that, you can be yourself. We agreed to be honest with each other, but most of all, you need to stop lying to yourself. No one said life was easy. I can see you're struggling. You want to move on, but you're afraid."

I rubbed my eyes with the tips of my fingers. "This is so fucked up."

"Yep. Come here." She circled her hands through the air at me. "Come."

I swiveled to face her. "What?"

"Do you trust me?"

"Nope."

She giggled, light and genuine. Or was she fucking acting? Pretending to care? *Damn it.* But if her laughter was a color, it'd be yellow like sunshine.

"Okay." Her tone turned serious. "Will you try something for me?"

"Try what?" I groaned. I was so over all this nonsense.

"Close your eyes."

"Why?"

"Just do it." She brushed her hands over my eyes, her touch gentle and soft. "You okay?"

"Yep."

"Good." She took my hands in hers, then rested them against my thigh.

Hmph. I curled my fingers around hers. The first time I held her hand wasn't supposed to be like this. It should've been at some fancy event, not when I was having a meltdown. Her skin was warm and silky soft. Her fingers were long and slender. And yeah . . . she could scratch those manicured pale pink nails of hers across my back when we were naked, anytime. *Shit.* I killed those thoughts with a shudder.

She held my hands so carefully, like I might break. *Highly possible.* She reminded me of my ex. Kind and caring.

Yep. Don't go there.

She gave my fingers a gentle shake. "What was the best show you ever played? Big or small—doesn't matter. Where did you perform?"

Behind my eyelids, lights flashed. Drums hammered. Images of Phil flickered and blinked. My heart pounded against my ribs. My head spun like a bowling ball, hurtling down the lane toward the pins. My breath panted. "I . . . I can't do this."

"Shh. Yes. You can." She squeezed my hands. "I've got you. It's just a simple question."

My fingers trembled in her grip. My palms turned clammy. "Shit . . . I don't know. I guess . . . um . . . it was this festival at The Rose Bowl in Pasadena."

"Oh." Surprise lilted in her voice.

Did she expect me to say The Billboard Awards? Some televised TV show or the largest crowd that we'd played to?

Nope. Not even close.

"Why was it the best?"

Phil jumping across the stage with his bass burned my brain. "Please. Stop."

"Flint." She stroked her thumb over the back of my knuckles, her touch, soothing and grounding. "It's okay. Don't think about Cole, or Slip, or Phil. Think about the feeling. Why was that performance the best?"

I closed my eyes tighter. Memories slammed and scrambled together inside my head. The lights. The crowd. The music. We'd just released our first album. It wasn't about our rising popularity or having a couple of hits; it was our home crowd.

My eyes shot open. "I loved seeing the fans dance and cheer and sing our lyrics. The songs *I'd* written. The crowd was there for us. Our music. Everyone was having a great time. Screaming. Hollering our names. That was the best feeling in the world."

A sly smile slid across her slender lips. "It was a festival, right?" Sarcasm slithered in her tone. "They could've been high on drugs."

Oh, she had a smart mouth. Was it wrong to like it? "Most probably were. Didn't change anything."

Her voice softened. "Remember that feeling. That magic. Don't you want that back?"

I sniffled and nodded. "Yeah. I do."

"Then don't think about plans and schedules. Just take another small step. Let's go see Kara. We'll have a fun afternoon trying on clothes. We have three days until the awards show. If you still want out by then, we kill the plan."

I pulled my hands free from hers, wiped them on my jeans. "You just want me to be your eye candy, don't you?"

"Yep. That's the deal."

Her positivity and bluntness made me nauseous. Why didn't she walk away and leave me be? "Can't you see I'm fucked up?"

"So is everyone in this town. I don't want to waste time finding someone else. Will you at least come with me this afternoon? Please?"

Could I?

I rubbed my temples. The tension threatened to bring on a headache. Maybe it was from alcohol withdrawals. I hadn't had a drop in days. "Do you always get what you want?"

"No . . . That's why I'm here."

Shit. This girl was putting her faith in me to help change her career. I couldn't even get mine on track. That was totally fucked up.

"Do you honestly believe that a few new dresses and going to events with me will land you a job?"

"It has to. I don't have a backup plan." Fear flickered in her eyes, but within a blink, a new fire replaced it. A mischievous smile inched across her lips. "We will cause a stir, Flint. We're going to shake up the headlines and have some fun. I believe that being in front of the crowds and fans and the cameras will remind you of why you love music, why you love to perform, and that you are ready to move on. At the very least, it will satisfy your record company."

I scratched at the burning ache in the center of my chest. Sutton was a downright pain in the ass. A hot, sexy, pain in the butt. Her focus was as annoying as a mosquito buzzing in my ear. It wouldn't go away. But then, maybe that was what I needed.

One step at a time, right?

I should get out of the house. I hadn't been anywhere in days. A change in scenery might be good for my health. "I can't promise anything."

She shrugged. "Neither can I. But I'm willing to try." Hope glimmered in her eyes. "Are you?"

I shook my head. "You're fucking crazier than I expected."

But . . . I wanted to stop spiraling downward, torturing and tormenting myself. Could I tolerate a few hours with Sutton? Watching her try on some dresses would be a sweet torture I could live with. Kara would be there, so that would make it easier. My aching dick didn't agree, but tough.

"Anyone who wants to put up with my shit deserves a chance. I could do with an afternoon out." I wasn't the only one banking on me getting my shit together. The boys needed me. Sutton did too. "So yes . . . I'm willing to try too. Let's go see Kara."

Chapter 5

SUTTON

I stepped out of my BMW, hooked my purse over my elbow, then put one stilettoed foot in front of the other to cross the parking lot. On the short drive to the private boutique near Rodeo Drive, Flint had hardly said a word. But I hadn't missed his constant quizzical glances. Each one warmed my blood and stirred my gut—not in a good way. He was more messed up than Charlie Sheen, but I understood why. I'd been the same when my mom died. I hadn't become a raging alcoholic at thirteen years old, but I'd certainly been crippled by grief. Despite his ongoing doubts about our plan, I wouldn't let him back down. We both needed this to work.

Focusing on the gilded door ahead, I cleared my mind. I could do this. Meet Kara. Find a few outfits. Start this charade.

Transform into someone new.

Fake it until you make it.

It sounded so easy compared to actual reality. Stripping away the innocent image that had paid my bills for years had me breaking out in a cold sweat. But growth didn't come from staying the same. Trends moved. People changed. It was my time to evolve.

And somehow, I had to do it all on a conservative budget.

Halfway to the entrance, Flint fell in beside me and fumbled for my hand.

I flinched, pulling it away. "What are you doing?"

He chuckled. "Practicing holding your hand."

"Oh. Oh, right. Yes. That's good." *God.* What was wrong with me? I slipped my hand into his. "Good idea."

"I promise I won't bite. Not hard anyway." He entwined his fingers with mine.

The little shake in his grip didn't go unnoticed, nor did the clamminess of his palm. Was he nervous too? With a gentle tug, he drew me closer. My stomach fluttered like I was on a first date. I lowered my chin, hiding the flush in my cheeks. *Damn it.* My body shouldn't react like this. I had to remember that every gesture from Flint was all for show. That this wasn't real.

I stomped on the butterflies in my belly, squashed them dead. I didn't need any emotional nonsense. The sooner my nerves aligned with my head, the better.

His new smile bordered on daring. "You ready?"

"Yes." I paused by the entrance. "Did you tell Kara about us?"

"I told her the basics." He squeezed my hand and stepped closer, leaving less than a foot between us. "I won't lie to my friends, but I didn't tell her the entire story either. I told her our managers set us up and we're attending some events. She'll assume that we're together."

I lifted my chin and met his gaze. "Then this will be great practice for when we're in front of the cameras."

"How so?" A devilish glint flickered in his eyes. "Are you planning to have your way with me?"

My pulse tapped to a new tempo. Despite his intimidating forwardness and his intense knee-weakening gaze, I'd do whatever it took to ensure Kara, and anyone else we crossed paths with, believed we were dating—no matter how anxious he made me feel. "Keep dreaming. But a little display of affection won't go astray."

"We'll see." He opened the door, then waved me inside. "After you."

The moment I stepped onto the plush cream carpet, the cool air conditioning soothed my flushed cheeks. *That's better.* Huge crystal chandeliers glittered and sparkled from the high ceiling. Glass tables displaying accessories and beige velvet chairs were spaced around racks of sequined and sparkly dresses on the right and men's attire on the left.

I recognized Kara immediately from online photos. She glanced up from her cell phone, then rose from the sofa. In towering stilettos, a Versace blouse, and tailored dress pants, she rushed toward Flint and hugged him. "Ooooh. It's so good to see you." She eased back and clutched his arms. "How are you?"

"I'm . . . okay." He shrugged, feigned a smile, then tilted his head in my direction. "Kar, this is Sutton."

"Hi." Kara hugged me.

The scent of Kara's floral perfume enveloped me, reminding me of my mother's rose garden. Timeless. Elegant. Beautiful.

"It's nice to meet you." Kara stood back and eyed me up and down. "Wow. I can see why you captured Flint's eye. You're stunning."

Warmth crept into my cheeks. *Oh. My. Goodness.* Kara Collins paid me a compliment. Even if it was just to be polite.

"Easy, Kar." Flint winced and chuckled. "Your flattery might go to her head."

"Well, it's the truth." Kara raised both eyebrows, blinked her long lashes. "Now be nice. You don't want to scare her away."

I pasted on an innocent smile, slipped my arm around Flint's lower back, and drew his side against my hip. "No chance."

He tensed, but played along, draping his arm over my shoulders. "Anyone who puts up with me must be a bit crazy."

"Yep. Totally." I giggled. *But Flint, you take the cake on being nuts.*

"Oh. You're adorable." Kara splayed her hand across her chest. "I'm going to love working with you." She turned to Flint. "Sorry Gem and the guys missed seeing you after the show on Monday night. We had to get home to the kids."

Flint scratched his cheek. "That's okay, Kar. I'd love to catch up with them while you're in town. Do they have any free time?"

"They're sleeping today. They need rest before the next run of back-to-back shows. But yes." Kara clasped her hands together. "We discussed having a few friends over on Tuesday before we leave LA. You two must come."

Oh hell, yeah! My heart leaped out of my chest and swung from the chandelier. *Meet Everhide? That'd be better than a concert.* I'd missed getting tickets to their sell-out shows, even after trying online and asking friends. *But wait.* My lungs deflated. Meeting and hanging out with Flint's friends wasn't part of our deal. I couldn't abuse our fake relationship. Asking to go with him would be overstepping our boundaries.

Damn it.

Flint glanced at me, then back to Kara. No doubt the same thought had struck him. "Um . . . Sutton might be busy. But send me the details. I'll be there."

My stomach sank a little, but I conjured a small smile. *Yep. Boundaries.*

"Awesome. But sorry, Sutton. Maybe next time." Kara clasped her hands together, her smile morphing from friendly catch-up to time-to-be-serious. "So, we better get to work. Would you like a drink? Perhaps some champagne?"

"I'd love some." I stood three inches taller. It had been nearly two years since I'd been in an exclusive showroom to source outfits for events, instead of just tagging along, watching my A-list friends shop. It'd been too long since I'd been treated like someone special. I tugged on the back of Flint's shirt. "What about you? Would you prefer vodka?"

"Hmm." He nudged his hip against mine. "You remembered."

"Hard not to." Not after you'd downed half a bottle in front of me at the bar.

"Thanks, but I'll have water."

"Giselle?" Kara called toward the adjoining dressing area room and office area. A middle-aged woman with her hair pulled into a neat chignon, dressed in a tailored jacket over a long skirt, walked toward us, the sway in her hips over-accentuated. "This is Sutton and Flint, who we'll be dressing today."

"Nice to meet you." Giselle shook our hands. "My, my. Aren't you a handsome couple?"

"Thank you." I soaked up the compliment, then glanced at Flint.

His lips twitched, almost forming a smile.

Kara placed her hand on Giselle's forearm. "This lovely lady has helped me dress my husband and friends for years. She's the hidden angel who works magic behind the scenes, sourcing outfits and accessories for every occasion. And she's a goddess for letting me use her boutique when needed."

"Oh, Kara." Giselle swiped the air, but her eyes sparkled as if she loved every second of the praise. "You're too kind. Let me grab some sparkling water and the champagne."

As Giselle headed toward the office, Flint took my hand and we followed Kara through the wide doorway into the dressing area at the rear of the boutique. A large, gilded mirror filled the wall between two velvet-curtained dressing rooms. This wasn't the first private showroom I'd been in, but it was one of the nicest.

"Flint?" Kara pointed toward a rack of men's clothes. "Can

you check out the suits and shirts I've selected for you while I help Sutton? There are some gorgeous blazers from Dolce and Gabbana and Versace, and some great colored and patterned suits from Burberry and Gucci."

"Thanks. I'm on it." He released my hand and walked backward toward the other side of the room. "Have fun."

I missed his touch the second it was gone.

"Oh. We will." Kara linked our arms and drew me across the room. Excitement hovered in her voice. "So, Flint has hardly told me a thing about you. How long have you been dating?"

"Um . . . just a couple weeks." *Shit.* We'd only known each other for six days.

"Wow." Kara's eyes widened. "And you're going public already?"

I shrugged, playing it cool. "Yeah. We're not into sneaking around."

"Beats the tabloids making up stories, right?"

"So true." Oh, I wanted to hit the headlines, but with a wow factor, not clickbait gossip.

"He's a top guy and loves a good party. His voice is to die for. And it doesn't hurt he's exceptionally hot." Kara halted in front of a rack of dresses and jerked her head in Flint's direction. "You've got yourself a good one."

"I hope so." I hadn't been privy to his wild side. I wasn't sure I wanted to witness it. Or . . . maybe I did? What would he be like, rocking up a storm? It was hard to imagine after seeing him struggle to face the day. But despite his battles, my heart understood what he was going through. Underneath his messy exterior, he had some admirable qualities. Warmth coiled beneath my skin as I watched him from across the room. "He's certainly intriguing. He loves his band. His music. He loved his brother. Losing Phil has been tough, but he's getting better. Oh . . ."—I nudged Kara's arm—"and you're right. His looks are a bonus."

"Oh yes. That they are." Smiling, Kara flicked her long hair over her shoulder, then ran her hand over a silky red dress. "But we better stop ogling or we'll never get you dressed. Thank you for sending me your size details and budget information via Flint. I googled you to see what you'd worn to past events. You've previously dressed rather conservatively. But you mentioned you want an edgier look. Is that correct?"

"I don't want to just amp it up. I want a complete overhaul. I'm dating one of the hottest rock stars in LA. I want to look the part. It's time to go from sweetheart to siren. Can you help with that?"

Kara scanned me up and down again. Not once, but twice.

A sweat broke out underneath my long hair. My pulse throbbed in my temples. Was there something wrong with me? Was I a lost cause?

Kara arched one manicured eyebrow. "How game are you?"

"Very." My stomach flipped. *Yes . . . yes, I can do this.*

Kara combed her red fingernails through my locks, draping the strands forward onto my chest. "Are you open to restyling your hair?"

"Sure. My current TV contract states I can't do anything too radical. You can cut it, color it, or put highlights in it, but I can't dye it black or green or anything like that."

"Oh, dear God, no. Do you have a preferred hairdresser, or can I call Carla, Everhide's hairstylist and makeup artist? She's magic and will know exactly how to cut it. We'll coordinate a time before Saturday. Does that work for you?"

"Absolutely." I nodded, but my insides cartwheeled. *Yay!*

"Excellent." Kara swept her hand over the top of the rack. "All these dresses are your size. Some of the gowns might need altering and maybe a touch over your budget, but don't hesitate to try anything on. Let's just work on style and find out what you're comfortable wearing. Once we've established that, Giselle will help me source dresses that fall within your price range." She straightened the sashes of a pink halter-neck on a hanger. "For some of the gowns, I might be able to call on favors for a loaner from a few designers. But anything from Bill Chante, no chance. He's an asshole, but his dresses are to die for." Then she smiled and waved toward a section of colorful sequined numbers on the end. "But if you like one or two of those dresses, they're yours. They're my designs. You're Flint's girlfriend; I'd be honored if you wore them."

Tears pricked my eyes. I sucked in a deep breath. Nausea pooled in my gut. How could I accept such kindness when I wasn't Flint's real girlfriend? I was a fraud. An impostor. "Oh, Kara. Thank you, but it's too much."

"Nonsense."

"Please. Let me pay. I don't expect anything for free."

"Sutton." Kara clutched my hand. "As far as I know, you're the first girl Flint has dated in over a year. Own that. I'll turn you into a sexy goddess. It's my specialty."

If I ended up half as dazzling as Everhide's Gemma McIntyre, I'd be ecstatic.

Kara rubbed my arm. "I'll have you and Flint on every best-dressed list this season. I promise."

Oh, I needed that. Not just for my career, but for my self-esteem as well. "Okay then. Show me what you've got?" Time to rock some frocks.

Chapter 6

SUTTON

Transforming into a rock star's girlfriend should be easy. Just another character to play. I could do this.

Turning to the rack, I surveyed the dresses—strapless silver sequins, bright blue sheaths, slinky scarlet slips, and daring off-the-shoulder cuts. Crop tops and miniskirts. Cut-outs and halter-necks. So many beautiful outfits.

I paused at a gorgeous black mesh dress with a plunging neckline and asymmetrical slim skirt. Rhinestone straps crossed over the back. The moment I touched the cool metallic fabric, my heart rate quickened. I'd never seen anything so exquisite. The swing tag with Bill Chante's gold-embossed logo shimmered in the lighting. The price burned my fingertips. *Three and a half thousand dollars! Shit.* It wasn't that expensive in the scheme of designer gowns, but it was beyond my budget. I closed my eyes and swallowed the lump lodged in my throat. *Don't even look at it.* Oh, but it was incredible. *No. No. Nope.* Keep moving.

"Sutton?" Kara caught my hand. "That reaction is just what I wanted to see. Your eyes lit up. Your beautiful smile filled the room. An amazing dress should have that effect. You must try it on. I promise I will find something similar within budget if it's what you like."

My knees shook. I was afraid that if I put it on, I wouldn't be able to walk out of this boutique without it. I wasn't destitute, but I had to watch my finances. "Are you sure?"

"Yes." She gave me an encouraging smile and grabbed the dress. "Absolutely."

After selecting a dozen dresses, Kara hung them in the nearby dressing room.

Flint came over and handed me a glass of champagne. "Find some dresses?"

"Yes. I think so." I took a tiny sip. The bubbles tickled my nose.

He downed a quarter of his bottle of water in a few quick gulps, then lowered his voice so only I could hear. "Are you gonna strip out here, or use the dressing room? We are supposed to be a couple."

"You'd like that, wouldn't you?"

"I'm a guy. Of course I would. But if you're not game . . ."

Oh . . . was that a challenge?

I narrowed my eyes, swallowed the rest of my champagne, then handed him the empty flute. Slowly, I popped open one button on my blouse, then another and another. His eyes went wide, then darkened as I toyed with the openings. With a flick of my wrists, I flashed him my black bra, then closed my top. "I'll use the dressing room."

A playful smile curved across his lips. "That all I get to see?"

"Yep." I spun on my heels and headed toward the dressing room.

"Tease." Flint's sultry voice resonated in my chest.

My heart stampeded with each step. Ripping the curtain closed behind me, I bit my bottom lip to stop myself from giggling. *Oh. My. God.* I covered my cheeks with my hands to cool them down. I'd never flashed a guy before. What had come over me? Flashing him had been funny, but foolish. I didn't want to lead Flint on.

"Sutton?" Kara called through the curtain. "Would you like my help with the gowns?"

"Yes. Yes, please." I took a calming breath, then stripped down to my black panties and strapless bra.

Kara came in and helped me into a dark green minidress. The bodice was firm, but not tight. It made my cleavage bulge. *Whoa!* I'd never shown off my boobs this much or worn anything this short to a public event before. If my father had seen me in a dress this short, he would've had a fit. Wouldn't allow it. Good thing he wasn't around to do that anymore.

Could I wear this? I clutched my breasts and grinned, then turned to see the back of the dress in the mirror. *Hell yeah.*

Kara drew the curtain open and led me toward Flint. He was dressing with Giselle's help in the center of the room.

My gaze fell to his chest. My mouth fell open, and my heart faltered. He had an amazing physique, an awesome six-pack of ripped muscles, but a large burn scar, red and inflamed, ran diagonally across his chest. *Was that from the accident? The seatbelt?* Smaller scars dotted his right shoulder. Giselle helped him shrug on a black button-down shirt. But every time he moved, he winced and groaned. As he raised his right arm, deeper grooves furrowed his forehead.

He quickly did up his buttons, tucked the shirttails into his suit pants. Then Giselle helped him into a dark green brocade dinner jacket that complemented my dress. He let out a slow breath. "I might need something stronger to drink."

"Would you like a beer, Mr. Glover?" Giselle straightened the shoulders on his jacket.

"No. It's fine. I was kidding. Just another water would be

great."

"I'll go grab one." Giselle disappeared into the office.

"Hey?" I took a few tentative steps forward. "Are you okay?"

"Yep."

Liar.

Hadn't he wanted me to see his injuries? He'd hidden his pain well. Maybe that was why he drank. The seatbelt burn looked nasty. Still raw and angry.

I lowered my voice so only he could hear. "Why didn't you tell me you're in pain?"

"It's nothing I can't handle. Physical therapy helps."

Didn't look like it. "Do you want to stop?"

"No."

"Let me know if you need a break, okay?" I slid my hands up the silky lapels of his dinner jacket. Straightening his shirt collar, my fingertips quivered. "You do scrub up nicely."

That was the truth. No lie required.

His electric gaze roamed over my dress. "You look nice too."

My chest expanded. Tingles sparked across my skin. *Geez.* He hadn't doused me in flattery or said anything mind-blowing, but my body still overheated and broke out in a fever. Maybe the champagne had gone to my head. *Wishful thinking.* Flint just had to look at me and I turned into a hot mess. That had to stop.

Kara sighed and joined us. "Flint? You can do better than that. She's gorgeous. Now . . ." She grabbed our arms and turned us to face her. "Stand together so I can see if these outfits work or if we change it up."

I wriggled and straightened the short dress, then smoothed my hands over the hipline. The gown fit perfectly; the slight stretch in the fabric hugged my slender curves. It was short, simple, and sexy.

"Stop fidgeting." Flint hooked his arm behind my back. "You

look fine."

He pulled me closer. As if unsure where to place his hand, he moved it from my hip, to around my arm, to my shoulder, then to the small of my back.

With a nervous giggle, I grabbed his hand and settled it on my waistline. Nothing like not knowing how to stand comfortably next to each other. More crap we'd have to work out. "There. Now. Smile for Kara."

"Perfect." Kara picked up the Polaroid camera off the coffee table and took a photo of us. "One outfit done. Next."

The following item I tried on was a red sparkly jumpsuit. It was fun and flirty. Something I'd normally wear. But nowhere near hot and sexy. I instantly tossed the garment on the unsuitable pile.

I tried on outfit after outfit, the dresses getting sexier and sexier. With each gown, my heart soared. My confidence grew a fraction. With the buzz of champagne kicking in, I showed off my legs to Flint through the thigh-high split in one of my skirts. I winked at him as I sashayed across the room. We laughed and fell against each other when our outfits didn't match, or my dresses were too big. With each photo taken, the rigidness in Flint's posture lessened. His hands seemed more than willing to wrap around my waist. His subtle smile threatened to tap into my heart.

But this was nothing but an act. A test to see if we could work together. I'd say we were passing. We were having fun. That was something I hadn't expected.

The last dress was the expensive Bill Chante mesh number. The dress cascaded over my body, draping like liquid silk down my sides. As I glided the rhinestone spaghetti straps onto my shoulders, my heart pounded against the plunging bodice. The metallic fabric cooled my fevered skin. The intricate short asymmetrical skirt hugged my hips and showed off my long legs.

I'd never worn anything so sexy. So stunning. So spectacular.

I could be in a *Mad Max* movie . . . or take up pole dancing . . . or be a rock star's wicked girlfriend.

Was this too bold? Too extreme?

Yep.

But the exquisite gown made my skin tingle, like I was worth more than the value on the price tag.

I stepped out from behind the curtain. Flint froze mid-tucking his shirt into his suit pants. His eyes widened. "Wow. That . . . is fucking amazing."

Heat flushed my cheeks as I headed toward him. I turned toward the mirror. "It's too *wow*, isn't it?"

Flint eased in behind me. He placed his hands on my hips and whispered in my ear, "I thought that was what you wanted?"

Goose bumps shot down my spine. The blazing fire in his eyes caught me off-guard. If I could attract his attention, surely others would notice me, too.

"It is . . . but . . ."

My heart plummeted to the floor. This dress was way over my budget.

His hands glided up and down my sides in slow, sensual strokes. His low voice came out all hot and seductive. "You will burn up the carpet in this."

His warm breath wisped across my fiery skin. Before I turned into a melted puddle on the floor, I spun around to face him. I slid my hands up his chest, over the silky ruby-colored button-down. "So will you. I like this suit and shirt. The cut is nicer than the last one. Shows off the shape of your arms better."

Yep. Focus on the clothes, not on him.

"You like my arms?"

There was too much satisfaction simmering in his eyes. "Yes." I patted his cheek. Twice. "But don't let it go to your head."

Kara angled the camera at us. "Face this way, please."

The second Kara finished taking our photos, Flint caught my hips between his hands. After spending the last couple of hours with him, I didn't flinch as much when he touched me. But my eyes widened when he nuzzled against my neck and guided me back toward the dressing room.

I faked a laugh and clutched onto his shoulders so I wouldn't fall. "What are you doing?"

"Helping you out of that dress."

Oh . . . oh, crap.

He ripped the curtain shut behind us, pushed me up against the wall, then planted his hands beside my head.

My heart pounded in my throat. My mind spun. Words failed me.

He burst out laughing, silently, so Kara and Giselle couldn't hear.

"You should see the look on your face?" he whispered. "You're terrified . . . and turned on."

"I am *not* turned on." *Okay, maybe a little.* I'd never had anyone so hot, so arrogant, and so intimidating invade my personal space.

"Yes, you are." He brushed the tip of my nose with his fingertip, then stepped back and folded his arms. His voice, still barely audible. "I'm just playing the game."

"We've shown off enough." I pointed to the curtain. "Now get out of my dressing room."

"No." He dialed up the sultry tone but didn't move from the wall. "Hmm, Sutton. Fuck . . . You . . . in this dress. So hot."

Holy. Shit! I gaped. His voice rumbling in his throat sent a shockwave to my core. *Wait.* This had to stop. Stop now. "Flint?" I hissed. "Get out. Kara and Giselle are outside."

"They won't care."

"Grrrr." I growled. He wanted to play? *Fine.* I stepped forward and ruffled his hair.

He caught my hand. Ice frosted his eyes. "What are you doing?"

"Disheveling you. Why?" I arched an eyebrow. "Did you think I was actually going to kiss you?"

"I wouldn't care if you did."

"Do you want me to?" My breath hitched. *What if he says yes?*

He licked his lips. Swallowed hard. His Adam's apple lurched. His eyes never left mine.

"Ergh!" I covered his face with my hand and pushed him away. "No chance. Get. Out."

"Gladly." He chuckled, yanked the curtain open and stepped outside.

"You two having fun?" Kara winked as she hung one of Flint's shirts onto the rack.

"Always." Flint half grinned, combing his fingers through his hair. "Sorry. We got carried away."

"That's perfectly fine." Unfazed, she grabbed another shirt to hang. "Hunter's exactly the same."

"Yep. I get it." Flint winked over his shoulder at me. "Sutt certainly drives me crazy."

I glared at him, then yanked the dressing room curtain closed. The nerve of him. How dare he come in here and . . . and . . . taunt me? *But shit!* He'd barely touched me.

I leaned against the wall, tilted my head back, and stared at the ceiling. He was so infuriating. Frustrating. Freaking insane. *Asshole!*

Wait. No, he wasn't. He'd just done what we'd set out to do. He'd pretended to be my boyfriend.

But for the briefest of seconds, when he'd pinned me against this wall, I'd thought he was actually into me. Wanted to kiss me. *Stupid, right? Stupid.*

I ran my hands over the beautiful dress. Flint's reaction to seeing me in it had been exactly what I wanted. Hunger had blazed in his eyes, his hands had roamed over my body, and his voice had weakened my knees. I wanted others to go *wow* like Flint had done. I wanted everyone to be mesmerized. But reality stabbed my heart. This gown was way too expensive. Closing my eyes, I ran numbers and options through my head. *What if I swapped the gold-sequined dress for the bright blue cutout, dropped the pink halter-neck and took two of Kara's dresses instead of one?* Nope ... not even then would my budget stretch to accommodate this dress.

But wait. What if I wore something I already owned to one or two events?

Oh, God forbid!

I blinked the tears from my eyes. I couldn't wear a dress a second time. My friends and the media would ridicule me to no end.

Rented something?

Again ... my friends ... no, just Georgia ... would laugh.

Then it clicked.

If I did my own hair and makeup—I'd perfected the smoky eye, thanks to YouTube—wore shoes I already owned—I had a similar sparkly pair in my closet—and skipped staying in the hotel for the night—a limo from home would suffice—I could do it. I loathed compromise and sacrifice, but this dress was worth it.

I only had one chance to make a huge impression. This gown was a must.

"Sutton?" Flint's voice hovered on the other side of the curtain. "Everything all right?"

"Yep." I carefully slipped out of the dress, then clutched it against my chest. "I'll be out in a sec."

"Cool."

A small smile curled my lips. But the ache in my head

mounted. There was only one other small problem with this dress. Flint hadn't been able to keep his hands off me. That wasn't the problem. The fact that I liked them on me was. Every glance from him and every touch of his hands raised my body temperature.

I didn't need more complications, and developing feelings for someone who was only pretending to like me would be a stupid mistake.

I had to pull myself together. We had an understanding. I didn't want to blow this opportunity. He was my ticket to being noticed. The dress would help. I could picture Sunday's headlines:

Hollywood's Hottest New Couple.

Sutton Summer's Wows the Red Carpet Beside Bad Boy of Rock Flint Glover.

America's Sweetheart Has Grown Up. Watch This Space!

Bring it!

It was time to say goodbye to the old Sutton—hello to the new.

This awards night would be spectacular.

As long as Flint turned up.

Chapter 7

FLINT

I placed my hand on the wall beside the intercom to Sutton's oceanfront condo in Santa Monica. The fresh breeze ruffled my hair and cooled my overheated skin. I needed the reprieve, or I'd pass out in my Versace suit in this first-week-of-summer heat. I wriggled my tie and swallowed hard. *Just press the button, idiot.* I wasn't looking forward to tonight. I was all dressed up for the awards show, but my band wouldn't be with me to tease, banter, or joke around with. Instead, I had to pretend to have a good time with Sutton.

I had no idea how that would go down.

She'd hardly spoken to me since going to the boutique on Wednesday. I'd apologized for the dressing room incident, but it hadn't helped. Her texts and calls had been few and far between. Was she still upset with me? *Probably.* But flirting with her had been too easy. Every time I'd touched her, she'd flinched. Every time I'd whispered in her ear, she'd blushed. Every time I'd stroked her hair, I'd wanted to wrap it around my fist and draw her lips to mine. I'd wanted to kiss her until she was delirious. I'd spent half the afternoon with a semi, checking her out in her dresses. I'd liked teasing and tormenting her and watching her tremble when I got too close. For the briefest of seconds, I hadn't thought about Phil. But that had freaked me out. I didn't want to forget. Once I'd gotten home, I slammed the door on the flirting game. *No more teasing, Sutton.*

I had to keep focused on one goal. My band's desperate plea drowned all other thoughts. *"Get your shit together. We don't want to lose our fucking contract."*

Until I got my head back on track, found music, and returned to the stage, the only relationship I could have was with myself. I needed this ridiculous publicity bullshit to work as much as Sutton did. So tonight, if she was still talking to me, we could just have some good fun . . . If not, this could turn into a complete shitfest.

There was only one way to find out.

My hand shook as I pressed the intercom.

"Hello?" Sutton's soft voice sounded tinny in the speaker.

"It's Flint."

"Come on up. Level fourteen."

She'd let me in. That was a good sign, right?

I entered the building through the security doors, then took the elevator up to her floor.

Before I could knock on her door, it swung open.

"Oh. Wow." My hand shot over my heart. Taking every inch of Sutton in, my gaze darted from her hair to her legs to her face. Gone were her sleek and smooth Barbie-blonde locks. In its place was a sexy, tousled bob with darker highlights. Her makeup was flawless, with smoldering smoky eyes and bright red lipstick. The satin kimono molding to her svelte body . . . wasn't the outfit I'd expected.

Still hot though. Still gave me an instant boner.

Clearing my throat, I threw her a sly smirk and glanced over her shoulder. "Um. I'm here for Sutton. Is she home?"

She tucked her hair behind her ear and blushed. "Yeah. Come in." She waved me into her living room.

The scent of the jasmine diffuser on the console table hit me as I walked in. A small kitchen with white cupboards and marble countertop lay to the left. Pale blue sofas and a large TV filled the living space. Seashells, coral, and seahorse decorations were scattered in glass bowls on the beechwood coffee table and painted in pictures on the walls. But the ocean view stole my breath. Full-length windows gave way to a balcony that had a one-hundred-and-eighty-degree uninterrupted view of the coastline. The lights of the Santa Monica Pier twinkled to the south.

I tossed my jacket onto the dining chair and took a small step toward Sutton. "You look gorgeous." My dick twitched, agreeing. "I love the haircut. But why aren't you ready? You're not pulling out on me, are you?" Wouldn't that be a laugh after she'd twisted my balls into submission to be here?

"Never. I just had trouble with my makeup."

It looked fine to me. Not a smudge or smear anywhere.

She held up her hand, splayed her fingers. "Give me five minutes."

"Okay."

She disappeared into her bedroom.

With time to kill, I wandered over to the bookshelves lining the far wall. Hardcover biographies and memoirs, and books about the history of Hollywood movies filled the rows. Photographs of her with girlfriends at a party and people I assumed were family or fellow cast members filled silver frames. A couple of statues from the Teen Idol and Young Actors TV Awards stood proudly, centered on the top shelf . . . the date on each was more than ten years old.

As I ambled toward her desk, the gentle crash of the ocean waves rolled in the distance. I ran my fingertips over the closed lid of her pink Mac laptop, a spiral notebook, and a script stained with coffee cup marks. At the rear of the desk was a mounted ring light and a small mic. Was that for showing off on Instagram and TikTok, or making showreels and videos for online auditions? *Probably both.* Next to them was a messy pile of papers that looked like bills. Her wire in-trays overflowed with more of the same.

But one with a bright orange logo caught my eye. "Barack Jones Lawyers. Final Settlement."

My heart thudded. I shouldn't snoop. I glanced over my shoulder toward the hallway. Sutton could walk out here any second. But temptation overruled. My fingers shook as I shifted the envelope off the top. The letter was dated February 3rd.

> *Miss Sutton Summers,*
>
> *Under the law within the State of California, mediation between you, MISS SUTTON SUMMERS, and the director of Bright Star Talent Management, MR. CHARLES SUMMERS, has been finalized. Mr. Summers has agreed to the settlement and the terms and conditions outlined in the attached appendix. The payment to terminate all existing management contracts, agent representation and service fees is due on April 12th.*
>
> *Mr. Summers will cease all contact with you, effective immediately. I am glad we have reached a resolution that is suitable to all parties. It has been a pleasure working with you. We are at your service if you require future representation.*
>
> *Yours sincerely,*
> *Kenneth Jones*

Barack Jones Lawyers

HOLY FUCK!

I wiped my hand down my face, then turned the page. A red PAID stamp burned bright across the invoice. I gaped at the three-and-a-half-million-dollar balance.

Shit!

I skimmed some of the other documents and bills from an accountant, a financial consultant, her new agent, and more letters from the lawyers.

What was going on? *Crap.* I should've pulled my head out of my ass and done some background research on Sutton. But Blake would've told me if there were any red flags.

"What are you doing?" Her icy voice slid down my spine and stabbed me in the balls.

I jumped, dropping the paper back into the tray. "I'm sorry. It was on top. I was just—"

Holy Jeezus! Her? In that dress? My blood rushed from my head to my cock. Total boner material.

"You were snooping?" Tears welled in her eyes. "Going through my stuff?

"I . . . I . . . shit." I slouched. "Busted." Own it, *dick*!

"Well, now you know." She thrust her chin toward the documents.

"Know what?"

She closed her eyes. "I loved the fact you didn't know about my past. You didn't seem to care. You never questioned me about it."

"Sutton, I don't put my nose in other people's business. I'm sorry; I didn't mean to find the letter." Nausea pooled in my gut. "Is . . . is that your father mentioned in the document? What did he do to you?"

"Don't you ever watch or read the news?" She swiveled

and rested her butt on the desk. Her long, tanned legs seemed to run for miles and miles. Sparkly stilettos highlighted her dainty feet, but it was the defeated look on her face that had me moving closer to her.

"Not if I can help it." I took a seat beside her.

"Bright Stars was my father's company. My dad was my manager, my agent, my accountant. He handled all my contracts, my money, and my career. He told me what shows to do, what to wear, where to go, and what to say, until I found out he'd been stealing money from me. Most had happened since my mom died. He'd taken advantage of me emotionally and in every financial way possible since I was six. What you saw was the financial settlement to get him out of my life forever." The pain rippling in her shaky voice speared my heart. "You happy now that you know?"

"Did . . . did he ever hurt you?" Bile pooled in my stomach at the thought of anyone laying a rough hand on her.

"Physically, no." She lowered her chin. "He was my father. I'd trusted him with my life. But he was nothing but a cunning, slimy asshole. He always ensured I had a healthy monthly allowance, so I never questioned my income. I lived a decent life. I didn't know any better."

"How did you find out?"

"I suspected something was wrong when I was eighteen after talking to my girlfriends about unions and agent fees and the new contracts I'd just signed. My trust account wasn't as healthy as it should've been. My expenses were exorbitant. That's when I hired a new lawyer to investigate him. They found that he'd been using my money to pay for his lifestyle and gambling addiction for years. My contracts were full of ludicrous service payments and way-above-industry management fees. My old lawyer, who I'd thought was an independent union rep, was actually taking a cut from him."

"What assholes—your dad and the lawyer. Has your dad gone to jail? For embezzlement?"

"I wish. But no." She shook her head. Her short, dangling diamond earring sparkled in the soft light. "We settled out of court. I had two very long, ugly legal battles. The first was against his accounting company for the fraud and embezzlement charges. That hurt. Every day of my life, he stood in front of me with a smile on his face and lied. Once I found out what he'd done, I wanted nothing to do with him. That document you saw was legal case number two against his talent agency. I had to pay him out to terminate the contracts."

"Fuck. I'm sorry you went through that."

She sucked in a deep breath and drew her shoulders back, her resilience reset. "I'm not the first childhood star to be taken advantage of, but I hated what he did to me. My own father! I've paid for his lucrative career and gambling addictions for long enough. Part of the settlement was he lost his license to represent actors. He can't hurt anyone again."

"Justice served?"

"Not even close. But it's over."

"Where is he now?"

She glanced toward the ocean; pain still rippled in her eyes. "Mexico, as far as I know. I honestly don't care. The past four years of sorting out this mess has left me exhausted, heartbroken, and cynical. I used nearly every cent I had to get rid of him. Now I want to put the hurt behind me. Move on. Start fresh."

God, I needed some of her positivity.

I covered her hand with my palm. "You could have told me this."

Tears pooled on the rims of her eyes. "I was afraid you'd think I'm naïve and pathetic. A victim."

"Why? What happened wasn't your fault. What you've done

to break ties with your father took strength and courage."

"Maybe." She fidgeted with my signet ring. "But I'm terrified. I've lived a sheltered existence. Starting over on my own is scary. But I have no other choice. I'm not broke, but I need a new job. Something that isn't tainted by my father and something that puts my past behind me. That's why I need your help."

Well . . . that added new weight to our plan. Nothing like more pressure.

"You got this." I squeezed her hand.

"Thank you." A tear fell onto her cheek.

"No tears. Don't ruin your beautiful makeup." I nudged her arm. "Going out with a fuck-up like me might help you work out what you *don't* want. Process of elimination can work too, right?"

She half smiled. "True."

"So, you ready?"

"Umm . . ."

"Sutt, I promise to be a gentleman and stick to our game plan. Remember, I need this as much as you do." I hooked my arm around her shoulders and gave her a hug. *Hmm. She smelled like cherry blossoms again.* "We're supposed to have fun, right?"

She wiped her fingertips beneath her eyes, then dabbed the corners. "Yes."

"Best way to face the cameras, shove the shit aside, and settle the nerves is to have a drink or two." I pointed to her sideboard. "Let's grab that vodka. Down a few shots. Then hit the show."

"You think we can pull this stunt off?" Worry flickered in her eyes.

"Some liquid courage will help. But with you in that dress?" I gave her a wicked smile. "Most definitely."

Chapter 8

FLINT

The four vodka shots at Sutton's place had sent a much-needed buzz through my brain and had dulled the ache in my chest. As the limousine crawled toward the Dolby Theatre, the fans' screams, and the photographers' flashes penetrated the car's windows. I was here now. There was no escape. I had to do this for Cole and Slip.

I stole a glance at Sutton. *And for her.*

I needed a dose of her strength, her determination, her will to change and move forward.

But despite her stoic front, she fumbled with the edge of her skirt.

I scanned the length of her gorgeous legs and placed my hand on top of hers. "Stop. You look incredible."

"Thank you." She threw me a quick smile, then ripped out her hand from underneath mine to check her lipstick in the mirror. "But I'm nervous."

Yeah. Me too. "Don't be."

The car jolted to a halt. An usher opened the door.

I let out a slow breath, but the crowd's clapping and the

cameras flashing pinned me to my seat. I couldn't move. Dizziness swam through my head. My pulse drummed in my temples. Maybe I'd had one too many shots. I hadn't eaten since lunch.

Move, idiot!

Get out of the car.

Get-out-of-the-car. Get-out-of-the-car. Get-out-of-the-car.

"Hey?" Sutton placed her hand on my arm. "You're okay. We're in this together. Just hold my hand."

Hmph. I used to joke and say that to Phil, who'd been camera shy. That was one thing I'd never suffered from. I was at home in front of the cameras as much as I was on stage or jamming in my studio. The zest for life was in me somewhere. I just needed to find it. This was one step in that direction.

I patted Sutton's hand. "I'm good. Let's get this shit over with."

I stepped onto the soft red carpet. The crowd in the temporary bleachers cheered, hollered, and clapped. Publicists and security guards herded the guests in front of us toward the main media section up ahead. TV camera operators glided around the carpet like they floated on clouds of air. Photographers jostled behind a roped off area, their telescopic lenses fighting for clear shots.

Did they remember who I was? I wasn't yesterday's news; I was last year's forgotten headline act. Then someone in the bleachers screamed my name. A small smile curled across my lips. *Sweet.* But tonight was about Sutton. I was just along for the ride.

I buttoned my jacket, then held out my hand to help her from the car. The moment her sparkly stilettos hit the carpet, her face lit with a smile as bright as a floodlight. Her energy levels soared. She waved to the fans. Blew kisses in their direction. Posed for the photographers.

Shit! Talk about a personality transplant. Where had this Sutton come from?

She let go of my hand and rushed over to the crowd for photos, then crossed over to the photographers. She zoomed from one side of the carpet to the other like a metallic comet shooting across the sky.

I stuffed my hands in my pockets and shook my head. Sutton was like no one I'd ever met before. She projected a vivacious confidence, but beneath the surface she was scarred and broken. Just like I was. But while I wore my wounds on my sleeve, she hid hers behind her alluring smile.

But what the fuck was she doing?

I may as well not be here. I didn't need this shit.

As she dashed back toward the fans, I caught her arm and swung her around to face me. I slid my hands onto her hips, drew her tidy body against mine, and whispered in her ear, "Sutton. Stop. What happened to the plan? Weren't we supposed to do the hot couple thing?"

She smiled and waved at the photographers over my shoulder. The loud *click, click, click* of their cameras remained constant and fast. "There are so many fans and photographers here. We need to see them all."

"We will. But not like this."

"Oh . . . shit." Her buzz plummeted like her plug had been pulled out of the wall. "I got carried away, didn't I?"

"Yep." I threw her a playful smile. "Tone down the Energizer Bunny and turn on that sultry, sexy siren."

Fear flickered in her eyes. "I . . . I've never done that before."

I'd gotten my ass here—I wasn't about to let her ruin her opportunity to blow away the media. I'd had enough training to know how to play the game. "We have one shot at this. Let me do my job. Do you trust me?"

"No."

"Good." It was nice to know she shared the same concerns I had about her. "But we're almost at the main media section. It's time to give them what they want. What you want. For the next couple hundred yards, you *are* going to trust me. Don't let go of my hand unless it's to grope me somewhere. Follow my lead. Ready?"

She tucked her flyaway strands behind her ear and nodded.

I drew her closer, flush against my chest. I grinned, enjoying her breasts crushed against me a little too much. I nuzzled my nose into her fine hair, just above her ear, and breathed her in. The intoxicating scent of her oriental perfume quickened my pulse. Was it wrong to just stand here and try to absorb her into every cell in my body?

Hmm. Yep.

"From now on, we go slow and steady. Every touch must be sensual. Every glance, seductive. Every smile, pure sex. Got it?"

"Uh-huh." Nervousness tittered her tone as she straightened my pocket square.

I swiveled her to face a photographer. "See that camera in front of you?"

"Yes."

I kissed the side of her head, then murmured in her ear, "Look down the lens like you want to fuck it. You are sexy. Beautiful. So damn hot. And you … in that dress … is making me hard." Semi anyway. I had to be careful, or we'd make headlines for the wrong reasons.

She giggled, bit her lip, then pouted perfectly toward the camera.

"See? Easy." I grinned and took her hand. I twirled her 'round once. Her gorgeous dress shimmered and sparkled in the spotlight. The fabric highlighted her sexy curves and cleavage. *Damn.* I'd love to see that gown pooled on my bedroom floor.

Shit. No. Focus.

Why did Kara's makeover have to turn Sutton into a tempting vixen? Temptation was dangerous. And I didn't need to enter that zone.

This was going to be a long walk.

Hand in hand, we hit the main section of the red carpet lined with reporters and photographers on one side. We posed. Cuddled. I whispered sweet nothings into Sutton's ears, but every one made her blush.

We had to stand waiting while the guests in front of us talked to a reporter.

Sutton's hand tightened around mine. "I hate waiting."

"No. This is perfect. This gives the reporters time to check the arrivals run sheets, work out who the fuck we are, and gives us a window of opportunity to attract attention. We need to make them want to talk to you."

"What did you have in mind?"

We were here for publicity; I'd make damn sure Sutton got it. She wasn't nominated for an award, so she wouldn't be on reporters' hit lists for interviews. But I'd make sure they wanted to talk to her. Every other couple just cruised the carpet, looking bored or bothersome in the heat. Single folk and groups posed politely for the cameras. We needed to stand out. Luckily, nothing created a commotion like a scandalous, hot new couple.

"Oh, I can think of several things." I pulled her close and stepped in front of her again. I threaded my hand beneath her hair and caressed the back of her neck. I threw her a sexy smile, then ran my gaze across her perfect lips, down the fine line of her neck, over her boobs, then back up. A hum hovered through my veins. My pulse thudded. No need to pretend . . . I liked what I saw.

Her lips parted. Her breath quickened. Then, the cutest wrinkles formed across the bridge of her nose. "You are good at this? Thought you couldn't act."

"I never said I couldn't. I said I *wouldn't*. I don't have to lie about appreciating and admiring the stunning woman in my arms. I'm making sure everybody here notices you, too."

She slipped her hands beneath my jacket, snaked them 'round my waist, then lowered them onto my ass. "Thank you. You think standing here, acting smitten with each other, will work?"

"Yes. But it's time to amp it up. You're the good girl gone bad, right?"

"Uh-huh."

"Let's give them something to talk about."

I leaned forward to kiss her cheek, but she turned toward me. Our lips connected. My heartbeat tripled. *Holy sweetness.* Her lips were so soft. Tender. Delicious, like strawberries. Her mouth lingered against mine, tempting and hot. *Hmm.* I wanted to flick my tongue into her mouth and taste more of her. But I kept it PG-rated. I smiled against her lips, expecting her to pull away. But she didn't. She kissed me back. No tongue, just gentle brushes and playful nips of her mouth against mine. I gladly returned every sensual motion.

Breathe. Stay in control.

But fire ignited in my blood. All the teasing had made the embers in my body smolder, but this had set them alight. I held her tighter. My heartbeat strobed in time with the flashing cameras. People hollered, clapped, and wooed, but the noise became muffled in my ears. *Shit. Too much. Too hot. Stop.*

I pulled back, breaking our kiss. Panting, I rested my forehead against hers. Could she feel my racing heart? "Sorry. I meant to kiss your cheek. That got a little hotter than expected."

Her cheeks had flushed redder than the carpet. Her fingers trembled as she fidgeted with my tie. "Not how I envisioned kissing you the first time."

"You've thought about kissing me?" Tasting her had crossed my mind more than once.

"Only for the cameras." She tapped my chest with her clutch. "That was brilliant. But no kissing on the mouth. We better move. We have a job to do."

Ouch. No ego stroking from her.

Behind me, a reporter called over the raucous, "Sutton? Sutton Summers? Over here."

"See?" I took her hand and entwined our fingers. "Slow down. Cause a stir. Then everyone will want to talk to you."

"Yay."

Sutton almost ripped my arm out of its socket as she dashed over to the TV reporter who had *Robyn—SC5TV Morning Show* printed on the front of her black blouse. The man beside her pointed his big black camera at us.

"Wow. Now this is a surprise." Robyn spoke into her mic, her voice too high-pitched for my liking. "Sutton Summers and Flint Glover?" After some standard questions, *"How are you?"*, *"How's your show?"* and *"What designer are you wearing?"* were out of the way, the reporter's interest seemed to pique. "I would never have picked you two as an item."

I didn't miss the cynicism in her tone.

Why was it so ludicrous for people to think I couldn't date someone like Sutton? Was my reputation that appalling? Did they honestly only see me as the ringleader for drunken parties and wild antics? Why did the smoke and mirrors I'd created suddenly sting? I loved to have a good time and never treated women like shit. Other than a few crazy stints in my life, I'd always had a girlfriend. *Fuck the reporter.* Maybe it really was time to clean up my act.

I drew Sutton's hand to my mouth, kissed it, and gave her a wicked wink. "Well . . . we are together. Crazier things have happened."

Sutton rested our linked hands against my chest. Her charm never faltered. "The moment we met, we just clicked."

Disbelief still rocked in Robyn's eyes. "Sutton, you look stunning. Has Flint inspired the change?"

Sutton threw her head back and laughed. "No. I'm not a high school sweetheart anymore."

"We can see that." Robyn scanned Sutton's awesome frock again. So did the three ogling cameramen standing nearby. I cast them the evil eye. *Back off, assholes. She's mine.*

Jealousy hadn't stirred my blood in over a year, but possessiveness flared inside my veins. Sutton and I may not have been officially together, but I would protect her when we were out. I slid my hand around her waist. Kissed her temple. Marked her as mine.

"And Flint?" Robyn angled the microphone toward me. "Please accept my late condolences for the loss of your brother. Can we expect to hear new music from you anytime soon? Any plans to replace Phil?"

It was as if a bulldozer had slammed into my chest. *Replace Phil? Phil . . . Phil . . . Phil wasn't here.* Dizziness swirled through my head. My lungs constricted. A sweat broke out on my brow. "Umm . . . umm . . ." *Shit!* "Yes. Soon."

Sutton flattened her palm against my pounding heart. The weight and warmth of her touch grounded me to her, calming me.

Concern flickered in her quick glance. "The Flintlocks will be back. I promise." She smiled at the reporter. "Thank you for your time. We must keep moving."

Sutton drew me away from the reporters. "Are you okay?"

"Umm . . . no. But thanks." I didn't need to have a meltdown in front of the cameras. That would make the headlines and blow up my music contract for not being mentally fit.

"Do you want to go inside?" She pointed to the fast-track

aisle that the non-celebrity, non-A-listers took into the theater.

I closed my eyes and took a deep breath. Somehow, somewhere, I found a thread of inner strength. "No. I'm okay. Let's just keep the focus on you."

"I can do that." She took my hand, giving it a soft squeeze. "But if you need to get away from the cameras, just give me a sign."

"Will do."

We continued along the carpet at a steady pace. Interview after interview, photo after photo, the process got easier. Sutton took control, answering all the reporters' questions. I never failed to touch her and admire her in that dress. I couldn't resist whispering sexy compliments in her ear and planting soft kisses against her cheek just so I could see her blush. I began to like that color on her a bit too much. *I'd better tone it down.*

But we certainly raised some eyebrows and attracted a lot of attention. The plan to be hot for each other and crazy in love worked. By the time we reached the end of the red carpet, my eyes ached from too many camera flashes, and my cheeks ached from plastering on the smiles.

I breathed with relief when we entered the foyer where hundreds of guests mingled and downed pre-function drinks.

Still holding Sutton's hand, I headed for the bar.

But halfway across the room, she pulled me to a halt.

"Oh. My. God." Excitement jumped in her voice as she clutched my forearm. "That was incredible. You were brilliant. We blew everyone away."

"I'm glad I could be of service."

"We need a drink to celebrate."

"Don't have to ask me twice."

"Now we can relax for a few hours before we have to do the whole act again at the after-party."

Hmm. Great . . . not.

If I had to keep touching her, I had to remain sober. I didn't need alcohol to mess with my head and cause me to do something stupid like make a pass at her. She'd made it clear from the start and again on the red carpet that she wanted to keep this professional. I respected that. I needed to do the same.

But I could have sworn I'd caught her staring at me more than once. She couldn't fake her pulse quickening beneath my touch, nor summon the blush to her cheeks. What if she *was* into me? *Fuck?* She'd certainly stirred something inside of my system. Whatever it was, it needed to be killed. I didn't need to lead her on and didn't need to add more complications into this mix. I'd played my part. Before I fucked this deal up, I'd best wind it down. I didn't need to drink to have fun. I could survive a few hours at the after-party.

I would stick to the plan. Do my job. Go home.

Surely I couldn't screw that up?

Chapter 9

FLINT

Hand in hand, Sutton and I meandered through the sea of TV personalities, the random movie stars and studio professionals. We occasionally stopped to chat with key people she wanted to network with before we finally reached the bar. The after-party at the Ritz-Carlton was overcrowded, loud and lively. It was full of people I didn't know. That was a good thing. No one was rushing up to me, asking about Phil or my music.

Sutton and I were still on show, but it wasn't formal anymore. To some degree, we could relax. Good. Because I was done. I wasn't in the mood to party. A couple of event photographers ran around the room snapping people, but they were mainly hunting down the award winners. I could get their attention if Sutton wanted me to.

I splayed my hand over her hip. "Do you want to go make out in the corner to attract the photographers or have a champagne?"

"No, to making out. Yes, to champagne."

"Spoilsport."

But that was the right choice. I should focus on why my ass

was here. Would hanging out, having a dance, and letting the DJ's tunes course through my veins kick-start the music in me back to life? Anything was possible, but I was doubtful.

I grabbed a champagne for Sutton and water for me. But as I handed her the flute, the color drained from her face.

"Oh, shit! What the fuck are they doing here?"

"Who?" I followed her gaze. Two young ladies dressed in glittery party dresses lingered near a console table covered in an enormous flower arrangement.

"My girlfriends. Georgia and Maddy."

"Why is that an issue? Don't you like your friends?"

"Maddy's awesome. Georgia . . . is, um . . . fab too." Her tone nosedived. Her shoulders sank like a tank in quicksand. "She's just very popular. And stunning. And—"

"You're best friends with Georgia Burrows?" I said with a thread of curiosity in my level tone. "The chick off *Unnatural Forces*?" The most popular TV show that rivaled *Stranger Things* was advertised all over town on billboards, buses, and buildings. It had been a huge hit for a couple of years, and the merchandise flooded stores.

"Yes. That's the one. Maddy and Georgia used to be on my show, but they went on to bigger and better things. Maddy's on the TV show *Vancouver Heights*. You'll love Maddy . . . but . . . you'll probably end up fucking Georgia."

My heart lurched. "What?" I'd never sleep with her friends. It was like the bro code I had with my band; you never touch someone else's girl . . . friends of, included. Georgia, with her platinum blond hair, her too tight, too short party dress, fake boobs and way too much makeup, didn't turn my eye for the right reasons. Sutton had nothing to worry about. "I'm here with you." I nudged my elbow against her arm. "We better make sure she knows that. Shall we say hello?"

"Can't we just go home?" All her earlier confidence had

dissipated into thin air.

Was she embarrassed to be with me around her friends? Or didn't she trust me? I'd love to go back to my house. Sit in the dark. Drink. Be alone and lost in thoughts of Phil. But I'd made it this far. I had to stick it out for a while longer and prove to her I had her back. "What happened to your end of our bargain? Are you piking on me?"

"No." Anxiety and concern flitted in her eyes.

I offered her my crooked arm. "We'll be fine. Promise. So please, introduce me to your friends."

"Am I gonna regret this?" She slid her arm around my elbow.

"You're with me, so anything is possible."

We crossed the room, but there was hesitation in Sutton's stride. She hugged her friends hello without her usual vibrancy.

"Holy shit! You cut your hair?" Georgia teased her fingernails through Sutton's tousled hairdo, then stepped back, holding Sutton's hands wide, to gape at her outfit. "And O.M.G. That dress . . . Wow . . . That is too hot. You can't be upstaging me."

What the fuck? Who did this chick think she was?

Hurt flooded Sutton's eyes, but she quickly blinked it away. "I wouldn't dream of it." She inched back to my side and wrapped her arm around mine. "Girls, I'd like you to meet Flint."

"Well helloooo, Flint." Georgia batted her long fake lashes and turned on a seductive voice that was more nasal than alluring. "I'm Georgia. Where has Sutton been hiding you?"

"We've just come out of the closet." I chuckled, but the girls didn't. *Ouch.*

"I'm Maddy." The bubbly brunette, with her long hair pulled into a high ponytail and a Zendaya vibe going on, politely shook my hand.

Georgia tilted her head to the side. "You look familiar. Where would I know you from?"

"Maybe my music." I shrugged. "My band is The Flintlocks."

"Oh. My. God." Maddy's hand shot out and clutched my arm. "I love your song 'Dusk to Dawn.'"

"Thanks." My stomach sank a fraction. I'd written that song with Phil after we'd been to a rave near Chinatown with Cole and Slip. That had been a wild night of booze, party drugs, and girls. I'd just turned twenty-one. But like always, Phil had drunk too much, taken way too many pills. The guys and I'd had to sober quickly to look after him. When I'd taken him home the next day, my parents had yelled at me for being irresponsible.

Fuckers.

"Sutton, I didn't know you were seeing anyone." Georgia tapped her clutch against Sutton's arm. "Why didn't you tell me? We tell each other everything."

"You've been away filming."

Georgia gave me the sexy eye. "If it doesn't work out with Sutton, give me a call. We all know Sutton can't keep a boyfriend."

Who was this chick?

Sutton wilted. Her head fell against my arm, and she lowered her chin. I didn't like that. Not one little bit. Maddy didn't look happy either. I kissed Sutton's temple, then glared at Georgia. "I can assure you, I won't be calling. I'm all Sutton's. I'm glad she hasn't kept anyone in the past because I was meant to find her."

Some twist of fate had brought us together.

Sutton tilted her head up to me and smiled, but it didn't touch her eyes.

I packed on the affection, just to prove my point. I wrapped my arms around her and buried my nose into the small of her neck, just beneath her earlobe. She flinched underneath my hot breath. Smiling against her skin, I whispered, "You're beautiful. Don't forget it."

I went to draw away, but the scent of her perfume filled my head. I'd smelled it all night, but here in the enclosed venue, it captivated me even more. *Damn!* It wasn't just her perfume, but all of her. It was getting harder and harder to stop touching her. Harder not to kiss her. Harder not to ravish her gorgeous body.

Sutton clutched the back of my jacket and melted against my chest. *Hmm. Nice.*

Maddy splayed her hand over her chest. "Oh Flint, that's so sweet about being meant to find her. Are there more like you hidden somewhere?"

"Nah. I'm pretty sure I'm one of a kind." I straightened, leaving my arm hooked around Sutton's shoulders.

"That's a shame." Maddy sighed. "You've got yourself a good one. Sutton's an angel, so be nice to her."

I liked this Maddy chick. "Always."

Georgia's eyes narrowed into catty slits. "You don't look like you're into nice girls."

"Don't be quick to judge. You don't know me. But a lady will always win my attention over a whore." *Truth.*

That shut Georgia up. Sutton gaped. But I'd just been honest and blunt.

Georgia threw me a bitchy smile, then pointed across the venue. "We're here with Xavier and Archer from my show. They've found a table. Would you like to join us?"

"Please?" A hint of desperation hovered in Maddy's tone.

"Um . . ." Sutton's voice faltered. "Okay, fine. One drink."

I rubbed her arm. "Babe, you sure?"

I didn't want Sutton to be uncomfortable I would've never picked her to suffer from low self-esteem, but her reaction to Georgia proved otherwise. Georgia had dented it somehow. I didn't need to know the details. But my role was to help Sutton land a new job. The biggest element in that was self-confidence. Was helping her with that part of my job description? Maybe not. But I wanted to put a smile back on Sutton's face.

She squeezed my hand. "I might need a bottle of vodka, not just one drink."

"I'm on it." I kissed her forehead. "Meet you at the table."

After visiting the bar, I joined Sutton and her friends. Following quick introductions to the guys, I slid onto the chair beside Sutton. Six people seated around a four-person square table gave me a good excuse to be close to her. Xavier sat on my other side. Georgia could keep her pouty, pumped lips to herself. I only had eyes for one girl tonight, and she was right beside me.

I wanted to see Sutton's face light up again. I wanted her to feel good about herself. She was sexy and hot and rocked that dress. Just looking at her made my blood rise one hundred degrees. I'd helped her bring out her inner goddess on the red carpet, I'd do the same for her in front of her friends.

A little more flirting wouldn't hurt, right? If I had to do that, so be it. All within her boundaries, of course.

Sutton had said no kissing on the mouth. So that didn't rule out touching her legs, teasing the hemline of her dress, or kissing other parts of her body. I'd make her friends believe we were together.

Shit. If I was going to do this, I needed a drink.

I poured everyone a shot. "Let's get this party started." I raised my glass. "To friends and a fuck-load of fun."

To hell with staying sober.

We downed our shots, then slammed the glasses on the table.

Her friends hit us up with questions. *"How did we meet?", "How long had we been together?"*

I let Sutton answer each one so I could kiss the tip of her bare shoulder, smooth my hand over her hair, nuzzle into the small of her neck, and smell her sweet skin. Each new question had her downing a shot. It was kind of cute she was nervous around me, but she needn't be.

I hovered my lips close to her ear. "Trust me. I won't cross any lines." *Hopefully.* "I'm just playing the game." *Unfortunately, but rules were rules.* "So, stop worrying about me and have fun. You are fucking hot." *Very, very hot.* "Half the guys here want to fuck you." *My name might be on that list.*

"Half?" Skepticism jumped in her soft tone. But then she threw me a flirtatious pout. Alcohol had restored some of her sassiness. She swayed, placed her hand on my leg and curled it around my thigh. "What about the rest?"

Her touch was like an electric pulse sparking through my body and igniting a low hum inside my dick. *Mmm.* I liked her touching me. "They're probably married or swing the other way."

She giggled and kissed my cheek. But she was quick to pull away and down a shot.

That had been the first time she'd kissed me at the after-party. I chuckled and downed another vodka, too.

"You guys are adorable." Maddy raised her glass. "I miss you, Sutt. Vancouver sucks. It's so far away."

Sutton sighed, but squeezed my thigh, hard. "The things we do for our jobs, right?"

So true. My balls were aching. I'd have to kill Blake for picking such a hot girl.

Another round of shots led to another, then Maddy, Archer, Sutton, and I hit the dance floor. We left Georgia and Xavier on the verge of hooking up. In the middle of the gyrating partygoers, I rarely let go of Sutton. Holding her around the waist, spinning around, and swaying to the beat seemed natural. Effortless. I had to keep reminding myself not to grab her, kiss her, or go rogue on our rules. But as alcohol messed with our senses and even though we kept our moves friendly, it was hard to ignore her heated gazes, her wandering hands over my ass and shoulders, and growing intoxication. I didn't need this to get out of control. I'd promised to remain a gentleman and I would.

Time to sober up.

After a couple of songs, we returned to the table to find Georgia and Xavier dueling tongues and groping each other. It was like bad porn. No, worse. Bad porn you could watch. This . . . you couldn't. But it didn't help my cause.

We grabbed the vodka and bottled water and sat at a nearby vacant table. After downing another shot, Sutton swayed on her seat. She slid her hand around my leg and smiled. Mission achieved. Even though she was drunk. It was good to see her let her hair down.

I draped my arm around her shoulders to make sure she didn't fall off her chair.

Maddy was engrossed in a conversation with Archer about some producer on his show. Georgia was deep-throating Xavier two tables away. But Sutton's hand gliding up and down my thigh held all my attention.

"You having fun?" She licked her lips. Slowly. Sensually.

I circled my fingertips over her bare arm. *God.* I wanted to taste the vodka on her mouth. Have that sweet, sticky, warm, alluring sensation on my tongue. Just once.

Nope. Stop. "Tough gig. But I've survived."

As she rubbed her hand in lazy strokes over my thigh, a teasing smile curled across her mouth. On her next swipe over my leg, her fingers froze mid-thigh. She then slid them toward the inside of my quad and inched a fraction toward my groin.

Shit. My pulse spiked. My dick jolted. I wanted her to touch me. Kiss me. Give Georgia a run for her money. *Should I let her?*

Sutton moved her hand another inch higher.

I didn't stop her.

Three more inches and she'd know the effect her tease was having on me.

Just how far would Sutton go?

I ran my fingertips across her shoulder, then cupped her

nape. I massaged the tension in her neck. Her eyes fluttered closed and a soft mewl fell from her lips. *So. Fucking. Hot.*

But a rush of sensibility sobered me. This wasn't a good idea. I lowered my voice so only she could hear. "Are you sure you want to play this game? What happened to your rules and boundaries?"

"Mine still stand. But you said you didn't have any." Her words were slurred. The vodka on her breath nearly knocked me out. "If I recall, you said anywhere, anytime."

Oh, she was a vixen. I liked that. But I had some hard lines. She'd had way too much to drink. So had I. Before I lost control, I had to get out of there. "I think it's time to go home."

"Yeah." She brushed her fingertips dangerously close to my groin. "We should go."

I swallowed hard. *Hmmm. Get her home safely. Call the limo. Get the fuck out of there.* That was the plan.

Right?

Yep. Stick. To. The. Plan.

No diversions.

None.

Chapter 10

FLINT

Rising to my feet, I downed the remains of my drink. "Folks, we're out of here." I placed my empty glass on the table and pointed to Maddy and Archer, and half-heartedly to Georgia sucking Xavier's face. "Nice to meet you, but Sutton and I are calling it a night." It was nearly two a.m.

"Sutton could never hold her alcohol," Georgia hollered from the other table. "She'll pass out before you're home."

"I'll make sure I tuck her into bed." I took Sutton's dainty hand and helped her to stand. She staggered on her feet as she said her goodbyes.

I hooked my arm around her waist, and we headed outside. The fresh air was the sobering hit I needed.

But in the limousine ride to her place, the façade was hard to drop. I still held her hand. Our fingers kept brushing over each other. Her head rested against my shoulder. I couldn't resist burying and swirling my nose against her hair and breathing her in. The night was minutes away from ending. But deep down, I didn't want it to.

Why?

Was it because tonight was the first night I hadn't thought about Phil during every waking moment? Was it because for a few short hours, I wasn't crippled by pain and grief? Was it because I'd enjoyed being with Sutton? It'd been nice to hang out with a girl who had no motive to hook up with me, even though alcohol had dared me to contemplate the idea more than once. But Sutton wasn't a one-night stand. I didn't need to tamper with our plan. I couldn't risk falling for anybody. Music had made me, but it also had destroyed my soul and those closest to my heart—Lena, my parents, and Phil. All were gone, thanks to my career. I couldn't risk losing someone I loved or cared about ever again.

Thirty minutes later, the limo dropped us off at Sutton's place. She stumbled into the building and entered the elevator. Swinging her stilettos from her fingertips, she clutched onto my arm for support. "You gonna keep your promise and tuck me into bed?"

"I'll at least get you a drink of water and some Tylenol."

"Oh. Where's the fun in that?"

On her level, she opened the door to her condo and banged it against the wall. *Thud.*

"Shit. Shh." She laughed, dropping her shoes onto the floor and her clutch on the counter, then held her finger against her lips. "Don't wake my neighbor. She's this cranky old lady with four cats. I don't want to end up like that." She wrinkled her nose. The cutest of creases formed across her bridge.

After following her into the kitchen, I tossed my jacket onto the counter, then grabbed two bottles of water from her fridge. "There's nothing wrong with cats, and I can't see you as a cranky old lady."

She cracked open her bottle, took a big sip, then wiped her lips on the back of her hand. She placed her water down, stepped toward me, and lifted her chin. "So what do you see me as, Flint Glover?"

I swallowed hard. My Adam's apple lurched, scrapping my throat like sandpaper. I had to keep my wits. "What do you mean?"

"I mean . . . what do you see?" She ran her hands up my chest and swirled them across my pecs.

I caught her wrists and lowered them to her sides so she couldn't feel my quickened heartbeat. My lips hovered three inches from hers. *Too close. Too tempting.* "I see someone who's had too much to drink."

"Am I sexy?" She pulled her shoulders back and jutted her chest slightly forward. "Am I someone you'd hook up with?"

Do-not-look-at-her-tits.   Do-not-look-at-her-tits. "Sutton. Stop."

But before I could step clear, she ran her hands up my arms and linked her fingers behind my neck. "Why?"

"You don't want this."

"What if I do?"

"Trust me. You don't." But my body had ideas of its own. Heat simmered in my blood and raced through my veins, engorging my dick. *So. Not. Good.*

"Flint?" She toyed with the back of my hair using soft strokes. "You can't deny there's something between us. You wouldn't be here if you couldn't stand to be in my presence."

"You're being presumptuous."

"Admit it. You want me."

I chuckled. Placing my hands on her hips, I gave them a little rub and pat, hoping she'd fall back a step, but she didn't. "Sutton. You've really drunk too much."

"So have you."

"I've had my fair share."

"Yep. But I sobered enough on the way home to know what I'm doing." Hunger blazed in her eyes. "It's been a big night. You found out about my father. We dazzled on the red carpet. You met my friends. You kissed me. Don't you want to do that again? You haven't been able to keep your hands off me."

True. "I was doing my job."

"You said you wouldn't act."

"Maybe I have a hidden talent." *Nope.* No acting. Just sheer willpower not to hit on her.

"Did you like it when I touched your leg?" She slid one hand onto my hip, raked her fingernails down the side of my suit pants. Shudders rippled down to my toes. "Did you like it when I played with your hair?" She teased the shaggy strands at the base of my neck. Goose bumps shivered along my spine. "Did you like it when we kissed?" She stood on her tiptoes and pressed her soft lips against my throat, then my chin, then my jaw.

My heart hammered as she edged closer and closer to my lips. *Please. Stop.*

"Flint?" Her breath was the softest of wisps against my face.

My pulse pounded in my head. My hands trembled around her waist. *Shit.* Why couldn't I stop her? *Yes . . . yes.* I could.

I grabbed her shoulders and stepped back. "Sutton. This isn't a good idea."

"I've had people tell me what to do my entire life. I want to make my own decisions. Maybe make a few mistakes."

"I don't want to be a mistake."

"I don't want that either." She slid her hands down my shirt and tugged on my loosened tie. "But haven't you ever had stupid, hot, crazy drunk sex before?"

More than I cared to remember. "Yes . . . but—"

"I want the hurt in my heart to stop ruling my head. I'm tired of pretending I'm okay when I'm not. I want to be crazy. Be spontaneous. Be me . . . with you."

Shit. Her words struck me in the chest. I wasn't okay either. I missed having fun. Being me. I caught her arms and locked onto her gaze. The desire darkening her pupils dug at my resolve. "This is a bad idea."

She circled her hands over my shoulders, erasing the gap between us again. "What if it isn't?"

"Oh no. I'm sure it is."

"Let's find out."

I groaned. My dick ached. "Sutton, you're killing me."

"Then stop making excuses and kiss me."

My heart raced like a metal riff. My life was a fucking mess; I didn't want to make it worse. I was sure I'd regret this, but my want for her overruled my head. My hands shot up and cupped her face. I kissed her. Hard. Wasting no time, I flicked my tongue into her mouth. The sweet taste of vodka tingled my taste buds. *Delicious heaven.* Parting her lips, she met my moves with the same hunger and urgency that burned in every cell of my body. My heart stampeded out of control. This was crazy. This was ridiculous. This was stupid. But . . . who fucking cared?

I shuffled her backward to the counter and lifted her onto the surface.

She wriggled to the edge and spread her knees. Clutching a handful of my shirt, she tugged me forward. Our lips connected in a fiery blaze as I melted against her. I ran my hands up her silky-smooth bare thighs. My fingertips burned to touch every inch of her skin. I'd forgotten what it was like to ache for someone, to savor every touch. Quick bangs or blowjobs in a bathroom at a bar were never this arousing, sensual, or fueled by days of agonizing, pent-up tension.

I hesitated at the hemline of her dress. *Shit.* The fabric had already gathered around her hips. Her crotch pressed and rubbed against my hardness.

"Something wrong?" she panted.

Oh. There was a whole lot of wrong with this. But fuck it.

"Do you kiss like this all the time?"

"What's wrong with the way I kiss?"

"Nothing." I drove my erection against her panties. "I think my dick is telling you how much I like it."

"I think my wet panties tell you how much I like your mouth on mine."

"They're wet?"

"Want to find out?"

Holy shit. What had happened to sweet Sutton? Drunk Sutton was fun, flirty, and dirty as fuck. *Hell yeah.*

I teased my lips against her mouth. Sliding my hands up her thighs, I eased them underneath her dress. "I might do that if you ask nicely."

She tilted her hips forward. "Please." Her breathy whisper burned my lips.

As I trailed my trembling fingers toward the edge of her panties, my need to touch her burned like an inferno. I dragged my thumb across the front of her panties, circled the soft lacy fabric, then pressed into her arousal. *Oh, yeah. Wet. Hot. Total turn-on.*

The breath rushed from her lungs. She rocked against my touch and moaned against my mouth. "Mmm."

Fuck.

This was madness. Ludicrous. But the wave of want had consumed me. Each dip and swirl of her tongue against mine had kick-started the rusty cogs inside my soul.

I fumbled for the edge of her panties, wanting to stroke her, touch and tease her, but she drew my hand away.

"Let's get naked. Take this off." She yanked my tie free and then popped open the top buttons on my shirt.

But before she reached the third one, I caught her hand. My breath snagged in my lungs. *Shit. My burn.* I closed my eyes and grimaced. *Fuck.*

She cupped my cheek. "Hey? It's okay."

"My scar."

"I know. I saw it at the fitting."

"It's . . . ugly."

She flattened her palm against my chest. "There is nothing ugly about you, Flint Glover. I won't scream or run away. I promise." She dragged her fingernail down to the next button. "May I?"

Lowering my chin, I nodded. My heart thudded as she popped open the remaining buttons, peeled the shirt from my shoulders, then dropped it on the floor. With delicate strokes, she traced the horizontal scar slicing across my chest.

"I hate it. It constantly reminds me of him."

"Shh." She placed a finger over my lips. "All scars have memories tied to them, so maybe I can give you something new to recall next time you look at it. Hopefully something good." Dipping her head, she pressed soft kisses, playful nips, and wicked licks along the length of my scar, then made her way up to my neck and lips. "That better?"

I swayed on my feet. Her kisses had left a trail of weird, almost-numb-not-quite-deadened tingles on my chest. I definitely hadn't thought about my brother when her mouth was on me. "Mmm. Yep."

"Good. I'll keep working on it." She clutched onto my waistband and tugged me closer. "Now . . . are you going to show me what you can do with this body of yours in the bedroom?"

"You're not a countertop girl?"

"The marble's cold beneath my butt." She wiggled, emphasizing her point.

"What if I can make you forget where you are?" I found the zipper on the side of her dress and lowered it.

"I'm hoping." A seductive smile skipped across her lips as she raised her arms. This was a whole new side of Sutton I'd never seen before. And damn, it made me rock-hard.

I gathered the dress in my hands and pulled it over her head. It joined my shirt on the floor. I raked my gaze over her black lacy bra, her breasts spilling over the top. *Fuck. So sexy.* After toeing off my shoes and socks, I kicked them aside, then edged between her legs. "You are hot, Sutt. Don't ever doubt that."

"You're sex on legs."

Chuckling, I swept her hair off her face. "Does that mean you want to do it standing up?"

"No. Bed."

I planted my lips against hers and deepened our fiery kisses. Each one injected fresh oxygen into my soul. Her hands on my back scorched my skin. The heat of her body against mine ignited my want for her. Every touch drove the tension higher. Each kiss turned my need to have her to dangerous levels.

She wrapped her long legs around my waist. "You better be more than a five-minute wonder."

Grinning, I picked her up and headed into her bedroom. "I'm at least a ten."

Entering her room, I placed her on her feet and guided her back against the wall. Caressing her face, I kissed her lips, her neck, and nipped and tugged on her earlobe. *Fuck.* She smelled like spring. I just wanted to taste every inch of her silky skin. Circling my hands around her back, I unclipped her bra, then slipped it off her shoulders.

Two perfect, peaked nipples taunted me in the soft light. *My God.* They were better than I'd imagined. And I'd pictured them a lot.

Her hands slipped from my neck down to my belt. She fumbled with the buckle, undid my suit pants, and yanked them to the floor.

She raised an eyebrow. "You're a briefs man?"

"What's wrong with briefs?"

"I thought most guys wore boxer briefs."

"I'm not most guys."

"I like that."

"Good." I spun her around and steered her toward her unmade bed. "You still sure about this?"

"Oh, yes." She drew me onto the mattress, shuffling up toward the pillows. "Absolutely."

As I crawled over her, I kissed my way up from her stomach to her chest. Gliding my hand over her smooth skin, I cupped her breast. The breath rushed from my lungs. The weight and size, perfect. *So soft, so silky.* I teased my thumb over her hardening nipples. Goose bumps danced across her flesh. My dick ached for some action, but it had to wait. Sutton came first. I dipped my head and flicked my tongue over one of her buds, drew it into my mouth, and circled the pebbled tip.

Her hands threaded through my hair as she arched toward me. "Hmm. I like that."

So did I.

I'd wanted to do that ever since she'd flashed me at the boutique.

She tugged my hair, then wriggled like she wanted to speed things up.

I wasn't going to argue. "Do you have a condom? I didn't plan on ending up here."

"Yeah. In my nightstand."

"Are you on the pill too?"

"I have an IUD."

"Good to know." I dipped my head, shuffled lower down the bed, and kissed across her belly. Skimming my fingers over her skimpy panties, I toyed with the top band. "Can I take these off?"

"Please."

I grabbed the edges of the silky fabric and eased them down her thighs, over her knees, and tugged them off her dainty feet. I raked my gaze over her creamy flesh and every tempting curve. *Hmm.* It had been too long since I'd had a woman sprawled out on a bed. My throbbing dick agreed.

She swiveled to sit upright, hooked her fingernail into the waistband of my briefs. "May I?"

"Go for it." I fell back onto the mattress and raised my hips.

She yanked down my underwear and my cock sprung free. Her eyes feasted on my erection. "Impressive."

"I'm glad you approve."

She crawled over me, reached into her nightstand, and found a condom. She waved it in front of my face. A sexy smile played across her lips. "This. Now."

"Bossy." I grinned, stealing it from her grasp. I ripped the packet open and rolled it on.

"Is that what you like? Bossy women in bed?" She lay down beside me, her hair fanning across the pillow.

"I like all kinds of sex." I hovered over her and kissed her gorgeous lips. "Good sex. Hot sex. Fast. Slow. Crazy . . . this here-right-now sex."

My head spun as I kissed her. I drank in her scent, her touch, her body. Something wicked within me had been unleashed, and I didn't want to stop.

Good thing neither did she.

Slipping my hand between her legs, I met her warm arousal. I dragged one finger up the length of her slit, then dipped into her depths to tease and torment her. *So wet. So warm. So sleek.* I smiled against her lips as I thumbed her clit, rubbed, and circled her. She moaned and rocked against my touch. Widening her legs farther, she pulsed against my hand.

Fuck. I wouldn't last long at this rate.

Taking my weight on my good arm, I moved over her and

edged my cock toward her opening. With a gentle thrust, I entered her. Slowly. Controlled. Restrained. Her heat enveloped me. *So, so good.* A shudder charged up my spine and pooled at the base of my neck. I stilled for a moment. Savoring her tightness around me. Her clenching. Throbbing. Pulsing.

But it lasted for a split second.

Sutton took hold of my hips and thrust upward, riding my cock from underneath me.

Jeezus!

She shattered my control. I pulled back a couple of inches, then drove into her.

Harder. Deeper. Faster.

Each time I thrust into her, she clutched and clawed my shoulders. Shudders and shivered coiled up and down my spine. Each time our lips connected, fire surged through my veins. All the teasing and flirting throughout the night had built up a crazed tension that needed to be released. This was nothing but alcohol-fueled lust. So why did my heart beat a strange tempo when I gazed into her gorgeous brown eyes?

I closed my eyes. Blocked her out.

"Flint?" She wrapped her legs around me like a boa constrictor and pinned my body to hers. "There."

With my cock buried inside her, she circled and rubbed her pussy against me. A gravelly groan escaped me as I drove into her deeper. Our breaths panted in a hot frenzy. Thrusting and rocking against her, I let her ride out the friction.

So. Damn. Good.

A soft moan tumbled from her lips. Her core clenched around me. Her fingernails dug into my back. *Fuck yeah.* Unable to maintain control, I let the brakes go and pounded into her. My muscles burned, screamed, and hollered. My right shoulder ached like a bitch. But I didn't relent.

Her eyes fluttered shut. Then she shuddered. "Oh yes,"

she gasped. Her head fell back against the pillow. She laughed, giggled, and panted. Her glorious body quaked and quivered beneath me. "Wow."

A grin curled across my lips as she orgasmed. Unable to hold on for another second, my release exploded. Spilling inside her, my dick throbbed. Pulsed. Thudded. Stars swirled before my eyes. My lungs heaved for air. "Jeezus, Sutt. That was hot."

"I so needed that." The smile lighting her face threatened to knock on the door to my damaged heart. *Nope. Not letting her in.*

Closing my eyes, I focused on the blissful shudders coursing through my body and the throbs still tapping inside my dick. *Damn.* I hadn't had sex like that in a long time. In a bed. Hot, sweaty bodies entwined. Mind-blowing kisses. Sensational, satisfying orgasm.

She swiped my tussled hair off my brow. "I was not expecting that."

I kissed her lips, then rolled off her to discard the condom, wrapping it in some tissues off her nightstand. "What were you expecting?"

"Good sex. But that was freaking amazing."

I tried not to grin but failed. "Are you trying to boost my ego or is it just because we're still kinda drunk and vodka makes you horny?"

"We are a bit buzzed, aren't we?" She shuffled onto her side and faced me. Her eyes glinted in the moonlight shining through the balcony doors. "So before we lose the rush, do you want to do it again?"

"Um . . ."

Could we take a breather for five minutes?

She zigzagged her fingernail down my chest and my scar, and across my stomach. My abs flinched and flexed beneath her torturous tickles. She straddled my hips, pinning my hands beside my head. She wriggled and slid her bare pussy over my cock. "I'm game if you are."

Shit.

She dipped her head and sucked my nipple into her mouth. As she flicked her tongue over the bud, a jolt of electricity sparked deep inside my dick.

What had happened to keeping our relationship professional? What had happened to our plan? *Fuck!* Things had gotten way more complicated than expected. I'd learned more about her tonight than I'd anticipated. My head spun with the shitfest sleeping with her had caused. Would this be the end of our arrangement? Was there any way out of this chaotic mess? *Nope. So fuck it.*

I hadn't had my fill of her yet. I threaded my fingers into her hair, drew her mouth against mine, and kissed her. I bit, sucked, and tugged on her lower lip, then I murmured, "I'm game. Definitely game. But once more won't be enough."

No freaking way.

I'd deal with the fallout in the morning.

Chapter 11

SUTTON

Cradling my head, I groaned and buried my face into the pillow. I turned away from the sunlight that slashed and sliced my skull like a sword from the curtain edges. I begged for the splitting throb pounding the center of my brain to stop. Last night came crashing back. *Flint!* Why did I have to drink so much?

I dared to open my eyes. The bed beside me was empty. The sheets were crinkled and crumbled from where he'd slept. His scent lingered on them, in the air, and on my skin.

What had gotten into me? Where had that seductress come from? I'd never done anything like that before. I wasn't spontaneous. I wasn't forward. I planned everything, lived to a schedule, played by the rules. But spurred on by vodka, the temptation to find out what it would be like to be with someone so hot had possessed me. His constant murmurs in my ear, his little compliments and teases, had gotten to me. They were just lines to get me focused on the task at hand—selling our fake relationship—but *damn*, after hours and hours of it and too many vodkas, I'd succumbed to his sweet whisperings.

Fool.

We'd gotten too drunk. Stupid things happened when intoxicated. Last night had been nothing but a one-night hookup. But breaking our rules had been mind-blowing.

And *wow* . . . He'd blown my mind and my body to smithereens.

I could still feel his lips against mine, him throbbing between my legs, his breath on my neck. *Amazing.*

The shower in the en suite turned on.

Oh . . . fuck!

He was still here?

Why couldn't he have just gone home? I didn't want to face him.

I flattened my hand across my stomach to ease the bubbling unrest. Last night had been a tangle of fun. But had I blown our publicity stunt? Would he want out? *Shit.* How would that go down in the media? Out one night with a hot rock star, dumped and single the next? *Ergh!* I didn't want to be seen as someone who was flighty and unlikeable.

Oh . . . but wait. *The Internet?*

I swung my feet off the bed and grabbed my robe off the chair. I dashed out to the kitchen, grabbed my clutch, and retrieved my cell phone. I quickly googled my name.

Holy. Moly. News item after news item, photo after photo of us, filled the screen. I stopped scrolling at an image of our kiss. Flint's eyes were closed. He leaned toward me, his hand fanned across my hip. My heart fluttered. *Mmm . . . super sexy.* We'd looked good. But did we convince the press?

I scanned the headlines.

New Duo Heat Up The Red Carpet At The Hollywood TV Awards

One Kiss Steals The Show

Sutton Sizzles This Summer With New Rock Star Boyfriend

Flint Glover Corrupts TV Princess

Oh, hell yeah. The corruption had been hot.

Harlow would be ecstatic. The plan had worked like a dream.

My vision blurred, and I swayed on my feet. Was I still drunk? *No.* But I was far from one hundred percent. I grabbed some Tylenol from the cabinet and a glass of water. I hadn't had a hangover in months.

Flint ambled into the living area wearing nothing but a fluffy white towel low on his hips. I coughed, choking on my tablet as I swallowed it. Droplets fell from his wet hair and trickled down his chest. My hands had been over every inch of his body last night. I'd licked and touched and tasted him. My gaze followed his thin happy trail from his belly button down to the top of the towel. I gnawed on my lower lip. *Hmm.* I knew what was underneath there now. *Nice. But nope.* I sucked in a sharp breath and snapped my eyes back to his. He really should put some clothes on.

"Um . . . morning." Standing on the opposite side of the counter, he rubbed the droplets into his torso. "Sorry. I didn't mean to wake you."

"Are you trying to take off without saying goodbye?" *Please. Yes. Go.* I peered over the rim of my glass.

He raked his fingers through his wet hair, leaving tousled tracks in their wake. "Kinda."

"Look . . ." I took a sip of water, then placed the glass on the counter. "About last night—"

He folded his arms and rested his hip against the counter. A small smile played across his lips. "It was . . . fun."

"But it shouldn't have happened. We were drunk. Things got out of hand."

"Maybe. But we're both adults. We consented. We fucked."

"That we did." Heat rose up my neck and burned my cheeks. "And it was good."

"But?" He grimaced.

"But . . . I don't want a relationship."

"Sutton, just because we fucked doesn't mean I want to be your boyfriend."

Thank. Goodness. "I understand if this messed things up." I rubbed at the ache behind my eyebrow. "Do you want to cancel our publicity plans?"

The grooves in his forehead deepened. "No. I don't. I have a lot riding on finding music again. Everyone but me thinks going out will help. But maybe next time we should stay sober."

"At least not drink any vodka."

"Say no to vodka." His eyes sparkled as he dipped his chin once. "Got that for future reference."

"Good." Relief flooded through my veins. "So . . . do you want to just forget last night ever happened?"

"I don't think I can do that."

Yep. There was no way I'd get him in my bed out of my head in a hurry. Somehow, I had to bury the desire to do it again. This was a short-term gig for the summer. He had his life; I had mine. I was just another notch on his bedhead. Last night had been wicked. A one-time fling. A not-to-be-repeated event. But it was one I'd never forget. "Me either. No regrets." *Hopefully.* "So, can I apologize for coming on to you and thank you for a great night over breakfast? I don't know about you, but I need greasy food, and fast."

"There's no need to apologize, and I'm down for food." He placed his hands on the counter. A hint of mischief flashed in his eyes. "Are you sure you'll be able to keep your hands off me?"

His ripped abs taunted me, begging to be touched. His toned arms flexed as he leaned against the marble. His ice-blue eyes sent an electric pulse straight to my core and a quiver between my legs. Everything about him tempted me. But I wouldn't fall into bed with him again. We had enough problems without adding more to the mix.

I drew my shoulders back and lifted my chin. "Yes. I'm not an animal."

"You were last night."

"Oh . . . God." I covered my face with my hand. Mortification crawled beneath my skin. "I'm so embarrassed."

He reached across the counter and drew my hand down. "Why?"

"That . . . wasn't me."

He chuckled. "Well, who the hell did I fuck last night in your bed?"

I burst out giggling. His quick comebacks put my mind at ease. He didn't seem to regret being with me. Maybe we could put this behind us. "Are you always this smart-mouthed?"

"I guess so. You're easy to stir." He straightened and rubbed his stomach. "Can we continue this conversation over breakfast? I'm starving." Smiling, he jerked his head toward my bedroom. "Go get dressed. I know the perfect place up the beach. I'll drive."

"Are you sober enough?"

"Other than a bit of a headache, I'm fine."

I arched one eyebrow. "Did I burn all the alcohol out of your system?"

"That you did."

I scanned his glorious half-naked body. Images of rolling around my bed with him flooded my mind—me riding him while on top, him licking and sucking my breasts, his body convulsing as he orgasmed. My heartbeat quickened. *Oh, yeah.* It had been hot. I needed to cool down. "Let me take a quick shower. Give me ten minutes?"

"Sure. Dress for the beach." He thumbed toward the door. "I have a change of clothes in my car. I'll run down and grab them."

"Like that?" *In a towel?*

"No. I'll wear my suit pants. Unless you want me to join you in the shower first?"

Butterflies fluttered in my stomach, but I set cement into my tone. "Um . . . no. Last night was a once-off. Whatever was simmering between us is over."

"Okay." He sighed like he didn't care one way or the other. "Can we just go eat?"

"Yep."

How could guys be so casual about sex? I needed to take the same approach and not make a big deal about it. What we'd done was done. If he was okay, so was I.

I walked over to the console table by the door and handed him my access card. "You'll need this to get back in the building. See you in a few minutes."

But when his fingertips brushed against mine, electricity shot up my arm and rippled in warm waves beneath my skin. Our eyes connected. Sparks zapped the air. *Oh, wow!* Did he feel that too?

He snatched the card from my grasp, then headed to my bedroom to dress.

Okay . . . maybe he hadn't.

But I had.

Crap.

I had to get Flint Glover out of my system.

Food and sunshine should do the trick.

Chapter 12

SUTTON

With my beach bag packed and my bikini on underneath my yellow sundress, I headed down to Flint's car in the visitor's parking bay. A good dose of his arrogant attitude would certainly erase any lingering want for him from my mind. We had our event at the end of next week to discuss, and hopefully we could also confirm all the appearances that would follow. While he seemed okay, I prayed sleeping with him hadn't screwed things up.

I ran my fingertips over the hood of his sleek silver Ferrari Portofino M. "Wow. Nice ride."

The smile that slid across his lips bordered on dangerous. "Thanks. Get in."

He opened the door for me. I slid into the car, stuffed my bag at my feet, and melted into the soft, black-leathered passenger seat. The smell of the new car and Flint filled my head. *Hmm. Nice.*

After tossing his suit and shoes into the trunk, he jumped in behind the steering wheel. He wiped his hands on his crumpled white T-shirt, then tugged and straightened his blue surf shorts that matched the color of his eyes.

He slipped on his black sunglasses. "Ready?"

"Where are we going?"

"You'll see."

He pressed the button, and the car roared to life. He reversed out of the parking space and headed north, following the coastline. The bright sun and the cool air-conditioning on my face did nothing to improve my hangover. Half an hour later, he pulled into a beachside parking lot. As I stepped out of the car, the fresh ocean air hit me, followed by the aroma of bacon and coffee tumbling out of the small café on the corner. My tummy grumbled. I hadn't eaten much last night at the awards.

"You want a breakfast sandwich?" he asked, stuffing his cell phone and keys into his pocket.

"Oh yes, please." I pulled my large floppy sun hat from my bag and jammed it on my head.

"Coffee?"

"I'd love one. I'll have a no-foam latte on half whole milk, half non-fat milk with one packet of Splenda, a dash of vanilla syrup, and a sprinkle of cinnamon, please."

He swept his hair back and yanked on a baseball cap. As he headed toward the café, he shook his head and mumbled something under his breath. While I waited, I took a seat on a bench that overlooked the beautiful stretch of beach and rubbed on some sunscreen. Surfers glided along gentle rolling waves. Seagulls swooped and darted through the air. Avid exercisers jogged along the water's edge.

Five minutes later, Flint returned with our order, and we headed onto the sand. Near the water, I rolled out two beach towels for us to sit on.

"This is the best food in the world after a big night." Flint handed me a sandwich and a coffee.

I inhaled the addictive scent of coffee and took a sip.

But . . . Ew! I licked and touched my lips. I struggled to swallow the hot liquid. "This isn't what I ordered."

"Nope. It's just a plain cappuccino. No flavors. No sugars. No shit."

"But—"

"No buts." He bit into his sandwich and chewed. "You don't need all that fancy crap. It ruins the flavor of the coffee. And it costs half the price. Just drink it."

Scrunching my nose, I took another tiny mouthful. Then another. It wasn't as sweet as I was used to, but . . . it was good. *Really good!* "Mmm."

He raised an I-told-you-so eyebrow at me.

Just when I thought I understood him, he threw me off-course. I placed my cup on my towel and grabbed my food. "So, you live in a multi-million-dollar house, drive a hot car, wear designer clothes on the red carpet, but you won't buy me a fancy latte or vodka cocktails? What's with that?"

"Fancy drinks and crap aren't necessary. I don't buy into the LA chic-fad-trending bullshit. Don't get me wrong. It's nice to have nice things—the house, the car. They're my rewards for hard work. But I don't make wearing designer gear and eating out at expensive restaurants a daily habit. That way, I can appreciate the finer things when I buy them or have to go to an event, film a video clip, or go to a photoshoot."

Wow. I couldn't remember a time when I didn't have the latest on-trend gear and fashion accessories. I'd never known any different. That had to change until I landed a new job. Budgeting was new and challenging. Maybe I could learn a thing or two from Flint, like appreciating a simple cup of coffee.

Hmph. When did I start drinking jazzed up lattes? Fancy cocktails? Cold-pressed juices? Had it started when hanging out with my A-list friends? Or was it from being primed by my pretentious father? *Ergh!* I couldn't remember. Did I even like those things, or did I just get them because everybody else did? My head ached, unable to think straight. But after tasting this coffee, I'd never order another over-the-top latte again.

It could just be my hangover talking.

I unwrapped my sandwich. Bacon, cheese, and egg protruded from the fresh white bread. Ketchup oozed down the sides. *Yum.* "You didn't change this on me, did you? It is real bacon and not tofu, right?"

"Guaranteed, this is the real deal. I'd never change bacon. That would be criminal." He took another bite, moaning as he chewed. "Greasy food and a swim are the best ways to cure a hangover."

I bit into the sandwich and heaven hit my mouth. "Mmm. This is what I needed. But I don't swim." I'd lived in California all my life and couldn't swim to save myself. When I was young, while other kids were in swimming lessons, I was at acting classes and already cast on a TV show. "I like looking at the water—not going in it. Venice Beach and Santa Monica are always crowded, often dirty, and full of too many tourists. I don't mind swimming in pools, but not the ocean."

"You should come up here. The water is great. I could teach you to surf."

"You surf?"

"Yeah." He glanced toward the waves. He sucked in a deep breath, then let it out slowly. "I used to come here with Phil and the guys."

"Um. I don't think teaching me to surf is a good idea. That would be beyond the rules of our agreement."

"Yeah ... but so is having breakfast together. So was having sex."

My shoulders slouched like my sun hat. "Please, don't remind me."

"Where's the fun in that?" He scrunched up his wrapper

and tossed it in the takeaway bag.

"Oh. I forgot to tell you." I sat taller. "We made *ET News* and several other entertainment sites. We looked so good in the photos." *Hot.*

He stared at the water for a few seconds, his face void of all emotion. Then one corner of his mouth curled. "How could we not? You rocked that dress last night."

"Thank you." Warmth touched my cheeks. But as I took another sip of coffee, my vision blurred. A sweat broke out on my brow. My hand shook as I wiped my forehead with the back of my hand.

"Are you okay?" Flint asked.

"I think I'm fermenting in the sun." I glanced at my half-eaten breakfast. Nausea swirled in my stomach. If I had another bite, my food might come back. "I can't eat any more."

I went to wrap it up and put it away, but Flint flapped his fingers at me. "Don't waste it. I'll have it."

I handed it over and he polished off the remains.

He let out a soft belch. "Okay. Now I'm full. Want to go for a quick walk up to the rocks before I take you home?"

Maybe the cool ocean air and a walk would settle my tummy. "Sure."

I gathered our towels and rubbish and stuffed everything into my beach tote. Side by side, we headed along the water's edge.

I looked up at him from underneath my sun hat. "So, take out our romp between the sheets. Did you enjoy last night?"

He pushed his sunglasses higher up the bridge of his nose. "Yeah. It was a touch crazy as always. It was weird being there without the guys. There were moments I missed Phil and my band. But I survived. Thanks to you." He scratched his chest. "The after-party was interesting. Not just because you were trying to feel me up. But your friend Georgia was a piece of work."

"Yeah." My stomach sank, but a wave washing over our bare feet distracted me. I tiptoed through the water. To my surprise, the temperature was pleasant and inviting. Pity I couldn't say the same thing about Georgia. Not last night, anyway. "She wanted you at the beginning. That was obvious."

"She had no chance." He tapped his elbow against my arm. "I was with you."

"Thank you." I focused on the rocks ahead to help keep my tone lighthearted. "Not many resist her charm. Xavier certainly didn't."

"No. But he could have her." Flint chuckled, but then his tone turned serious. "Is she always like that?"

"You mean all over guys? A man magnet? Totally sexy? The one who owns the room?"

"No. I meant a total bitch for not respecting us being together, and for putting you down, thinking she's the shit."

"Oh." Flint had nailed Georgia. She'd always been a queen bee. She attracted attention and had guys falling at her feet with a click of her fingers. I'd learned to just step back and let her take what she wanted to avoid getting hurt again. "That's just Georgia."

"Why do you let her get away with it? Maybe it's different for guys, but we call each other out if someone is being a dick."

"We've known each other for a long time and been through a lot together—boyfriends, breakups, auditions. Maddy and Georgia stood by me when shit went down with my dad. We've always been there for each other."

"But you didn't even want to introduce me last night? Why?"

"Do we have to talk about this?"

"No." He shrugged. "Not if you don't want to."

He continued to stroll beside me, not saying a thing. It really was as if he was content for me not to say anything about

Georgia.

God, he infuriated me.

"I didn't want you to meet Georgia because I knew she'd want to hook up with you. I didn't want to risk you running off with her." Was it wrong I wanted to keep Flint to myself? Have my moment being seen with the hottest guy in the room? "She's hit on every guy I've liked or shown an interest in since Beau, my ex, and I broke up eight months ago." Some of her conquests still hurt too much to talk about.

"On purpose?"

"I don't think she realizes she's doing it. She gets drunk, she flirts, men fall for her."

"I won't. Promise." Sincerity warmed his gaze, but I didn't buy it. My past experiences had left me too scarred.

"Georgia always gets what she wants. Deep down, she's a nice person. She helped me find a lawyer to take on my dad and picked up the issues in my new contracts. But she's changed since being on *Unnatural Forces*. Fame has gone to her head. Maddy and I have had so much going on in our lives—me with my court cases and Maddy moving part-time to Vancouver—so we haven't had time to worry about her. She's done some mean things that we've let slide, hoping they don't become the norm.

"Last night, I didn't want Georgia drilling me about you in case I gave our plan away. I have an awful tendency to spill everything after a few drinks. If she found out we weren't actually dating, she'd be all over you. If I let slip any information about the auditions I'm going for, she'll sweep in on them and steal them away from me again."

"Again?" His stride faltered.

Shit. That didn't come out right. Maybe I was still a touch drunk. "I'm not jealous of Georgia's and Maddy's successes. They've worked their butts off and deserve to do well. But some days, it's hard not to be overwhelmed by self-doubt. Georgia landed the role on *Unnatural Forces* ahead of me and was signed for small parts in two movies we both auditioned for. I can accept that I might not have been the right casting choice. Absolutely." I splayed my hands across my chest. "I love my friends, but right now, I just want to keep some distance from Georgia. She's a force I can't compete with. I want to score a new role, something I can call my own, while she's not around."

I had to do whatever it took to improve my chances of landing a new job, even if it meant avoiding her for a while.

"You did." He nudged my arm. His voice hovered with a velvety sexiness. "You scored with me last night."

I play pushed his shoulder, sending him stumbling sideways. "You turkey."

"Me? Why you . . ." He ducked his head, caught me around the waist, and picked me up over his left shoulder. He grabbed and tossed our hats, sunglasses, his keys, and my bag onto the sand, and headed into the waves.

"Flint? No." I shrieked and smacked his butt. "No. Put me down."

"No one calls me turkey."

I kicked my legs, but his laugh was contagious.

"No. Stop." I wriggled but failed to escape his clutches. "I can't swim."

"I've got you." He waded out farther. Once he was thigh deep, he dunked me under the water.

Resurfacing, I screamed. "Argh. Why did you do that?" I wiped the droplets from my eyes. My hair clung to my face. My sundress had glued to my body.

"It's hot." He flicked the water out of his long hair. "And it's a great hangover cure."

His ice-blue eyes glinted, as clear as the gorgeous water. His saturated white T-shirt had turned transparent, molding like a glove across his chest, showing off every fine muscle of his physique and highlighting his peaked nipples.

Maybe being dragged in here had been worth it.

But a big breaking wave approached. The blood drained from my face. "Oh, shit." I flung my arms around his neck. "We're gonna drown." I wasn't lying. I really couldn't swim.

"No, we're not." He took hold of my hand. "I've got you. Take a deep breath. Duck under the wave. Ready? One. Two. Three. Go."

I sucked in oxygen until my lungs hurt. I closed my eyes and bobbed down.

The wave rolled over my head. The water swirling around me was cool and refreshing. As I popped up above the waist-deep water, Flint clapped. "You survived."

My heart raced. "That wave was huge."

"No, it wasn't." He swam out a few feet farther beyond the break. "It was a baby."

I waded toward him. "Stop. That's far enough."

"I got you." He wrapped his arm around my waist, gliding me over another wave. "See?"

"Hmm." I rested my arms over his shoulders and linked my hands behind his neck. "Was this some ploy to get me into your arms again?"

"No. I just wanted to cool off. You needed to do the same."

His gaze fell to my chest. My low-cut dress revealed too much cleavage. Every time he checked me out, my breath hitched, my nipples hardened, and goose bumps prickled my skin.

A sly smile slid across his lips. "I'm not complaining about seeing you wet."

I swept some damp strands off his brow. "You're a hard one to work out, Flint Glover."

"I don't need you to work me out."

"I don't believe that for a second." I ran my fingertips down the chiseled line of his jaw, then rested my hand against his shoulder. I preferred his T-shirt off; I'd much rather be touching his bare skin. "Is your arm okay? After carrying me?"

"Yeah. It only hurts when I raise it above my head."

"So no volleyball, tennis, or golf?"

"No." He chuckled. "None of those."

"What happened?"

"It was dislocated in the accident."

"Ouch." A bone popping out of its socket, then being rammed back into place slammed into my mind. *Ergh.* I didn't need that. "Does it affect you playing guitar?"

"I don't know." He twirled me around in the water, floating over another wave. "I haven't played since then."

"Not even at home?"

"No."

"What are we going to do about that?"

"We?" His brows pinched together. "Nothing. I don't need your help."

"But that's part of our plan. I have to help you find music again. I'm just not sure how to do that."

He tugged me closer so our hips connected. With the softest of strokes, he ran his fingertips down the side of my face, then hooked my wet hair behind my ear. "Do you really want to help me?"

"Yes. Did you have something in mind?" Watching his lips move made kissing him again tempting. Ripples of warm air sizzled between us.

He tilted his head to the side. "Maybe we should see some live music. Hang out with some musicians."

"That sounds okay. When?"

A smile quivered across his lips. "Do you have to work on Tuesday?"

Tuesday? What was on Tuesday? What day was it today?

Oh ... Sunday. I combed my fingers through the back of his hair. "I'd have to check my scene schedule. Why?"

His lips inched toward mine. "Would you like to go with me to Hunter and Kara's get-together at Kyle and Gem's place? It starts at six."

My heart leaped into my throat. I slapped my hands against his chest and pushed backward. Water swooshed and splashed around us. "Get the fuck out. Are you serious?" *Holy. Freaking. Wow.* "I ... I ...would love to but ... but ... are you sure you want me around your friends? That's not part of our agreement."

His laugh rumbled, low and husky in his throat. He grabbed my floating dress underneath the water and drew me toward him. His hands circled my waist as he rested his forehead against mine. "I think after last night, and here, now, we've broken every rule we had set."

Shit! What was I doing? I didn't want to give him the wrong idea.

"Flint." I flattened my hand against this chest to keep him at bay. "We can't do this."

"Sutton. It's just an invitation to hang out at Kyle and Gemma's house and have dinner. That's it."

Yeah. Look how breakfast had turned out. I was seconds away from making out with him again. *Fuck!*

I pushed out of his hold and floated backward over a rolling wave. "I'd love to meet Everhide and the guys in your band, but I don't know if spending more time together is a good idea."

"It's not a party." He waded over to me. Any distance I put between us, he erased instantly, like magnetic ends constantly drawn to each other. What was with that? "There won't be many people. I'll drive, so I won't drink. We can reset and make sure we can go out without tearing each other's clothes off at the end of the night."

Oh, there'd be no more sex. That was for sure. But

reestablishing our boundaries in a calm and controlled environment would be a good idea.

I lowered my feet onto the sand and put on a playful grin. "Okay. But you'd better make sure there's no vodka around."

He hooked the strap of my sundress back up onto my shoulder. "No vodka. Not since it makes you hot for me."

"No, it doesn't." *Lie.*

"You sure about that?" He drifted closer and closer.

"Yes." My gaze fell to his lips. Not sure I needed vodka or anything else to raise my body temperature around him.

"Well, if it does?" He grabbed my hands and hooked them around his waist. "I'll just have to do this."

As we floated over a wave, he cupped my face and kissed me. Long and slow and deep. His tongue flicked into my mouth and teased across my teeth. Jolts of electricity sparked in my core, and I melted into him. *Shit.* My heart pounded against his chest as his hands circled my back and dug into my flesh. I crushed my breasts against his ribs. The friction of clothing and skin rubbed my nipples until they ached. I parted my lips and surrendered, kissing him back, slowly. Sweetly. Seductively. He smiled against my mouth, then sucked on my top lip, bottom lip, and flicked his tongue against mine again.

I'd never been kissed by someone who made me lose all my senses. I lost track of time. I couldn't get enough. Which was stupid. Because this had to stop.

Soon . . . Maybe . . . In a minute.

His hand swept over my shoulder, trailed down my side, then cupped my breast. Water swirled around us as I drove my crotch against his hardness, needing more pressure.

Fuck. Shit. Fuck!

"Flint?" I tugged on his hair. My breath panted against his. "Stop. I'm sorry. This has to stop." I swam back a foot. "This is wrong. I don't want this to turn into something. We live different lives. Want different things. I don't want our involvement to get ugly?"

"Sutton, you're overthinking this. It was just a kiss."

That . . . was not just a kiss. Not to me anyway. Between my legs was as wet as the ocean. "Fine. Please don't do it again."

Grinning, he held up his hands. "If you insist."

The glint in his eyes held too much humor.

Oh, the nerve of the guy. Was he playing me? This might just be fun for him, but it wasn't for me. His kisses were hotter than the sun's surface, and I couldn't risk getting burned again. "Yes. I insist. No more kissing."

What had I been thinking? Clearly, I wasn't.

Frustrated at myself for falling for his seduction, I staggered and stumbled toward the shoreline and glanced at my palms. "I've turned into a prune. Can you take me home please? I need to learn my lines for tomorrow."

Laughing, he took my hand and helped me to the water's edge. "Anything for you, princess."

The moment we reached the shore, I tugged my hand free. I raced up the beach, grabbed our belongings, and rushed toward his car. My mind spun with dizziness. The taste of his lips lingered in my mouth. *Crap.*

After Everhide's party, it would be best to only see each other for our scheduled events and not drink excessively. Nor swim. Nor have breakfast. Nor have sleepovers, sex, or steamy kisses. Nor hold each other close.

Damn.

My list of rules of engagement grew longer and longer. But I needed them in place to stop being tempted. And he was certainly tempting.

But wait?

Would breaking the rules be so bad?

Oh, yes . . . it would be bad. Very, *very* bad.

And I was worried that I'd like it.

Chapter 13

FLINT

Weaving around the several cars that blocked the driveway to Gemma and Kyle's house in Pacific Palisades, I headed for the front door with Sutton by my side. She was dressed in a white cropped tank top and tiny pink denim miniskirt; her curves were on full display. Her silky long legs tempted me to touch and kiss every inch of them again. Knowing how they felt hooked around my waist was killing me.

But she'd thrown me more personas than a choose-your-own adventure book over the past two weeks. From nervous yet bossy at our first meeting, to fun and flirty at our fitting, to sultry and sexy on the red carpet, to a wilted flower when I'd met her friends, then . . . hot and seductive in the bedroom. *Damn actresses.* She constantly did my head in. Which one was the real Sutton? Maybe she was all of them. *God.* Was she more messed up than I was?

This get-together was a test to see if I'd be able to go to more events with her . . . and to see if I could keep my hands to myself. Unlike at the beach two days ago. Nursing a mild hangover, spontaneity had taken hold of me for the first time since the accident. The fun I'd had carrying her into the waves, helping her swim over them, and floating around in the water had surprised me. Having her cling to me like a lifebuoy had been an unexpected bonus. Kissing her had been impromptu and unplanned. Something about her just drove me crazy. Fooling around in the ocean had been the first sign of my old self in months.

She might be helping me after all.

But bringing her here to meet my friends was a big deal. As we neared the door, the nerves flitting in my stomach hit overdrive. I was protective of Kyle, Gemma, Hunter, and Hayden's privacy, and treasured how much they'd supported my band's career over the years. They wouldn't care that Sutton and I had been set up, or that we hadn't been together long. So why was I on edge?

The answer jolted my chest and squeezed my heart. *Crap.* This was the first time I'd been out to visit friends since Phil had died. Was I mad for doing this?

Yep.

I scaled the two front steps and stopped by the huge wooden door. I turned to Sutton. Excitement and concern swirled in her eyes. "Sutt, you cool?"

"No." She fidgeted with the tie at the bottom of her top, then smoothed her hands over her miniskirt. "I'm about to meet my favorite band. Do I look okay?"

I reached out to touch her, rub her arm, but stopped myself. "Yes, you look . . . good." Too good. "These guys are easy-going. Just relax and have a good time." I really needed to listen to my own advice.

"But I want to impress them. Do you want me to be fun and flirty? Shy and meek?"

Why did both of those options send a fevered rush over my body and my blood south? I wiped my clammy palms on the back of my cargo shorts. "You don't have to put on an act. Just be yourself. These are my friends, so just chill."

"If you want me to chill"—she threw me a saucy smile—"maybe I should've had a few vodka shots before I left home."

My heart skipped a beat. "Ah. No. Not unless you want a repeat of Saturday night?"

"Oh…um…" She lowered her chin. Her fine hair fell forward across her face. No matter what she did, she couldn't hide the reddening of her cheeks. She scooped the loose strands behind her ear. "No, I don't. I'm sorry."

My chuckle rumbled deep and low in my throat. We'd agreed to reset our rules, but damn . . . she made it hard not to break them. I liked taunting her. Maybe a bit too much.

I pressed the doorbell. The huge door opened, and a big burly security guard with arms as thick as tree trunks greeted us.

"Hey, Flint."

"Hi, Sam." I clasped palms with him and slapped his shoulder. "How you doing?"

"Superb as always."

"Sam? This is Sutton."

"Nice to meet you, miss." Sam bowed his head, then waved us inside. "Head on through. Everyone is out by the pool."

I took Sutton by the hand. It was the safest place to touch her without my fingers wanting to wander. I'd never thought being a fake boyfriend would test my ability to maintain control and practice restraint. I'd never had to do that before. So far, I'd failed dismally. When I had more mental issues than a back catalog of *Rolling Stone* magazine, were suppression and constraint good things? I clearly sucked at abiding by rules.

But that made every second with Sutton a challenge.

Would I follow the rules or break them?

As we walked through the foyer, laughter and music hit

my ears. The succulent, sweet smell of grilled meat filled my nostrils. This was supposed to be a small gathering, but when we entered the open-plan living area, more than forty people filled the room and overflowed out into the entertainment area by the pool.

Sutton tugged on my arm. "Shit. I thought you said this wasn't a party."

I shrugged. "Guess their plans changed."

"Flint?" She tightened her grip on my bicep. "Do you know all these people?"

I scanned Everhide's friends and entourage. "Most. Why?"

"I'm a little starstruck. This place is crawling with huge rock stars."

"But you hang out with TV and movie people. What's the difference?"

"They're my friends."

"And these are mine. Come on. They won't bite. I promise."

Hand in hand, we strolled out to the pool. Stepping free of her hold, I held my arms out wide and headed toward Hunter, Kyle, and Gemma, who were talking to some of their friends. "Guys? How the fuck are you?"

Hunter's broad smile lit his face. With beer in hand, he rushed over and gave me a big hug. "Flint. You made it."

"Sure did."

"Flint. Dude." Kyle flung his arms around me, then ruffled my hair. "You are looking good, man. Great to see you."

"You too, Kyle."

"Flint, baby." Gemma held her arms open.

I embraced her extra tight and rested my head on top of hers. "Hey, gorgeous. How's tour?"

"Freaking awesome."

"Guys?" I placed my hand on the small of Sutton's back. "This is Sutton."

"Hey Sutton." Hunter swooped forward and gave her a kiss on the cheek. As he stood back, she touched her face. Stars appeared in her eyes, like she was a teenager who'd just been kissed by her idol and never wanted to wash her cheek again. *Totally adorable.*

Kyle swept forward and kissed her other cheek. "It's nice to meet you."

Then Gemma hugged her hello. "Hi." She fell back a step and clutched Sutton's hands. She jerked her head toward me. "I hope you have the energy to keep up with this one. He loves a good party."

I feigned a smile. In the past I'd been like that, but I wasn't that same guy anymore. Not when a huge chunk of my heart had died with Phil. Life before the accident seemed like a distant memory, a dream. The after-party last Saturday had been tame compared to my usual antics of crazy dancing, excessive drinking, and sometimes stupid shenanigans.

"But if you ever get into trouble or need help"—Gemma patted my forearm—"he'll always be there for you."

"That's good to know." Sutton curled back beneath my arm and rested her head against my shoulder.

Closing my eyes, I brushed my nose against her hair and inhaled the scent of her oriental perfume. When she cuddled me like this, it grew harder to believe that this was all for show. Every touch made me question my sanity. *Every. Single. Second.* But the mention of Phil kept my reality in check.

I had to change the topic to not dwell on Phil or linger too long on touching Sutton. "Where are Kara and the kids?"

Hunter waved his beer toward the house. "She's upstairs with Diego, our nanny, settling the kids in to watch a movie. She'll be down soon."

"Cool."

"Would you two like a drink?" Gemma clasped her hands

together. "Beer is on ice in the cooler by the door. Spirits and champagne are inside. What will it be?"

"I'll have a beer." I swept my hand underneath Sutton's hair and rubbed her neck. "Is champagne good for you, Sutt?"

"Yes, please."

"Awesome." Gemma shuffled forward and grabbed Sutton's hand. "Flint, you stay here. I'm gonna steal Sutton for a few minutes. We'll be back in a sec."

Before I could argue, Gemma linked arms with Sutton and dragged her off toward the kitchen. Sutton threw a quick glance at me over her shoulder. Her eyes were wide and lit with excitement, then she turned and dashed away.

My gaze drifted directly to Sutton's gorgeous legs and her miniskirt that rode to the perfect height up her thighs. *Not a bad sight. Not at all.*

"Hey?" Hunter handed me a beer. "She's not too shabby."

"No. No, she's not." I cracked the lid off my bottle and took a mouthful.

My phone pinged. I grabbed it out of my shorts pocket and read the message from Cole.

RUNNING LATE. FLAT TIRE. BE THERE ASAP.

Crap. I needed the guys here to help me through tonight. I quickly replied:

OK. I'M WITH SUTTON.
BUT GET YOUR ASSES HERE.

"Everything all right?" Kyle asked me as Hunter and I followed him over to a nearby outdoor bar table.

"Yeah. Cole and Slip got a flat. They'll be back from Palm Springs soon."

Cole and Slip had jumped at the opportunity to play some gigs to help our friends' band. One guy was sick; another one's girlfriend had had her first baby. My guys missed playing. I hated that I was such a mess and fucking with their lives.

Kyle placed his beer down and rested his elbow against the surface. "Cole rang us earlier today. He filled us in on what's going on . . . about your recording deadline. I'm sorry to hear you've been struggling since Phil died. If we'd known, we would've done anything to help. Touring keeps us locked in our own bubble for way too long."

"It's okay." An icy sweat swept over me, rushing from my head down to my toes. "Did he tell you? About Sutton and me?"

Hunter shrugged and sipped his beer. "Yep. He said Blake set you up as a means of therapy for you and re-imaging for her. We've done that throughout our careers. Don't worry about it. It looks like Blake has done all right, though. You two seem to have hit it off."

Relief flooded my veins. I'd never wanted to lie to them. It didn't matter that I'd met Sutton through our managers. That wasn't any different to meeting someone online these days. We'd agreed to go out. We'd slept together. We'd come out tonight.

Shit. Were we actually dating?

Contemplating that concept hurt my head. There were too many issues with that notion. The biggest one . . . neither of us *wanted* a relationship.

I summoned a faint smile. "There are some sparks, but we're not taking things too seriously. She's hell-bent on her career and somehow, I have to grasp onto mine again." That was no lie.

Kyle twisted his beer back and forth on the table. "We're glad you're making the effort to move on. Doesn't matter how. Losing Phil sucked. The music will come back when you are ready. Don't force it."

My heart struggled to beat. Music used to fill my soul, but it had been replaced by a vast, bottomless pit. "There's nothing at the moment."

"Maybe something new and unexpected will ignite your fire." Kyle jerked his chin in Sutton's direction. Hope shimmered in his eyes.

With champagne in hand, Sutton hugged and kissed Kara and Lexi and Carla hello. Her eyes sparkled and her laugh resonated through the air, hitting my chest with a thud. It was nice that I didn't have to babysit her. She wasn't clingy. Timid or shy. Nothing like my ex, Lena.

"Have you fucked her yet?" Hunter asked as casually as if he were enquiring about the weather.

Grinning, I savored a cool mouthful of beer before swallowing. "Yep."

Kyle chuckled and shook his head. "Good. So you can stop eye-fucking her now and come help me grill some more steaks." Kyle shoved me toward the barbecue at the far end of the pool. "I wanna tell you about the production company we're looking at buying."

"Awesome." They'd be so good at that.

But within a few steps, I halted. I thumbed toward the house and walked backward. "I'll join you in a sec. I'll just check on Sutton. Make sure she's okay."

Hunter drained his beer, then tossed the empty bottle in a nearby trash can. "Dude. You got it bad."

No. No, I didn't.

Did I?

Chapter 14

FLINT

Zooming into the kitchen, I headed over to Sutton as she talked and laughed loudly with Hayden and Lexi. I waved hello to them as I snuck up behind her. I slid my arms around her waist and nuzzled her ear. We had to practice faking for our events, right? Even though we didn't have to pretend here, I wanted an excuse to touch her. "You having fun?"

She let out a soft giggle, snaked her hands around my forearms and leaned against my chest. "Yeah."

"Are you meeting all my friends without me?" I circled my hands over her bare belly, her skin smooth and soft beneath my fingertips. Her little muscles fluttered and tensed beneath my touch.

I like that.

I dipped my fingers beneath her waistband, but she flattened her palms over my hands to stop my ticklish onslaught. "Yes. Is that okay? Why? Did you miss me?"

"Yes," I whispered with more want and need in my voice than I should've.

"Sorry." She smiled and touched my cheek. "Hayden was

just telling me about Hunter's bachelor party in New York. Were you drunk at some club, trying to out-serenade some girls with Hunter and Kyle? Is that true?"

I rested my chin on her shoulder. "Unfortunately."

Hayden wiped laughter tears from his eyes as if he'd had way too much fun retelling the tale.

Sutton gave me a sideways look. "And then went skinny-dipping in the hotel pool?"

"Yep. Also true." I nodded.

"And trashed your hotel room?"

"Ahh . . . no." My heart stilled. "That was Phil."

That night slammed into the forefront of my mind. Being drunk had always fueled Phil's outbursts. He'd lost his stash of party pills and gone ape shit in the hotel room looking for them. "He didn't break anything too serious—just the bed lamps. He knocked over a chair. Kicked the crap out of the trash can. Smashed an empty bottle of tequila against the wall. The neighboring room complained about the noise, so we got kicked to the curb."

"Oh . . ." Hayden's eyebrows shot skyward. "Phil told us it was you who trashed the room."

Sutton squeezed and rubbed my hand.

"Nope." I closed my eyes. Pulling Sutton closer, I inhaled the sweet scent of her perfume. For some strange reason, it stopped my heart from splintering. "I just had to pay the bill."

"Wow." Hayden ruffled his hand through the back of his short hair. "Sorry, man. You copped some flack in the news for days after that."

"It wasn't the first time, and I'm sure it won't be the last." I'd learned not to take notice of the gossip. Most of it was lies. Most of it was to cover Phil's ass.

Lexi splayed her hand across her chest. "Some good times and crazy memories. We loved Phil. I still can't believe he's gone."

"No. Neither can I." My chest shuddered. But before this conversation went further down a Memory Lane I didn't want to travel on, I had to get out of there. Talking about Phil was too hard. Too raw. I rubbed Sutton's arms. "I'm gonna get some fresh air. You wanna stay here or come with?"

Concern flickered in her eyes. "I just need to use the restroom. I'll be out in a sec."

"Okay." I waved across the counter to Lexi and Hayden. "Catch up soon."

On shaky legs, I ventured outside. Drawing oxygen into my lungs was easier in the open air.

At the barbecue, Kyle had two guys standing around helping him cook. It didn't look like he needed any more hands. I grabbed another beer and drifted over to the edge of the pool to talk to the guys from Kill Hive, Everhide's support band.

"Hey, Flint." Mason, their lead singer, shook my hand. "We didn't have time to catch up after the show last week. We're so stoked we got the gig to play for these guys after you pulled out. But we're sorry about Phil, man."

"Thanks." Every time I heard Phil's name, my chest constricted like I'd been punched. My heart crumbled and ached. I let out a slow breath. *I could do this. I could be here, be social, be out. Breathe.* "You guys are nailing it. You're really good. I hear your songs everywhere."

Fuck! That should be my band flooding the airwaves. I hated letting them down.

"It's been an incredible ride," Kieran, their drummer, said. "Everhide are awesome to tour with."

It should've been my band touring with Everhide. "Yeah. They're great guys."

Bryson, their bassist, clutched my shoulder. "So sorry about your brother. Are you playing again?"

"Um . . ." A low, deep throb drummed in the back of my head. The tension in my temples tightened. "Hope to soon, man."

Where was Sutton? I scanned everyone present. There she was. By the bar. Sidetracked, talking to Kara again.

Where were Cole and Slip?

They still hadn't arrived.

I made my excuses and dashed over to a clearing by the doorway. I ripped out my cell phone and called them. No answer. No new texts. *Shit!*

Sophie, Everhide's manager, and her partner, Gayle, came over to chat about Everhide's tour. Then, of course, they changed the conversation. "Sorry about Phil. You doing okay?"

No. No, I'm not. I wish everyone would stop saying his name!

I did my best to accept their sympathies graciously, but my blood pressure had skyrocketed. I headed inside to get a drink. *Vodka. Neat.* I was quick to down the shot, followed by another.

Then Rita Morgan, one of my super-cool solo-artist friends, came over to talk. "Condolences. Phil was awesome. Sorry he's gone."

Shit! I knocked back another swig of vodka.

After Rita, Carla came over. "Sorry for your loss."

More vodka.

Then Chester, Gemma's bodyguard, offered his commiserations. Then Bec, Everhide's PA. Then friend after friend.

Fuuuuck!

A knee-buckling dizziness swam through my head. My lungs were so tight I couldn't draw in air. It was too crowded. Too hot. Too much. My ears rang. My vision blurred. *Shit. Shit. Shit.*

Then a hand appeared at my waist. Oriental perfume filled my head. *Sutton.*

"Hey? Come walk with me." She drew me outside. We

crossed the lawn to the far fence line, where an outdoor sofa bordered a coffee table. Holding my hand, she sat and patted the cushion beside her. "Sit."

I collapsed onto the sofa and buried my face into my palms. My body trembled all over. I struggled to breathe. "Fuck."

Sutton peeled my shaky hands away from my face and held them in hers against my leg. "You're okay. I've got you." Her voice was calm and soothing, like the voices on those meditation apps. "Close your eyes. Breathe."

"I can't." Air sliced through my lungs, tightening and burning my chest. "It hurts."

"Shh." She stroked her thumb across my fingers. "Yes. You can."

"This is so fucked up." Tears welled in my eyes. "This is why I don't want to go out. Everyone just asks about Phil."

"You have to face conversations about him at some point."

"And have a panic attack every time?" My heart twisted and shuddered. "No thanks."

"It gets easier. After a while, people will stop asking." She ran her hand over my hair in slow, rhythmic strokes.

"When?" I swayed. *Damn.* Those vodka shots had hit me hard. "Tell me, when does it get easier?"

"Slowly. Every day. With time."

I rested my head back onto the sofa and stared at the murky, black evening sky. "How . . . how do you know how to deal with this?"

"Maddy used to get crippling panic attacks. Every event we attended, and even some days when shooting, she'd suffer from them. But she's better now she's on meds."

"I'll stick to vodka."

"You can't keep drinking."

I rubbed my palms into my eyes. "I know. I'm sorry. I warned you I was fucked up."

"Yes, you did. But you haven't scared me off."

I slumped forward and rested my elbows against my knees. "I know it's early, but I think I should just go home. You can stay if you want, or do you want me to call an Uber for you?"

"No." She rubbed my back, each stroke warm and melty. "I'll come with you and make sure you get home, okay?"

"You don't have to do that. My place is too far."

"It's only eight in the evening. I'm sure I'll make it back in time for my beauty sleep."

I twisted my head toward her. A touch of flirtation slipped into my voice. "Are you just looking for an excuse to come home with me?"

"Yeah." Sarcasm rolled off her tongue. "That would be it." Her tiny smile helped me to calm down.

She grabbed my hand and hauled me to my feet. I stumbled and crashed into her chest. Gazing down at her, I brushed my fingertips over her soft cheek. "Sutt, you don't have to look after me."

"We came together. So, yes I do." She lowered my hand away from her face. "I'll drive. I've only had two champagnes. I've been too busy talking to drink."

"Why doesn't that surprise me?"

"Where are your keys?"

Smirking, I held up my hands. "In my pocket."

"Which one?"

"Why don't you find out?"

My skin tingled as she ran her hands down my chest, across my stomach, then around my waist. Her eyes stayed locked on mine. She patted the back of my cargo shorts, then slid her hand around to the front. She dipped her hand into the front pocket and pulled out my car keys.

"Nothing other than these down there." She dangled the key-fob before my eyes. "Let's get you home."

With her arm hooked around my lower back, she drew me toward the house.

Kyle placed a platter of cooked food on the table and rushed over to us. "You need help?"

"No." Sutton shook her head. "We're fine."

"I'm sorry." I placed my hand on Kyle's shoulder. "I gotta get out of here. Being asked about Phil . . . is still too hard."

"I feel you, man. I was the same after my parents died. Thanks to Hunt and Gem, I made it through. You'll get there too."

"Thanks, bud." I pointed toward the entrance. "We're just gonna slip out. Can you say goodbye to the others for me? We'll catch up once you finish the tour."

"Sure." Kyle nodded. "I look forward to it."

With my arm linked around Sutton's shoulders, we headed toward my car. But as we approached my Ferrari, nerves and nausea swirled in my gut. Panic seized my lungs.

"Sutton. Please. Be honest. Are you okay to drive?" Phil's Porsche slamming into the light pole flashed before my eyes. *Shit.* I shouldn't have drunk. "I was supposed to drive. I'm sorry."

"Flint." She placed her hand on my chest. My heartbeat flew as fast as a torpedo. She stepped forward and kissed my cheek, then swept her fingertips across my brow. "I swear I'm okay to drive. Trust me."

Why did her touch have to be so soothing? Why did it ease my troubled mind?

"Now hop in." She opened the door, and I fell into the seat.

She didn't raise her voice or get angry or mad. She stayed calm, collected, and compassionate. Whatever she did or said, I obeyed without question.

As Sutton drove toward my place at Mt Olympus, I turned my head toward her to avoid the bright streetlights flickering in my eyes. She drove steadily. Carefully. But kept glancing at me.

Damn. She was beautiful.

She wrung her hands around the steering wheel. "You let me know if you're going to throw up so I can pull over in time."

"I don't feel sick. I didn't drink that much."

"Good."

But I felt something. Something new. Unexpected. Terrifying. All for her.

By the time she pulled into my huge four-car garage next to my motorcycle, I'd sobered a fraction. I was far from totally coherent but well enough to know that what was tumbling through my head wasn't from intoxication.

And it frightened me.

As the garage door closed behind us, I hopped out of the car and met Sutton at the front of the vehicle.

"Your garage is massive." She scanned the stacked rows of equipment trunks containing amps, lights, and music equipment that filled two of the car spaces and lining the rear wall. "What is all this stuff?"

"Gear for our shows." Another constant reminder Phil was gone.

I took her hand and shuffled backward. The moment my knees connected with a metal trunk, I sat down. I didn't have a plan. Didn't know what I was doing. But I didn't want her to leave either. She made the pain in my chest more tolerable.

She held out my keys. "Home safe and sound, as promised."

"Thank you." I placed them beside me.

"Let's go inside." She hooked her purse over her shoulder. "I'll grab you some water."

She went to step past me, but I blocked her path, catching hold of her hip.

"Sutton?" I glanced up at her. "I'm sorry about tonight. I messed up."

She combed her fingernails through my hair and tucked

it behind my ear. "No, you didn't. Tonight would've been hard, having all those people ask how you're doing and talking about Phil. There's no need to be sorry. I'm just glad I could help."

"Why do you do that? Help me?"

"That's what fake girlfriends do. Take care of their fake boyfriends."

"No, they don't. They run. Walk away. Give up." I drew her toward me. I turned my head and rested my cheek against her belly. Closing my eyes, I wrapped my arms around her legs. "Why don't you run?"

She circled her hands over my shoulders, her touch soothing and warm. "Because I know what you're going through."

I glanced up at her. Kindness, understanding, and concern darkened her eyes. I'd never had someone who barely knew me care about me so much before. I was the one who always looked out for my bandmates and my brother. I always stood up for them. I'd always reassured my ex-girlfriend that I was loyal and faithful and true. Sutton wanted nothing from me, and I had nothing to give . . . other than more complications.

Who'd want anything to do with a screwup like me? *Nobody. Right?*

With my eyes locked onto hers, I slowly slid my hands down her hips, skimmed her bare thighs, tickled over her knees, then curled my hands around her calf muscles. *Hmm.* Silky, smooth skin. My heartbeat quickened as I worked my way back toward her thighs.

"Um . . ." She fisted a handful of my T-shirt but didn't move. "I better call an Uber."

"Is that what you want to do?" I teased my fingers along the hemline of her skirt.

Her eyes fluttered closed. She swayed on her feet. "It's for the best."

I circled my hands around her thighs and caressed her sexy

ass. "Why?"

"This is dangerous."

"How so?"

"Because . . ." Her voice was barely above a whisper. "You make me feel things I haven't felt before."

"Like what?" I leaned forward and brushed my nose across the front of her exposed abdomen, then skimmed lower over her skirt and buried it against her groin. She smelled of floral fabric softener . . . and her.

"Shit." She clutched my shoulders. "Things I shouldn't. Like sexy. Desired. Adventurous. *Needed*."

"Then we have a problem."

"What's the problem?" she whispered.

My heart beat too fast. I flattened my cheek against her tummy and took a steady breath to clear my mind. "You frustrate me, taunt me, and drive me crazy. But then, you calm the noise in my head. Stop the ache in my chest. Make the abyss in my heart not feel so bottomless. I haven't felt anything for months other than grief. Then you came along." I ran my hands over the back of her thighs in slow, sensual strokes, then skimmed them underneath her skirt. I dug my fingers into her flesh. "You make me feel hopeful. Scared. *Wanted*. So the problem is . . . I don't want to play games anymore."

She tugged on my hair and drew my head off her belly. Hunger, doubt, fear, and excitement darkened her eyes. The same combination lurked in my veins.

"So, where does that leave us?" Her brow furrowed. "You want to call it quits?"

"No." I swept my hands around her legs to her inner thighs. I was waiting for her to pull away, but she didn't. Trailing my fingertips upward, I ventured underneath her skirt toward her crotch. "Do you?"

I brushed my thumb across the front of her panties, then

rubbed and pressed against her arousal. Her warmth enveloped me. Her dampness coated my fingertip. *God*. I wanted her. My whole body ached for her.

Her eyes fluttered closed. Her lips parted. "Flint?"

"Sutton, I want to get better. To do that, I can't lie about how I feel. I never expected this. I'm not sure if you and I are a good thing. Healthy or not. But I like you."

"Yeah?" Her hips pulsed against my fingers pressing into her slit. "That's good, because I like you."

My breath shuddered in my lungs. With both hands, I grabbed the edge of her panties and eased them down slowly to her ankles. My dick strained and swelled in my shorts. "Do you want me to stop?"

She dropped her purse on the floor and stepped out of her panties. "No."

"Good." Leaping to my feet, I crushed my lips against hers.

Chapter 15

SUTTON

My hands shot up and clutched the back of Flint's head. His kiss scorched every cell in my body. His anxiety worried me. I wanted to help him in any way possible, but I wasn't sure if this was the right way to go about it. *But holy hotness.* Unable to deny it, I was drawn to him in inexplicable ways. I was tired of resisting him. Tired of lying. Closing my eyes, I exhaled and surrendered to his hypnotic touches. He was the first guy I'd been with who had set my soul on fire, twisted every thought and decision, and made me hungry for more.

But I had to keep my wits intact and my heart in check. No matter how hot this was, or how intense, we had an expiration date. Keeping that in mind was the only way to survive without being burned to a cinder.

With a gentle nudge, Flint walked me backward until my knees connected with the front bumper of his Ferrari. He wasted no time in yanking off my tank top, unclipping my bra and unzipping my skirt. Proficient and to the point. Clawing and tugging at his T-shirt, I ripped it over his head. His shorts and briefs were quick to follow. Clothes were so overrated.

Supporting my hips, he lowered my bare butt onto the hood. I sucked in a short breath. The surface was hot from the drive against my sensitive skin but not unbearable. The heat escalating between us was much more combustible.

"Lie down," he whispered over our kisses.

As I furled backward, he kissed a trail down my neck, over my breasts and across my stomach. His hands swept across my skin in swirling motions, warming every inch of my flesh. Every hair on my body shivered.

"We're crazy, right?" I threaded my fingers through his gorgeous black hair, loving the way the long strands fell across his face, and the way his ice-blue eyes shimmered with a devilish glint just before he kissed me.

"You are, definitely." He grazed his teeth over the top edge of my hipbone.

"Ow!" I flinched. "You said you didn't bite."

"Not hard, anyway."

I clipped him on the head. "Be nice."

"Okay." He chuckled and headed toward my groin. His searing breath rushed across my skin as he nipped and licked and sucked, heading lower and lower.

Anticipation burned in my core like a delirious fever. Closing my eyes, I conceded control. No more fighting. I had other battles to face. But resisting Flint wasn't one of them. "I've never done it *on* a car before."

"I like being your first, then." He curled his hand beneath my thigh and widened my legs.

Burying his finger into my slit, he stroked me up and down. Every muscle inside me clenched. My hips pulsed as he circled my clit and dipped into my arousal. He threw me a mischievous wink, parted my folds with his fingers, then lowered his mouth onto me. *Oh yeah.* His hot tongue licked the length of my pussy, circled and flicked my aroused bud, then delved into my wetness.

I bit my lip, arched my back, and gasped. *Oh. Fuck. Yes.*

No other lover had made me this hot with want, this crazy with lust, this mad with hunger. And this was only the second time I'd been with him.

Each lashing of his tongue made my toes curl. Each swirl made my core tighten. Each suck made me moan. Fire coiled up my spine and pooled at the base of my neck. I was completely submissive to the tip of his tongue.

Reaching up with one hand, he cupped my breast and tweaked my nipple. I covered his knuckles with my palm, not wanting him to stop.

"Oh, God. That feels good," I murmured, lifting my pelvis in time with his licks.

My thighs tensed and tightened. Quickening his pace, he lapped me harder. Fingered me. Then fucked me with his tongue.

More. There. *YES*.

My eyes fluttered closed. My breath panted. My body burned and clenched, spiraling and coiling, higher and tighter. Every muscle screamed for release. With a hot rush, my orgasm ripped through me, jolting up my spine and shuddering through my system. My thighs quivered, trying to close. But Flint didn't relent, tasting and torturing me until I tugged on his hair to stop. "Holy shit. Flint, enough."

I collapsed against the hood, panting.

But he caught my hand and helped me sit upright. "You like that?" He grinned, wiping my arousal off his lips with his fingertips, then he licked them. *So hot!*

His rock-hard cock glistened before me. I took him in my hand, cupped his balls, and ran my fingers up the length of his shaft. "Oh, yeah. I'm hoping it's not over."

"Not even close." He edged between my legs and bent his

knees. He nudged his cock against me, but frustration rippled across his brow. "Wait. The car's too low." He picked me up and carried me around to the side. Placing me on my feet, he spun me 'round and bent me forward. "This okay?"

Blood rushed to my head. "Yeah." I'd never done it bent over a car either. There was only one way to find out if I'd like it. "I just want you inside me."

"Fuck. Condom."

I swept my hair off my face. "There's one in my bag. In the side pocket."

He dashed to where it laid on the floor, delved inside, and found the condom. "Were you expecting some action?"

"I'm a modern woman," I said, leaning against the side panel. "I'm allowed to carry condoms."

"Thank God you are." He tore open the packet with his teeth, then rolled the rubber on.

Stepping behind me, he brushed his fingertips across my collarbone and along the side of my neck, then teased them through my hair. Goosebumps danced across my skin. Every touch was amplified, electric and hot. Standing with his chest flush against my back, he glided his hands across my tummy, then headed upward, cupped my breasts and taunted my nipples. Arching into his touch, I let my head fall back against his shoulder. His warmth enveloped me as he dipped his head, kissed my neck, nibbled on my earlobe, breathed me in.

Brushing his nose around the rim of my ear, he whispered, soft and sultry, "I didn't expect to be doing this tonight."

"No." Every cell in my body still hummed from coming before. I turned my head and kissed him. "But I'm not complaining."

"Good." Bending his knees, he nudged his erection between my legs.

I leaned over the car, placing my palms flat on the hood.

He eased into my wetness. His breath hissed through his

teeth. With a thrust of his hips, he drove into me, hard.

Shivers shot up my spine. I moaned and gasped. *Oh, yeah. So good.*

With deep, delving pushes, he plunged into me, burying every inch inside. My toes curled. My fingers clawed at the hood to no avail. If this was what he did to me in the garage, what would he do to me inside the house?

"Fuck, you feel good." Flint's steamy thrusts turned into frantic poundings, obliterating my thoughts. His hard hammerings rammed heaven into my core. I met his moves, rocking back against him. Our bodies slammed together. Then he dug his fingers into my hips to hold me still. His breath singed my skin. "Oh yeah, babe." With a deep drive, he found his release. Shuddering around me, he chuckled and moaned. "Damn. Sutton. What have you done to me?"

My orgasm ripped through me, coiling through every cell. My knees weakened. Collapsing, I lay flat, panting against the Ferrari . . . my new favorite car. A blissed-out smile curled across my lips as he kissed my spine, my shoulders, and my neck. His sensual nibble on my ear spiraled sparks through my body and tingled my toes. "Not sure. But that was hot."

"Absolutely." He withdrew and handed me his T-shirt to clean up. "Let's go take a shower."

"Okay."

As I pulled my clothes on, I couldn't stop staring at his body, those arms that had wrapped around me, that chest that was so firm and tight. We had an undeniable chemistry—that much was clear.

But fire and passion this hot risked burning out. Such intensity often left a path of destruction in its wake. That scared me. Neither of us wanted to get hurt. Was there a way to contain this blaze now we'd set each other alight?

I didn't know. Only time would tell.

Hand in hand, we threw each other sheepish grins as we walked along the hallway and into his bedroom. A king-sized bed, neatly made with a black quilt and sheets, dominated the large room. A mounted flatscreen on the opposite wall was at least seventy-five inches. Canvas pictures of The Killers, Oasis, and Green Day lined the other wall. I could see their influence in his music. A walk-in closet, the size of half my condo, stood beside the en suite. Best thing of all . . . his room smelled like him. All citrusy and cinnamony. All Flintified.

He grabbed a towel from the linen cupboard in the bathroom and handed it to me. As I clutched it against my chest, he cupped my face, kissed my eyelids, my cheeks, then my lips. "Since we didn't eat at Kyle's, would you like to stay for dinner? I have Italian on speed dial. Do you eat lasagna or pasta?"

He'd just given me two incredible orgasms, it would be rude to leave, wouldn't it? But the distance looming in the depths of his eyes went beyond just being nice. It was as if he didn't want to be alone. He had nothing to worry about. I wasn't going anywhere. Not yet anyway. Just like him, I could do with some company.

Thirty minutes later, after showering and dressing in one of Flint's plain black T-shirts, I sat adjacent to him at the end of his dining table with a glass of red wine in hand. Steam rose off our loaded plates. My belly grumbled at the decadent aroma of lasagna and garlic bread filling the air.

I cut and piled a tiny amount of lasagna onto my fork. Flint had been quiet since showering. So had I. But we had to address the elephant in the room. That being . . . us. "So, are we going to talk about what happened before?"

"The party or the sex?"

"Both." I covered my mouth with my fingertips and finished my mouthful of rich sauce. *Delicious*. "But party first. Are you okay?"

"I am now." He pressed his lips together, as if he was trying not to smile, but after a moment, it spread across his mouth. "The sex was gooood."

My insides did a running-dance and a couple of cartwheels. Warmth touched my cheeks. We'd had phenomenal sex. "Um . . . we got carried away . . . again."

"I'm not complaining."

Neither was I. But I was concerned about him. "Why don't you do something about your attacks?"

One of his eyebrows shot skyward. "You want to have sex again?"

He wanted more? Oh, boy. I ran my gaze over the ink on his bare arms and his broad chest, and met his smoldering gaze. Could I jump on his lap and do it a second time? *Hmm.* Maybe after dinner. "Not right now. I'm still recovering from the round we just had." I took another bite of my food. But was he using sex to avoid his problems? "Have you been to a doctor? Maybe they could give you some meds to help manage the anxiety. For the near future, people are going to ask about Phil, you and your music, every time you go out."

He stared at his food. "I don't need a doctor."

"What about a therapist?" I rounded my shoulders. "They helped me after my mom died."

"They're useless." He slumped back in his chair. "I went to one after a friend died a few years back. It was a waste of time. No amount of talking will ever bring him back . . . or Phil."

"No, it won't. But they can help you work toward feeling better."

"And what?" Fear flashed in his eyes. "Forget Phil ever existed?"

"No. Never." I clutched his hand across the table. "Is that what you're afraid of? Forgetting him? Trust me, it's not possible. I lost my mom years ago and I still dream about her.

I see things, smell things, hear things that always remind me of her. You never forget someone you've lost, but you learn to cope."

"Thanks. But I'm not seeing any doctor or therapist." He pulled his hand free and loaded his fork with another mouthful of lasagna. But before he lifted it to his mouth, a puzzled expression flitted across his face. He puffed out a short breath, and a hint of a smile returned to his lips. "Sutt, for some strange reason, you're helping. I'm not in bed, or sitting outside in the dark, or staring at the wall." He tilted his head toward me and raised a suggestive eyebrow. "Maybe you're the therapy I need. Can I stick with you for now?"

My pulse jumped, but trod with caution. "In what capacity? Where and what are we?" What was this between us? I didn't know how to help him. I wasn't a doctor. But I didn't want to walk away.

"We clearly can't keep our hands off each other." Hot wickedness shimmered in his eyes as he took a sip of wine.

"It seems that way." I pursed my lips to stop grinning like a goof. "So, what do you want to do about that?"

He leaned forward and lowered his voice. A blend of seriousness and seductiveness rippled through his tone. "I think we need to renegotiate the terms of our deal. Change the rules."

Hmm. This could be interesting. But we were on the same page.

"Okay. Let's renegotiate." I spiked a cherry tomato and popped it in my mouth. The vinegary dressing tingled my tongue. His eyes darkened as I slowly chewed and swallowed. Heat flushed my cheeks every time he looked at me like that. But we had to keep this thing between us in the fun zone. "I'm still adamant about not getting serious or too involved, but I'm open to enhancing our arrangement. So . . . do you want to add sex into the mix? Just for the summer?"

My insides flipped as I ate another mouthful of salad. I couldn't believe I was being so direct and considering this. But I didn't want to be a wound-up ball of sexual frustration every time I was around him. "I've never had a fling before."

"Neither have I." A playful smile inched across his lips. "I was hoping to add kissing into our agreement, but your plan is so much better."

"What?" I gaped. "You did not. You wanted more."

"True. Kissing was just a segue to more sex. So we're good." He winked and nudged his knee against mine, then drew his brows together. "But why do we have to end whatever this is at the end of the summer?"

His question pulled me up short. No deadline? No way. That would end in heartache. "Our lives will pull us in different directions. You'll return to music, gigs, and touring. It's highly likely I'll leave LA for a new role. Filming schedules are always long and draining."

"What if you get a job here in LA?"

I drew my shoulders back and took a deep breath. Nothing would change my mind. "Doesn't matter. This still ends. You admit to hooking up with a gazillion chicks. There is no way I'd trust you to be faithful when you went on tour or promo."

I wasn't willing to gamble with my heart. I'd done that with Beau and it had broken me. Never again.

Hurt flashed through his eyes, but he flushed it away with a sip of wine. "What if you fall for me or vice versa?"

"We won't." I shook my head and softened my tone. "We have a lot of issues we're dealing with and have to stay focused on our careers. This is just a bit of fun without getting emotionally attached." We had more baggage than a LAX luggage carousel. Altering our plan put us into murky territory, so we had to keep our involvement with each other as light as possible. "Let's just stick to seeing each other for our events. That's about once a week. If we end up going home together for the night afterwards, so be it."

"I have a problem with that." He licked his lips and placed his glass down. "I won't make it through an event without wanting to tear your clothes off."

His heated gaze made me wriggle on my chair. I liked him taking my clothes off, especially my panties. "Um...well...what about seeing each other one other time through the week? Just for...ah...you know...um..." *Crap!* Heat burned my cheeks, my neck, and the tip of my ears.

Flint chuckled, low and sexy. "So, you want to hook up for sex, then go to our events with maybe a bonus round after?"

I winced. Hearing it out loud was so much worse than saying it in my head. "You make it sound like we're just fuck buddies."

"Isn't that what you'd call it?"

"I guess." I sighed, swiping my long fingernail across my eyebrow.

"Deal, if it includes sleepovers."

"No. That's too intimate."

"Sutton?" He drew my hand down onto the table and covered it with his palm. "If I only have you for the summer and only for two nights a week, you won't be making it home or kicking me out before dawn. So if you want to get a few hours' sleep in before work, sleepovers are included."

"Fine." Butterflies swarmed through the nausea swirling in my stomach. I withdrew my clammy hand from beneath his and rested it in my lap. "I've never had a casual sex partner, friends-with-benefits situation. I've only ever had boyfriends."

Grinning, he took a bite of lasagna, then waved his fork at me. "Have you had many boyfriends?"

"No." I fumbled with the hemline of Flint's shirt, which I was wearing. "Some didn't last more than a couple months. I've only had two serious relationships."

"What were they like?"

I wrinkled my nose. "You want to know about my exes?"

"Only if you want to tell me about them." He broke a slice of garlic bread off the loaf and popped it in his mouth.

There he was, doing that *I-don't-care-one-way-or-the-other* thing, like he'd done at the beach when we'd talked about Georgia. And for some reason, it made me spill my guts. His laid-back attitude helped me relax. I liked that he was easy to talk to.

I topped up our wine glasses. "My first boyfriend was Christian Webber. We met when we were sixteen at the studio. He filmed on the sound stage next to mine. My father approved of him big time because his parents were A-list movie stars. Christian and I would meet for lunches, hang out, go to events together. I lost my virginity to him on my seventeenth birthday. He broke up with me two weeks later when he moved to South Carolina for a new show. I haven't seen him since."

"Ouch."

"Yeah. That sucked." I took a sip of my drink. Christian had been my first love. It had hurt my heart when he left.

"And the second one?" Flint asked as he loaded his fork with leafy salad.

Nothing, not even alcohol, could drown the heartache Beau had caused.

I sucked in a shaky breath. The rich red wine gurgled in my gut. Just thinking about my ex hurt every fiber in my body. I'd never been able to talk to anyone about what had happened, but maybe I should. *Therapy, right?* This conversation had certainly taken an unexpected turn.

"Beau. We met at a friend's party. He was a couple years older than me and played for the Dodgers. He was handsome and charming, sweet and funny. We dated for nearly two years before he was traded to the Mets and moved to New York. We did the long-distance thing for about another six months. But then ... he cheated on me. We broke up via text."

"He cheated *and* text dumped you?" Shock rocked his tone. "Asshole."

If only that was only the worst of it. "I suspected something was wrong the moment I got the '*Oh, I can't fly out and see you this week. I'm busy*', '*Sorry I missed your calls and texts. I trained late*' messages for five days straight. Then photos of him with girls at parties were posted online. They became more frequent." I closed my eyes, wishing I could erase seeing them. "Every time I questioned him, he'd say it was nothing, that I was paranoid, delusional and imagining things. On top of dealing with my dad, I got sick with stress, worrying about him. But when pictures of Beau in bed with some blonde appeared all over social media, he tried to convince me that it wasn't what it looked like. I wasn't that naïve. We argued. We were done. Over. Confirmed by text."

"That's so fucked." Flint placed his hand on my knee and gave it a gentle squeeze. "I'm sorry. Was it with Georgia?"

"What? No." But it may as well have been. Flint's concerns over Georgia were justified. "A couple months after I broke up with Beau, she hooked up with this guy, Dwayne, I'd liked. We'd only gone on one date, but it didn't work out."

"That's just as bad." Shards of anguish flickered in his eyes. "Interests or exes, of any kind, are off-limits."

I wish. "Dwayne and I were never serious, but I loved Beau like mad. He broke my heart. Broke my trust. The sporting world is just as bad as the entertainment industry. The star players are always surrounded by fans and temptation. He couldn't resist it." My voice slid down a sloping scale. "We didn't see each other often enough. Long-distance destroyed us."

Flint shook his head. A muscle ticked in his jaw. "Distance

shouldn't be an issue for true love and commitment."

"It always is." I picked up my wine and downed a large mouthful. "Love doesn't survive across the miles. With my future uncertain, I don't want to be tied down or be worried about what someone else is doing or where they are or who they're with. I don't ever want to question if they're being faithful or be concerned about giving someone enough of my time. I want to be able to relocate and not worry about anyone but myself."

"You sound like my ex, Lena." His eyes clouded over, and he slumped in his chair. "We were together for two and a half years. I would've followed her to the ends of the universe, but I wasn't part of her plan. When she was at college, studying marketing, she worked part-time for a soda company setting up in-store merchandise displays and promotions. At the end of her degree, they offered her an internship in Atlanta. She couldn't move interstate fast enough. I wanted to keep seeing her, but she wanted out. She broke up with me backstage, right after we'd performed at Coachella."

"Who does that?" My hand shot across my chest. "What a way to kill an epic night."

"No shit." Scoffing, he scratched the tip of his stubbly chin.

I threw him a sympathetic smile. "See? Distance kills relationships." That was the truth. We both knew it. I finished my last mouthful of lasagna and placed my cutlery on the plate. "So . . . has there been anyone since Lena?"

"Not anything that lasted longer than a few minutes." He half grinned, then took a sip of wine. "After Lena left, I went a bit crazy. For the first time in years, all of us guys were single. We went wild, drinking, partying, and had our fair share of women. But after Phil died, the couple hookups I had just made me feel shittier. So, I stopped."

He waved his glass at me. "What about you? Anyone since

Beau?"

I shrugged one shoulder. "I've had a few dates, but the guys have often fallen into Georgia's web."

He lifted his index finger off his glass and pointed it at me. "You need the dibs rule."

"What's the dibs rule?"

"It was this rule Phil and I made in high school." He put his glass down and rested his arm on the table. "The only thing we fought over were girls. In senior year, I liked this chick, Shelby. When I finally grew the balls to ask her out, he went ballistic. He'd liked her too but never said anything. We got into this huge fist fight. There was a lot of blood. I'm sure he broke my nose. Our parents were called to the school. But the principal let us off with a stern warning because I was a stellar student and took the blame. So, after that incident, we made a pact." A tiny smile played across his lips. "If one of us was into a girl, wanted to ask her out, hook up or were dating, we'd call dibs. The other person was never allowed to interfere or hit on her. Not ever. Even if the girl rejected you, told you to fuck off, or it didn't work out. No chick would ever come between us. Even Slip and Cole live by it. It's our bro code."

"Such loyalty is kinda cool. But what about after summer?" Rubbing my hands against my bare thighs, concern loomed in my tone. "If you ran into Georgia somewhere, would you hook up with her?"

"God no. First off, she doesn't do it for me. But the dibs rule bans you from hooking up with each other's exes and close friends. There's always baggage."

"Hmm." I placed my elbow on the table and rested my chin on my hand. I injected a touch of sauciness into my tone. "I haven't met all of your friends yet. What if they're super-hot?"

"Don't care. It's a rule."

"Touchy subject?"

"Yeah. You could say that." He picked up his last lettuce leaf and tossed it in his mouth.

"Care to enlighten me?"

Pushing his empty plate aside, he took a deep breath and stared at the cityscape. The kitchen light flickered behind me, and the wall clock ticked. He lowered his chin. "The night of the accident, Phil hooked up with this girl, Rici, I'd liked. The first one I was kinda interested in since Lena left. She was this flight attendant chick. Super sexy. A friend of one of our lighting guys. I'd called dibs, but Phil ignored me. He flirted with her and fucked her right in front of my face. I was so pissed off and hurt and angry. I got totally wasted."

"I'm sorry."

He took hold of my hand and clasped it tight. "I swear, I won't touch your friends. Rici texts me every month and I never respond. I don't want anything to do with her. She was with Phil. That's it. So this thing between us is, whatever it turns out to be, is exclusive. You down with that?"

My heart fluttered, filling my chest. "You really want to be with just me?" I stroked my thumb over his hand, melting with the warmth permeating from his skin. Melting because he wanted me. *Me!* Even if it was only temporary.

"Yes, Sutton." His eyes glinted as a smile quivered across his lips. "Is that okay?"

I wanted to scream and shout and run outside and holler to the Boulevard below, but I just blushed and tucked my hair behind my ear. "Yeah. That's okay."

"So, you're dibbed."

I scrunched my nose, loving that I was his. "It sounds kinda intense."

"Maybe. But it's just for the summer." There was an edge to his tone, one that suggested he didn't like the deadline. But tough. That was the rule. He leaned back in his chair, but still held my hand. "It's casual. No strings attached. My goal is music. Yours is a job. But I have one more condition I'd like to add. It's non-negotiable."

"What is it?" I held my breath.

"We go bareback. I'll go get tested for you and vice versa. I hate condoms. You cool with that?"

"Oh . . . um . . ." The air shot from my lungs. My heart stampeded. We were doing this? *Holy. Shit.* "Okay."

"And since this is our first bonus night, I call sleepover." He stared at our entwined fingers. "It's been a crazy night. So much has happened. I'd like you to stay."

Stay? My heartrate doubled. Nothing like jumping right into our new arrangement. No breather. No time to settle and sleep on it. But I wouldn't have agreed to the conditions if I wasn't ready for them. I glanced at the wall clock. 9:27pm. "That'd be nice, but I have work tomorrow. I don't have a change of clothes."

"Don't you just have wardrobe at work? Does it matter what you turn up in?"

"No. I guess not." It really didn't.

He tilted his chin at me. "What time do you start?"

"Ten on Wednesdays. We have writers' room meetings and scene read-throughs."

"I'll drive you there, pick you up, then take you home."

I slipped on a sly smile. "Are you just looking for another excuse to get your hands on me?"

He drew my hand toward his mouth and kissed my fingers. "What if I am?"

"I won't say no."

"Then you better help me clear the dishes away."

Chapter 16

SUTTON

I ambled into Flint's kitchen to find something for breakfast. I couldn't wipe the smile off my face. I'd worked up an appetite after spending a wicked night in his bed. Watching a movie and hanging out were probably more intimate than what was deemed acceptable for casual partners, and the sex had been phenomenal. Slow and tender and sensual.

But I had to put it out of my mind. We had a little more than a week until our next event. Nine days. It felt like a lifetime away. I'd drown myself in work like always and try not to think about Flint during every waking moment . . . once the tenderness between my legs eased. *Damn* . . . last night had been hot.

I opened Flint's fridge; the bright light stabbed my eyes. Squinting to see straight, I scanned the shelves. There weren't many options available—half a loaf of bread, some old-looking apples, cheese, and leftovers from last night's dinner. The pantry wasn't much better—oats, pasta, noodles, packets of potato chips. Nothing really excited my taste buds, but I needed to eat something before work. I returned to the fridge and grabbed some ingredients. A grilled cheese sandwich would do.

Searching through the cupboards, I found the sandwich maker. It was easily located; he didn't possess many gadgets and appliances. No slow cooker. No air fryer. No mass array of frypans and saucepans. But I admired the fancy coffee machine.

Just as I placed my cheese sandwich into the grill, the doorbell chimed.

Who made house calls at seven a.m.? *Shit.* Would Flint wake and answer the door?

The bell sounded again.

Guess not.

Shit. Should I answer the door? In Flint's shirt? I glanced downward. The hemline hovered near the top of my thighs; it was long and respectable enough.

Licking butter from my fingertips, I headed to the foyer and peered through the peephole.

A guy dressed in running gear, with floppy short brown hair and handsome devilish green eyes, leaned with one hand pressed against the wall.

Cole?

I opened the door with one hand and held the kitchen turner in the other.

"Hey? Sutton?" His eyes widened. Straightening, he jerked his chin back. "What are you doing here?"

"Hi. Nice to meet you, too." I turned and headed back into the kitchen.

Cole followed. "Sorry. I forgot my key for the front door, and I didn't expect to see you."

"We went to Kyle and Gemma's last night. Flint drank too much, so I drove him home and stuck around to make sure he was okay."

He sank onto the kitchen stool. Slouching his shoulders, he rested his elbows on the counter. "What happened?"

I stared at the sandwich maker and inhaled the aroma of

melted cheese. "Everyone kept asking about Phil. It got to him. Then he hit the vodka."

"Shit. We should've been there. But we got a flat tire. Slip didn't have a spare. We waited for hours for roadside assistance. By the time they arrived, it was late. Was Flint a write-off?"

"Not quite. I talked him 'round." I scooped my grilled sandwich onto a plate. Gooey cheese dripped from the sides. Cole eyed my creation and licked his lips. With toned arms to die for and zero body fat, he had the build of a marathon runner. He'd burn off the calories in seconds, whereas they'd go straight to my hips. I pointed to my food. "You want one?"

"Um . . . sure."

I pushed my plate over to him, made myself another sandwich, and popped it into the grill. "Did Flint suffer from anxiety or panic attacks before Phil died?"

"No. Before, Flint loved going out. Loved life. Music. Everything. Losing Phil has broken him. It's like he's a different man."

"Did you have plans with him today?"

"No." He bit into one of the toasted triangles. "I just wanted to get him out of the house. I came over to haul his ass out of bed to go for a run up the canyon."

"Do you do that a lot?"

"Run? Yeah. We hate the gym. Running outdoors is much better. But it's been impossible to get Flint to go for months. He'll be so unfit when we play again . . . *if* we play again."

I threw him a mischievous smile. "There was nothing wrong with his endurance last night."

"Wait? What?" Cole sat four inches taller, licking grease from his fingertips. "You and Flint? When you said you stayed to make sure he was okay, I assumed you crashed in one of the spare rooms or on the sofa."

"Yeah." I grabbed my sandwich off the grill and slid it onto a plate. "The fake dating clearly didn't work out."

"Wow." Cole rubbed his chin. "Flint never brings girls back here. Never."

I stilled, hovering the cutting knife over the toasted bread. "Should I feel special he asked me to stay?" I pressed my lips together to stop smiling as I cut my sandwich.

"He did? . . . Wow."

"Can you stop saying that?" I scrunched my nose. "It's freaking me out."

"Sorry. We thought going out would be good for him but dating for real might be even better. It will give him something new to focus on."

"Don't get too hasty there." I picked up half my sandwich. "We're not dating . . . We're just . . . keeping it casual until the end of summer."

Cole coughed and cleared his throat. "Flint agreed to that?"

"Yeah. Why?" The concern in Cole's eyes jolted my gut.

"Flint doesn't do things by halves." He rested his elbows on the counter. "He's an all-in-or-nothing type of guy."

"Neither one of us want to get hurt. We have an end date."

"Do you know about what happened with Lena?"

"His ex? Yeah. They broke up when she left."

"Yeah . . . but he fell for her hard and fast. He molded his life around her. We had to schedule practice around her timetable. She wasn't a fan of the attention he got, but they were so good together. In love. It was such a shock when she upped and left and wanted to call it quits. It gutted Flint. I don't want to see him hurt like that again."

Shivers skipped across my skin. What would it be like to have a guy adore you so much that he built his life around you? I'd never experienced love like that. But I understood heartbreak.

Cole pushed his empty plate away. "Flint was a mess after

she broke up with him. He bordered on being depressed. Similar to what he's like over Phil."

Shit. What had I got myself into?

I'd handle it. We had experience under our belts and had ground rules set. "I appreciate your concerns. But I promise we're being careful and won't go down that path."

"*Damn it.*" Cole grinned a sly grin and slapped his hand against the counter. "I lost the bet with Slip. He said you'd end up fucking."

Warmth curled in my belly and touched my cheeks. "Yeah. I would've lost the bet too." I nibbled on my hot sandwich, then covered my mouth with my fingertips to talk. "But the goal hasn't changed. We're just going to have a bit of extra fun in the process."

"Good. I don't want to see him worse than he is now. Ultimately, I don't care what you do as long as we get the old Flint back. I want to play with him again. I miss that magic."

"Didn't you get *magic* at the gigs you just played, filling in for your friends in Palm Springs?"

"It was fun." He drummed his fingers against the counter. "But it's not the same as playing with your own band."

"You miss it, huh?"

"Sure do."

The love Cole had for Flint blew my mind. It was the same regard Flint had for the guys. Envy prickled my skin. I'd never experienced that dedication and devotion. Acting was too cutthroat. Everyone was out for themselves. For them, losing Phil went beyond losing a family member or friend . . . It was like they'd lost a limb. "Have you found a replacement for Phil?"

"No." Cole shook his head. "They'll be hard shoes to fill. We need Flint back playing first."

"What was Phil like?" I leaned my hip against the counter and licked the last crumbs from my fingertips. I'd been hesitant to ask Flint about Phil as I was afraid it might upset him too much. But maybe Cole could give me some more insight.

"Phil?" His eyes clouded over as he glanced toward a photo of the four of them hanging on the side wall. "He was like a brother. But he was a crazy, larger-than-life motherfucker. He loved fast cars. Fast women. He was smart-mouthed and lived to play bass. He was electric on stage and thought he was invincible. But he couldn't hold a candle to Flint. Flint has a charisma, this magic energy and aura when he performs, unlike anything I've ever seen before. He sings because he loves it so fucking much. You can feel it in your bones. He's not there for the girls or the fame or the money. Phil, on the other hand, was all about those things." Sadness loomed in Cole's green eyes. "Phil had grown reckless. He drank bourbon like it was water, took too many drugs, and was always getting into trouble—hitting on girls that had boyfriends, picking fights with assholes, being a dick at parties. We were waiting for him to grow out of the stupid phase. We were days away from intervening and telling him to clean up his act. But we never got the chance to do it."

His anguish tore at my heart. "I'm so sorry, Cole."

"Flint has been my best friend since we were nine. I hate seeing him this cut over Phil. It's chewing him up inside that we didn't help Phil sooner. The toxicology report showed that Phil was high the night of the crash. Flint didn't know. Nobody did. We would've never let them get in the car otherwise."

"No one would've. It's not his fault."

"He doesn't see that." Cole rubbed his jaw. "Flint may be a touch arrogant and cocky, but underneath all that, he'd do anything for those he loved. It crushes my heart when he says he wished it had been him who died in the car accident, not Phil. I didn't want to lose either of them. But Flint puts everyone he cares about before himself—even the fucking cat they nearly hit."

I jerked my chin back. "What cat?"

A faint smile curled across his lips. "When he woke up in the hospital . . . Flint kept mumbling, asking about Phil, but also if the cat was okay. We didn't know what the fuck he was going on about until we watched the dashcam footage. Phil swerved to hit it and lost control of the car."

He *tried* to hit a cat? That was awful. "Was the cat okay?"

"Yeah. No dead cat was found at the scene."

"That's good to know." I breathed a sigh of relief, picked up the dirty plates and put them in the dishwasher. "Can you be honest with me about something?"

Cole nodded.

"Flint and I have only been out twice, but both times he has ended up drunk. Should I be worried? Is the drinking an issue?"

"Nah." Cole scratched the scruff on the tip of his chin. "Like most guys our age, he likes to drink. But he's usually telling us to slow down. He's had a couple rough weeks with the passing of Phil's birthday and us intervening. So please, give the guy a break."

"But what about all the stories online about your partying and drinking?"

"Don't believe everything you read." Cole puffed out a short breath. "Phil caused most of those stories. Flint often took the blame to protect him or copped the flack because he's the lead singer."

"Doesn't that bother him? That he has been accused of things that Phil did?" I'd be horrified and have my publicist working overtime to rectify any false accusations. "Did he cover up for Phil a lot?"

"Yeah." Cole rubbed his hands down his thighs and shrugged. "I guess it's brotherly love. But he wasn't always innocent. The publicity, the good and the bad, never hurt us. We know the truth. That's all that matters. The public sees what they want to see. They see us dressed in black clothes, performing on stage, and partying, and think we're reckless, randy rock stars. You thought that. To some degree, we have been and fed that fire. We wouldn't be as popular as we are if we were the cherubs of rock."

"I'd be mortified if someone wrote lies about me."

"You're with Flint." He smirked. "I'd be prepared. Isn't that why you're doing this publicity stunt? To heat up your image?"

"Yes. But we want to tone his down. I don't want lies circulating about us." I'd never been trolled on social media or slandered in the press. "I don't want things to get worse for Flint and for you to lose your contract."

"Neither do we." His tone was light but had a sharp edge of seriousness. He placed his hand over his heart. "We want him back. Music is our life. We'll do anything to help. If you can get Flint playing again, you're a fucking miracle worker. Slip and I will be in debt to you for life."

"If I land a new job, I'll be indebted to him."

Cole smiled and shook his head. "You're so much like my younger sister—a touch crazy and determined to do whatever it takes to land a role. Just like she is. It's cool."

I straightened my shoulders. "Your sister's an actress?"

"Yeah. Tia's in Chicago working on that firefighter series, *Through the Smoke.* Since we were little kids, she always wanted to be an action star. Our parents loathed the idea. But after she graduated, she went through all this insane fitness training and stunt work to get a part. I'm always afraid she'll get hurt. What they do on that show is nuts. She's always flung around on harnesses, climbing up crap, and doing dangerous tricks."

"She can have that." I snatched up the leftover ingredients and put them back in the fridge. Stunt work was not on my bucket list of career ambitions. The most strenuous forms of exercise I'd ever done were yoga and Pilates . . . and sex, of course. "I'll stick to dating Flint. That comes with enough risk. I'm not cut out to be an action star . . . but hey, if a show will pay me enough, I *will* do anything."

Cole chuckled. "Dating Flint might be your most challenging role ever."

I placed my hands on the counter and rounded my shoulders. "It has its perks." Hot guy. Great sex. What could go wrong?

Laughing, he rose to his feet. "I like you, Sutton. Just be careful. That's all I'm saying."

"Thanks. We will."

"Before it gets too hot, I'm gonna go for that run. I'll catch up with Flint later."

"I'll tell him you dropped by." We headed toward the front door. "It's nice to finally meet you."

"Same."

I farewelled Cole, then headed toward Flint's room. I had to get his ass out of bed so he could take me to work. But halfway down the hall at the first door opposite one of the spare bedrooms, I stopped.

What is in there?

I slowly opened the heavy door. My eyes widened. My heart leaped into my throat.

Holy. Shit.

Holding my breath, I slipped into the studio.

Chapter 17

FLINT

The bed beside me was empty. But the scent of Sutton lingered on my sheets. I rubbed the sleep from my eyes and glanced at the digital clock on my nightstand. 7:52a.m. *Fuck.* It was way too early to be awake. Good sex had delivered the first decent night's sleep I'd had in months. I'd only made it halfway through the movie before I buried myself inside Sutton again. Once on the sofa, then here in my bed.

She'd certainly gotten underneath my skin. Unexpectedly. But our new rules to see each other only twice a week didn't sit well in my gut. I didn't like restrictions. I'd never had a relationship deadline. I didn't know how to keep my heart in check. Would losing Sutton at the end of summer hurt as much as it did when Lena left? Would it be as crippling and heartbreaking as Phil's death?

I fucking hope not.

All I could do was take one day at a time. At least today, I actually wanted to get out of bed.

But where was Sutton?

I sat upright and put my feet on the floor. Her clothes from when we'd arrived home from Kyle's were still in a pile by the en suite door. Was she wearing my T-shirt or nothing? *Hmm.* I'd be happy with either.

After using the bathroom, I headed for the kitchen. The aroma of grilled cheese drifted down the hallway. She'd found something to eat. *Cool.* Scratching and combing my fingers through my messy hair, I halted.

My mouth ran bone dry.

My breath formed icicles in my lungs.

The door to my music room was ajar.

No. No. No. Shit. Shit. Shit.

My heart clenched as I opened the door wider. I wanted to see a vacant room but had no such luck. Sutton, wearing my T-shirt, hovered near the desk, holding several pieces of paper in her hands. Her lips moved as she read the lyrics scribbled across the page.

Fire ripped through my veins. My nostrils flared. She shouldn't be in there. That was my private space. My studio. As I sucked in a razor-edged breath, my heart smashed against my ribs. *Shit.* Closing my eyes, I clenched and unclenched my hands. The tension twisted and pulled in my neck. *Calm . . . the fuck . . . down.* She didn't know this was a no-go zone.

Breathe. *In. Out. In. Out.*

After a couple more steady inhalations, I cracked my neck from side to side.

After fucking her senseless last night, I wouldn't be an asshole.

I took a few steps inside the room. I kept my voice low, so I didn't startle her. "What are you doing in here?"

She spun toward me. Her hair flicked against her face. She dropped the page onto the desk and bit her lip. "Oh. Um."

"Snooping?" I scanned the room. Had she touched anything else? Moved something? Had she tampered with the only connection to Phil I had left?

"Fair's fair, right?" she whispered. "You went through my things. Now, we're even."

"Is everything a game to you?" I strode over to her, my hold on my emotions close to slipping.

"No. I just wanted to see this part of you. Understand why you haven't been able to play since you love it so much."

I swayed on my feet. "Can we please just get out of here?" I grabbed her hand and turned for the door, but she didn't move.

"Wait." She placed her free hand over mine. "This room is awesome. All the instruments, the tech, the mics. There's so much energy and creativity within these walls. There's magic in the air."

"No." I lowered my chin. "It died with Phil."

"Didn't you write most of the music?" Her tone was just too bright and fucking chirpy for this hour of the day.

"Yeah . . . but some was with Phil."

She yanked her hand free from my grasp and scanned the pages piled on the desk. "I read these lyrics. Are they yours?"

I rubbed my tired eyes. I didn't want to be in there. "Yeah."

"I love this one." She picked up one page and read it out loud:

> *Morning sunlight touches your hair,*
> *The scent of you lingers in the air.*
> *The bed sheets are crumpled from where you lay,*
> *Wanna stay wrapped in your arms for all the day.*
> *Will you let me be your man? What do you say?*
> *Do you dare to take . . .*
> *Dare to take the chance?*
>
> *And stay.*
> *Stay until the sun . . .*
> *Until the sun goes down.*

Nighttime breezes touch my skin,
Dancing with you feels like heaven.
Kissing you is my reason for living,
My love for you has no ending.
Will you let me be your man? Will you give in?
Do you dare to take . . .
Dare to take the chance?

And stay.
Stay until the sun . . .
Until the sun goes down.

My heart splintered as I fell back a step.

"Hey?" She caught my forearm. "These words are beautiful. They just resonated with me after spending the night in your bed."

I snatched the page from her and put it back on the desk. In the pile. Neat. Straight. Perfectly aligned. As they were before. Like no one had touched them. "Yeah, well. They aren't about you." *Shit.* I didn't mean to be short.

"I know." Her tone softened. "Are they about your ex?"

My brain throbbed. The walls pressed against me. The room grew smaller and smaller. I didn't want to talk about the lyrics. Or Lena. "It was a long time ago. It never evolved into a song."

"And what about these?" She rushed across the room to the sofas and pointed toward Phil's journal on the coffee table. My sheet of lyrics now rested beside it.

Oh, shit!

Panic seized my heart. Following her, I held out my hand. "Don't touch—"

Ignoring me, she opened the book, grabbed a few loose pages and read the words aloud:

You think this is a game, but your words sting,
The light shines on you, 'cause you're everything.

What's it gonna take for you to see me?
I stand in the shadows, never the light,
My heart has to follow you every night.

"And this one." She flicked another page straight and read:

I think I wanna go out and get drunk tonight,
Dance with some girl under the disco lights.
Feel her body crush next to mine,
Do anything to get you out of my mind.
Just want a day without you in my head,
Just want a night not alone in my bed.

I think I need to go driving up the coast,
Feel the cool wind in my hair the most.
Wash away the darkness in the waves,
Bury my thoughts deep in a cave.
Before I scream at the city for breaking my heart.
Before I hate the world for tearing me apart.

Nausea flooded my stomach. I'd never read or seen those lyrics before. Who were they about? *What the fuck?*

"Sutton." Tears pricked my eyes. "Please. Stop."

"No." She put the sheets down and took my hand. While an element of compassion swirled in her eyes so did a fair level of grit. "You need to face this. Whatever this is. Just talk to me." She pointed toward the page. "Did you write those?"

I shook my head.

"Was it Phil?"

I nodded. My chest squeezed tight. "Why are you doing this?"

"Because you can't stay hidden from the world. Or your music. It's who you are. It's your life."

"You don't know anything about me." I clenched my teeth to contain my pain. "Or Phil. Or this." I flicked my hand at the room.

"Then tell me." She grabbed my hand and held it against her chest. "You have amazing talent. Why don't you want to embrace it?"

"This is nothing without Phil."

"I love that you loved your brother so much. That you thought so much of him." She lowered my hand along with her tone. "I hardly talk to my brother."

"I . . . I didn't even know you had one."

"Steven is three years older than me. We're slowly reconnecting now my father is out of my life. He and Dad never got along. Steven is super smart and works for some tech giant in Bakersfield." She patted my hand. "But enough about me. Back to you."

"Sutton, I'm sorry." My knees buckled. "I'm not ready to do this."

"Yes, you are. Time for a baby step."

I groaned. Why did she never listen?

"Sit. Now." She pointed to the sofa.

Fuuuuck! I collapsed onto one of the black leather sofas. Just being in this room felt like a ton of lead lay on my shoulders.

"So?" She glanced around and rubbed her hands together. "Which guitar is yours or which one can I use?"

"What?" I clutched my knees as if somehow that would magically stop the dizziness swarming through my brain.

"You need to play something."

I keeled forward and cupped the side of my head. "No. Please. Stop."

"If you don't, I will. And you don't want to hear that. So quick. Which one?" She waved toward the two guitars on stands by my microphone, then the one laying on the opposite sofa. "Hurry up and tell me, or I'm just gonna use this one."

Tears stung my eyes. Breathing hurt.

"Fine." She reached toward the guitar on the sofa opposite

me.

I shot out my trembling hand. "No. Not that one." *Shit.* Didn't she know anything about guitars? That was Phil's electric bass. It needed power. No one touched that guitar. I jerked my chin toward the guitars by the mic. "They're mine. Grab the acoustic on the left."

"Right." She zipped over to it.

Nausea flooded my stomach. A sweat broke out on my brow. This wasn't happening. *No, it wasn't. No, it wasn't. No, it wasn't.*

But then she came back and stood in front of me, holding my guitar.

Crap. Yes, it was.

The sight of her dressed in my T-shirt that had ridden up and barely covered her panties was fucking sexy and almost distracted me from what was happening. I struggled to take my eyes off the strings in her hand. She sat next to me and propped the guitar over her lap.

I swallowed the dry lump that was the size of an Arizona bolder in my throat. "I thought you didn't know how to play."

"I don't. But if you won't play, I will."

With no notes or chords held, she strummed the strings.

You broke my heart with just one text.

I winced. She was flat, but . . . her voice didn't sound too bad.

Left me alone, made me your ex.
I was lost didn't know what to do next,
Hurting so hard was my only reflex.
After months of going nowhere,
Took a leap of faith and took a dare.
Now I'm sitting here, facing the unknown,
But I'm willing to try.
All I had to do was let go-oh-oh.

All I had to do was let go-oh-oh.

I rubbed my brow. I didn't know the lyrics or the tune. "What song was that?"

"I just made it up about my asshole ex." She rested her arm on the guitar. "After years of ad-libbing and singing in acting classes, I can pull the odd thing out of a hat. Don't ask for more—that's about the extent of my rhyming capabilities."

She never ceased to shock me. "It was actually pretty good. For your first attempt at songwriting."

"Your turn." She held out the guitar.

I stared at my Gibson. I hadn't touched her since Phil died.

"Baby steps, Flint. You can do this."

She swung the guitar around and placed it across my lap. My legs molded to the familiar shape as it pressed against my stomach. Butterflies screamed inside my gut. "I . . . I can't."

"Yes. You. Can. Close your eyes." She swept her hand over my eyelids. "Just breathe. Listen to my voice. Nothing else. Don't think about Phil. Or your guys. Think about something new. Recent. Think about the night we met. What comes to mind?"

"How crazy you were."

"Nuh-uh. You're not allowed to talk. Sing. Play." She took my hand and wrapped my fingers around the neck of the guitar. "Sing whatever is in your head."

My voice evaded me. I didn't have the soul to form a tune. But I rolled out words, talking in time with the chords I strummed.

> *You are the craziest girl I've ever met,*
> *Do my head in every sec.*
> *Why are you doing this, wasting my time?*
> *Just leave me here, please let me die.*

Her breath hitched. The light in her eyes dimmed. "Is that what you want? To die?"

"No. It was just a line."

"Oh. Thank God." She sank into the sofa beside me.

I slid my fingers slowly over the frets. It felt good to hold my guitar again. I positioned my fingertips over the strings and struck them gently. My heart palpitated with the reverberations. *Shit.* My gaze locked onto Sutton as I spoke softly and rhythmically, not quite able to sing.

> *You drive me up the wall, turn me on.*
> *Make me scream, make me shout all night long.*
> *Why are you doing this, playing with my heart?*
> *Just let me be, I want to play no part.*
>
> *Playing games is too dangerous,*
> *We shouldn't be this adventurous.*
> *I'm the biggest train wreck in this town,*
> *Don't need to derail you and bring you down.*
> *This will end, you'll just leave.*
> *In the end, there'll just be me.*

Tears welled in her eyes. She splayed her hands across her breast. "Oh. My. God."

"What?" I played a few more chords and let the sound settle deep inside my chest. The words jolted my heart. They were about her. The fate that lay ahead.

"You just played and did that weird talky-sing thing." She lunged forward and kissed me on the lips. "We made a breakthrough."

"Don't get excited. It was just some stupid notes. Nothing serious."

"Can we focus on the positives, please?" She rubbed my cheeks, hard. "You played. How did it feel?"

Scary. Sick. Surreal. I held up my trembling fingers. "My hands are still shaking."

"You did good. The lines were depressing. But yay."

A blanket of warm air settled over me. My fingers fell effortlessly to the strings. Strumming came as natural as breathing. But I couldn't find my voice to sing. This block... this blackness had swallowed it whole. As I played the tune, I spoke softly:

> *My compass always pointed north,*
> *I knew what I wanted, I set my course.*
> *Always knew where I'd come from,*
> *Always knew where I belonged.*
> *Then with one searing kiss,*
> *You stole the air I was breathing,*
> *Stopped my mind from thinking.*
> *I lost my foundation,*
> *My feet weren't grounded.*
> *My heart kept racing,*
> *My fever, escalating.*
> *Because... damn, girl.*
> *You are the one.*

I stilled the strings and stared at my hands. *Fuck.* Adrenaline coursed through my veins at breakneck speed. My whole body shuddered. I'd just played a verse from one of our hits. *Holy shit.*

Sutton rubbed my leg, gentle and coaxing. "You want to play some more?"

I shook my head, dumbfounded. Shocked.

She pried the guitar out of my hands and put it aside. Placing her hands on my shoulders, she straddled my lap, then combed her fingers through my hair. "See? You're okay. You did good. But that's enough therapy for today."

"Therapy?"

"Yeah. I'll send you my bill next week." She ran her hands down my chest scar and rested her palm over my thundering heart. "Oh... shit. Are you all right?"

I caught her hand. Closing my eyes, I took some deep breaths. "I may be having a medical episode. Just give me a sec."

In silence, we sat. With my eyes still shut, I absorbed the room, reaching out to find that magic I'd always felt in here. A faint glow, although distant, flickered in my system.

I'd played. Sutton had gotten me to play. "Thank you. It felt good to hold my guitar again."

I ran my hands up her bare legs to her waist. But when I did that, my fingers couldn't stay still. Slipping them underneath her shirt, I circled them over her back. Her skin was cool beneath my blazing fingertips.

Her scent filled my senses. Her warmth surrounded me. Touching her calmed my mind.

"Do you know what else feels good?" She wriggled on my lap, rubbing her crotch against my groin.

"No idea." I grinned, getting harder by the second.

She reached between us and cupped my dick. "This."

I clutched her ass and flipped her down onto the sofa. My knees fell between her legs as I crawled over her. "You are trouble, aren't you?"

"Maybe this could be the process? You take a step with your music, then we have mind-blowing sex."

"Not sure that's a stable solution."

"No. But we get to have sex."

"You might be the death of me, Sutton Summers."

"I hope not. Life is good, remember?"

"Is this good?" I eased up her T-shirt. Dipping my head, I teased her nipple with my tongue. The taste of her sweet skin fed new hunger into my bloodstream. Licking and sucking and nipping her sparked a fire inside me.

"Oh, yeah." Her voice came out as a breathy whisper.

"You are not what I expected. I never thought you would be a sex fiend."

"Honestly? I've never been like this. Maybe you're my therapy to discover new things."

"With sex?" Peering up at her, I flicked my tongue over her hard nipple. "Then, in my professional opinion, you'll need more sessions. Seeing you once or twice a week is not enough."

"Nice try." She tousled my messy hair. "But it has to be."

"We'll see." I dashed over to the duffel bag beside my desk. I found a stash of condoms and headed back to the sofa.

Sutton sprawled out on the sofa, in my T-shirt, and with her panties peeking out from underneath the hemline, made my dick as hard as the hills.

I ripped off my boxer shorts, slipped the condom on, and kneeled before her. With no hesitation, I grabbed the edge of her panties and eased them down her legs. Crawling on my knees, I closed the gap between us. As I kissed her soft mouth, I teased my cock against her hot opening. With a gentle thrust, I plunged inside her.

Moaning against her mouth, I shuddered. I'd played my guitar. I'd stumbled through some lyrics. That was a huge step forward. All thanks to Sutton.

Lost in the pleasure of her body, I drove into her. My fingertips quivered as I stroked her skin. My nose tingled with the scent of my citrusy shower gel on her flesh. My tongue savored the taste of grilled cheese on her lips. Every inch of her was delicious.

Needing more depth, I drew her onto the floor. I turned her around, pulled her on to my lap and entered her from behind. My cock throbbed inside her hotness. On my haunches, with her straddled backward across my thighs, I fingered her clit with one hand and caressed and fondled her tits with the other. Rising up and down, I drove into her.

"Oh, wow." She panted, gripping onto the sofa for balance.

But I had her. She wasn't going anywhere.

No. Not. Anywhere.

She pushed back, meeting every one of my thrusts. Cupping my hand between her legs, she guided me where to touch her hot, swollen bud and apply more pressure. "There."

I smiled against her back and brushed my lips over the smooth skin. I never relented on pleasuring her, but it took all my self-control not to blow my load. Her hips bucked and rocked. Bucked and rocked.

"Flint. Holy. Crap." Her head fell back. A guttural groan escaped her sweet mouth as she came. Her fiery core clenched around me. Her body shuddered and convulsed.

I wrapped my arm around her waist and held her flush against my chest. The air sizzled around us. "I've got you." Driving into her, I found my release. Pouring into her, my cock throbbed. My hips jerked. "Hmm . . . fuck. That's so freaking good."

I sucked in hard lungfuls of air. My heart raced like a rocket man's. Making her come might be my new addiction. I could definitely get used to this.

She reached back and cupped the side of my head. "Wow. I mean, fuck. I didn't even know that was a position."

I nipped and kissed the sensitive spot beneath her earlobe. "You've been missing out."

She wriggled off my lap, and I wrapped the condom into my boxer shorts. I'd deal with it later. Right now, I just wanted to hold her. Grabbing two cushions, we lay on the rug. As her head rested against my shoulder, my heart still pounded from the exertion.

She lifted her chin and kissed my lips. "That was a great therapy session."

I chuckled. "If therapy *was* like this, I would've gone ages ago."

"There are options. You can pay for what we just did by the

hour."

"No thanks." Chuckling, I kissed the top of her head. "This was way better." Not that I'd ever hired a hooker to know if they were worth it.

She glided her hand across my chest in lazy strokes. "Are you okay?"

"Yeah." I circled my fingertips up and down her spine, then combed them through her hair. "But you need to get ready for work. Would you like some more breakfast? I can make a killer omelet."

"That would be nice." She pressed her lips against my collarbone. "And coffee. I need coffee."

"I only make plain coffees or cappuccinos. I don't have any fancy add-ins or flavors."

"I can live with that." She glanced up at me with a saucy smile. "I'd love a cappuccino."

"Okay. Let's go."

After breakfast and dropping Sutton off at the studio, I counted down the hours until I picked her up tonight at nine.

I still tried to comprehend what had happened last night. It went beyond good sex . . . and a lot of it. For the first time in months, life simmered through my blood. I felt lighter. I didn't want to waste the day.

As I revved my Ferrari's engine and drove toward home, music pummeled my head.

Without overthinking the morning, I dialed Slip's number.

"Flint?" Slip's sleepy voice droned through the speaker.

"What the fuck happened to you last night?"

"I didn't have a spare tire. Roadside assistance took forever," he mumbled. "Why are you calling this fucking early?"

"I just dropped Sutton at work."

"Oh." Surprise jolted his tone. "Did she stay the night?"

"Yeah. I need to fill you in on what's happening."

"Okay. When? You want to catch up for lunch?"

"Actually . . . now would be good if you're up for it. I'll call Cole. You want to come over? I think I want to jam."

"Holy. Fuck." His tone spiked skyward. "I'm so there. See you in twenty minutes."

Chapter 18

FLINT

I rushed around, cleaning my house before the guys arrived. Dishwasher on. Laundry on. Trash taken out. I had no intention of hiding the fact I'd been with Sutton; my place just needed some order. After putting the cushions back on the sofa, there was no evidence of her being there . . . except the subtle scent of her perfume lingered in the air. The emptiness in my heart twisted. *Damn.* She'd only been gone an hour, and I missed her.

But before the guys got here, I had one room to check . . . the music room.

At the door, I sucked in a deep breath and entered. As I moved around the studio, making sure everything was straight and in place, my mind hurtled. I couldn't believe Sutton had gotten me to play . . . or that I'd slept with her in there. Both had been phenomenal. For a few brief moments, the darkness inside of me had eased. The way she pushed me to do things I didn't think I was ready for scared me, but I liked it too.

For the first time in months, I was ready to pick up my guitar and play with the guys.

At the far end of the room, I swiped the cushions off the

floor and rearranged them on the sofa. The visions of my body entangled with Sutton's were still fresh in my mind. I did like her form of therapy.

I reached for my guitar resting against the end of the sofa when the lyrics lying on top of Phil's journal caught my eye. Something about them troubled me. I sank onto the seat, picked up the sheet of paper, and scanned the words again.

> *You think this is a game, but your words sting.*
> *The light shines on you, 'cause you're everything.*
> *What's it gonna take for you to see me?*
> *I stand in the shadows, never the light.*
> *My heart has to follow you every night.*

Who had Phil written this song about? Who did Phil hate so much?

Pain speared the center of my chest. *Was this about me?* No . . . no, not possible.

My hand trembled as I flipped open Phil's journal. Loose sheets and Post-it notes stuck out from within its pages. It was sacrilege to read another musician's notebook—their innermost thoughts, moods, and feelings. But Phil was gone. I had so many good memories of him. Was reading it another way to tattoo him onto my heart? Be closer to him? Feel like he was still alive?

No . . . don't touch it. Put it down.

Wait . . . maybe read one or two pages . . .

No . . . don't touch it. Put it down.

Shit . . . just one or two.

I fanned through the journal; it was only half full. I found a page toward the beginning, dated twelve months before he died.

> *You are like a thorn in my side,*
> *Seeing you with her kills my vibe.*

My blood burns the words from my tongue.
I hate every word that we've sung.
Chains keep my hands tied to my side.
Livid fury hurtles through my mind.

My breath shot from my lungs. *What the hell?* My hands trembled as I flicked forward several pages. Another song, a month before the accident, was scribbled across the page.

Storm clouds keep rolling through my head,
Darkness consumes everything.
The ocean drowns out my words,
When all I want is to run screaming.
Waves wash away what I should be saying,
Wind fills me to keep me flying,
Then slams me to the ground, leaving me crying.
It kills me inside, but I can't take this no more.
It kills me inside, that I can't stay anymore.

More than once you've stood in my path,
Played me for a fool, blinded by stars.
I'm not gonna take this lie no more,
I won't stand in your shadows anymore.

Tears welled in my eyes. My heart twanged, hard. I clutched at the crippling pain.

Fuck!

Was this about me? Was this what Phil thought?

No. It couldn't be. We were brothers. I loved Phil.

My eyes squeeze shut, releasing the tears that had formed. A loud, excruciating thud drummed inside my head.

Phil? Why didn't you say something?

The door crashed open and in strolled Slip and Cole.

"Dude?" Cole rushed over and sat beside me. "What's happened? Is it Sutton?"

I flicked a tear from my cheek and handed the journal to

Cole. "Did you know about this?"

Slip sat on the sofa opposite, next to Phil's bass. "About what?"

"About Phil? Was everything I've ever known a fucking lie?"

"What do you mean?" Cole scanned the pages.

"He hated me. It's there." I jabbed my hand toward the journal. "In his fucking lyrics."

Cole read page after page of Phil's notes and lyrics. "I've never seen these before." He handed the book to Slip. "But they could be about any one of us. Or anyone."

Slip's brow furrowed as he read several entries. "This is some dark shit. Was he jealous?"

"If he was, I never suspected anything." I wiped the dampness from my eyes with the back of my hand.

"So this last entry . . . did you read it?" Fear darkened Slip's eyes.

"No."

"Shit. It's fucked up."

I didn't want to hear it, but I had to. "Read it."

Slip's eyes flicked to Cole and then back to me before he reads my brother's words out loud:

> *Tonight, I'm gonna be the man that she needs,*
> *Tonight, I'm gonna give her all that she wants.*
> *You can have any girl, but this one's mine,*
> *Don't care what you think, I'm gonna blow her mind.*
> *Don't stand in my way, no, don't you dare,*
> *Revenge is a bitch, but I don't care.*
> *I want you to know what hurt feels like,*
> *Things I've felt every day of my life.*

I shot forward, bending over my knees. Tears streamed down my face. I struggled to talk over my sobs. "It's about Rici, isn't it? I told him I liked her about a week before the party. *Oh God.* He used her to hurt me. Why? I've never done anything to hurt him. Not ever. I've only ever loved and protected him. *Fuuuuck!"*

Slip closed the journal and put it on the coffee table. "Guess this puts a different twist on the dashboard camera recording of the accident."

My head pounded and throbbed. I'd watched the accident footage once, but I didn't need to. It was common for people in severe accidents to not recollect a thing. Go into shock. Block the trauma. But I wasn't one of them. I remembered every minute detail. Every second. Every word that had tumbled from Phil's mouth:

"I got Rici, man. I scored the hot chick. I was on fire tonight. Oh, she wanted me . . . not you. I'm the fucking rock star. Me. Not you."

"I thought he was just stoked he'd been with her. I was happy that he was happy. But he was gloating? Using a nice girl to hurt me? Who does that?"

Everything about that night was still crystal clear in my head. Phil had hit on Rici the moment we'd arrived at Slip's party. Our bro code had meant nothing to him that evening. Phil had pursued Rici like she was water after he'd crossed a desert, right in front of my face. I'd refused to let some girl come between us again, so I'd let Phil be.

Catching them banging on the billiard table had hurt. That was when I'd hit the vodka, ending up shitfaced. I'd been too drunk to stop Phil carrying me to the car. Too wasted to even walk. Too incoherent to stop him from driving.

I cradled my head between my hands and clutched at handfuls of my hair. "Why can't I forget that night? I remember every fucking second of the drive home. Every word he said. I can still see the cat on the side of the road he swerved to hit. Every sound—the squealing tires, the crash into the pole, the breaking glass—is all on repeat in my brain. I can still hear the voices of the paramedics. See the flashing lights. I can recall every fucking detail until they put me into the ambulance."

"It's okay, man." The rims of Cole's eyes burned red. "It will get better."

The pounding in my skull didn't relent. "How? He died hating me. How am I supposed to live with that?"

"No. No, don't think that." Cole rubbed my back. "Phil was awesome. Don't let some stupid words tarnish the good times."

"How can I not? He lied to me. For how long? Years? Is nothing real?" Anguish tore me apart, ripping through my gut. "Phil hated me. My parents don't want anything to do with me. My fake-come-real girlfriend lies for a living. Are you two fucking bullshitting me, too?"

"God no. Never." Cole drew me into a hug and let me sob against his shoulder. "This is just as much of a shock to us as it is to you. We had no idea."

"I loved him." I wept. "He was my brother. My fucking brother. I'd have done anything for him."

"We know. So would've we." Slip came over, sat on the arm of the sofa, and clasped my shoulder. "If Phil had issues with you, he would've had a ton with us. Maybe the drugs had affected him more than we'd realized. I hate we didn't help him in time. We should've done . . ." His voice snagged in his throat and he sniffled. ". . . more. Sooner. But we can't bring him back. We can't change what's happened. We will never know the truth. All we can do is remember the great time we had together."

I sat straight, but tears burned my eyes.

Cole wiped the dampness from his own eyes with the ball of his hand. "Yeah. Remember the time we went up to Big Bear for a weekend to write? It was freezing, close to snowing. We'd had a few drinks and Phil ran outside and jumped into the lake. Just because we dared him to, and he refused to be a pussy."

Slip leaned forward, ruffling his hand through his long hair.

"And the time we played up at San Francisco and we couldn't get the crowd hyped? Phil stripped down to his boxer briefs and jumped across the stage, playing his guitar, like Angus Young in AC/DC. He was so fucking out there and funny at times."

"That's just it." My head was stuck in a wormhole, warping through space at the speed of light. "He was. So why did he hate me? Was it because I sang lead?"

"You sing lead because your voice is fucking phenomenal," Slip said. "You're a better singer than him by a million miles. He knew that. We wouldn't have been signed if he was on vocals. He never had the range you have."

I couldn't argue with the truth.

Slip sighed and rubbed the tip of his chin. "Maybe Phil craved more attention. I don't know why when none of us lacked in that department."

I stared at Phil's journal. "Maybe it goes back to Shelby in high school? Maybe he liked Lena. Maybe he should've just told me he had a fucking problem with me." I pointed to Cole, then Slip. "If you two are losing your shit with me, you fucking tell me."

"We have." Slip shrugged. "That's why we had an intervention. We want our life back. We want *you* back. That's why we agreed with Blake to set you up with Sutton."

"How's that going?" Cole nudged me in the ribs. "I dropped by on my way out for a run this morning and met her. She seems nice."

"Yeah. That's a whole different bucket of worms. Where did he find her?" I rubbed at the tension throbbing in my temples. "Somehow, she's weaved her way under my skin and twists everything around. Then she makes me do shit I don't want to do, and fucking turns me on. We fucked like crazy last night, then again in here this morning. We're now kinda hooking up for the summer."

"How is that a bad thing?" Slip raised an eyebrow.

My heart shuddered, snagging against my ribs. "Because . . . I forget Phil. Now . . . all I want to do . . . is forget him."

"No, you don't," Cole said.

"How can I sing the songs we wrote together without thinking how much he loathed me?"

"Then we write new music." Slip clasped my shoulder. "We only sing the songs you wrote. You take the lead; we'll follow. We're not going anywhere. There's no rush to play gigs. We just want you back behind the mic and to hit that recording studio in a few months."

No. No. NO!

I jumped to my feet. Anger burned my veins and twisted every muscle in my body. "Phil fucking lied to me. How dare he? I told him everything. Loved him. I wanted to die instead of him."

"Finally!" Slip splayed his hands in the air, relief flooding his voice.

"Finally, what?" I hissed through clenched teeth.

"You're angry. You've progressed on to the next stage of grieving. You're one step closer to recovery. This is brilliant."

I clenched my fists. Before I punched Slip in the face, broke every piece of equipment in our music room, or smashed the windows, I had to escape. "Please. Get me out of here. I promise we'll jam. But right now, I need air."

Cole jumped to his feet. "Let's go for a run. Up through the canyon. Burn off that rage."

"I haven't exercised in four months. I'm as unfit as a fat cat."

"Excellent." He rubbed his hands. "We'll make you hurt. Let's go. Get your running shoes."

Five minutes later, I pounded up the dirt track with Cole and Slip by my side. I wanted to believe that Phil's lyrics were just random thoughts about someone else, just venting some steam. But the truth slammed into me with every stride.

They were about me.

Every. Fucking. One.

The toxic truth blistered beneath my skin. The rocky track crunched beneath my shoes. My muscles burned, frustrated I couldn't run faster.

At the top of the hill, I pulled to a halt, sucking in and gasping for air. I leaned over and clutched my knees. Sweat dripped from the tips of my hair, ran down my face, and soaked my tank top.

"You are one unfit motherfucker." Slip slapped my back.

"You used to outrun us. This is a first." Cole stood, barely panting, with his hands on his hips.

"Fuck you."

"Feel better?' Slip asked, retying his shoelace.

"Not even close."

"Well . . ." Cole pointed down the hill. "We better push you harder on the way home then."

With grit in my veins, I raced back to my house, then we hit the studio. I grabbed one of my electric guitars, plugged in the power cable, and struck the steel strings. The vibrations invaded my soul. I was hungry, needy, desperate to jam. Cole took to his drums and Slip, his electric guitar.

For two hours, we belted out music. No singing—just playing. My hands ached. The steel strings cut my fingertips. They'd softened after months of not playing. My shoulder hurt, but I pushed through the agony.

Strum. Strike. Slay.

No matter how hard I hit the strings, it didn't kill the pain hurtling through my bones.

Strum. Strike. Slay. Strum. Strike. Slay.

Phil's cutting lyrics broke my heart and crushed my soul. But at least now I felt something other than emptiness. Anger was new. Sutton had helped push me forward. If this was some stupid step I had to take, so be it. I wasn't going to back down.

God help anyone who fucking got in my way.

If this was the process of getting better . . . bring it.

But how long was this fucked up phase supposed to last?

And what would get me through it?

Chapter 19

SUTTON

I paced the floor in my condo with script in hand. Nerves twisted in my tummy as the lines tumbled from my lips. On Friday, three days ago, Harlow had scored me a closed-call audition. For today. Just one and a half weeks after Flint and I had hit the red carpet. The publicity had worked quicker than I'd expected.

Flint wasn't what I'd expected.

There was so much more to him than the drunken, debauchery-filled douchebag of a rock star I'd read about online. He wasn't who I'd thought he was after our first meeting. Sleeping with him had not been on my agenda. Not after the awards night and not after Everhide's party last week. But something about the way he looked at me, needed me, touched me, had awoken a desire inside of me that had never been alive before. The constant hum of hungry, hot tension that hovered between us was an aphrodisiac.

Shit. Focus. I had lines to learn. I'd taken the day off work and had five hours until my audition. *Stop. Thinking. About. Flint.*

This potential movie role was huge. Bigger than anything

I'd ever done before. The YA dystopian thriller would be filmed in LA and had a massive Hollywood budget. My hand went to my stomach, trying to settle the waves of nausea. Was this role out of my league? I ticked all the selection criteria boxes. I was the correct age. I had the required appearance and possessed the necessary experience.

Yes. I could do this.

Only six girls had been called for the audition, so I had a decent shot.

But why couldn't I memorize the lines? I'd never had issues before. Failing to deliver the part off by heart was cause for immediate culling. I had to get this right.

I sank onto the kitchen stool and stared at the script. The lines blurred before my eyes. Flint kept bombarding my mind.

On the drive home after work last Wednesday night, he'd said he needed a few days to sort out some band business with the guys. He'd been quiet, distracted, not his usual flirty self. I'd been tired after our huge night together and a long day at the studio, so I hadn't thought anything of it. Until I'd tried to touch base with him.

He hadn't answered any of my calls or returned my voicemails. I'd texted him several times about our next event this coming Friday and which outfit to wear. I'd messaged him over the weekend about my audition . . . maybe too many times when I'd had too much wine. His replies had been brief and to the point—*Yep. Okay. Sure. Great. Good luck.* There'd been no hint of a hookup. It was almost as bad as being ghosted.

Every hour of the day that passed, worry mounted in my mind. Had I pushed him too far last week, getting him to play his guitar? *Shit.* I hoped he was okay.

Maddy and Georgia had reassured me over Snapchat not to overthink things and wished me luck for today. But I couldn't get him off my mind.

Was there a protocol for booty calls? A time frame? A process? Between my legs, I certainly felt the need. I couldn't hold out until Friday.

Huffing out a breath, I strummed my freshly manicured baby-pink fingernails against the counter. I was so out of my depth with a casual affair, it wasn't funny. I'd never done this before. But I'd waited long enough. After the audition, I'd call him. Drop by his place on the way home. Say . . . *hi*.

A smile curled across my lips. *Perfect.*

My cell phone pinged on the kitchen counter.

I grabbed it. Flint's name lit the screen. *Finally.* My heart rate doubled. I swiped the screen to read the message.

> WHAT ARE YOU DOING?

I typed, my long nails tapping against the screen.

> LEARNING LINES.
> I HAVE MY AUDITION THIS AFTERNOON.

His response was instant.

> WANT HELP?

What? No. I was perfectly capable. I didn't need interruptions or distractions. I needed to focus. Concentrate. Be diligent.

> NAH, EVERYTHING IS UNDER CONTROL.
> BUT . . . I COULD COME OVER AFTER?

My intercom buzzed. Had my cranky neighbor locked herself out again? Stupid woman. I rushed over to the door to answer it. "Hello?"

"I'm here. Downstairs."

"Flint?" My heart leaped into my throat. "What are you doing here?"

"Just let me in."

"Um . . . okay."

Shit. I didn't have time for visitors. I scanned my living room for clothes laying around, used coffee cups, and mess on my desk. *All good.* I wiped my hands over my oversized Universal Studios T-shirt and cotton shorts. *Yep. Respectable enough.*

Two minutes later, he knocked on the door.

I unhooked the latch and pulled it open.

Oh. My. Lord.

A feverish wave washed over me. Between my legs clenched. Flint rested one hand against the doorjamb and held a water bottle in the other. His sweaty tank top clung to his chest and every one of his ripped stomach muscles. Damp strands of hair clung to his forehead and his face was as red as Spiderman's suit.

I swallowed the hard lump in my throat. "What have you been doing?"

He stepped inside and headed into my living room. "I went for a run along the beach."

"But this is nowhere near your house." I closed the door and followed him.

"It's nice weather." There was no sunshine in his tone— more like surly aggravation.

Something was off. But I wouldn't let him get to me. I straightened my shoulders, crossed my arms, and leaned against the counter. "Again. Nowhere near your place. I thought you did nothing but sulk at home and never went out."

"Yeah. Funny." He grunted as he paced the room, fidgeting with his empty water bottle, wringing it between his hands.

Every step he took tightened the tension between my shoulder blades. This wasn't the reunion I'd wanted to have with him. If he had a problem with me, he should just come out and say it. "Is there something wrong? Do you need anything? I have work to do. I need to prepare for my audition."

He waved his bottle. "I need to refill this."

"Um, okay." I tipped my chin toward the beach. "Why didn't you just use a water fountain on the beach? And can you stop moving?" I waggled my finger at him. "You're dripping sweat all over my floor."

He halted, pinning me with his gaze that shimmered with a primitive hunger. The icy fire in his eyes caught me off-guard, weakened my knees, and sent a jolt between my legs. *Oh wow . . . Totally. Wickedly. Sexy.*

But everything else about him—his jaw, his hands, his posture—was like a rubber band about to snap. The mixed signals radiating off him were like wildfire, unsettling but bewitching. Intoxicating. Strangely captivating.

I gripped onto the counter to steady myself.

"Do you have to make everything difficult?" A sinful grin slid across his lips. "I went for a run and wanted to say . . . *hi.*"

"Hi." My voice came out in a breathy whisper. My pulse quickened just being in the same space as him.

Before I could blink, he rushed forward, cupped my face, and kissed me. Hard. All-consuming. Mind-bending. *Oh . . . so this was what he meant by "hi."*

But what the hell? I pushed against his chest. "What are you doing?"

"I needed to see you."

The gravelly raw need in his voice coiled and tugged at my core. I pressed my thighs together to stop the sudden throb. "Your timing sucks."

He curled his hands around my neck. Driving his fingers through my hair, he tilted my head back to meet his fiery gaze. "I. *Need.* You."

My mouth gaped. The intensity and urgency in his voice reverberated through my body and hummed through my veins. "But . . . you're all sweaty and gross and wound up."

"Not for long. Not because of you." He picked me up. Hooking my legs around his waist, he headed for the shower.

"Flint. Stop." *Damn*. I'd win a Razzie Award for that pathetic performance.

He pinned me against the wall inside my shower and slayed kisses down my neck. His musky, sweaty scent enraptured me. His hot breath on my skin made me delirious.

Dragging his thumb over the arch of my breast, he teased my nipple. "Say . . . I don't want you to fuck me. Say . . . I don't want to come. Say . . . I don't want an orgasm or two."

My knees buckled. *Oh sweet Lord!* "I have . . . um . . . an audition."

"It's at four. There's plenty of time. Promise." He lowered the zipper on my shorts.

Unable to resist him, my head fell back against the tiles. I dug my fingers into his biceps. "I'm so mad at you. You should've returned my calls."

"You're mad? Good. Let's have angry sex."

Was that what he wanted? He was clearly upset over something. We should talk about whatever was bothering him . . . later. *Oh yeah. Later.*

He dipped his hand inside my panties and teased his fingers through my slit, circled my clit, then slipped them inside me.

My body shuddered. This was crazy. Out of control. Ludicrous. But so, so hot! Maybe I needed this too. "I could use some stress relief before this afternoon."

"So, is that a yes to fucking?" His husky voice rasped in my ear.

"Yes. Now shut up and kiss me." I curled my hand around his head and drew his lips to mine. Our tongues connected in a fiery duel.

He flicked the shower on.

"Argh!" I shrieked and gasped as the cold water shot over our bodies and saturated our hair. Our clothes glued to our skin.

A lopsided grin curled across his lips. His icy gaze darkened as he raked his eyes over my hardened nipples. "You are definitely what I need. My plan to see you worked."

The water was quick to warm. He yanked off my T-shirt, unclipped my bra, and ripped off my shorts and panties. He kicked them to the far end of the shower in a soggy pile. His clothes were quick to join them.

"I'd wanted to see you later tonight." I dragged my nails down his chest and across his stomach. Leaning forward, I licked salty droplets from his nipple, then grazed my teeth over the tip.

"Yeah?" He moaned. "I'm glad we're on the same track."

I took hold of his hardness and rubbed my hand up the length of his shaft. Circling my thumb over the head, I whispered against his lips, "Did you get your results? Are you clean?"

"Yes." He kissed down the length of my throat. Millions of goose bumps shot down my arm and side. "I'm all good. You?"

"I did." My eyes fluttered closed as he dipped his head, licked and flicked his tongue over my nipple. I tightened my hold on his cock and pumped him faster. A wicked smile inched across my lips. "I have chlamydia. Herpes. Warts and some other weird bacterial growth. We used condoms before, so you should be fine. I don't think you would've caught anything from going down on me the other night."

"What the fuck?" His head shot up. He reefed his dick out of my hand. "Did your ex give you all that shit?"

I burst out laughing. The shock on his face was priceless. "I'm fucking with you." I placed my hands on his chest. His heart pounded wildly. "I'm clean. Honestly. The results are on my phone if you don't believe me."

"Shit." He wiped the water off his face. "You scared me half to death. Total mood killer."

Nope . . . his cock still stood at full mast.

He splashed water in my face. "Not funny."

"Oh . . . yes, it was." I giggled, wiping the spray from my eyes. "Were you afraid your dick might fall off?"

"No. I was afraid I wouldn't be able to do what I wanted to you."

I caught him around the waist and drew him against me. I took hold of his balls and massaged them gently. "And what is that, exactly?"

"Hmm." He groaned, low and gravely. Leaning into my touch, he murmured against my mouth, "Take you hard. Bareback. Make you scream as you come."

My insides clenched in anticipation as he pressed me back against the tiles. Standing on tiptoe, I curled one leg around his thigh and guided him toward my opening. "Then what are you waiting for?"

"Nothing."

The water spray cascaded over us. He widened and bent his knees, then thrust inside me. Sparks spiraled up my spine and tingled my scalp. *So good.* With a rush of warm air, his mouth claimed mine. His kisses were electric enough to light the Sunset Strip at night. Every taste was like hot honey. Nothing was sweeter or as addictive. Wrapping my arms around his shoulders, I clawed at his skin and crushed my breasts against his pecs. I shouldn't be this ravenous for him. This wild. This hungry. But I wanted more. Harder. And harder.

He withdrew a fraction, then slammed into me again. "That's for being mean." His tone purred like a puma. Then he thrust into me again. "That's for being so freaking tempting." Then he took hold of my hands and pinned them above my head. "And this is just because I want to fuck you."

He drove into me time and time again. Each thrust, deeper and deeper.

Exquisite pain and pleasure coursed through me. My back

slapped against the tiled wall. Hooking my leg higher around his hip, I glued my body to his. I wanted it harder. I wanted all the pent-up frustration over work, and him, and my audition, and my future, pounded out of me.

This . . . was what I needed.

Curling his hand around my thigh, he quickened his pace. The guttural, animalistic moans rumbling in his throat reverberated through my body. *Fuck!* Why did that do strange things to my heart? Whatever reason had fueled his need for this crazed, bone-melting sex, I'd be down for it anytime. Every time he slammed into me, my toes curled, my breath came out panted, and my insides clenched tighter around him.

With a deep thrust, he buried himself inside me and stilled.

"Oh, shit. That's good," I whispered against his hot lips.

He slowly pushed deeper and deeper. I didn't think it was possible. Then, he hit something far inside me. I wriggled for more friction. More connection on that spot. *Holy. Fuck. Yes.* "Flint?" I tried to free my hands. I wanted to touch him, but he tightened his hold on my wrists.

Tilting his hips, he closed his eyes and let out a slow breath. "Want more?"

"I won't be able to walk after this."

"Sutton?" He traced the tip of his nose along the edge of mine. His hair tickled my face. "I want to hear you scream."

"No." But twisting tension built inside me. Like a fuse about to explode. Was this one of those deep orgasms I'd read about online? Everywhere between my legs craved release. My hips pulsed against him. I sought his lips, crushing my mouth against his. Our tongues tangled, tasting each other.

His cock was a hot rod, ramming into me. Pounding and pushing me closer and closer to the edge. I dug my nails into his hand, holding mine above my head.

A wicked smile curled across his lips, then he drove into

me. Harder. Deeper.

I screwed my eyes shut, willing myself not to cry out. But it was futile.

"Flint," I screamed.

My head fell back, and my body ignited. The most intense orgasm of my life ripped through my core, catapulting through my veins, and zapping every follicle on my body. My chest heaved, panting for breath. My heart beat so loud that it reverberated in my head, fuzzing the sound in my ears.

"I got you, babe." He curled his hands around my waist just before my knees gave way. He jerked and thrust. His hot release spilled into me in throbbing bursts. "And you got me. Fuuuuck."

As he rode out his waves of pleasure, his body spasmed against mine. He kissed every inch of my face. I didn't think I could melt any more, but the tender, gentle brushes of his lips on my skin turned me to molten liquid.

"If that's angry sex"—I raked my fingernails across his chest—"I rate it."

"Hmm. I needed that." He grabbed my shower gel and soaped my shoulders. "You okay?"

"Yes, but my legs are jelly. I might not walk for a week. But that was worth it."

"Told you I could make you scream."

"Smart ass." I play-punched his arm. "Let's clean up and hop out."

I grabbed Flint a clean towel and threw his clothes in my dryer. Guess he'd be sticking around until they were done.

"Are you hungry?" I asked, tying my robe. "I could make chicken and salad wraps for lunch."

"That sounds perfect." He followed me into the kitchen with the towel wrapped low around his waist. His black hair curtained his gorgeous icy-blue eyes. Last time he was here after the awards show, he'd worn the same thing. *Hmm.* This couldn't become a habit.

I dug into my fridge, gathered containers and packets of ingredients, and lay them out on the counter. He stepped in beside me to help. He cut the chicken; I washed the lettuce.

"You gonna tell me why you needed angry sex?" I scattered the lettuce onto the wraps I'd set out on two plates.

"I feel better now." He dropped a shred of meat into his mouth. "That's all that matters."

"No, it's not. What happened?"

Trouble etched his brow. "Just dealing with Phil crap. In the studio the other day, those lyrics you read created a tsunami of shit."

"How so?" I sprinkled grated cheese over the lettuce, piled on the chicken, then squeezed mayonnaise over everything.

He tossed the dirty knife and cutting board into the sink. "I'm trying to get my head around it. So are the guys. They came over and we went through more of Phil's journal."

"What's so bad about that?" I handed him his folded wrap, and we headed over to the sofa to eat.

"We read more of his lyrics. I'm convinced Phil hated me."

My steps faltered. *That couldn't be right?*

He sank onto the sofa and stared at the wrap on his plate. "We never knew he had issues. It's imploded every memory we had of him."

"Why? How?" I wriggled on the seat beside him to get comfortable. "What did he write?"

"On every page, the lyrics he wrote suggested he wanted me out of the way. He wanted to sing lead. That girl, Rici, I told you about? He used her to hurt me. He hated that the other guys and I got more attention than he did. We don't know if it was the drugs getting to him, or if he'd just loathed me for years. But his words were dark . . . angry and cruel. It's fucked with my head to think that every conversation we'd had, every song we'd written, every fun time we'd had was all bullshit and backloaded with lies."

"Oh my God. That's awful." I rubbed his thigh. "So, what are you going to do?"

"So far, I've just been angry, mainly at myself for not seeing it. I didn't think I was stupid and naïve. I don't know what to do or how to process it. I've run miles a day. I've jammed with the guys. But nothing has put out the fire raging through me. I thought sex might help." He grinned at me before taking a bite of his wrap.

"And did it?" I picked up my food and took a bite.

He nodded and chuckled. "Funny thing . . . yeah, it did. I don't feel like I want to smash the shit out of everything now."

"Please don't." I glanced around my condo. "Everything I own is in this apartment."

"You're safe. I promise." He took another mouthful and chewed. "Cole and Slip were excited that I've moved on to the next stage of grief. I just fucking hope I don't stay in this phase as long as the first one."

"The sex was freaking hot." I licked mayonnaise from my fingertip. "But we can't do that every day. We have rules, remember?"

"I don't like rules." His gaze raked up my legs. A smile curled across his lips. "Maybe just jerking off while thinking about you will be enough until we see each other again. Or . . . a picture of you in that robe would do the trick."

I giggled as I smoothed my hand over the short skirt of my kimono. "This old thing?"

"Fuck yeah. It shows off your sexy legs. There's a hint of cleavage at the top. I know what's beneath it. I could totally get off to that."

"Well, in the name of therapy . . ." I put my plate down, grabbed my cell phone off the counter, and returned to sit by his side. I eased the robe off my shoulders and clutched the silky fabric low over my breasts.

"What are you doing?" His eyes widened.

I grabbed his plate and placed it next to mine. Tousling my wet hair, I pouted at the camera, and took a selfie. Then I took another one, licking my lips, then another kissing his cheek. But that wasn't enough. I straddled his lap, drew his face into my chest, and took a few more snaps. He chuckled as he planted a kiss above my left boob. I wriggled against his groin. *Hmm.* I did like him between my thighs, even if I was still sore from the wild sex. I added the images to a message and sent them to him. His cell phone on the coffee table dinged. "Now you have material to help."

"You are fucking crazy." Seeing him smile again was worth it. "Don't you have an audition soon?"

"Yes. I need to run through my lines again."

I went to crawl off his lap, but he caught my hips. "Want some help?"

"You want to run lines with me?"

"Sure. I don't have plans with the guys until tomorrow afternoon after physical therapy. Jamming with them has been good."

I linked my fingers behind his neck. "You really playing again?"

"Yeah." He rubbed my sides. "I'm still not straight in the head. I'm not up for singing yet. Too many songs remind me of Phil. There are no lyrics zooming around in my mind. But it's progress."

"So true."

His hands moved to my arms, sliding upward. "I have you to thank for it. Again."

"You can thank me by accompanying me to the Children's Hospital Charity Dinner on Friday night."

He tugged the robe off my shoulder and kissed along the ridge to the base of my neck. "Can't I rock your world before then?"

"No. I have work to do."

"But this hookup isn't over yet, is it?" He untied the bow on my robe, dipped his head, and took my nipple into his mouth. His hot tongue swirled around my bud, sending electric charges straight between my legs. My eyes fluttered shut. *Oh, wow.*

But no . . .

"Flint. No." I yanked my robe shut. "This audition is too important to me."

"I'd never jeopardize that." Mischievousness glinted in his eyes as he nudged his erection against my panties. "So, let's have sex while we rehearse your lines."

Hmm. I'd never done that before. *But no.* This had to stop. *Now.*

I teased my lips against his, then pushed off his chest to stand. "Nice try. But your booty call is over."

He leaned forward and curled his hands around my legs. "You are one tough woman. I like that."

"I just have my priorities straight." I retied my robe. "You've been enough of a distraction."

"Hopefully a much-needed one. You seem much more relaxed than before. I certainly feel better. So thank you." He rose to his feet and kissed my forehead. He grabbed my script off the kitchen counter. "Now . . . you want help with these lines?"

For the next hour, we walked around my living room, running through my script. We laughed. We joked and teased each other. With each run-through, I tweaked my delivery. I'd nailed it.

I changed into a pair of smart dress pants and fitted top. After putting on a touch of elegant makeup, I headed out into the living room to Flint. I twirled around and smoothed my hand over my hips. "Do I look okay?"

"That you do." He put on his clothes he'd retrieved from my dryer.

"Funny. I'm not nervous anymore."

"See? . . . Sex helped you to chill."

"I can't deny that." I gathered my purse and shuffled him toward my front door.

With his water bottle and cell phone in hand, he wrapped his arms around me and kissed me—all tongue, with knee-buckling hotness and belly-quivering hunger. "Good luck with your audition. Call me if you need to see me again before Friday. I'm happy for you to break our rules anytime."

I took a deep breath. It took a second for my feet to come back to the ground. I tugged him toward my door and opened it. "I won't be breaking our rules. Thanks for helping me with the lines. I'll see you Friday."

"But—"

"No buts. Bye." Giggling, I pushed him out the door.

The latch clicked shut.

Time to focus. Time to nail my audition.

Chapter 20

SUTTON

I strode into the casting agent's office with an extra spring in my stride. My head was held high, my smile stitched into place, and confidence was in each step. I knew the lines. I was relaxed. I was ready. Thanks to Flint. Angry sex—as he'd called it—had been wicked. I'd never had a rough, hard, *need-you-now-or-I'll-lose-my shit* ravishing before. Between my legs still ached, raw and tender. My body tingled from my head down to my toes. Was *I've-just-been-fucked-senseless* written all over my face? *Oh yeah!* There was no need to wear blush; warmth still colored my cheeks. The catchup had totally been worth it.

No matter how much I pep-talked myself into maintaining control around Flint, every time he walked into the room, I slipped under his spell. And each time he left, I had to tether my grasp on reality—otherwise walking away from him at the end of summer would break what remained of my fragile heart.

Pushing Flint out of my mind, I zoned in on the task ahead. *Audition time.*

I checked off my name at reception and proceeded down the hallway of seated women, waiting for their turn. No faces were familiar. All but one. My stomach hit the floor with a glass-shattering smash.

What. The. Fuck?

Georgia sat perfectly posed on the farthest yellow upholstered chair. Her makeup, flawless. Her hair, perfectly straightened. Her *I'm-better-than-you* attitude plumped her perfect pout.

"Oh, Sutton." Georgia leaped to her feet. She skipped forward and hugged me.

"What . . . what are you doing here?" My mind spiraled in tight, tiny circles. Georgia was supposed to be in Phoenix, filming. Not here. Of all the casting calls, why did she have to be at this one?

"I'm auditioning too. I flew in at lunchtime and fly back tonight." Georgia grabbed my hand and dragged me to sit on the chair next to her. "This role would be awesome, wouldn't it? The moment you told me about it, I called my agent. He knows the casting director and called in a favor. He loved that I was interested and got me on the list."

"That's . . . great." *Shit!* Hurt stabbed my chest, denting my confidence. Bile bubbled in my belly and burned my throat. Georgia wouldn't be here if I hadn't mentioned the closed audition to her on the weekend. Too much wine and not seeing or hearing from Flint for days had flustered me. *Me and my big mouth.*

"But what about your show?" I kept my tone light and airy, but each breath tore my lungs. Could I blame Georgia for jumping at an amazing opportunity? *No.* I guessed that was why she was so successful. She seized every moment regardless of who she hurt along the way. "You can't fit this into your schedule, can you?"

"Sure, I can." Georgia relaxed back into her chair. No one exuded self-importance like she did. "Filming for this movie falls between seasons. It's perfect."

"That's … awesome." I hugged my purse against my curdling gut. Were my chances obsolete if Georgia's agent knew the casting director? This town was all about who you knew, not what you knew. Doubts poisoned my mind. Georgia was prettier. More popular. More outgoing. She had experience in this genre. *Fuck*. Georgia may have those things, but this audition had been offered to me; she'd had to make a call to get in. I had talent, skills, and experience. I wouldn't be here otherwise. I gathered my frayed confidence, stitched it back together, and injected *I'm-not-going-down-without-a-fight* gusto into my smile. "But if there are delays or unforeseen issues, as there often are on big films, I'm much more flexible. It will be so exciting to work on a project that has the potential to be bigger than *The Hunger Games* and *Divergent*."

Georgia flicked her long hair over her shoulder and raised one mocking eyebrow. "I can't believe you're even considering this role. It's all action, grit, and injustice. Wouldn't rom-com or another sweet remake of *Cinderella* be more suitable?"

Her condescending tone furled fire through my arteries. Why couldn't Georgia be supportive and encouraging? She'd never used to be a snob, but she'd become more of a diva than all the Kardashians combined since her show had become a hit.

Her attitude hadn't bothered me until Flint had come along. I'd been blind to it. Flint talked about his band and his brother with true love and respect. They shared a true, loyal friendship. He'd made me feel special and worthy when he'd barely known me. I'd never been treated like that before. Not by family, friends, or lovers. Flint's fame and loss hadn't changed him from being a decent person. I couldn't say the same about Georgia anymore.

Flint had come into my life at just the right time. With the mess with my father behind me, he'd given my confidence the kick it needed. "I'm ready to try new things. Diversify. This role is perfect."

Georgia pouted and patted my arm. "Oh, that's sweet. But I think you're too late. You'll be a *Gilmore Girls* for the rest of your days, not a ball-breaking dystopian star."

Was this Georgia's weird way of preparing me for rejection? I didn't need it.

I dug my fingernails into my palm. She'd transformed from being one of the *Mean Girls* into a paranormal fighter for her show. Why couldn't I morph into a new character for a movie? I was an actress. That was my job.

It wasn't too late. I wouldn't let her get to me.

Drawing my shoulders back, I lifted my chin. I had as much chance as any other girl here of landing the role. I knew the lines. I fit the requirements. I had way more experience than Georgia. As I inhaled slowly and deeply, I conjured a warm smile. One thing that would never fail me was my manners—even though Georgia pushed them to breaking point. "Well, we'll see. I wish you luck in your audition."

"Oh, thank you." Georgia slathered honey into her tone. "This would be my dream role."

Yeah, what actress didn't want to score the lead in a potential blockbuster franchise? "Mine too."

"And Cory Holt is the lead guy." She squeezed my hand like an overzealous fan. "He's so freaking hot. I met him last year. I'd love to work with him."

My stomach hit the floor. "How do you know that? They haven't announced castings?"

"I told you. My agent knows everything and everyone." Georgia curled her arm around mine and leaned against my shoulder. "Isn't this exciting to see who gets the part?"

"Yeah . . . totally." *Not anymore.*

"I'm so nervous." She squeezed my arm. "Distract me. How's Flint? Are you still together?"

Why did she want to know? So she could sweep in on him if we weren't?

I hoped Flint's dibs rule stood the test of time. She had no hope in hell of being with him. Was it wrong to have some small sense of satisfaction in knowing that fact?

"Yes, we are." My lips were still sore from his brutal, hungry kisses. My nipples were still tender from his torturous fingertips. *Oh. So. Good.*

"I'd love a piece of hot ass like that. He's *nasty* hot."

Hot. Sexy. Amazing in bed. "That he is. So hands off." *Crap!*

Georgia puffed air through her nose. "Why would you say that? You're not still hung up on what happened with that guy from Miami, are you? That was months ago."

"Dwayne? No." I wasn't. We'd gone on one date. We'd never got the chance to get to know one another. The moment he'd met Georgia we were over. "But every guy I've liked since Beau, you've made a pass at, made out with, or fucked."

She shrugged. "Then they're not the one, are they?"

Shit. She had a point.

"I just really like Flint." I really did. I didn't want to jeopardize my limited time with him by putting temptation in front of his face. "So, as my friend, please respect that."

"Only if he feels the same way."

"Why wouldn't he?"

"Come on, Sutt?" The corner of Georgia's mouth quirked. "Be honest with me. Everyone in this business knows Harlow has a reputation for creating controversy. Is that why he set you up with Flint? For some PR? It's just for show, right? I can't comprehend how else you'd be with someone that smokin' hot. Flint's way out of your league."

Georgia's words speared my heart. She may have been right. I may have never caught the eye of someone like Flint without being set up. But we were together for now.

I turned to Georgia and met her cool glare with defiance. "Harlow is my agent because he's damn good at his job. I'm with Flint because we hit it off. Setup or not, it doesn't matter anymore. Meeting him has been the best thing that has happened to me in a long time. Any hype that surrounds us being together is all thanks to this town's hunger for idol gossip."

Ain't that the truth!

That was why Harlow's plan was working.

My breath shuddered in my lungs. Flint really was the best thing that had happened to me. I hadn't expected that.

"Chill. I'm just stirring you. There's no need to be so defensive." Georgia grimaced as she dug into her purse and pulled out a pale pink lip gloss. Staring into a compact mirror, she sheened the glittery gel across her lips. "God, anyone would think you're in love with the guy. You haven't even been together for a month."

Love him?

Our connection and chemistry were a touch intense, but there was no way I could've fallen for him in such a short time frame. *Nope.* Definitely not. Nope. Nope. *Nope!* "I haven't dated anyone in a long time. I don't want to fuck it up."

Georgia put her gloss away and folded her hands in her lap. "Well, if you are so into each other, don't keep him locked in a cage. When I'm back in town next week, we should all go out. You. Me. Maddy. Flint. I'd love to get to know him."

I bet you would. So, nope. "He's super busy with band stuff. He probably won't be able to make it."

"He's not playing, right? So, get him to change his plans." Georgia pointed at me. "Thursday night. At Dalton's. Make it happen."

Nope. "No promises." I pulled a folded print-out of the script from my purse and waved it at Georgia. "If you don't mind, I'd like to run through my lines one more time."

I needed Georgia to stop drilling me about Flint. And I needed to get him out of my head. He couldn't become a permanent fixture—not when we were destined to part.

The audition room door at the end of the hallway opened. A man and Barbara Healy, an actress I knew from another network show, stepped into the hallway. She shook hands with the casting agent, bade him farewell, and strode toward the reception area, her high heels clicking on the tiled floor. "Good luck everyone. May the best girl win."

"Georgia Burrows?" the casting agent called.

"Oh. That's me." Georgia sprang to her feet and hooked her purse over her shoulder. "Wish me luck . . . oh, wait. I don't need it because I'm awesome."

Georgia winked at me, then strode into the audition room.

As the door closed behind Georgia, my shoulders sank three inches. *Shit.* I was wasting my time. I should just leave. When Georgia wanted something, nothing stood in her way. A heaviness settled in my stomach. I hoped Flint wasn't in her sights.

I cared about him too much. I understood why he and the guys had a dibs rule. Seeing her with Flint would cut me up too much. I couldn't bear it.

Taking a deep breath, I cleared my mind. I was here now. I'd see the audition through.

I unfolded my printout and smoothed the pages straight.

My hand shot over my heart.

Flint had scribbled comments above several of the lines and in the side columns. In the villain's line: *I want to kill you*; he'd crossed out the word *kill* and had written: *kiss*. Instead of: *I want you to die*; he'd written: *I want you to come.* Next to the line: *Get down on your knees*; he'd written: *I would LOVE you to do this.* He'd bolded and underlined that.

I covered my mouth to stifle my giggle. I traced his

handwriting with my fingertips. He'd done lines with me. Kissed me. Made me come. And yeah . . . I would get down on my knees for him. How could I not fall for him just a little when he made me laugh? He did little things like this that brought a smile to my face. He made me feel good about myself and like anything was possible.

This role could be mine.

I had a one in seven chance.

I would give it my best shot.

Fuck Georgia.

And I would thank Flint for helping me . . . on my knees, as requested.

Chapter 21

FLINT

Thursday night, I stretched out on an outdoor sun lounger by my pool and stared at the lights of Hollywood Boulevard below. After our wicked hookup last Tuesday, and the charity dinner on Friday, I had to wait two more painful days until I saw Sutton again. Phone calls and texts just didn't cut it. This whole limitation on seeing each other was ridiculous. My balls ached. No amount of jerking off to the photos of her was as good as real sex. I'd run more miles through the canyons in the past week than I had in the past two years to help alleviate the mounting tension. Jamming with the guys hadn't released my frustrations. Phil's lies and my lingering anger still twisted and tainted my thoughts. Before the accident, my mind used to constantly roam, form lyrics, crave music. But since the crash, there'd been nothing but darkness and an eerie silence. Now, my brain just wanted to scream.

I strangled the neck of my beer bottle between my hands. What if I hadn't drunk the night of the accident? Phil would still be alive. We could've worked out any issues. I'd do anything to have that opportunity.

If I'd seen signs that Phil had problems, I could have helped him. Changed things. I'd have let him sing the occasional song—even though it would have taken a lot to convince Cole and Slip. But most of all . . . if Phil was so unhappy, I could've let him go to follow his dreams—even though that would've broken my heart. There were so many things I could've done. Could've changed.

I rubbed the ache in my forehead. I hated that I'd never have a resolution. How was I supposed to find peace with this?

Somehow I had to fight this clusterfuck in my mind. I wanted to live and breathe music again. I wanted to sing and find my voice and enjoy life.

As I closed my eyes, Sutton slammed into my mind. She flitted through my brain as frequently as Phil did. Picturing her smile plucked at my heartstrings and hardened my cock. Recalling her touch eased the tension at the base of my neck. I took a deep breath and a wave of calm blanketed me in warmth.

Why did she excite and scare the living shit out of me?

Dick! That was a no-brainer. Her light softened the blow of Phil's death. She made it easier to breathe. Was I finally moving forward?

With her, hope dared to simmer in my soul.

Shit. Hovering my beer near my lips, I chuckled. She had me by the balls. That pissed me off. But I also liked it.

Hmm. Maybe I needed to renegotiate the terms of our agreement again.

I needed to speed up this bullshit process of moving on from Phil. I had to stop slipping into bouts of depression and darkness and drinking. She seemed to be the key. I refused to lose my record deal, so there was only one solution.

I wanted her in my bed every night until the end of summer. Starting tonight.

The guys would be here soon. They'd insisted on dragging

me out to see some live music. But I'd ditch them for sex with Sutton.

I picked up my cell phone and sent her a text.

You home? Can I come over?

No point in beating around the bush. I inserted the emojis of an eggplant and the hand displaying a peace symbol. I hoped she understood that meant I wanted my cock inside her.

I added the tongue, the pointed finger and the droplets to make sure she knew I was hell-bent on making her come. My dick twitched, hardening just thinking about it.

No reply.

Maybe I'd grossed her out. Some manners wouldn't hurt.

Please?

Three minutes later, my cell phone buzzed. Sutton's message lit the screen.

I'm not home.
Out with the girls.
Celebrating.
Georgia got the movie role.

Oh, shit. Sutton would be devastated. I quickly dialed her number.

She didn't answer.

I called her again.

This time, she picked up.

"Flint," she whimpered. "I can't talk right now."

Music blared in the background, but I didn't miss the sadness in her voice.

"Georgia got the part? Are you fucking with me?"

"No," she sobbed. "Me and my big mouth. I should've never mentioned the role to her. She knows how important it is for me to find a new job. I was so excited to get an audition and had a really good chance at being selected. But the minute I told her about the casting call, she pulled her strings, had her agent call the fucking casting director. No one else stood a chance . . . Shit." Her voice took on a toughened tone. "I'm sorry. She's my friend. I'm happy for her."

"No, you're not."

"Yes. I am. The best girl got the part. It wasn't meant to be. I'm just not at that level."

My jaw clenched and I dug my fingers into my thigh. She projected so much confidence but around Georgia, it withered and wilted. Why couldn't Sutton see how amazing she was? She may not have been on the highest-ranked TV show, but damn, she'd survived working in Hollywood since she was six. That was a tremendous achievement. She shouldn't feel less worthy just because Georgia was more popular.

"Sutton, you are that level. Okay, this role wasn't meant to be. You will land something soon. You're super talented. Any casting agent or director who turns you down is an idiot."

Whoa.

Was that how Phil had felt about me? That he wasn't good enough? *Shit.* As the lead singer, I had no control over attracting more attention than the other guys. I never actively sought the spotlight. When I was with my band, hanging out, making music, playing or performing, I never gloated or boasted about being more popular. I shared our fame and bore the flack. I never made the guys feel like they were less than me. Not ever.

No. The difference between Phil and Sutton? Phil had been jealous, envious, and reckless. Phil hadn't suffered from thinking he wasn't good enough; he'd thought he was better. Deserved more. Sutton didn't have a jealous bone in her body. She was quick to squash any fleeting flurry. She'd put her friends on a pedestal and failed to see she sat beside them. I couldn't do anything about Phil, but I could help Sutton.

"You're just saying I'm good to make me feel better." Her voice remained flat and strained.

I struggled to hear her over the background music. "You're amazing." I took a quick sip of beer. "I watched some of your *Brentwood* show on Netflix. How old were you at the start? Seventeen? Doesn't matter. I got a total boner." I now understood why teenage boys may have had pictures of her pinned to their bedroom wall or saved on their cell phones. She was a babe back then and a total siren now.

She sniffle-giggled. "You're sick."

"I know. But it's okay to be upset and pissed at Georgia. So get drunk. Let off some steam. Curse like Gordon Ramsay, and then . . . move on."

"What? Like you?" Sting snapped in her tone. "Like you've done with Phil?"

Ouch! That was a low blow. But she was right. Who was I to preach to anyone when I couldn't move on myself? "Okay . . . fair point. You win." I picked at the label on my beer bottle, held between my thighs. "So, you wanna come over and mope with me?"

"No." Her fragile voice sounded like she would shatter at any moment.

Was she wiping the tears from her eyes? Were her long lashes damp and stuck together? *Fuck!* All I wanted to do was hug her and make her feel better.

"It just hurts." She sighed, letting out a long breath full of exhaustion. "Georgia won't stop going on about it. Maddy's told her off so many times, but she doesn't stop. Georgia said I had no chance at landing the role because I'm too sweet and innocent."

"There's nothing wrong with being sweet." A wicked smile slid across my lips. "But I can vouch that you're not that innocent. My dick is still recovering from Tuesday night."

Her soft laugh was like summer sunshine, but it was short-lived. "Fuck! This just sucks."

"Yeah, babe. It does." I wanted to put a smile back on her face. I could do something about that. She'd been there for me when I'd had my panic attacks. For one night, could I stuff my hurt, grief, and anxiety aside, stuff it down into the depths of my stomach, and be there for her? A cold sweat broke out on my brow. My blood pressure spiked.

No. I could do this. "Where are you?"

"At Dalton's on Sunset."

That would be right. One of the hottest bars in Hollywood.

"Flint. I gotta go. The girls will be worried. It's my turn to buy drinks. Thanks for the texts. But that's not gonna happen."

Maybe not, but I could always hope. "The night is still young."

"I gotta stay. I won't see Maddy or Georgia for weeks. I'll call you tomorrow after work and see you on Saturday night."

After she hung up, I clenched my cell phone. Saturday was too far away.

Seconds later, Slip and Cole walked through my house, stepped outside, and headed toward me.

I drained the remains of my beer and placed the empty on the side table. I'd put it in the trash tomorrow. Or the day after that.

"You're ready." Cole waved at my clothes. "I'm impressed."

"Yep. I made an effort to shit, shower, and shave." I'd put on a pair of designer jeans, a button-down dress shirt, and polished combat boots. I'd shaved off my two days of facial growth and washed my hair. Pushing it, I felt like I was worth five bucks instead of a dime. There was no million-dollar dazzle about me. I stood and shoved my cell phone in my back pocket. "But there's a change of plan. Let's go to Dalton's."

"Dalton's?" Cole grimaced. "Why the fuck would we want to

go to some hyped-up nightclub?"

"Sutton's there."

"So?" Slip sneered. "We'll need security."

"Nah. I guarantee she'll be with her girlfriends in the VIP area. We'll call April to get us on the entry list." April, our publicist, wouldn't have any issues getting us into the club and helping us to avoid queues. "But Sutton's upset. So, let's go."

"Saving a damsel in distress, are we?" Cole chuckled. Grasping my shoulder, he shoved me toward the house. "I'm just glad we're going out."

Sutton was no damsel. But I cared about her.

"Yeah. Me too." I locked the bi-fold doors behind us, grabbed my keys and wallet, and headed for the front door. "Oh . . ." I spun to face the guys. "I've gotta reinforce the dibs rule. Do not hook up with her friends." I pointed at Cole, then Slip. "Not ever. Especially Georgia. She's done some shitty things to Sutton. Got it?"

"It's Dalton's." A mischievous grin slid across Slip's mouth. "It's full of hot, easy chicks. It won't be a problem."

"Good. Let's go."

Chapter 22

FLINT

Thirty minutes later, Cole and I climbed out of Slip's Camaro in front of Dalton's Nightclub. Slip tossed his keys to the valet parking attendant, and the three of us rocked into the club like we owned the place. Ignoring the evil, how-dare-you and overzealous glares from the people waiting in the queue, we checked in at the counter. At eleven p.m., the venue was packed. Booming dance music thudded off the walls. A DJ was on stage, spinning out the tunes. Laser and disco lights flashed across the room. Sweaty bodies gyrated on the dance floor. The bar was at least four people deep, waiting for service.

Shit. This club was massive.

But just like a missile hitting its target, I zoned in on Sutton sitting at a table in the VIP section with her friends. Two guys hovered and swooned around Georgia. Sutton and Maddy sat opposite her, knocking down some drinks.

I tapped Cole and Slip on the arm and jerked my head in Sutton's direction. Dodging the partygoers, we weaved through the crowd. We waved our VIP wristbands we'd collected at the door to the security guard and headed over to the girls.

Slipping on to the seat beside Sutton, I hooked my arm around her shoulders. Before she had time to think, I kissed her sweet lips. My heart beat faster than the DJ's mix.

"Flint?" She pulled back. Her eyes widened. "What are you doing here?"

"Hey, beautiful." *Hmm.* Those words rolled off my tongue too easily. "We came for a boys' night out."

"Here?"

"Yeah." I roamed my gaze over her, devouring her emerald-colored party minidress. Shoe-string straps I'd love to peel from her arms. A loose skirt my hands itched to slip underneath. Silky fabric that I'd love to ease off her body. *So sexy.* But before I got a raging hard-on, I waved at my friends and introduced them to the girls. "This is Cole and Slip. My bandmates."

"Evening, ladies." Cole dipped his head.

Georgia fanned her face. Her eyes smoldered in Cole's direction. But he ignored her.

I chuckled. I loved my buddies. Loved our dibs rule. I had nothing to worry about. Georgia wasn't Cole's type. Blondes weren't his flavor. Not ever.

Georgia tilted her head toward the two arty, plucked-from-the-pages-of-*Vogue* guys in designer suits next to her. "This is Brandon and Nolan. They're models on the new Gucci campaign."

"Hi. Nice to meet you." Slip waved half-heartedly at them as he drank in every inch of Maddy. But he wasn't one to break a bro code. He cleared his throat and thumbed toward the bar. "I'll grab some drinks. What's everyone having?"

"Vodka and cranberry." Sutton held up her empty glass.

"Hmm." I teased her lips with another quick kiss. "You have good taste. But you don't need the cranberry."

"We'll be back in a sec." Cole shoved Slip on the shoulder and disappeared into the crowd.

Shock still blazed in Sutton's eyes. "I can't believe you're here. Why?"

I brushed my thumb beneath one of her eyes, then the other. There were no tears, but her mascara had smudged a little from crying. I skimmed my fingertips down her cheek, caught her chin, and angled her head back. "I needed this."

I pressed my lips to hers. Warmth flooded my veins. The storm clouds that constantly bombarded my head evaporated. With a flick of my tongue, I sought hers. Every muscle in my body melted when she kissed me back. Each brush of her lips was soft. Delicate. Sweet. She tasted of cranberries and vodka, smelled of cherry blossoms and fit perfectly into my arms. Everything about Sutton was dangerous and intoxicating. One drink could send me over the edge. Problem was . . . I wanted the whole damn bottle. I buried my fingers in her hair and deepened our kiss.

Within two seconds, she relaxed, moaning against my mouth. Her hands tugged at my shirt, then shot into my hair. *God.* I needed her closer. Tugging her sideways onto my lap, I wrapped my arms around her. My heart thudded in time to the loud dance music. There was no way I could hide the affect she had on my body. My hardening cock strained beneath her.

She smiled against my lips. "Is that your eggplant?"

I chuckled, pressing my forehead against hers. "Would you like some?"

"Maybe later."

"Are you okay?" I swept her tousled hair off her face. "I was worried about you."

Her eyes twinkled as she toyed with my top button. "I'm better now."

"Wanna go somewhere and talk?" I glanced around the club. There weren't any obvious quiet nooks or corners. The guys who had been hovering like flies near Georgia had left for the bar and were already chatting up new girls. Had they been intimidated by me and the guys? We had just waltzed in and claimed Sutton and her friends.

Sutton shook her head. "Nah. You're here. That's all I need for now."

"Phew, girl," Maddy hollered and fanned her face. "You two need to get a room. *Damn!* That was fucking hot. I wish I could find a guy who kissed like that."

Georgia rolled her eyes. "Oh, please." She flicked her talons in my direction. "You can drop the act. We know you're just one of Harlow's publicity stunts."

"Were." Wickedness slipped into my tone. "You're just jealous that Sutt and I have turned into something real. You're even more envious that we're attracting attention and dragging the spotlight away from you."

Sutton stilled on my lap. But she needn't worry. I'd met a ton of girls like Georgia who acted like divas. I didn't stand for it. Georgia needed to be put in her place.

"Real?" Georgia sneered at me. "You're as real as my boobs."

"Enough." Sutton wriggled to slide off my legs, but I tightened my hold on her waist. She wasn't going anywhere. "Flint? I'm okay." She pushed against my arms and pulled at my hands. I just held her tighter.

"Sutton." I caught her face between my hands. I lowered my voice so only she could hear. "Don't let Georgia get to you. She's jealous. I'm here. For you. This between us *is* real. Out of all the chicks in this club, I'd pick you. Why? Because you've got that sweet something I dig. Maybe it is your good girl vibe. Whatever it is, it's what I like. You are the hottest, baddest, sexiest girl I've ever had. I don't want anyone else. Just you."

"Flint?" She closed her eyes and winced.

What was she struggling with? Me? Georgia? Losing the role? I didn't want to stress her out. I was here to put all our shit aside for one night and have fun. "Hey?"

Her eyes locked onto mine. A million concerns rippled in their depths. Light. Dark. Good. Bad. For. Against.

I skimmed my thumb across her lower lip. "Tonight, there are no deadlines. No deals. No doubts. Let's just enjoy hanging out. Okay?"

She caught my hand hovering near her lips. As she entwined our fingers, my heart beat so loudly I was sure she could hear it.

A tiny smile played at the corner of her mouth. Then she parted her lips and sucked my thumb into her mouth. She licked and kissed it, swirled her tongue around it. *Holy fuck. So Hot. Warm. Wet.* Electricity jolted right through the center of my dick and coiled around my heart. *Oh, yeah.* I was in trouble.

"Deal." She threw me a mischievous wink.

I just grabbed her and kissed her again.

Georgia clicked her fingers. "Okay, lovebirds. Tonight isn't about you, it's about me. We're celebrating." She picked up her cocktail and swirled the cherry around in the pink liquid. "Flint, did Sutton tell you? I'm going to be in a huge movie." She fluttered her excessively long fake lashes. "I'm so excited."

Sutton's spine deflated, and she fell against my chest. Her hair fell forward across her face, covering her eyes.

I didn't want her to hide. Not tonight. Not ever.

I leered at Georgia. "What you did was low. You shouldn't have gone to that audition. You wouldn't have even known about the movie if it wasn't for Sutton. You went over her head and hurt her in the process."

Georgia froze. Her cocktail hovered halfway to her mouth. Then she let out a fake, pathetic laugh. "Don't be silly. I didn't hurt her."

"Flint. It's okay," Sutton whispered against my throat. "Let it go."

"No." I clutched Sutton's arms and sat her straighter. "Tell her the truth. She's the one who should feel like crap. Not you. Don't bottle this shit up and regret it."

I wished Phil had never kept things from me.

"Tell me what, Sutton?" Georgia sipped on her cocktail, feigning innocence.

"You can do this," I whispered to Sutton.

She clutched my hand, trembling like a leaf. But then she took a deep breath. Fire sparked through the golden flecks in her eyes. She nodded, then turned to Georgia. "I am hurt. And pissed. And angry. You shouldn't have gone to that audition. Whether or not I got the part is irrelevant. As my friend, you should've left it alone. I hope you got the role based purely on your acting skills. Or did you bribe, blackmail, or bang someone?"

Holy shit! I wasn't quite expecting her to be that forthright. But I loved it.

The air between the two girls zapped and crackled. Georgia's hand shot to her throat and fidgeted with her blingy necklace.

Maddy choked on a mouthful of her drink. "Holy crap, Georgia? What did you do?"

Cole and Slip returned with a tray loaded with drinks and handed them out—vodkas for the girls, beers for the guys.

"What are y'all yapping about?" Cole pulled up a chair. Slip took the one next to Maddy.

Sutton downed half her vodka in one gulp as I took a sip of my beer. I wrapped my arms around her and kissed the tip of her shoulder. "Sutton just asked Georgia how she secured her huge movie deal?"

All eyes turned to Georgia.

She sat straighter. Defiance gleamed in her eyes. "I did what was necessary to stand out."

"Oh, shit!" Cole downed a mouthful of his beer. "Did you fuck someone for the part? Isn't that frowned upon these days?"

Sutton clutched my hand so hard, she almost cut off the circulation to my fingers. "Georgia, tell me you didn't?"

"Georgia?" Doubt clouded Maddy's eyes. "Did you?"

Guess Maddy had the same concerns about Georgia as Sutton did. Did she have the same history with Georgia? *God.* Why were these girls friends?

Georgia's face remained Botoxed-blank, then she sighed and shook her head. "Y'all are too high-strung. I *did not* sleep with anyone for the part. But after talking to Cory . . . and the chemistry that sparked between us . . . who knows what will happen in the future?"

"You spoke to Cory?" Sutton snapped.

"Yes. We had a great chat." Georgia smoothed her hands over her short, silky skirt. "We totally hit it off. Just like you and Flint, right? We had a great time talking about you and the other girls who had auditioned."

"What . . . what did you say?" Sutton stammered.

"Oh. I told him you were sweet, that you'd never done anything like this before and might struggle breaking away from your TV persona, and it'd be physically challenging for you." A cunning smile drew across Georgia's lips. "We also discussed marketing potential. Cory wants this movie to be a success. So do I. Compared to you and the other girls, I have the biggest following. I'm a sought-after influencer and I'm hot. I was the best candidate. He agreed. So, my agent talked to his agent. They talked to the casting director, who talked to the production team and the film's director . . . and voila . . . the part was mine."

"What the fuck?" Sutton cried. "You dissed me and pulled strings again?"

"Geez. What is with you?" Georgia rolled her eyes and flicked her long blond hair extensions over her shoulder. "You're normally quiet as a mouse."

"At least I'm not a rat." Sutton's sharp tone could cut diamonds. "You knew how excited I was to be invited to that audition and how much this role would've meant to me. But you went out of your way to make sure I had no hope of even being considered. Why?"

Wow! I'd unleashed a lion. I may have only known Sutton for a short time, but I loved it when she didn't take any crap.

"I'm not a rat." Georgia laughed and swatted her hand through the air. "I can't help it if Cory requested to work with me because I'm talented. I'm a star like he is. We're the right choice for the franchise."

"You fucking bitch." Sutton shrieked, slamming her glass down onto the table. She shot to her feet, fisted her hands against her head, and paced behind Cole and Slip. "That's so not fair. You've undermined everyone and broken so many rules. You didn't give anyone else at that audition a chance."

I jumped up to comfort Sutton. Drawing her against my chest, I wrapped my arms around her shaking body.

Maddy shook her head at Georgia. Tears glistened in her eyes. "Oh, Georgia. This is low. Even for you."

Georgia shrugged. "This is Hollywood. You gotta do what you gotta do to get ahead."

"At my expense?" Sutton twisted to face Georgia. A tear slid down her cheek. "Or at the expense of the other girls at the audition?" She jabbed her finger against her chest. "I'm supposed to be your fucking friend. You should've never gone to that casting call."

"Hey?" I rubbed her shoulders. "Let's get out of here."

Sutton closed her eyes. She sucked in a shaky breath. Her jaw clenched. Then she shook her head. "I just need a sec to process this. I . . . I . . ." She tapped her hand against her chest. "My heart's racing. I can't breathe. It hurts everywhere."

Now that I could relate to. I didn't want to think about

the club being too crowded, or about the fans eyeing us with cameras posed our way, or the security guys keeping tabs on our group. I just wanted to get Sutton and my friends out of there. I was more than ready to leave.

"I got you. Come on." I turned for the exit, but she didn't budge.

"Just hold me for a moment so I don't kill her."

She snaked her arms around my middle. Hugging her tight, I rested my head against hers. I would love to see her lunge at Georgia, slap the bitch across the face, and beat her to the ground. Maybe have a full-on catfight. But that wasn't in Sutton's nature. Well . . . I didn't think it was.

She trembled in my embrace, clutching onto the back of my shirt like it was a stress ball.

The color had drained from Maddy's face. "You've gone too far this time, Georgia. It's cruel. Unprofessional. Unforgivable."

Georgia laughed. "You're just jealous."

"You're unbelievable." I threw her a scathing glare. "Don't you care about your friends?"

"As if you can talk." Georgia's tone turned so cold the room temperature dropped by ten degrees. "You're rock stars. I bet you didn't get to where you are by playing innocent."

"Actually, we did." Slip rolled his beer bottle between his palms. "We became successful thanks to hard work, talent, and a bit of luck. We've never fucked over anyone to get where we are. We never set out to be huge stars. We just wanted to play our music and make enough money so we never had to get real jobs."

"Here's to that." Cole chinked his beer against Slip's, then took a swig. "Doing what we love everyday kicks major ass over being famous. We just take that in our stride and don't let it get to our heads."

"See Georgia?" I jutted my chin toward the guys. "We are

loyal and true to each other. These guys come first. We're thicker than blood. We always have each other's backs. Pity you don't respect yourself or your girlfriends in the same way."

"What? I love my girls." Georgia shimmied her shoulders. "They'll get over it. They always do. They're my sisters."

Was Georgia delusional?

Sutton shook her head. "No, Georgia. Friends can only forgive each other so many times. You just lost your last chance. You've gone too far. Hurt us too many times. I'm done. I have done nothing but support you and have been your friend for years. I looked up to you. Admired you. But now . . . I can't stand the sight of you."

"Sutton, sit down." Georgia patted the empty chair beside her. "You don't mean that."

"Oh, I mean every word." Sutton's tone was calm yet chilling. "Karma's gonna be a real bitch to you. You better watch your fucking back."

Georgia straightened. "Are you threatening me?"

Sutton wavered. I was quick to take her place. I got up in Georgia's face. "Yes. You fuck with Sutton, you fuck with me. And you don't want that. We know a lot of people in this town. No one will want to work with you if they know you're nothing but a conniving, backstabbing bitch."

Georgia half grinned as if she didn't care, but fear rippled in her eyes.

Good.

"I can now see why you're perfect for Sutton." She raised an eyebrow. "You care too much about everyone else and not yourself. You can't survive in this town with that attitude."

"You're so wrong. The guys and I survive because we have each other."

I was there thanks to Cole and Slip. Their unfaltering support and crazy ultimatum were because they loved me and wanted me to get better. Finding Sutton had been a bonus in their plan. I stepped over to her and gazed into her big brown eyes. I brushed my thumb down the side of her cheek. "Now I have Sutton too. She's awesome. She's my balance. My Zen. My balls are in her hands. She's a keeper." I had to work on that last part.

"Thank you," she whispered. "Can we get out of here?"

"Yep. Let's go, guys." I jerked my head toward the exit. "Maddy, you want to join us? There'll be live music, cheap drinks, and greasy food. You in?"

"Hell yeah. That sounds awesome." She grabbed her clutch and jumped to her feet. Tugging down her tiny tight dress that barely covered her panties, she sidled up to Slip. He smiled with complete approval.

Sutton sneered at Georgia, then waved around the club. "You can stay here with all your other friends. You're not invited."

I chuckled. There was no one near Georgia. No one looked her way. No one was interested.

"Come on, beautiful." I entwined my fingers with Sutton's and led her out of the club.

Outside, the warm summer breeze rustled along the Boulevard. It was just before midnight, so people were still jostling into the club, or hovering around, waiting for their rides elsewhere. I was just glad to be in fresh air, away from the crowds. My blood pressure thanked me for it.

While we waited for the valet to retrieve Slip's car, I held Sutton against my chest and kissed the top of her head. For the first few minutes, she trembled. No doubt adrenaline from going off at Georgia still coursed through her veins. But then she relaxed. Her hands went from clutching my shirt to slipping into the back pockets of my jeans.

"I can't believe I just lost one of my best friends." Her soft voice was muffled against my shirt.

I loved how she'd stood up to Georgia. She'd had to get that shit out or it would've eaten her alive. Like it had done to Phil. My heart felt her pain. Being betrayed by a friend was beyond brutal and cruel.

We'd had too much hurt inflicted on us by people we'd loved and trusted. I may have more issues than a Julia Michaels song, but I swore I'd never hurt or betray Sutton.

"Yeah. I'm sorry." I rubbed her arms. "That sucks. But she was a tad toxic."

"A tad?" She giggled. "I can't believe it took me so long to do that. I don't think I would've ever stood up to her if it wasn't for you. So, thank you. I actually feel good. Lighter. Free."

"You deserve the best. Nothing less."

I'd come out to make Sutton feel better. It had taken an unexpected turn. Georgia had been the casualty. But she'd put that target on herself. Now, it was time to put that behind us, keep my simmering anxiety locked away for a while longer, and get a smile onto Sutton's face.

The valet handed Slip his car keys, and we all climbed into his red Camaro. I squeezed into the tiny back seat between Sutton and Maddy. As Maddy rattled on to Slip and Cole about music over the loud tunes playing through the stereo, I drew Sutton sideways onto my lap so her back faced Maddy.

But holding her in my arms warmed my temperature. I nuzzled her ear, and whispered, "You okay now?"

"Yeah. Much better." She tilted her head to the side, giving me easier access to the side of her neck.

That didn't help my cause to stay cool. But the sparkle in her eyes hadn't returned. I had the solution for that.

"Want to feel even better?" Out of sight from the guys and Maddy, I slid my hand underneath her floaty skirt and brushed my thumb across her panties.

It wouldn't be the first time I'd made out or felt up some

girl in front of the guys. Hell, they'd done the same thing in front of me more times than I cared to remember. But this was different. The way Sutton's body leaned into me, the way her lips seared mine . . . it was like a need, not a cheap thrill. It was as if she wanted more but was afraid to ask.

She didn't have to. I was happy to oblige.

She shuddered against me. Her breath was a hot vapor against my lips. Wriggling on my lap, she widened her knees.

Oh, yeah.

All the way to Pasadena, we made out like teenagers. I tugged her panties to the side and fucked her with my fingers. Slowly. Torturously. Tenderly.

I made her come and quiver. Every murmur and soft moan against my lips did something strange to my heart. I was in more trouble than I'd first thought. I couldn't deny it. Didn't want to. Yep . . . I'd fallen for Sutton Summers.

I was a lost cause.

And the night wasn't over yet.

Chapter 23

SUTTON

"You have fun in the back seat of my car?" Slip ruffled the top of my head as we took seats at a small wooden table in the center of Hayley's Bar. The half-full music venue in Pasadena was a cross between a tavern and a trendy wine hangout. The laid-back, chilled atmosphere was a welcome relief after the noisy, overcrowded nightclub.

"You saw?" My cheeks blazed hotter than a Californian wildfire. I didn't know whether to crawl under the table and die . . . or, while I was down on my knees, blow Flint. He just made me feel alive, like there were no boundaries.

"Don't be embarrassed," Slip hollered over the classic rock hits the band was playing. He grabbed a peanut from the tin bucket on the table, cracked the shell open, then popped the nut into his mouth. "I had a great show in my rearview mirror. But now I'm fucking horny and need to get laid."

"Sorry." I tucked my bob behind my ear. "We got carried away."

"Don't apologize." Cole lazed in his padded wooden chair and tilted his head toward Flint at the bar. "Flint's out, not sitting at home in a dark room, manically depressed. Keep fucking him or doing whatever it is you're doing. You're the steel for our Flint."

"You were just kissing, right?" Maddy nudged my arm.

"Um . . ." I wrinkled my nose and caught my bottom lip between my teeth. "We may have got a little more carried away than that." I leaned over and whispered in her ear, "Flint felt me up. My panties are sopping wet and really uncomfortable."

Maddy burst out laughing. "Holy shit, girl. I love you more each day."

"It's not funny. I'm serious."

She waggled her finger at my crutch. "Then take them off. I'm sure Flint won't mind."

"No. I can't do that." *Could I? No . . .*

The guys chuckled, tucking into more peanuts. They were the most laid-back guys I'd ever met. Just like Flint. No hype. No bullshit. No flamboyance.

Waiting for Flint, I glanced around the urban-chic venue. Exposed wooden beams lined the ceiling, the dark floor was planked timber, and the lit bar was black with copper panels. Huge round light bulbs hung from a wrought-iron rack above the counter. At the far end of the room, a four-member band and their equipment filled every inch of the small stage.

But what struck me was the patronage. Everyone sat at tables or stood in small groups eating food, holding conversations, or downing drinks. No one was yelling or pushing and shoving at the bar. The people dancing in front of the band had plenty of room to jump around. They weren't all squished like sardines, as they had been at Dalton's.

I also noticed everyone's attire. Jeans, shirts, long dresses or neat skirts were the most common clothing. No rhinestones, ridiculous high heels, or raunchy outfits. I glanced at my sparkly party dress, then at Maddy's tiny outfit. *God.* Everyone here would think the guys had picked us up on Sunset and were paying us by the hour.

I leaned in and lowered my voice so only Maddy could hear. "I feel overdressed . . . or maybe not dressed enough."

"Um . . . what about me?" Maddy made no attempt to turn her volume down. She waved her hand at her outfit. "I'm wearing something that's half the size of a slip."

"But you look hot," I admitted.

"I know." Maddy winked.

"If you need help to get out of that thing later, you let me know." Slip tossed a peanut shell at Maddy. It fell right between her breasts. She peered down at her cleavage, then back at Slip, and burst out laughing.

"I'll pass. But thanks for the offer." Maddy dug the shell out of her cleavage and tossed it back at him.

Cole clipped him on the head. That made Slip snarl. But he stopped teasing Maddy.

"What's taking Flint so long?" I glanced at him resting his elbows on the counter, chatting to the much-too-attractive female bartender. A tinge of jealousy swirled in my guts as the bartender leaned toward him. They smiled. Laughed. *Flirted?*

"That's Molly." Cole jerked his head in their direction. "She's the venue manager. She's been wanting us to play here again for months. Flint, of course, has been AWOL. I bet she's trying her hardest to convince him to do a gig.

"Do they, or did they, have a *thing*?" Had my face turned green?

Slip laughed, resting his elbows on the table. "Molly and Flint? God, no. Her hubby is that biker dude of a bouncer on the door. They'd both break your balls if you tried to hit on her. I'd know. I've tried."

"Oh." I giggled. "That's funny."

"No harm done." Cole slapped Slip's shoulder.

"It only bruised my ego." Slip scratched the fine stubble on his cheek. "But they love us and want us back. We're good at attracting the crowd."

"Why don't you play then?" Maddy asked.

Cole threw me a questioning glance.

I hadn't told Maddy the full extent of Flint's battle with Phil's death, so I'd better come clean. "Um . . . Flint hasn't sung since his brother died."

"Oh." Maddy's shoulders slouched. "That sucks. He's amazing."

"We know," Cole said. "We miss playing so much."

"And we need to do something drastic to make it happen." Slip dipped his head at me.

"Why are you looking at me? What else can I do?"

Slip's eyes glinted, and a sly smile curled at the corner of his mouth. "You seem to be able to get him to do anything. You want to put your pussy power to a test?"

"My what?"

"A challenge?" Slip chuckled. "Are you up for a dare? I'm willing to put money on it."

"What's the challenge?"

"Get Flint to sing. Right here." Slip jabbed his finger against the table. "Right now. We know Duke and the band. They'll be down with anything we ask or need them to do. I'll give you one thousand dollars if you get Flint on that stage in front of a mic."

"Fuck, I'll do it for that kind of bet," Maddy piped in.

Sing? My heart cinched. The desperation in Slip's voice grabbed my heart. I had no idea how I could get Flint up there, but I'd give it a damn good go. I wanted to help Flint and didn't need a bet to convince me. "I don't want your cash. But if you think he'll benefit from this, then challenge accepted." Before they got too excited, I held up one finger. "My only condition is that whatever I do to get him up there isn't filmed, recorded, or repeated in any way. Okay?"

"Cross my heart." Slip sliced his finger across his chest, then made the scout's honor symbol.

"We gotta get a mic in his hand." Cole shot forward. "What do you want us to do?"

My stomach somersaulted. My pulse quickened. No plan came to mind. "I need a couple of shots to give me the nerves to do this. I'll come up with something. If I need help, I'll ask."

Slip rubbed his hands together. "Bring it on, baby."

Flint finally joined us and placed a fresh bottle of vodka in the center of the table. He lined up the shot glasses in a straight row. "Sorry I took so long."

"We've been entertaining the girls." Cole chewed on a peanut. "It's cool."

Flint poured the shots, then glanced my way. "Is that true?"

"Yes. They were perfect gentlemen." I picked up a shot glass. "Please don't let me get too drunk. I have work tomorrow."

He slid onto the chair beside me and hooked his arm around my shoulders. "You can always crash at my place. It's closer."

"We'll see." Depending on how long this challenge took, I might take him up on the offer. *Oh . . . who was I kidding*? Of course, I'd be crashing.

Could I bribe him to sing with the promise of sex? But what if that backfired? I didn't want to miss out on some action later.

After he kissed my cheek, we chinked our glasses with the others and downed our shots. The cold vodka burned the back of my throat but warmed my chest. I wiped the corners of my mouth with my fingertips, then grabbed the bottle to refill our glasses.

The cogs in my head turned. How would I coax Flint to sing?

I needed a plan. Another shot might help.

Downing another vodka, I let the music take over. Maddy and I swayed and sang along to the classic rock songs. But I rarely lost contact with Flint—I curled my hand around his thigh, held his hand, or hooked my arm around his. I laughed and joked with Maddy and the guys. It had turned from one of the most devastating nights of my life to one of the best. By one a.m., the bar was crowded but not jam-packed. The band rocked. As they churned out the first few beats of "Summer of '69" by Bryan Adams, over half the bar cheered, clapped, and rushed to the dance floor.

Tickled with vodka, I jumped to my feet. "Oh, I love this song."

"Well then?" Flint stood and took my hand. "We better dance."

"You dance?" Where had this Flint come from? I was certain his effort at our first awards show had been under sufferance, to get me away from Georgia and to be polite.

"Absolutely." The sexiest smile inched across his lips. "Come on."

"We're up too." Cole jumped to his feet. "Dude, it's been forever since you've hit the dance floor."

"Shut the fuck up." Flint growled, then smirked.

Slip pushed his chair back and rose to his feet. "Maddy? Care to join us?"

"Yay." She clapped. "Yes, please."

Hand in hand, Flint and I weaved through the crowd and headed toward the band. The staff had cleared away several tables to make more room for people to dance. Flint spun me 'round. He hooked his hands around my waist, and we swayed in time to the music. The others joined us.

For the next half an hour, Maddy and I danced up a storm with the guys. A few patrons recognized Flint, Cole, and Slip but didn't make a fuss. It was so nice not being harassed and asked for selfies and autographs like people often did when Maddy and I were with Georgia.

As I spun around in a circle with Flint's arms around me, an idea popped into my head. *Oh, wow.* I'd definitely had too much vodka. *So be it.* The plan was crazy, but worth a try.

I jumped over to Slip and whispered in his ear.

He threw me a doubtful glare, but then nodded. "Hope you know what you're fucking doing."

"Nope. But it's worth a shot."

Flint edged in behind me and wrapped his arms around my waist. "What was that about?"

I turned and linked my fingers behind his neck. "Doing something crazy."

"Like what?"

"This." I drew his lips against mine, kissed him hard and long and deep. My knees weakened when he groaned against my mouth. *Hmm.* That sent tingles straight between my legs. But out of the corner of my eye, I saw Slip talking to the band. Then he gave me the thumbs up. Time to execute.

I hovered my lips an inch from Flint's "How bad do you want me to stay at your place tonight?"

"I think my constant hard-on tells you how much."

"Nah . . . you have to be more convincing."

"How?"

"Better follow my lead." I teased a kiss across his lips just as the band played the first few notes of "Summer Lovin'" from *Grease.* I patted his cheek, then, at speed, I took off toward the stage and scaled the four steps.

"We have a special guest tonight," Duke hollered into his mic as he handed a spare one to me.

I curtsied and scanned the inquisitive crowd. Over one hundred sets of eyes stared back at me. Butterflies spiraled in my belly. *Shit!* How did musicians do this? Perform in front of the masses?

Duke waved his hand toward me. "Please give a warm

welcome to Sutton Summers."

The crowd cheered, clapped, and whistled.

Would that turn to booing? *Oh, God . . .* Nausea mixed with the vodka in my gut. *Not good.* I wrung the mic around in my hands. The music pounded in my head. *Well . . . here goes nothing.*

Flint stood in the middle of the dance floor with Maddy and the guys. He glared at me and mouthed, *"What the fuck?"*

Winking at him, I sang. I knew this song backward, upside down and back to front. I hit the first few lines with Duke. The patrons joined in, clapping and singing along to the classic hit. But Flint remained frozen to the spot. I pointed to him, then at the stage, wiggling my finger for him to join me.

He didn't budge.

Slip shoved him on the shoulder, but he stood his ground.

God. I hoped Flint could do this. He needed to do this to push through his block. No matter how far out of my comfort zone I was, singing in front of all these people, I refused to give up. I'd make the most of it if my plan backfired.

Vodka spurred me on.

But Flint hadn't moved an inch.

Before the second chorus, I sliced my hand at Duke to stop singing, but the band kept strumming the beat.

Da-dada-dada-dadadadadada-da dada.

It was perfect for a little ad-libbing. I pulled out my best bad-ass bitch attitude, strode to the very front of the stage and sang in my best *Grease* voice . . . more Rizzo than Sandy.

> *What kind of boyfriend,*
> *Won't sing a so-o-ong.*
> *Says he's a rock star,*
> *But I think he's wr-o-ong.*

I animated every line with my hand, pointing at him, looking at the people on the dance floor who had *what-the-fuck* looks plastered on their faces. Then I sweetened my tone and splayed my hand across my chest as the band kept playing.

> *I'm just a girl,*
> *Crazy for him.*
> *He's just a boy,*
> *Who will not si-i-ing.*

Striding from one side of the stage to the other, I was getting the hang of this performing thing. Sweeping my arm and pointing to everyone in the venue, I ad-libbed again.

> *What do you think,*
> *We should all do-oo-oo?*
> *Show him the door,*
> *Give him a big boo-oo-oo?*

I stopped in the center of the stage and put my hand to my ear. I ignored Flint's fire-filled gaze, the steam coming out of his ears and nostrils, and his sheer desire to send me to hell.

> *Oh-wella-wella-wella-huh.*

> *What was that? What was that?*
> *Did you just tell me 'fuck you?'*
> *What was that? What was that?*
> *Oh babe, you so know I want to.*

Sliding my hand sexily over my body, I swayed my hips. Lowering my voice, I added some extra John Travolta spice into my tone.

> *All you have to do,*
> *To get what you wa-a-ant.*
> *Is get your ass up here,*

Sing the damn so-o-ong.
You can take me home,
My panties will come dow-ow-own.
You can have your way with me,
Or I'll ride you to tow-ow-own.

Those lines brought a smile to his face. *Progress. Sweet.* And I scored laughs from the crowd. *Bonus.*

But then I stopped. I stood straight and still. I held the mic in two hands before my lips and dialed down my voice.

What do you say, Flint?
Will you make my day-ay-ay?
Or will you disappoint this crowd?
Send me on my way-ay-ay?

Duke and the band stopped playing.

Silence fell across the entire venue.

Everyone stared at Flint.

My heart pounded so loudly in my chest, I was sure the mic picked up the erratic beat and amplified it through the speakers. If his icy gaze could've been a samurai sword, I would've been slayed and annihilated.

The crowd chanted and clapped. *"Sing. Sing. Sing."*

Dizziness swam through my head. *Shit!* This hadn't worked.

Cole's and Slip's shoulders sank.

Tears welled in my eyes. I took a deep breath, locked my gaze onto Flint's and sang just above a whisper.

I look at you,
Feels like a dream.
Oh baby, please,
Come sing with me.

He closed his eyes and clenched his fists. "Fuck!"

He flicked his hair back. His mouth contorted and twisted as if he were in pain. But then . . . it transformed into a warm *I'm-gonna-kill-you* grin.

He headed for the stage.

The crowd erupted and hollered.

My heartbeat soared through the roof.

Flint bounded up the stairs and strode over to me. He wrapped his arms around me, picked me up, and swung me 'round. Dipping me backward, he planted a hard kiss against my lips. "You're crazy."

I half laughed, half sobbed as pure relief flooded me. "I should say no to vodka, right?"

"I like it when you drink vodka." He gave me a quick kiss and helped me straighten.

Over the whistles and clapping from the patrons, Duke handed Flint his mic.

In the middle of the dance floor, Slip and Cole hugged each other and jumped up and down. Their eyes glistened.

Flint got up in my face. His eyes blazed with a new hunger. "You wanna sing this song the right way?"

"Yes. Please."

"*Grease*? Really?" He arched an eyebrow.

"Yeah."

"All right, then." Flint turned to the band. "From the top. Hit it, boys."

I couldn't stop jumping and twirling around as we sang "Summer Nights." Everyone in the venue joined in. They nearly shattered every light and glass in the place with their screeching tones when they hit the last note.

But Flint's voice . . . *wow!*

Him. Singing. Pure magic.

At the end of the song, he was about to hand the mic back to Duke when the band played the opening chords to one of The

Flintlock's songs: "Don't Stop".

He glanced over his shoulder at me. His eyes smoldered underneath the stage lights. "Was this part of your plan, too?"

"Yes . . . it's my favorite." The crescendoing rock tune that hinted at obsessive love had threaded something wicked into my soul from the very first time I'd heard it a few weeks ago.

He held my gaze, and tingles spiraled all over my body and up my spine, and pooled in the center of my chest.

Oh shit.

Was I falling for him? Could I give him a piece of my heart and walk away at the end of summer in one piece? *Damn it.* I really shouldn't drink vodka. It made me do crazy things. Made me think crazy thoughts.

I swallowed the dry, sticky lump in my throat and wiped my clammy palms on my dress. "Will you sing the song for me?"

He stared at the ground. Then at Duke. Then out at the venue.

The overture to the song boomed through the speakers.

Flint? Please sing. Please sing. Please sing.

He turned to Duke. "Do you mind if my boys help?"

"No, dude. We'd be honored." Duke relieved me of my mic. "Ladies and gents? Would y'all mind if The Flintlocks played a song or two?"

"Woohoo!" they screamed and whistled. "Yeah!"

Flint clipped the mic into the stand and spoke into it. "Cole? Slip? Get your asses up here."

They charged up on stage, hugged Flint, then relieved Duke's band of their instruments. Cole took to the drums. Slip, the electric guitar.

"Evan? You good on the bass?" Flint asked.

I didn't miss the shake in his voice. But he was there. Singing. Taking another baby step.

"Sure am." Evan's fingers galloped across the thick strings, the thrum reverberating through the amp. "Let's rip."

I kissed Flint on the cheek and turned to leave. But he caught me on the back of my dress. "Nuh-uh. You're not going anywhere. You're gonna sit here, right beside me." He dashed to the side of the stage and grabbed a wooden bar stool. With an evil smile, he plonked it right beside the mic. "Sit."

Oh, God. I'd been on stage enough tonight to last a lifetime. But I did what I was told. I slid onto the seat and folded my hands in my lap. This was more embarrassing than ad-libbing. But if he needed me by his side, then that was where I'd be. *Oh boy.* What had happened to my head and heart? *Ergh!* I didn't want to think about that right now.

As I pasted on a smile, Maddy waved to me from the floor. She gave me the thumbs up, then formed a heart shape with her hands. A huge grin lit her beautiful face.

I blew her a kiss. I loved her so much.

"All right, folks." Flint took to the mic. "Seems like I've been roped into this. I haven't sung for a while so my pipes might be a bit rusty. But I'll give it a shot. This song was written a long time ago. It was off our first album. Some of you might know it. And this lovely lady beside me is my new inspiration to sing it. This is 'Don't Stop.'" He clicked and pointed at Cole on the drums. "Let's do this. One. Two. Three. Go."

My pulse jumped to a new tempo, and it had nothing to do with the music. Flint, with his hand wrapped around the mic, his hair teasing his long lashes and his lips poised, ready to sing, was pure sex on legs. I burned this image of him into my brain, wanting to hold onto it for a lifetime.

The lyrics fell from his lips. His beautiful voice filled the room.

> *How did we end up here?*
> *Thought it would take a couple of years.*
> *I never thought I could feel this way,*

Where I lost all track of the time and day.
But now I can't stop.
Don't wanna stop.
Falling deeper.
Deeper into you.
Falling.
Falling in love with you.

He unclipped the mic and slid over to my side. He hooked his arm around my shoulders and sang—half to me, half to the crowd.

But the partygoers may as well have not been in the room. All I saw was Flint. Every word was etched into my heart. That wasn't part of the plan.

How did we fall so fast?
Thought this wasn't supposed to last.
I never thought I could feel this way,
You sent my heart into disarray.
But now I can't stop.
Don't wanna stop.
Falling deeper.
Deeper into you.
Falling.
Falling in love with you.

Then he leaned closer to my ear. He lowered his voice. A gravelly husk rumbled in his throat as he sang.

I don't care if you've possessed me.
Poisoned me.
Hypnotized me.
Just hit me.
Hit me with your love,
Again and again.
Whatever you've done,
Please, don't ever stop.

No, don't stop.
Not now. No, never.
'Cause baby,
I want this feeling,
To last forever.

Holy shit! I closed my eyes. Thank God I was sitting down because my knees had weakened. A low hum throbbed between my legs. This was insane. Being serenaded and sung to like this had me breaking out in a feverish sweat. How could words he'd written for someone else hit me so hard?

It's-just-a-song. It's-just-a-song. It's-just-a-song.

But I liked it.

At the end of the hit, Flint drew me to my feet and kissed me. I didn't know which way was up or which way was down. Who knew music . . . that he . . . could affect me like this?

"Thank you," he whispered against my lips. "My God. Thank you. For persisting. For not putting up with my bullshit. For getting me to sing."

"You're welcome."

"Do you mind if I play one or two more songs? Would you like to join Maddy or stay here?"

There was no way I wanted to make more of a spectacle of myself. "Maddy. Definitely Maddy."

"Okay. But after this," he purred in my ear, "you'll be coming home with me. So be prepared. I will be fucking you until the sun rises."

I squeezed my thighs together. My core ached in anticipation. "Promises. Promises."

"Oh . . . I promise."

Chapter 24

SUTTON

With a constant headache and fatigue embedded in every bone in my body, I made it through the long day at work. On less than three hours' sleep, I delivered every line, every scene, and every reshoot perfectly. Multiple coffees and Tylenol had been my savior.

But nothing stopped Flint's new proposal from bombarding my mind—not even a grilling from my producer for turning up to the studio looking like hell. Flint wanted to renegotiate our agreement. After we'd gotten home from the club and had toe-curling sex, he hit me with a new proposition. He wanted to spend more time together. Wanted me to stay with him every night. Torn between wanting to and fearing how much it would hurt at our inevitable end, I'd needed time to think.

He'd driven me home after work. I'd been so tired I'd fallen asleep while he navigated peak-hour traffic. But now . . . sitting on my balcony, eating the takeout Chinese he'd bought, the air simmered between us.

My time had run out.

He wanted an answer.

I was still unsure of my response.

"What did you do today?" I sipped on my soda. My body needed a total detox from vodka . . . for weeks, if not months.

He loaded his plate with more teriyaki chicken noodles. "Slept for most of it."

"That's so unfair."

"I love my life some days." He hit me with a sexy smile that was just too adorable.

"How are you feeling? After singing last night?"

The breeze caught his long hair, brushing it against his cheek. It didn't seem to bother him. He stared at his food as if contemplating how to answer. "To be honest . . . numb. But also dazed. Shocked. Pissed. Mad. Freaked out and excited. That about sums it up."

"You were incredible on stage. The crowd loved you."

"I think you took that crown." He grinned, digging into his food. "The night still feels surreal. I can't believe you ad-libbed all those lyrics and told everyone you'd take off your panties."

Oh, God, don't remind me. "You think you'll be able to sing now?"

"I hope so. But singing isn't the only problem. It's being able to write new songs. Normally, I constantly have them forming in my head. That's not back yet. There's this black void still consuming my brain."

"It will come." I took a mouthful of noodles. I had no idea how to overcome his writer's block. The guys should be able to help him with that. I didn't have a musical bone in my body.

Flint poked his chopsticks toward my cell phone on the table. "Have you seen the Internet today?"

"No. Why?" My stomach tightened at the wariness in his tone.

"Last night, we were videoed and photographed by onlookers. The posts about your fight with Georgia, and our stint at Hayley's bar, aren't flattering."

Shit! I swiped on my cell phone, searched and skimmed the articles. Photos of me with rage contorting my face as I fumed at Georgia topped the headlines. *Not good.* There were several stories with images of me charging out of the club with Flint. *Not bad.* Then there were pixilated pictures of us at Hayley's, downing vodka shots, and a grainy video of my little impromptu performance. *Ergh!* "We knew there would be good and bad publicity. It's okay." I hoped it would be. "It was worth it to get you singing."

The whole night had been emotionally challenging. Standing up to Georgia had been empowering and well overdue. Walking away from our friendship had been hard. But hearing Flint sing live had been one of the most incredible, spine-tingling moments of my life.

"Not if it hurts you." Flint finished a mouthful of his food. "There has been nothing good reported. I don't want shit like this to ruin your chances at landing auditions. I've talked to my publicist. She's made a statement saying that the headlines don't depict the truth. She reinforced that your song was innocent fun to coax me onstage. We toned down how much you drank. It was me and the guys downing all the vodka, and it was my bad influence, taking you to Hayley's and keeping you out partying all night."

"What?" My eyes widened. My grip on my chopsticks tightened. He'd taken the blame for my actions? No one had ever done that before. But then, I'd never done anything that warranted covering up.

My father had always kept me on a leash with curfews. He'd constantly grilled me and limited the quantity of drinks I had when out. He'd managed every element of my perfect public profile. Now, I was free from my father's shackles, but I didn't need Flint to take over my life. "Why did you do that without telling me?"

"You didn't return my calls or texts."

Shit! I'd had my cell phone on silent. I'd been too tired to even look at it during the day, opting for a power nap during lunch break in my dressing room.

"I went into damage control. You want to show the world you're a sexy and confident woman ... not a rebellious, partying alcoholic, right? I've done what I can to tame the situation. You wanted to avoid drunken debauchery, remember?"

"I don't regret what happened last night. We did nothing wrong." The fallout rattled through my weary brain. "You shouldn't have done that. Your record deal is on the line. What if your label still thinks you're a mess?"

He slumped back in his chair. Concern flicked in his eyes. "I didn't want you to be slandered in the media. What you did for me was incredible and beyond brilliant. But the public doesn't care about the truth. How can I not want to protect one of the most amazing people I've ever met?"

My heart fluttered and swelled. How could I be upset with him when he cared about me? He'd always looked after his band and his brother, taking the fall for everyone. Now, he'd done it for me without considering the consequences it could have on his career. It was selfless *and* stupid.

"Thank you. It was very thoughtful of you." I sweetened my tone but backloaded it with warning. "Just don't do it again without talking to me first. I'm a big girl and can handle some idle gossip."

A muscle ticked in his jaw, but then he relaxed. "Okay. You're right. I'm sorry. Noted for next time."

Let's hope there weren't any more incidents. But my worry mounted. I didn't want his reputation to take a hit from the progress we'd made. I needed to ensure last night didn't damage our plan. We were about to hit a busy schedule over the next few weeks. We needed to be on our best behavior.

I dug through my noodles, searching for a piece of chicken. "What do you say to lying low for the next couple weeks? When we're at our scheduled events, we keep the drinking to a minimum. I won't have any catfights in clubs or perform drunken singalongs. We'll make sure we're home at respectable hours." Most of the incidents last night had been my doing; he didn't need to suffer any ramifications. We needed some quick damage control. I owed it to him. "Let's play the media into our hands. We need to show them we're blissfully happy, living a normal everyday life, and that partying isn't the norm."

"I'd be happy to do that if you stayed with me." Grinning, he shoved more noodles into his mouth.

Damn. I'd walked right into that one.

"Flint." The lock on my heart rattled. "The consequences of that scare me."

"Me too." He lowered his chin. "It scared me to wake up every day, unable to breathe without Phil. It scared me that I'd never play or sing again. But you've changed that. I'm not afraid to face each day now. But every day, the end of summer creeps closer, and that scares me even more. I don't want us to end. I don't see why we have to. But if you're adamant about calling it quits, I don't want to waste the time I have left with you."

More involvement meant risking my heart, and I wasn't prepared to do that. But was I already a lost cause when I cared about him? I didn't trust this fling to survive beyond the end of the summer. Our futures inevitably involved being apart by distance or long periods of time. That would break us. When I wasn't around, he'd fall for someone more tempting. Just like Beau had done. I lowered my hands onto my lap and fidgeted with my fingers. "I don't want us to get hurt."

"Neither do I." He wiped his hands on a napkin, scrunched it up, then tossed it on the table. "But it's a risk I'm willing to take.

I'm getting better because of you. I like having you around."

"I'm not going to pack my bags and move in with you. We've only known each other for a few weeks."

"Well . . . let's renegotiate." He lifted his chin. A daring glint shimmered in his eyes. "What is acceptable?"

It blew my mind that for the next few weeks, he wanted to be with me. I loved spending time with him. I'd be mad not to enjoy this while it lasted. Putting on my game face, I placed my elbow on the table and rested my chin on my hand. "Isn't seeing each other twice a week enough?"

"Nope."

"I don't want to just hook up for sex. If that's what this is about, it's a no." My hand fell to the table. Tiredness from the long day seeped into my bones. "I can't have sex like we've been having every day. It's exhausting."

He grinned and nodded. "But it's good, right?"

Warmth flooded my cheeks. "Yes. It's awesome . . . but—"

"Sutton." He clutched my hand across the table. "I want to take you out to dinner. Hang out at the beach. See bands play. I want to take you clubbing or whatever it is you want to do. We can sit here on the weekends, lazing around, reading or watching TV. I just want to be with you."

My heart sailed over the balcony, glided over the waves, touched the moon, then slammed back into my chest. "What about your music?"

He chuckled, low and sexy. "My hours are very flexible. At the moment, anyway."

I squeezed his hand. "You should be writing."

"That is something I can't force."

"So, writer's block is the next issue we have to overcome?"

"No." He shook his head. "Getting you more auditions is."

"I'd like to work on both. That okay?"

"Yes." He entwined our fingers and rubbed his thumb across

the inside of my wrist. "I don't want to always have a plan or run to a schedule. I want to see you whenever and for you to come over just because you feel like it. I want to hang out. I want you to be mine, with no end dates, no deadlines, no bullshit."

I can't do it. He'll break my heart, and I don't know if I'd recover from it. "Flint. I like you. But—"

"But nothing." He softened his tone. "Life is too short. Phil lost his too soon. So did your mom. I don't want to waste mine. I don't want to live with any regrets. You are funny and crazy and sexy. I love spending time with you. So no pressure. No rules. Just be with me."

Are all musicians this intense?

But he was right. Life was precious. I'd been burned badly but survived. I knew what I wanted. My career meant everything to me. I wouldn't lose my head or my heart to him totally. I couldn't. No matter how much I liked him. No matter how much I was attracted to him. No matter how much I felt *something* for him. I had to keep my wits about me. I couldn't do that if he broke my heart. "You make it sound so easy."

He jumped to his feet and dragged the chair around to sit beside me. He covered my hand with his palm and gazed into my eyes. "For once, let's make it easy. Everything else in our lives is so messed up and complicated. We have so much going on. But let's make us simple. Just friends, hanging out, having sex when the opportunity arises."

"Why do I think you want the last part the most?"

"Because it's fun." He raised my hand and pressed it against his lips.

"I have conditions."

"I wouldn't doubt it. Lay them on me."

"I don't want to spend every night together. I like my independence, and I need time to learn lines for work."

He bobbed his head. "Work comes first. Got it."

"I like the idea of seeing more live music. I've never seen bands like that before. I loved it. The bar. The atmosphere. The company. So yes to that."

"Awesome."

I held up my finger. "But I promise not to sing."

"Come on. You weren't that bad," he teased, recapturing my hand in his and resting them together on the table. "But I don't think you will be signed in a hurry."

"No. That's for sure." I fidgeted with his signet ring. The platinum band was scratched and dented, far from perfect. Just like us. "If we go out to dinner, I don't need it to be at fancy restaurants. Just local cafés, Thai, pizza or burger joints would be perfect. That okay?"

He grinned and chuckled softly. "You don't want me to take you to The Ivy?"

"No. Not at all." I shook my head. "Oh, and can we go Dutch?"

"How about we alternate? I pay one night, then you pay the next."

"We can do that." But the low ache hovering in my chest flared. I stared at the ocean, watching the lazy waves crash onto the dark shoreline. "But Flint . . . I make no promises about changing our deadline. I will go to every audition possible. I will move across the country or the globe at a second's notice if I need to do so for my career."

His eyes darkened. He rubbed his cheek and nodded. "You wouldn't be the first girlfriend to leave if you did."

Ouch! But at least he understood our situation. "I'm not Lena. I'm not blindsiding you or leaving you unexpectedly. That's why we have rules in place. I'm being honest and realistic. And that reality includes you returning to gigs and touring and screwing around with girls."

He leaned in close and clutched the back of my neck. His grip, firm but tender. Fire blazed in his eyes. "As long as you are mine, there will never be another girl."

My heart melted another fraction, fluttering against my ribs. I whispered, "Okay."

"Good." He threaded his fingers into my hair and grabbed a handful of the strands. As he hovered his lips a few inches from mine, his warm breath teased my face. "Are there any other terms and conditions?"

"Probably. But I can't think of any more at present." With him this close, I couldn't think of anything but him. "I'll let you know if something comes up. You want to add anything?"

"No. I'm a go-with-flow type guy, remember?" His eyes narrowed and glinted. "So, do we have a new deal? You and me, doing whatever, whenever."

I swallowed hard. My heart twisted and shuddered. He wasn't the crazy one. I was. Because I wanted to be with him. "Until the end of summer, if we take it day by day . . . yes."

He arched a sexy eyebrow. "Can I officially call you my girlfriend?"

A smile pulled at my mouth. "I like the sound of that better than fuck buddy."

"So true."

He closed the gap between us and brushed his lips against mine. Flicking his tongue into my mouth, he deepened our kiss, sending shivers to my core. Warmth coiled through my veins and pooled in my belly. My tired body hummed, waking up, wanting more of his touch and connection. But he sat back.

Grinning with satisfaction, he licked his lips. "You are very tempting. But our new deal can start tomorrow. I'll help clean up and do the dishes, then I'll head home."

He stood and cleared the plates off the table.

"Oh." Somewhat disappointed, I rose to my feet and gathered the empty takeaway containers. "You're not staying?"

"No. Not tonight. You need sleep." Heading for the kitchen,

he called over his shoulder, "Unless you want me to stay over?"

"Yes. No." I dragged my feet, following him. My gaze fell to his backside. *Damn.* His ass was hot. It filled out a pair of board shorts just as sexily as a pair of jeans. My fingers twitched, wanting to clutch and dig my nails into his flesh. But my head ached with drowsiness. I tossed the trash into the garbage can underneath the sink, then closed the cabinet door. "No. I'm exhausted. I have work tomorrow."

Flint loaded the dishwasher and put it on. But before I escaped the kitchen, he caught my waist. He spun me around, pinning me against the kitchen counter with his hands braced on either side of my hips. "Just know that every second away from you will make me want you more and more. Don't keep me waiting too long."

I lifted my chin. "What if I do?"

"You won't. Your eyes give you away."

Stupid eyes. "I'm sure I can last a couple days. I have until now. How about we just see each other on Sunday for the movie premiere?"

"You gonna last that long?" He kissed my forehead, my tired eyes, my weary cheeks, then my lips.

I flattened my hand against the hard plain of his chest, then clutched onto his T-shirt. "Uh-huh." *Yes. No. Crap.*

He skimmed the tip of his nostrils along the edge of my nose. His breath, hot against my face, melted my bones. I wanted him in my bed, his arms wrapped around me, and his warmth enveloping me. Why did he affect me like this?

He whispered against my mouth, "Call me if you change your mind."

"Okay." *No. Wait.* I flicked my head back and broke out of his spell. "I won't change my mind. I'll see you Sunday. Your place. At eleven." We had to head down to Anaheim for a Disney movie premiere. We'd booked a hotel for the night. I couldn't wait to spend the evening with him but wasn't looking forward to the early start the following morning to make it back in time for work.

"I better go, then. Night." He cupped my face and kissed me until my knees weakened. Kissing him could be my new favorite pastime.

Just as I hooked my hands around his neck, he pulled away. He shook his finger at me and gave me a pained grin. His hard-on bulging in his shorts wasn't my fault. He'd kissed me. But I loved having that effect on him.

"I'm gonna go now." He grabbed his keys and cell phone and headed for the door. "Get some sleep. You'll need it, because you won't be getting much on the weekend. See you soon, beautiful."

After one last kiss, he dashed out the door.

He'd kept his promise. He hadn't stayed.

Now I had to keep mine. I had to wait until Sunday to see him.

The hours couldn't tick by fast enough.

Chapter 25

SUTTON

The next month disappeared in a hot rush. We went to two movie premieres, an album launch, the grand opening of a theater production, another award show and charity dinner, and a VIP evening at Michael Kors. Outside of our publicity engagements, we hung out with friends and went to see a couple of bands play at small venues. I stayed at Flint's one night a week. He crashed at my place the same. On weekends, we rode up the coast on his motorcycle, and he helped me with my lines and cooked me dinner. We toned down our partying and still had incredible fun. He made me feel special in a way I'd never experienced before. I was the center of his world, but only for a little while longer. When he found music again, I'd be forgotten. But our publicity had soared. Being with Flint had worked much better than I'd imagined.

At events, the press loved seeing us together. We were interviewed on the red carpet and sought after by photographers. But not all the media coverage glowed. Gossip headlines read:

Rock's Bad Boy Wrecks TV Princess

Flint Glover's Drunken Antics Take Down TV Sweetheart

Another Hollywood Starlet Falls From Grace

The paparazzi snapped us at dinner, on the beach, and while we had coffee at my local café. We gave the photographers nothing scandalous to feed off, but that didn't stop their clickbait-loaded stories appearing online. Luckily, the good articles outweighed the bad. Spending time with Flint had finally attracted the right eyes of casting directors and industry professionals.

One Saturday afternoon, I'd just arrived home from the salon to dress for the Pacific West Music Awards when Harlow called me.

"I've got you three red-hot auditions with lead roles, Sutton. All TV series with huge potential." Enthusiasm skipped in his voice followed by a hearty wholesome laugh.

"Three?" I shrieked, jumping around my living room, unable to contain my excitement. "Awesome. What are the details?"

"The shows are for Netflix, HBO or HazelStream. The casting directors are sending me the audition requirements over the weekend. Let's have lunch on Monday so we can go through them. Sound good?"

"Yes. Yes. Oh my God, yes."

"I'll text you a time and place."

"Okay. See you then."

With my heart pounding in my chest, I slipped into my outfit for tonight. Yep . . . I was being on trend *and* recycling a dress I'd worn last year. Alice, in wardrobe at work, had altered the top for me. I loved this gown. I loved being able to wear it again.

I kept glancing at my wall clock. Flint would be here at any moment. I looked forward to an evening that celebrated his industry—the artists, the songwriters, the producers, the videographers and more. This publicity stunt wasn't all about me. This was his night. We'd meet Cole and Slip at the venue before we walked the red carpet together. I wished he'd hurry so I could tell him about my auditions.

Ten minutes later, my intercom buzzed. I rushed over to let him in.

But as he walked through the door, his eyes remained dark and distant. His hair wasn't styled. The top buttons on his shirt weren't done up. His tie was loose. His jacket hung limp in his hand. He smelled like heaven, looked like hell.

An ache gripped my chest. I hadn't seen him this withdrawn since we'd first met. Why had he slipped backward? What had happened?

I closed the door behind him. "Flint? What's wrong?"

"Nothing." He tossed his car keys on the counter. He draped his jacket over the kitchen stool and dropped his overnight bag onto the floor near his feet. "I'm good."

"Bullshit. No lies, remember? Come . . . talk to me. I'm nearly ready." I headed into my bedroom to finish putting on my shoes and accessories that matched my gorgeous turquoise now off-the-shoulder minidress.

He followed and sank onto the edge of my bed. "Umm . . . today was my mom's birthday. I stopped by the house with flowers and her favorite wine, but they wouldn't let me inside. They were there. Their cars were in the garage. I heard one of them drop something in the kitchen. I called and sent a dozen texts. But they never answered or replied."

"Oh, shit." Pinning in my dangling rhinestone earring, I sat beside him. "I'm sorry."

"They won't even talk to me."

"That's awful." I hooked my arm behind him and rubbed his back. "I'm sorry. I don't know why they'd do this to you."

"I'm tired of waiting." The sadness in his tone crushed my heart. "I miss them. I miss Sunday dinners. My dad's bad jokes.

My mom's cooking."

I swept his long bangs off his face and kissed his beautiful lips. "Is there anything I can do to help?"

"No." He clutched my hand and held it against his thigh. "The thing is, that wasn't the worst thing that happened today. I expected Mom and Dad's bullshit but not the call from Blake. Our label wants a couple demo songs within two weeks. I've got nothing. I've not written a word. Not a line. Not a lyric. *Fuck!* I'm so screwed. I don't want to fuck up our record deal."

"Hey?" I caught the tip of his chin and turned his face toward me. "I'll help you. Sometime next week, let's sit in your studio and play around with music. It might inspire you."

"I've done that with the guys. It hasn't worked. I just can't break through the block inside my head."

"You haven't tried with me."

He lowered his head and shook it. "I usually write alone. It's the way I work."

"Well, clearly that *isn't* working." I jabbed my finger against his arm. "So let's try something new."

Fear lurked in his eyes. I didn't want to intrude on his creative process, but I wanted to help him kick it back to life.

He slowly nodded. "Maybe. No promises."

"No, but we'll give it a shot." I jumped to my feet. His solemn mood couldn't tamper with the buzz zipping through my veins. Maybe I could infect him with some of my vibe and brighten his day. "But this might cheer you up. I have some great news. I've got not one, but three big auditions. Three!" I clapped my hands, then clutched them against my chest. "I'm so excited."

"Three?" He straightened. The tension eased in his brow. A faint glimmer sparkled in his eyes. "That's awesome. What are the roles?"

"All new TV series." I counted on my fingers. "One is for HBO, one is for Netflix, and one is for HazelStream, that new network everyone is raving about."

"Wh-where are they being filmed?" His voice snagged in his throat. His shoulders slouched.

No. This was good news, not more bad to add to his day.

"I don't know. Harlow doesn't have all the details yet." I kept my tone light. My energy electric. But my heart faltered. We knew what it meant if the shows weren't filmed in LA. I'd be gone. But I didn't want to think about that now or have the unknown ruin our night. "I'm having lunch with him on Monday once he's received all the information. I can't wait."

"Me either." He feigned a smile. "I'm happy for you."

"Good." I hooked my hand beneath his chin and raised it up. "So tonight, Mr. Glover, we're going to celebrate the wins, drown the losses, and unlock that brain of yours. We deserve a night of wicked fun. It's time to let our hair down and party until the sun comes up. Shall we have some vodka?"

He rose to his feet, sliding his hands up my legs and pressing his body flush against mine. "I love it when you drink vodka." There was that genuine smile, the one that reached his eyes.

"Are you sure you can handle me?"

"Anytime. Anywhere." He tugged on my earring. "You look beautiful, by the way."

"Thank you." I teased my fingers through his hair. "So do you. I like this *I've-just-been-fucked* look you've got going on."

"Want to make it authentic?" He kissed the side of my neck, sending shivers down my spine.

Giggling, I stepped out of his hold and grabbed my sparkly stiletto pumps. "No. We have to go in five minutes. I don't want to ruin my hairdresser's hard work." I hadn't sat at the salon for two hours to have him mess up my hairdo and makeup before the red carpet.

In my kitchen, we knocked back a few shots before heading down to our waiting limousine. We climbed into the backseat and took off toward The Forum in Inglewood. If the traffic was good, it'd only take us thirty minutes to get there.

The moment the driver pulled out onto the road, vodka tingled and buzzed through my veins. Flint, sitting next to me in his black designer jacket paired with suit pants covered in tiny metallic discs, electrified every hair on my body. I flicked the switch on the door panel and closed the privacy screen so the driver couldn't see us. Before the glass panel had shut, I'd hitched up my skirt and straddled Flint's lap.

He tilted his head back against the seat. A devilish grin charged across his lips. "What are you doing?"

"Have I ever thanked you for agreeing to go out with me?" I slid my hands over his chest, toying with his tie. "If I haven't, I want to. I honestly don't think I would've landed these big auditions or have been noticed without you. So thank you."

"Thank me when you get a part."

"I'll thank you then, too." I tilted my hips and rubbed my crotch against the zipper of his suit pants. "But I've scored three auditions. I wanna thank you now."

I brushed my lips against his, then slithered off his legs, sinking onto the floor between his knees.

Looking up at him from underneath my glittery lashes, I winked at him. I reached for his belt and unbuckled it.

He caught my hand. "Babe? We'll be at the venue soon."

"I'll be quick." I unzipped his pants and stroked his hard shaft, bulging inside his sexy black Calvin Klein briefs.

"Sutton?" His voice was nothing but a breathy rasp.

"Flint?" I licked my lips. "I know you want me to. *I* want to."

"You should not drink vodka. It makes you horny."

"I haven't heard you complain."

"No. I won't ever." He leaned forward. Catching my face between his hands, he kissed me. "God, you turn me on."

As the car bumped and glided along the road, I savored

the sweet taste of Flint's lips and the intoxicating smell of his cinnamony cologne. Then I pushed him backward. He collapsed against the seat. His eyes blazed with blue fire as I reached for his suit pants and wriggled them lower. He lifted his butt to help me. As I tugged his Calvins down, his huge, hard cock sprang free. I licked my lips and clenched the muscles between my legs. My panties were wet from just looking at his hot, hard nakedness.

How many times had he been inside me? Made me come? How often had we gone down on each other? I'd lost count over the past few blissful weeks. But this was another first. *Wicked!* "I've never done this in a car before."

I took hold of his thick cock and glided my fingers up his length. I lowered my head and licked the warm droplet glistening on the tip. *Mmm. Salty.*

His hips bucked. The leather seat squelched beneath his body. "Geez, Sutt. You're gonna kill me."

"You want me to stop?"

"Fuck, no."

I dipped my head and took him into my mouth, slow and gentle. Deeper. I flicked and rolled my tongue around the knob, then slid up and down the groove. A guttural moan rumbled deep in his throat. His hand shot into my hair, clutching at the loose strands. So much for wearing it neat and straight. It would be a tousled mess in a minute.

Bobbing my head, I licked and sucked him.

"Oh, yeah. That's my girl." He hissed through his teeth. Widening his legs, he thrust his cock toward the back of my throat.

I dug my nails into his strained thighs beside my head. My body ached to have him. Running my hands over his legs and ripped abs turned me on and drove me wild. His musky scent mixed with his cologne made my head spin. Lapping and licking him, tasting him, poured more heat into my core.

I glanced up at him. His eyes locked onto my gaze. Something new flickered in their depths. A warmth I'd never seen before. His lips parted. His breath quickened as I teased my tongue around the tip of his cock.

"Let me inside you," he panted.

"No."

"I'm close."

"Good. I wanna come with you."

"Okay. Move. Let me touch you."

"No. I got this." I lowered my mouth onto him again. Sucking him harder, I quickened my pace. But my body was as tense as a tight wire. My core screamed. I needed my own release. Slipping my free hand underneath my dress, I dipped my fingers into my wet panties. My hot arousal sleeked my fingers as I delved inside my opening. I rubbed small circles over my clit. *Mmm!* I worked my other hand around Flint's cock, pumping his hardness in time with the rhythm of my mouth.

"Oh, fuck." Flint clutched and tugged my hair, massaging my scalp. "That . . . you touching yourself? . . . So hot."

I fingered my swollen bud harder and faster as he surged and bucked his hips. His breath morphed from pants to hisses. Driving him insane made me lose my mind. I was unable to hold on. Touching my clit sent me over the edge. I shuddered. Shivers shot up my spin and skipped across my skin. Unrelenting, I pumped Flint's cock. Swirling and circling my tongue around him, I sucked him deeper into my mouth.

"Oh yeah, babe. That's it. There." He rocked his hips forward. His hot release spurted into my throat. Lapping and licking, I swallowed the warm, salty rush. His body convulsed. His cock pulsed and throbbed in my mouth in time with my racing heartbeat. Chuckling, he sank into the seat. "Shit. That was, without a doubt, one of the hottest blow jobs ever. Extra hot watching you get off."

Unable to contain my satisfied grin, I grabbed some tissues from the box in the door compartment to clean myself up and handed a few to Flint. He zipped and re-buckled his pants. Grabbing a bottle of water from the holder, I cracked the lid off and took a sip. "Now we'll both look disheveled on the red carpet."

"You are crazy." He drew me onto the seat and cradled my face. "But I like it a lot. You're my kind of crazy."

His intense gaze deepened, captivating my soul. I forgot how to breathe.

"But you want to hear something even crazier, Sutt?" he whispered, smoothing his hand over the back of my hair. "I've fallen in love with you."

Oh . . . shit!

No. No. No! That wasn't supposed to happen.

A cold sweat broke out on the back of my neck. I shot forward and kissed him. I kissed him to smother his words, make them disappear, and to stop my heart from hammering against my ribs.

I couldn't admit it out loud. But I knew it was true.

I was falling in love with him, too.

Chapter 26

SUTTON

At noon on Monday, I took a seat at a table in the Olive and Thyme café-restaurant close to the studio. I ordered a cappuccino for myself and a vanilla latte for Harlow. He paced the pavement outside, talking to someone on the phone. I rubbed my arms, wishing I'd brought a light jacket. While the air-conditioning was cool and welcoming from the heat outside, it was a touch too cold indoors.

The vibrant cafe with its white marble countertops, raw wooden tables, and exposed white beams bustled with people on quick breaks, devouring salads, fancy sandwiches, and to-die-for treats. The aroma of spicy chicken wafting from the kitchen made my mouth water. But my head was still stuck on the weekend.

Flint had said he loved me.

My heart pummeled my chest with every beat. I hadn't been able to say it back. Luckily, Flint hadn't seemed to care. But how I felt about him scared me. Could we have a future together? Be a couple regardless of his work or mine? He was one of the hottest new rock stars in this city and he and his band would only get bigger and more famous. He'd always be surrounded by women, always be traveling, always have someone vying for his attention. Temptation would always be around him. But he wanted me. Loved me. Flint Glover fucking loved me.

But for how long?

Would he just be another Beau?

"Hey?" Harlow patted my shoulder, shattering my thoughts. He took the chair opposite. "Sorry about that." He poured glasses of water from the pitcher on the table. "Looks like you and Flint had fun on Saturday night."

I sucked in a deep breath and straightened my shoulders. Now wasn't the time to think about Flint. I had to focus on finding a job and hope my luck was about to change. "Yeah. It was a great night. The awards show and after-party were awesome."

"You certainly are a convincing couple." Harlow flicked his napkin, placing it across his lap.

"We're excellent actors, aren't we?" I hadn't told Harlow we were together. I didn't want it to influence him in sourcing roles for me. I was not bound to LA in any way. Well . . . I hadn't been. My stomach sank at the thought of leaving. *Damn you, Flint.*

"You sure there's nothing going on between you two? Some pictures online are hot. All the kissing. The touches. The longing glances you give each other. From my observations, you look great together. He seems like a decent guy."

"He's okay." He was more than okay. He was kind and thoughtful and made me question my heart.

"Okay?" Harlow's voice pitched skyward. "I'm as straight as a straw, but I'd tap that ass in a second."

I giggled. "I'll be sure to tell him that next time I see him." Tonight. After work. At his place.

"Go for it." Harlow chuckled. "I'm quite confident he's not into men."

"Yeah. I don't think so either. Sorry." Warmth rose in my cheeks as I knew that for a fact. But enough sidetracking. I was here for business, not to talk about Flint. "Now, stop stalling. Tell me about the auditions."

"Little lady, you are gonna love these." He dug his cell phone out of his jacket.

The waiter interrupted us, placing our drinks on the table and taking our lunch order—a Cobb salad for me and a spicy chicken sandwich for Harlow.

"Won't be long." Daphne, the waitress, flicked her braided pigtails over her shoulder, took our menus, and headed for the kitchen.

Harlow took a sip of his coffee, then placed it on the saucer. "Do you want me to start with the good news or the bad?"

Why did there have to be bad news? "Hit me with the worst first."

"HBO are delaying face-to-face auditions for their new series for now. Something about unforeseen scheduling conflicts. It's not dead in the water, but we don't have a new date yet. So I'll keep you posted on that one."

That wasn't awful news, but not great either. "Okay. So what's next?"

"The next one sounds interesting. It's for the Netflix series *Fallow Creek*. It's that show that's a cross between *Gilmore Girls* and *Virgin River*. They've just renewed for two more seasons and are casting new characters."

I knew the show. It was a sweet, everyday small-town drama where everybody was in everybody's business. I was aiming for something a little more exciting and to steer away from the same typecasting, but I was getting desperate. "Okay. Are the auditions online or face-to-face?"

"They've requested self-taped online submissions. I'll have the script extract for you tomorrow."

"Awesome."

"Now the role for HazelStream excites me. This could be huge. They've secured the rights to the bestselling paranormal book series, *Hidden Cove*. There are twelve books they can draw upon."

My heart took the fast-track to my throat. I'd read some of the series a few years ago; a twenty-one-year-old girl comes into magic, and it's her family's duty to protect the town against evil. This was the type of role I'd been hoping for, something so far removed from what I'd done in the past. "That's awesome. What are they after?"

"You've been invited to a face-to-face next week. They loved your showreel and profile. But . . . the series will be filmed in Maine . . . near Portland."

"Maine?" I couldn't catch my breath. My pulse pounded my head. "As in, the East Coast, Maine?"

"The one and only."

The waiter placed our food in front of us. "Folks, y'all enjoy your lunch. Call me if you need anything."

"Thank you." In a daze, I waved the waitress away. *Maine? Oh no . . . Flint.*

Harlow unrolled his cutlery from his napkin. "Maine isn't a problem, is it? You said you'd move anywhere. This show could be massive. Think *Vampire Diaries*. Think *Teen Wolf.* Think *The Order* and *Buffy.*"

A role like this was a dream come true. So why did my stomach sink to the bottom of the ocean? "No. It's not a problem."

Fuck! Yes, it was. Just when I'd contemplated for one second the possibility of being with Flint past our deadline, my career dangled a shiny carrot in my face. Leaving would break his heart and mine, too, if I was completely honest with myself. He loved me. *Fuck!* I should've never gotten involved with him. This was what I'd wanted to avoid. Hurt blistered my skin. This was all my fault. For making deals. For falling into his bed. For caring about him.

Shit. Shit. SHIT!

I sucked in a deep breath, refusing to let the tears looming at the back of my eyes take hold. There was no need to worry about anything until I'd landed the role, right?

"Great." Harlow snacked on a crunchy fry, oblivious to the torment in my head and heart. "I'll have the audition script for you by tonight."

Nibbling on a tiny piece of chicken, I ignored the crack in my chest by pasting on a smile. "Thank you. I look forward to it."

Harlow took a bite of his spicy chicken sandwich and finished his mouthful. "Yasiv Mesik is the director and Leo Wilcott is producing the show. These two have been in bed together for years, creating hit shows. I've never worked with them before. I've contacted colleagues, clients, and industry reps to see if I could dig up some inside information, but no one has said anything good or bad about them. That concerns me."

"Why?"

"This is the third studio and network jump they've made in seven years. I wanted to make sure they were legitimate career moves for these guys and not because they were assholes to work with. I want to make sure you, my client, are looked after and respected."

Harlow seemed to have my best interests at heart. It was nice to have someone on my team. After the dealings I'd had with my father, I wasn't going to be screwed over again by anyone in this industry. If I got offered the role, I'd be going over every fine detail in the contract with my lawyer and union reps. "If Yasiv and Leo have had hits and signed with HazelStream, they have to be reputable, right?"

"Here's hoping." Harlow grabbed his napkin and wiped off

the mayonnaise that had caught on his upper lip. "These guys have only handpicked three young female actors to audition for the lead. They need to make a quick decision on casting because pre-production starts in New York at the beginning of November. That makes you the ideal candidate as the other casting options are committed to other projects until January. They won't want any delays."

Oh, wow. A rush charged through my veins. This sounded too good to be true. "That's great. But what's the catch?"

"So far, the only one is you have to live in fucking Maine during winter. You can have that shit. Give me LA and sunshine all year round any day."

Yeah. I would miss that . . . if I got the part. But there were many hoops to pass through before being awarded a role. Many other things to think about. I had to pass the audition and then have the director, production, casting, marketing teams, and the studio give me the tick of approval.

Harlow sipped his coffee. "Oh, one small fact I found out about Yasiv. Supposedly, he loves his gin. Future reference, if you need gift ideas for Christmas or a special occasion . . . like when you land the role."

"Good thing it's not vodka," I mumbled, munching on a lettuce leaf. But I liked his optimism though.

"What was that?"

"Nothing. Thanks for the tip." Heat touched my cheeks, recollecting all the crazy, sexy things I'd done with Flint while under the influence of vodka. No other alcohol affected me in that way. But I didn't need a drink for every one of my senses to be heightened when around him. His kisses made me melt. Making love to him set my soul on fire. The laughs we'd had warmed my belly. Just looking at him turned me on. All that thick black hair, his gorgeous eyes, and his body to die for made me sizzle. Closing my eyes, I fought off the stabbing ache in my heart.

Maine? Why Maine?

"Sutton?" Concern lilted in Harlow's tone. "You okay?"

"Yep. Yep, I'm fine." I pushed my salad around my plate with the fork. My appetite had wilted like the limp lettuce leaves.

Harlow licked crumbs from his fingertips. "So Yasiv will be here in LA next week for the auditions on Tuesday and the Hollywood Production and Film Awards on Friday. I've got you and Flint on the list to attend the awards. Make sure you get in front of Yasiv's face."

Oh my. The HPFAs? They were as big as the Directors Guild of America Awards. I'd never been to either. "Absolutely. I'll be there." I wouldn't let the opportunity pass me by.

I stuffed my growing feelings for Flint into the depths of my gut and locked them away. The chance to work on a huge project was only one audition away. This was my dream. I wouldn't blow it. Not for Flint. Not for anyone.

Determination set into my soul.

This was why I'd dated Flint. To be noticed. To be in front of directors, producers, and casting agents. The plan had worked. I had to see it through to the end.

***

The following week, I nailed the audition.

Then I got a phone call that changed everything.

Chapter 27

FLINT

I took Sutton's hand to walk another red carpet. Smile. Kiss. Wave at the cameras. There was a new lightness in my step. It grew every day, all thanks to Sutton. Was I fool for falling for her? Probably. It had crept up on me . . . fast. Unexpectedly. Unintentionally. But now . . . I never wanted to let her go.

She posed in front of the photographers in a stunning black halter-neck sequined dress, the thigh-high split super sexy. But tonight, she wasn't her usual vibrant self. She hadn't been for the past few days since her audition and a few private phone calls. Ever since she'd arrived at my house late this afternoon, she'd been extra quiet. On edge.

So had I.

Butterflies flurried in my gut.

Blake had arranged for me to meet Paulo Scott, a producer who was interested in me writing the headline song for his new movie. It was a massive opportunity that had come around from dating Sutton. An unforeseen bonus. Slip and Cole would meet me at the after-party to be part of the casual introduction. But I hadn't written any new songs in months. The void still dominated my brain. I didn't want to overpromise and under-deliver.

Over the past two weeks, I'd tried to rework some old tunes to submit as demos to our label, but nothing had grabbed my soul. We had a meeting with our record company in a few days and I'd have to get down on my knees and plead for an extension. I just had no idea how long I needed. But I didn't want the chance to write a hit for a blockbuster pass us by. If I could unlock the barrier, that gig would be fucking awesome, and the royalties would be off the charts.

I had no concerns about nailing the meeting with the producer, but nerves still hovered low in my gut. Until then, Sutton and I had work to do. This was a massive industry event and networking opportunity for her. This place would be crawling with directors, writers, casting executives, and producers she'd want to meet.

We shuffled along the red carpet. Cameras flashed. Reporters conducted interviews. I stole as many kisses from Sutton as I could before the production crew ushered us into the venue.

But nothing I said or did put her at ease. Her hand perspired in mine. Her gaze darted across the chattering crowd downing pre-dinner drinks. She tugged on her sparkly earring, then fidgeted with her clutch. I half grinned, kissing the back of her hand. She shouldn't be nervous. We'd work this room and meet every damn person here if that was what she wanted to do. I'd do anything for her. We were in a good place. For the first time in months, I was happy. Content. Hopeful. *In love.*

I had to convince her to kill our deadline.

She was the first girl I'd met who'd understood the ups and downs and the highs and lows of our volatile industries. She worked hard, was ambitious, and knew what she wanted. But most of all, she got me. She didn't take any bullshit and had never turned away from my scars, my heartache, and struggles, and vice versa. I'd fallen head over heels for her. Phil no longer clouded my every thought. She'd been the key to moving forward.

So why, since I'd told her I loved her, had she been distant? She loved me. She couldn't hide the truth. Her gorgeous brown eyes gave everything away. So did her touch, her kisses, and her body when we made love. Was she down because her show wrapped filming in two and a half weeks? Was she disheartened that no role had come to fruition? I had no doubt she'd land something soon. But tonight, I didn't want her to worry. We were out. Dressed in black-tie. Together. Ready to have a good time.

She fidgeted with my fingers again.

I wrapped my arm around her waist and whispered in her ear, "Sutt, what's wrong?"

Glancing sideways, she eyed a group of men in tuxedos and ladies in long gowns heading for the theater, then a couple chatting to Steven Spielberg. Even I was a little starstruck to be in the same room as him.

She placed her hand on my chest and gave it a little rub. "Nothing. I'm just intimidated by all these executives in one place."

Totally understandable. "Well . . ." I kissed her cheek. "We'd better make a good impression."

She pursed her lips and nodded just a fraction. "I'd like that."

But her gaze flitted past my shoulder. My skin prickled. The unease in my stomach wouldn't settle. "You want a drink to calm the nerves?"

"Yeah. That would be great."

We headed to the bar to grab a drink, but Sutton tucked in behind my arm. It was like she didn't want to be seen.

That wasn't like her.

I grabbed her a champagne and a beer for myself from the bartender. As I took a sip of the frothy cold ale, my cell phone buzzed in my jacket pocket. I whipped it out and read the notification. *Shit.* Rici again. Without fail, she'd messaged me every month, wanting to see me, since Phil had died. If she wasn't a good friend of one of my band's stage crew, I'd block her. Didn't my silence tell her I wasn't interested? I ignored the text and stuffed my cell back into my pocket.

"Who was that?" Sutton took a dainty sip of her bubbles.

"No one important."

"Good." She wriggled my bow tie straight. Damn thing always choked me. Threading her arm around me, she crushed her chest against mine and clutched my ass. "Because you're mine tonight."

Hmmm. A hint of sassy Sutton had returned. The possessive underlying current in her tone tingled my balls. *I love you* had never passed her lips. But she didn't have to say it. Our connection went beyond words. I felt her love in every cell in my body.

"Forever and always," I whispered against her lips.

"That's a long time."

"I'm not going anywhere."

"I am."

My heart jolted. "What?"

"I just need to use the restroom." A wicked smile drew across her lips as she held her flute toward me. "Can you hold this, please? I'll be back in a sec."

Geez! I puffed air through my nose and shook my head. My heart slowly slid back into place. Even after spending over two months together, she still did my head in. *Damn actress.* There was never a dull moment. Maybe that was why I loved her. She was unpredictable . . . maybe too much like me.

"Sure." I took hold of her glass and waved it toward a spare bar table by the far wall. "I'll wait for you over there."

"Okay. I won't be long."

Ogling her sexy ass, I couldn't wipe the goofy grin off my face as she weaved her way through the crowd, nodding and saying hello to the men and women she passed. I didn't know who most of those people were, but like at most awards nights, there was an electric hum in the air. Maybe it was because I was with Sutton. I was happy. I hadn't felt this good in months.

I placed our drinks on the table and leaned against it. I should mingle and socialize but I didn't want to do that without Sutton. This was her gig, not mine.

As she disappeared into the restrooms on the other side of the foyer, a veil of warmth enveloped me and penetrated my skin. I took a deep, lung-filling breath, and a fevered rush shot through my bloodstream. Every pore tingled. *Strange.* Did I feel okay? I think so . . . *Oh, wait. Oh, fuck.* My head spun. My heart pounded. The clouds that had been covering the dark recesses of my mind since Phil died had cleared. Music and words flooded and formed in my brain.

Holy. Shit.

I grabbed my cell phone, swiped it on and opened the notes application. My fingers flew across the screen.

> *It happened just last summer,*
> *When I wasn't feeling right.*
> *I wasn't looking for a lover,*
> *But then you walked into my sight.*
> *You said just hold my hand and breathe,*
> *Even if it's just for a while.*
> *Let's throw caution out to sea,*
> *See how fate unfolds tonight.*
>
> *Now the snow is falling,*
> *And it's bitterly cold outside.*

You're the one I'm still loving,
Can't seem to get you off my mind.

"Hey?"

I jumped, startled by Sutton's return. My vision blurred. I couldn't see for the lyrics swirling before my eyes.

"Who are you texting?" Suspicion hovered in her tone.

What? Was she crazy?

"Me?" I blinked and shook my head. "No one. I was just—"

"Sutton?"

A tall lady with flawless dark skin and black hair sleeked into a high bun approached. She held out her hands toward Sutton. "So good to see you."

"Shona. Hi." Clasping the lady's hand, Sutton kissed one cheek, then the other. Sutton placed her slender fingers on my arm, gripping it hard, and introduced me. "This is my . . . boyfriend, Flint Glover."

I threw Sutton a quizzical look. Why did she hesitate? Was she upset at me for writing lyrics while I'd waited? Surely not. I let it slide and shook Shona's hand. "Good evening."

"Flint? Shona used to produce my show." Sutton smiled, slipping into friendly catchup mode with Shona. "Where are you now? I haven't seen you for over a year."

"I'm at Warner working on a show similar to *Suits*." Shona peered past Sutton and waved at her nearby colleagues. She held up her finger for them to wait one minute. "It's a temporary gig but so much fun. What about you? I miss working with you. Have you got anything lined up after *Brentwood* wraps?"

I only half listened to their conversation. Lyrics. Music. Guitar riffs formed in my head. I rubbed my brow and swayed on my feet, overcome by the bombardment. Chords. Notes. Bridges.

Concern flickered through Sutton's eyes before she turned to Shona. "Nothing yet." She remained upbeat and drew her shoulders back. "Do you know of anyone casting?"

"Hmm." Shona's eyebrows pinched together. "Not off the top of my head. But I'll keep my ears open. Let's catch up for coffee in a few weeks and I'll see what I can find."

"That would be awesome." Sutton dug into her clutch and pulled out her cell phone. "Can I grab your contact details and call you?"

"Sure can." Shona typed them into Sutton's cell and handed it back. "It's great to see you. Nice to meet you, Flint. But please excuse me. My friends are waiting."

"Have a good night." I waved, then turned to Sutton. Songs pounded and played in my head, but I pushed them aside to focus on Sutton. Hope for her filled my chest. "That's kinda promising. She might stumble across something for you."

"That would be nice. But you know I'll take any job." Hardness set in her tone.

She didn't have to remind me. But I didn't want her to take any old job that came her way. I wanted her to wait until she found something she loved.

Now wasn't the time to discuss that she could take as long as she needed to find a role. I'd help her out until she landed on her feet. Hell, she could move in with me.

Whoa!

Was that too quick?

Maybe. We'd only known each other for a couple of months. But I'd do anything for her. Most of all, I wanted her to stop stressing about finding work.

I slid my hand beneath the back of her hair and brushed my lips against her mouth. She tasted of strawberries and smelled like oriental flowers. Fresh. Delicious. Like the summer I never wanted to end. "Your job, if I recall correctly, is to network and show me a good time. My job is to make you stand out from the crowd. So how about it?" I took a step back and held out my hooked arm. "Can I interest you in schmoozing some of the hobnobs here, and another drink before we head inside?"

I needed a distraction to stop the symphony of songs blaring in my head. But now they were back, I was afraid they'd disappear. I didn't want them to stop.

"I thought you'd never ask." She snaked her hand around my arm. "But no vodka."

"Spoilsport."

After a drink and some mingling, we headed into the auditorium for the dinner and awards. We sat at a table toward the back of the room with a few TV producers and writers Sutton had a vague knowledge of. I made casual chitchat but found it hard to concentrate. My mind was alive with lyrics. Tunes tumbled in my head.

The host had the audience in stitches. Award after award, speech after speech rolled on. We were halfway through the presentations when I couldn't fight it anymore. The need to write burned hot inside me. I pulled out my cell phone. Holding it beneath the table, I typed every crazy line that popped into my mind like a madman.

"Who are you texting?" Sutton's voice was barely above a whisper, but it was cutting.

"No one. One sec." I finished a couple of lines, then switched off my cell phone. But pure adrenaline coursed through my veins. My fingers twitched, wanting to write more. I flicked my hair back, leaned over, and kissed her cheek. Breathing her sweet scent always calmed my mind. "All done."

"Good." She curled her hand around my thigh, then gave it a playful but firm tap. "Now behave."

"Never." I grinned against her hair. I never wanted to behave when she was around. "I'm sorry. But . . ." Sitting back, I closed my eyes. Lyrics hit me with a vengeance.

I never knew what was wrong with me,

I lived a life I didn't want to lead.
I didn't want to be in a world where you didn't exist,
Where you were nothing more than a memory in the
mist.

They wouldn't stop. My bow tie strangled my throat like a noose. I wiggled it free, but it didn't ease my breathing. My leg jiggled. There was too much noise in the auditorium. The music, the acceptance speeches, the laughter and constant chatter clanged and clobbered inside my head. I needed fresh air. Just for a minute. Just to settle my mind.

"Sutt?" I hooked my arm over the back of her chair and spoke low into her ear. "I quickly need to visit the men's." Any excuse to get out of there.

She arched a dubious eyebrow at me. "Okay. Hurry back."

I headed for the exit at a pace that was nowhere near casual. I pushed through the heavy auditorium doors and stepped into the vast foyer. There were only a few souls to be seen—a few ladies and gents floating to and from the restrooms, a couple of security guards standing at the entrance to the building, and half a dozen hotel staff carrying trays of cups toward the tea and coffee station they were preparing for after the ceremony.

I didn't need the restroom. I needed space. Somewhere quiet. Somewhere away from the noisy auditorium.

There. At the bar. On the far side of the foyer.

I crossed the carpet in long strides and slid onto a bar stool underneath the dim lights. *Perfect.*

The bartender, drying a wine glass with a linen cloth, ambled over. "What can I get you?"

"Nothing. Sorry, bud. I just need a sec before I head back inside."

"Fair enough." The guy shrugged, then hung the glass in the wire rack above his head. "I'm Hamilton. Holler if you need anything."

I ripped out my cell and typed. Lyric after lyric. Verse after verse. Chorus after chorus.

"Are you, by any chance, Flint Glover?" Hamilton stood halfway down the bar, resting his hip against the counter, drying another glass.

Still typing, I nodded. "Yep. The one and only."

"What are you doing at a gig like this?"

"I came with my girlfriend." I kept my eyes glued to my screen.

"Oh. That's right. You're dating Sutton Summers, aren't you? She's a total babe."

"Thanks." The words kept coming. I couldn't type fast enough.

"Sorry to hear about your brother. You doing okay now?"

The pain that usually erupted inside my chest when someone asked about Phil only tugged like a dull twang instead of stabbing like a spear. That was new. Tolerable. Manageable. "Yeah, thanks."

"You sure you don't want a drink?" Hamilton asked.

"Nope. I'm nearly done." My fingers typed faster.

> *I was lost in the darkness, not knowing what to do.*
> *But like a shooting star, you swept into my view.*
> *Didn't understand the strange feeling I had deep inside.*
> *One chance meeting dared to change my life.*

Words kept coming and coming. Every line was an addictive high. I couldn't stop.

"Yo, dude." Hamilton tapped his hand on the counter beside him. "You've been here fifteen minutes. Won't your girlfriend be wondering where you are?"

Probably. Shit. I'll just finish this verse. "She'll be fine."

Sutton would have everyone at the table entertained with stories and jokes about her show. She'd be drilling each one of them for potential auditions and opportunities. She'd survive a couple more minutes without me.

> *Did Heaven send out a search party,*
> *The moment they knew one of their angels had gone?*
> *Will they see how we're meant to be and be long gone?*
> *You brought me salvation, yeah, you're my saving grace.*
> *With you by my side, there is nothing I can't face.*

"Whatever you're doing must be serious." Hamilton placed a beer on a coaster beside him. "Looks like you could use this."

"Thanks, man." I took a sip. But all my focus was on my words. Screen after screen, I jotted song after song. Exhilaration pumped through my veins. After months of not writing a word, the black shroud had fallen. I barely drew breath as the profound quantity of lines fell from my fingertips.

"Um . . . Mr. Glover?" Hamilton tapped the counter again, then pointed across the foyer. "Here comes trouble."

I glanced over my shoulder. Sutton stormed toward me. Her black dress sparkled in the soft lighting, but fire blazed in the wake of her quick steps.

Shit.

Chapter 28

FLINT

"What are you doing out here?" Anger and worry furled through Sutton's voice. "You've been gone for more than half an hour."

Had I been that long? *Shit.* "I'm sorry. I was just—"

"Texting?" She stabbed her finger toward my phone. "Who is so important? Rici?"

"What? No." How could she be insecure over some chick I wasn't interested in anymore? That had died the night she'd touched my brother.

"Then what? Whatever it is, tell me." Tears pooled on the rims of her eyes, but she held them in.

Oh no. Rising to my feet, I cupped her face. I pressed my mouth to hers. Her lips were tense, tight, thin lines. Not even a flick of my tongue softened them. I smoothed my hands over her bare shoulders. "Babe, I'm not texting anyone. I'm writing lyrics."

Her eyes widened. She sucked in a sharp breath. "Lyrics?"

"Yep. Look." I grabbed my cell and scrolled through the lines I'd written.

"What? When? How?" She scanned my face. More tears

shimmered in her eyes. All traces of anger disappeared.

I rubbed the back of my neck, still dazed by the songs forming in my head. "Just tonight. When we got here. They hit me. I can't turn it off. It's brilliant."

"That's . . . that's amazing." She flung her arms around me and held me extra tight. Really tight. Squeezing the breath from my lungs. *So good.* Her lips murmured against my throat, "Why didn't you tell me?"

"I did . . . well . . . I tried. But we kept getting interrupted."

"Oh, Flint." Stepping back, she smiled, but it didn't touch her eyes. She clutched my hands, trembling all over like she was about to shatter. Her voice came out soft and fragile. "This is incredible."

So why did she look like she was about to break? "But?"

"But nothing." She sniffled and shook her head. "You did it. You'll be able to write and record and . . . tour."

My heart leaped for the ceiling, but then crashed to the floor with a thud. Her eyes glazed over. Did she think this was the end of us? Just because I'd written a few lyrics? No fucking way. "It's all thanks to you. I'm not letting you go. Not ever. I promise."

She winced, then lowered her chin. "Please don't make promises we can't keep."

"I won't." I caught her delicate jaw in my palms, then tilted her head back to look into her eyes. Fear and dread stared back at me. My heart hurt. I had to erase her doubts. But how? "I promise."

She pursed her lips and nodded. "Okay. We better go back inside, or do you need more time to write?"

"I'm good." I took her hand to lead her into the auditorium.

But by the end of the ceremony, Sutton's spark had faded further. Her hand hung limp within mine. What could I do to reassure her I wasn't going anywhere? We'd survive any future touring schedule. Or her filming locations. I would never be away from her for long. I'd make sure of it.

After the show, guests hung around in the foyer, chatting, praising award winners, and drinking before heading off to various after-parties.

"Let's have one more drink before we get out of here." I steered her toward the bar.

She tugged on my hand, pulling me toward the door. "No. Let's just go. Please?"

I pointed to the swarming congregation of partygoers waiting for their limousines, taxis, or valet-parked cars outside the hotel. "It's too busy." I checked the time. I had ninety minutes until I had to meet Cole and Slip. "One drink to avoid the stampede, then we'll head off. Promise."

"Shit." Her fingers trembled as she tucked her hair behind her ear. "Fine. One drink. Then we're out of here." Why was she so anxious?

As we mingled with a few guests, Sutton shielded herself in front of me as she peered around the room. The hairs on my arm stood on end. Who was she avoiding?

She'd downed three champagnes to my one beer. On top of all the wine she'd drunk throughout the dinner, she was beyond tipsy. It wasn't like her to drink that much that quickly. Usually, she got all touchy-feely when drunk—her hands would slip beneath my jacket, clutch my ass, or glide across my chest—but tonight, I'd had nothing. She clung to her drink instead of me. She wouldn't even look my way. Unease swirled in my gut and burned my throat.

As the people we'd been talking to left, we stepped up to the bar to finish our drinks.

"Sutt, what's bugging you?" I drained my beer and placed the empty glass on the bar. "Are you pissed at me for writing lyrics or is it something else?"

Sadness swallowed her eyes. "No . . . Oh, shit." The color drained from her face as she stared over my shoulder. "We need to go. Now." She grabbed my hand and yanked me toward the door.

"Sutton?" a man's deep voice hollered across the room.

She halted and winced. The blood drained from her face. "I'm sorry. It's Yasiv. Just let me say hi and I'll be right back."

Yasiv? Yasiv? How did I know that name? Who was he?

A short man in his forties, with thinning blond hair, headed toward her. Dressed in a Hugh Hefner-like paisley maroon dinner jacket with a black ascot cravat, he held out his hands and met Sutton a few feet away.

"Sutton." He swayed on his bowed legs. "Nice to see you again."

"Hi, Yasiv." Taking his arm, she tried to draw him away to talk in private, but he waltzed and twirled her around and she ended up back beside me.

"How's my girl?" Yasiv gave Sutton's arm an overly friendly rub that lasted way too long.

I didn't like that. Not one bit. I fired a back-off glare at him. He snapped his hand free.

He raised an eyebrow at Sutton but jerked his head toward me. "This one isn't going to be a problem, is he?"

"No, of course not." Sutton paled further and took a step toward the clearing at the end of the bar. "Yasiv, can we please talk in private?"

What could she possibly want with this guy who reeked of more cologne than a Macy's men's fragrance counter?

"Sure . . . after you meet someone." Yasiv waved and hollered at a gentleman in a navy pin-stripe suit, who headed over and joined us. "Sutton, I'd like you to meet Leo Wilcott." Yasiv hooked his arm around Leo's shoulder and overzealously kissed the dumpy man on his temple. "I love this guy. He's my best buddy and will produce the show."

Holy shit. Was Yasiv drunk? Or just weirdly over-the-top eccentric? No . . . it wasn't that. *Ohhhh.*

The darting eyes. The little smirks. The high-octane levels of energy. These fuckers were as high as the Wilshire Grand.

"What a night, hey?" Leo held his arms wide. "Shame I didn't win *Best Producer.* Fuck 'em. That's what I say." He sniffed and rubbed the tip of his nose. "But the night is still young and we're in the mood to party."

I smirked. *Oh yeah.* They'd been fucking partying. No doubt on cocaine.

"Please, Yasiv?" Sutton pleaded. "May I talk to you?"

"Oh, we'll have plenty of time to talk. Tonight, we celebrate. We're so excited." Yasiv tousled Leo's hair as he threw Sutton a lit smile. "Miss Summers, are you ready to join us in Maine?"

My heart stilled. *What the fuck? Maine?* A chill shot down my spine. It seized my throat, my chest, and my lungs. No words came out. I just glared at Sutton. My eyes burned like frost bite.

"Yes."

I could barely hear her timid voice over the pounding in my head. She wouldn't look at me. I clutched onto the back of her dress, digging my fingers into her hip. She flinched but ignored my desperate need for answers. I didn't want to make a scene and embarrass her in front of her . . . her . . . what? . . . New fucking boss?

Yasiv swiped a glass of wine from a waiter passing by and took a sip. "We hope to finalize your offer in the next day or so."

"Whoa. Whoa. Whoa." Leo tapped Yasiv on the chest. "We have more details to discuss."

"True." Yasiv raised his glass toward Sutton and winked. "But until then . . . we're having a little get-together back at my place. Just a couple of friends and partners. Why don't you two join us? We can discuss the project in more detail."

"Sure." Sutton nodded, but a brick wall had shot up between us.

My insides burned.

She'd lied to me.

She hadn't told me she'd been offered a role or was in negotiations. Was that what the phone calls had been about? She hadn't mentioned any role being based on the other side of the fucking country.

"Wait." My voice scratched and scraped my throat. "We can't. Not tonight. I have to meet the guys at the after-party."

"That's okay." Sutton glanced my way for less than a split second. "You meet the guys and I'll go with Yasiv."

Like hell she would. "You're not going to some party without me." As far as I knew, she'd never been around drugs, and these guys were semi-loaded. I'd been to more parties than I cared to remember that had been inundated with booze and drugs and sex. I didn't want her to be in a situation that could get out of hand. I didn't care who these turkeys were, I wouldn't leave her alone with them.

Chuckling, Yasiv swayed as he circled his finger at us. "Why don't you two have a little chat while I get my car? I'll see you outside in five." He winked at Sutton. "Don't keep me waiting."

Oh. He could fucking wait.

I grabbed Sutton's hand and charged outside the hotel into the fresh evening air. I needed to cool down. I dragged her over to the far side of the venue's driveway, away from listening ears. The hurt, anger, and frustration twisting through my body overruled any happiness I may have had for her landing a role.

"Flint. Stop." She tried to tug her hand free from my hold. "Just stop."

"Shit. I'm sorry." I released my fingers and spun to face her. My breath ripped at my lungs. I clutched at handfuls of my hair and tugged. "You got an offer, and you didn't tell me? Why?"

"There was no point." She closed her eyes, the chilling calm in her voice unsettling me. "I haven't signed anything yet. We're negotiating final terms."

"This is why you've been acting weird the past few days, isn't it? Why you've been acting weird tonight."

The grooves on her forehead deepened. "No."

"Don't . . . lie to me." Fire furled beneath my skin and burned my chest.

"Fine. Yes. I didn't want to upset you."

"Upset me?" I had to keep it together. There were cameras and too many people about. "I'm upset you didn't tell me. But . . . you have a job offer. That's . . . that's . . . great. But—"

"No," she snapped. "There is no but. You know the deal. I'm prepared to move anywhere for work."

My shoulders sank. Nausea pooled in the pit of my stomach. "It's just fucked that it's so far away. I like having you around. But we'll survive. We'll make it work."

"Long-distance?" She said it like it was a dirty, crass word. "Come on, Flint. Be real. This isn't going to work long-distance."

My heart splintered. The shards pierced the center of my chest. "Why wouldn't it? I'll come see you as often as I can. Between filming seasons, you'll come home."

She shook her head. "They've secured two series. But if the show is successful, it could go on for five to seven years. Maybe more."

"Fuck." I paced the pavement. One step. Two steps. Three. Turn. *Think. Think. Think. Shit!* "I don't care." I stopped in front of her and clutched her arms. "We'll be fine. The guys and I can spend some time on the East Coast. We'll rent or buy a house. Base ourselves over there for a while."

Tears welled in her eyes. "I can't ask you to do that."

"You don't have to." I brushed my thumb across her blotchy cheek. "I'll move for you."

She grabbed my hands and lowered them. "Please. Don't."

"Why not?"

Her chin quivered. "Because I don't love you."

My heart shattered across the driveway. I took a step back, unable to draw breath. "What?"

Lies. She was lying.

She shook her head and wiped the tears from her eyes with her fingertips. "We've had an amazing summer. But just like a vacation, it has to end. We've had a great time. We got what we wanted out of this deal." She splayed her hand across my chest. "You're better. You're playing, singing, and writing again. I got my TV role. We're in good places. Let's just leave it as it is and move on with our lives."

"Not without you." I clutched her hand against my hammering heart. "I'm better because of you. I want you in my life."

She shook her head.

"Why are you doing this?"

She pulled her hand free. "Because I care about you."

"But you don't love me?"

She closed her eyes. Her chin quivered. "No."

"Liar." The word left a bitter taste on my tongue.

"I'm not lying. I gotta go."

She turned to leave, but I caught her arm. "Don't get in that car. They're high. Half drunk."

"No, they're not." She yanked her arm free.

"Yes, they are. Please? Let's talk this out. Come with me to see the guys, then I'll take you to Yasiv's."

"I'm a big girl." She stood her ground, hardness set into her jaw. "I can take care of myself."

"Oh, I know you can. But what about at the drug-fueled party they'll be throwing?"

"Flint. Enough." Fire flared in her eyes. "Stop telling me

what to do." She stabbed her finger at my face. "God, you're just like my father. All you want to do is control every part of my life, and I won't have it. I'm not a child anymore."

Ouch! Being protective and caring wasn't controlling. "That's bullshit and you know it."

"Then let me go," she pleaded. "This is for my career."

"Sutton. I beg of you. Don't get in that car. Don't end up like Phil." Did I sound desperate? Scared out of my wits? Too fucking right I was. "I'll call the guys. I'll meet Paulo another time."

"No. Go." Ice set in her eyes. "We're done. I don't need you anymore."

My knees buckled. Her words ripped my insides apart. Every muscle ached. "Don't say that. You do."

Tears rolled down her cheeks. "No. I don't."

A black Lexus sports car pulled into the driveway and stopped by the hotel's entrance. The concierge tossed Yasiv the keys.

"Sutton?" Yasiv called across the driveway. "You coming?"

Fuck!

"Yes." Sutton headed toward him. "Where's Leo?"

"Oh, he got a lift with Helena." Yasiv waved his hand toward the road. "He'll met us there."

Alarm bells wailed like sirens in my head. "Sutton. Stop." I stormed after her. "Let me come with you. We'll catch an Uber."

"No. I got this." Sutton dashed toward the car.

"Stop." I rushed over and blocked Yasiv's path. Several people and countless cameras turned to watch the commotion I'd caused. I didn't care. "Yasiv. Don't be a dick. You're high and drunk. Don't get behind that wheel."

"What are you talking about? I've hardly touched a drop. Or a gram." He tapped the side of his nose with his fingertip, then slipped me a business card. "Here's my number. Text me and I'll send you my address. Come party with us, rock star."

Yasiv pushed past me, but I shoved him on the shoulder. "Give me your fucking keys. Now."

"Sir?" A security guard who had been standing next to the concierge, stepped onto the driveway. "Is there a problem?"

"Yes." My voice sliced through my teeth. "This asshole is drunk, high, and about to get behind the wheel."

Yasiv held up his hands. Innocence played in his pompous tone. "This fool is just upset his girlfriend wants to come to my party."

"Ma'am?" The security guard turned to Sutton like she had all the answers.

"Sir. Everything is fine." A cool smile hid the shake in her tone. "We've just had a small misunderstanding." But there was no hesitation in her hand as she opened the car door and slipped into the passenger seat.

Yasiv sucked up to the guard. "I assure you I'm perfectly fine to drive. See?" He closed his eyes, stood on one foot and touched one fingertip to his nose, then another. He walked a straight line along the driveway and back again.

I didn't believe his act for one second.

The guard's eyes narrowed, watching Yasiv's every move.

Yasiv winked at the security guard. He pulled out a one-hundred-dollar bill from his jacket pocket and slipped it into the man's hand. "Sorry to trouble you. We'll be out of your way in a second."

"Good. Clear this driveway now." The guard got up in my face. "You, sir? Please vacate the premises."

Steam blew from my nostrils and ears as Yasiv glided past me with a grin loaded with satisfaction. He hopped into his Lexus and yanked the door shut.

I charged past the guard and slapped my hand on the hood, then rushed around to Sutton's door. "Sutton? Please? Get out of the car."

I pulled on the door handle, but she'd locked it. *Fuck!*

She stared out the front window, then turned to glance up at me. Her chin quivered. *"I'm sorry,"* she mouthed. *"Go. Please. I'll be okay."*

Yasiv revved the engine, took off, and pulled out onto the street.

"Fuuuuck!" I screamed and sank to my knees. I covered my head with my arms. *This-isn't-happening. This-isn't-happening. This-isn't-happening.*

Air burned my lungs. My skull thudded and throbbed.

"Sir." The guard hooked his hand beneath my arm. "Will you please leave the premises, or I'll call the police?"

I got to my feet. Yanked my arm free. Straightened my jacket. "Fuck you. I'm outta here."

Storming toward the road, I ripped out my cell phone. I had to call an Uber to follow Sutton and contact the guys to reschedule our meeting. *Fuck.* They'd be pissed. I was pissed. Just when my life had fallen into place and was back on track, it had derailed again. But I had to make sure Sutton was safe. All I needed was Yasiv's address.

I glanced down the road. His Lexus's taillights disappeared in the distance. Fucker drove like a rally-car driver. *Like Phil.* Every cell in my body shuddered. Tears burned at the back of my eyes.

She'd broken my heart. Left me stranded. Put her life at risk.

Surely the night couldn't get any worse.

Chapter 29

SUTTON

I stared out the windshield as Yasiv drove, but I couldn't focus on anything. My chest crushed my heart. I hated hurting Flint. I saw it in his eyes—the moment his soul shattered. I heard his heart break when I told him I was leaving and I didn't love him. Lying broke me in two. I loved him like crazy. But I had to hide the truth. This was the best thing for us, for our careers. I needed this new role and he needed to focus on his band. He'd reconnected with his music and was writing lyrics again. My heart soared at the breakthrough. He'd done it. But worrying about me and relocating would only create new problems, and he'd end up resenting me for it in the end. My jealousy didn't help—I'd thought he was texting some other girl when he'd been writing music. How would I go without seeing him 24/7? Why did the right decisions have to hurt so much?

Champagne gurgled in my belly and bubbled up my throat. *Ergh.* I rested my head against the window and closed my eyes. All I saw was Flint. I was too young to be serious about a guy. I'd learned that from being with Beau. I wanted to support myself and follow my dreams. I wanted no restrictions, no rules, no curfews or controls. I wanted to live my life—not be tied down in a relationship. But no matter what I told myself, or how much I reasoned with myself, it didn't ease the pain contorting and ripping apart every cell in my body.

Flint? I clutched my chest. *I'm so sorry.*

Yasiv gunned his Lexus down the Boulevard. Avoiding him at the ceremony tonight hadn't worked. I hadn't wanted Flint to find out about my job offer by running into Yasiv. I'd wanted to wait until I'd signed a contract before I'd told him about it. It had sounded better and less painful in my head than in reality.

God. I was a fool.

I flattened my hand against my belly to settle my nausea. Having to lie to Flint about the calls with Yasiv over the past few days had exhausted me. It had blown up in my face. Maybe I'd taken the wrong approach. I should've told him about the offer. But it was too late now. What was done was done.

A tear fell onto my cheek, but I was quick to swipe it away. I didn't want to leave Flint. But I couldn't do long-distance. Not from Maine. It would be cruel to both of us.

He deserved to be free. Have no commitments. Have fun with his band. Be with girls. Travel and tour the world. I couldn't be the reason he put any of that on hold.

I'll need to focus on the show.

"Your boyfriend was a piece of work back there." Yasiv weaved through the light traffic. "Are you okay?"

"Yes. I'm fine," I lied, blinking the tears from my eyes. "He's just protective." I swallowed the dry lump in my throat. I loved that about him. No one had ever cared for me like he had. "He's upset about Maine."

"Doesn't he support you?"

"Yes. He's not the problem. I am. I'm worried about our relationship surviving long-distance. I want to give my all to this role," I said. Yasiv didn't need to know I'd just broken up with Flint.

"That's what I loooove to hear. We're gonna have so much fun."

Yasiv swerved sharply around the car in front of us. I hit my head against the door. "Ow! Could you slow down? Are you trying to kill me?"

"Never." Laughing, he stepped on the gas, charging down the road. "We're moving to Maine, baby. This is so exciting. Tonight, make sure you pay some attention to Leo. He was keen for Bridget, the chick from Boston, to take the role. But I swayed him my way. So make sure you chat to him and *stroke* his ego. He'll love that. I'll powder his nose. You need to convince him you're the perfect fit for our little family."

"How am I supposed to do that?" Panic crept into my bones as the lines of the road zipped in white flashes toward me. I pushed my feet flat against the floor like I wanted to brake. I gripped onto the door's armrest. "Please. Slow down. You're scaring me."

"You're fine. I know what I'm doing." He veered left, then right, around another car. "Come on. You're a party girl, right? Like living a little dangerously? After all, you're dating Flint Glover."

"What's that got to do with anything?"

"That's why I liked you for the role. You're sweet on the outside, but spicy on the inside, right? You love having a good time? That's the kind of person we want on our show. Someone who's a talented actress and will be fun to work with."

"Great." I clutched my seatbelt. Sweat broke out on my brow. I didn't know if it was from being terrified at the speed we were traveling or from too much alcohol or both. "But this isn't fun. Was Flint right? Are you high?"

Shit! How had I not seen this? I'd been too messed up in my head to notice.

"I always have a little something to make the evening more enjoyable. Want some?" He dug into his jacket pocket and pulled out a vial half full of white powder. "Here."

My pulse thudded in my temples. "No. Thank you. I don't do drugs."

"You don't?" He jerked his chin back. "Are you serious? This is Hollywood. You're with a rock star. Everyone takes something. Uppers. Downers. Painkillers. Coke. Weed. Valium. Come on. What's your poison?"

"Nothing." Maybe vodka. When with Flint. But Yasiv didn't need to know that.

Oh shit. Flint. Why didn't I listen to you? "Can you please stop the car? I want to get out."

"Sutton. Don't be silly. We're nearly there."

"No. Please. Stop."

He kept on driving.

"I'm going to be sick."

"No, you're not." He smirked and sped up.

"Stop."

But as I glanced out of the windshield, my eyes widened. A homeless man pushed his grocery cart out from behind a parked car to cross at the pedestrian crossing.

Yasiv didn't see him.

"Look out." I pointed.

"Oh, fuck!" Yasiv swerved hard to miss the grocery cart but clipped the front of it. *Thwack.* Tangled metal clanged through the air.

Yasiv lost control.

The car spun around. Tires squealed.

I hit the door, hard. I covered my face with my hands. A scream ripped from my throat. "Arrrrgh!"

The world blurred before me as the car spiraled out of control. One-eighty. Three-sixty. Another turn. I lost all sense of direction.

Then *smash.*

Glass shattered as the driver's side slammed into a parked SUV. Pain shot through my ribs and neck. The airbag exploded, smashing into my nose as it pinned me against the seat. The car's alarms beeped and blared.

Panic gripped me as tears streamed down my face.

I shook all over, from my head down to my toes.

Oh-my-God. Oh-my-God. Oh-my-God.

I glance sideways. Blood covered the side of Yasiv's face. His head rested against the broken window. His eyes were shut. He didn't move.

Oh, fuck! Was he dead?

"Yasiv? Yasiv?" My voice sounded distant. Not my own.

The airbag held me hostage. I couldn't move. I couldn't free my hands.

My gut roiled and rumbled. Then . . . I threw up. I couldn't free my hands to wipe it away. *Yuck.*

"Ma'am?" An old man's voice drifted near my ear. "Stay still. I've called for help. Ma'am. You're okay. Help is on its way."

Who was that?

Where was that voice coming from?

My eyelids fluttered. I couldn't keep them open.

I tried to fight it. I wanted to keep alert.

My vision blurred, closing in from the edges.

Then . . . *vwoomp!*

Blackness swallowed me whole.

Chapter 30

SUTTON

Blip. Blip. Blip.

I winced at the unfamiliar sound. My head ached. My shoulder and ribs screamed in pain. I forced my eyes open.

Oh, shit.

My heart rate quickened. Propped up in a hospital bed, I wiggled my legs against the blankets that were tucked tightly across my waist. My right shoulder was bound in a blue sling. A foam brace strangled my neck. Monitors had been stuck to and pulled at the sensitive skin on my chest, and a heart-rate reader covered my index finger.

What the fuck had happened?

I was alive. But every-fucking-thing hurt. Even my toes.

"Sutt? You're awake?" My brother leaped from the chair, clutched my hand, and kissed my forehead.

"Steven? Wh-what are you doing here?" Grogginess swam through my voice.

"You're okay." He rubbed my hand. "You were in an accident last night. Do you remember?"

Unfortunately, I did. I closed my eyes and tried to nod, but my neck hurt.

"I got a call just after midnight and rushed down here as quickly as I could. I don't have Dad's number. You don't have him listed as your next of kin anymore?"

"No. I don't." I didn't need my father. Not at all. I didn't care if I needed a kidney; he'd lost the right to be part of my life.

"You scared me half to death." Worry darkened his big brown eyes. His tousled blond hair looked like he hadn't brushed it in weeks.

"I'm sorry." A tear leaked sideways out of my eye and trickled its way toward my hairline. "What's the damage? Why do I hurt so much?"

He kept stroking my hand. It was nice. Soothing. But it wasn't Flint. Where was he? Was he here? *Stupid*. Of course, he wasn't. I'd broken his heart. I shouldn't miss him like I did.

Steven softened his tone. "You have two cracked ribs. A sprained wrist. A busted nose from the airbag. Some cuts and bruises. Whiplash. You're lucky to be alive."

I licked my dry lips in search of some moisture to talk. "What about Yasiv?"

"The guy who was driving?" Steven scratched his stubbly cheek. "He's worse off than you but all right. He got a nasty knock and gash to the head. Broke his arm, hip, ankle, and a ton of ribs. But the police are all over him thanks to the quantity of drugs they found on him. His friend, Leo someone, was here when the police were questioning Yasiv about half an hour ago. They'll charge Yasiv with possession, use, dangerous driving, driving under the influence, and a ton of other stuff, plus there's talk of rehab."

Rehab? What about the show?

Steven squeezed my fingers. "Sutt, please tell me you haven't fallen into taking drugs? Did Dad fuck you up that much?"

"No," I whispered. "I just made a stupid mistake getting in

that car." The crash flashed before my eyes. My chin trembled with a painful quiver. Flint's cat story from his accident pummeled my brain. "Is the homeless man okay?"

Steven chuckled, low and husky. "He's fine. He wasn't hurt at all. He stopped someone to call for help."

"Oh." Stabs of pain shot through my ribs on my lower right side. *Damn.* Broken ribs. "Remind me to find and thank him."

"You might owe him a bit more than that. If I were him, I'd be pissed at you for destroying my grocery cart and spraying my worldly possessions across Hollywood Boulevard."

"I'll replace everything." I jerked my chin toward the glass of water I spotted on the nearby bed table. "Water. Please?"

Steven grabbed the glass and stuffed the straw into my mouth.

I took slow, quenching sips. Nothing had ever tasted so good.

"Um... There's someone outside who wants to see you." His eyebrow arched upward but returned to neutral territory just as quickly. "He's been here all night. He was here before I was. But the nursing staff wouldn't let him in to see you because he's not a relative."

"Who?"

"Flint."

My heart split in two again, like it had been sliced with a Katana. Tears filled my eyes. He shouldn't be here. Not after what I'd said to him.

"He's the boyfriend, right? He told me you'd had a fight." He put the empty glass back on the table and took a seat beside me on the bed. He took my hand in his again and rested it against his knee. "I wasn't sure if you wanted to see him. I may not be around much, but when I am, I've gotta look out for my little sis."

"Thank you." I squeezed his fingers. "I miss you."

"Yeah. Me too. We need to change that, hey?"

"I'd like that."

"So . . ." He straightened his shoulders and thumbed toward the door. "You want to see this Flint guy, or shall I tell him to fuck off?"

The throb behind my left eye drilled through to the center of my head. What could I say to the guy whose heart I'd just broken? Who I hadn't listened to because I was too pigheaded and stubborn? Who I loved but couldn't be with?

I drew the blanket up higher over my waist and clutched at a handful of the soft waffle cotton. My chest shuddered. Flint hadn't done anything wrong. I had. All he'd ever done was care for me. Help me. Be everything I needed. *Fuck!* He deserved to know I was okay after I'd been an idiot and gotten in the car with Yasiv. He'd be freaking out, especially after losing his brother. "Yeah. Just for a few minutes."

"You want me to stay with you?"

"No. I'll be fine."

Steven leaned forward and kissed my forehead. "You just hit the emergency buzzer if you need me. I'll come running as fast as I can. After I've had a coffee."

"I'd kill for a cappuccino." I attempted to smile but even that hurt. *Shit, I'm a mess.*

"I'll bring one back for you." Steven stood and headed for the door. He paused and turned to face me. "I don't know this Flint guy. But Sutt, he loves you. Not sure if that helps or not."

No. It didn't. It made it worse.

Steven left the room. Before the door clicked shut, Flint strode in, still wearing his tux shirt and suit pants.

He tossed his jacket and bow tie onto the chair and rushed to my side. "Oh, Sutt." He kissed the top of my head, lingered there as he breathed me in like he always did. "I'm so glad you're okay," he murmured against my hair. "I'm sorry for fighting. For getting upset. For letting you leave with that asshole."

"Flint, this wasn't your fault. It's mine, all mine."

"I thought I'd lost you." He pressed his forehead against my brow. "When I heard you were in an accident, I went out of my freaking mind."

"How did you find out?"

He sank onto the chair beside my bed and took my hand in his. I was too tired to pull it away. Besides I didn't want to . . . his touch was comforting. Warm. Tender. The soft strokes of his thumb eased the throb inside my skull.

"When I was at Yasiv's."

"What?"

"After you took off, I was pacing the road outside the hotel. Once I called Cole and Slip, I dialed Yasiv's cell for his address, but he didn't answer. I called you, but you wouldn't pick up. I knew you were pissed at me, but I wasn't going to leave you with Yasiv. I asked everyone who walked past where he lived. No one had a clue. Then, this stretch limo pulls up beside me and the window winds down. Leo, with his cock half hanging out of his pants, leaned out of the car. The poor chick who'd just shagged the fuck out of him was still pulling on her dress beside him. But anyway. He recognized me and asked me if I needed a lift to the party. So I hitched a ride."

"To Yasiv's?"

"Yeah. I ended up somewhere in Beverly Hills. You weren't anywhere to be found. I panicked. Yasiv's car wasn't there, but it didn't stop me searching every room in the house. I've been to some insane parties, but man, the place was covered in blow. There were these topless chicks walking around in thongs, carrying trays lined with coke. Everyone was snorting lines. It was fucking nuts, and it scared the shit out of me when I couldn't find you."

My head hurt from information overload. But Flint had

gone after me? To make sure I was safe? Even after I'd broken up with him? "So how did . . . when did you get here?"

"Leo got a call. We jumped in a limo and arrived here just after one a.m."

"What's the time now?"

"Nine." Tiredness and exhaustion swam in his eyes, but he rubbed it away with his fingertips.

"Thank you." I wriggled the neck brace. *Damn* . . . that was fucking uncomfortable. "But you didn't have to come."

"Yes. I did." A smirk tugged at the corner of his mouth. "But you need to sack your brother as chief carer. Have you looked at yourself in a mirror?"

"No. Why?"

"You'd scare a bear right now. Your makeup has run everywhere. There's a bit of dried blood on some small cuts. Would you like me to get a hot washcloth and help clean your face? Unless Morticia Addams is the look you're going for."

What? God no. I blinked. Yes, mascara had clogged like glue on my lashes. At least someone had wiped away my vomit and stuffed me into a pale blue hospital gown.

Flint disappeared into the private bathroom and returned with a steaming cloth. I went to raise my good arm to take it, but pain sliced through my side. "Ow!"

"Broken ribs hurt like a bitch, don't they?" Understanding softened his eyes. He held up the face towel. "May I?"

I nodded.

He sat on the bed beside me and swiped my loose hair off my brow. He then dabbed, blotted, and removed the makeup and blood from my face. "The cuts are tiny. You won't have any scars. There . . . Done. Beautiful as always."

"Thank you."

But then deep grooves etched his forehead. "Did . . . did you get a burn from the seatbelt?" He touched the scar peeking out from the opened top buttons of his dress shirt.

"I don't know. I haven't looked." I didn't want a scar but deserved it if I did. It was my own stupid fault for going with Yasiv. "It hurts too much to move."

"It's fine. I just remember it stung like hell, resting my broken arm against my chest."

"Well, I don't have that." I adjusted my strapped wrist within my sling to rest more comfortably against my tummy.

"That's a good sign, then." He tossed the cloth on the nightstand. Turning to me, he entwined his fingers with mine. He drew them to his lips and kissed my knuckles. "Sutt?" Agony swayed in his tone. "About last night?"

"Flint?" I winced. "I don't want to do this now."

He looked at me through the fine strands of hair hanging over his eyes. The sadness rippling through them pierced my heart.

He rubbed his thumb over the back of my fingers. "Well, we are. Things got out of hand. We had a few too many drinks. We said some hot-headed things. But I meant what I said. I don't want to lose you just because you'll be on the other side of the country."

"It's not that simple." My voice was as meek as a lamb.

"It can be."

"No. It can't." I lowered my gaze to stare at the blanket. Looking at his gorgeous face hurt my heart too much. "It will be too hard. I want us to end on a high note. I loved being with you. We had so much fun and helped each other out. But it's over." My chin quivered, but I had to stay strong. "Can't you understand that? Our whole publicity stunt was about getting our lives and careers on track. We've done that. We weren't supposed to get involved."

"But we did." He softened his tone. "I fell in love with you. I know you feel the same way."

Shit. Why did he have to steal what was left of my heart? But I'd made my decision. "It doesn't matter. We can't do this. I won't do this."

The rims of his eyes reddened. Water pooled on the edges. "When are you gonna be honest with me?"

"I am. I'm protecting us to avoid being hurt down the track."

"You don't know that will happen. I want to give us a chance to find out."

"I. Don't. I can't." The muscles in my jaw ached from keeping it together.

"Fuck." He leaped from the bed and stormed over to the window. He stared at whatever street, building or tree was outside. Or maybe just nothing at all. He rested his hands on the sill and lowered his chin. "When do you move?"

"I'll sign the contract sometime this week. Then I'll move toward the end of October." If the show wasn't delayed with Yasiv out of action.

"So?" Hope jumped in his tone. "We could have another two months together."

"No. Don't make this harder than it already is."

"Why are you doing this?" He raked his fingers through his hair and paced the floor. "You're fighting for the wrong things. Career and money and lifestyle are great. I'm all for you following your dreams. I will support you no matter what. But none of those things matter if you don't have someone to share them with. Fight for us. Fight for what we have."

I was fighting. To protect my heart from total destruction. "We had a hot fling, Flint. That's it."

"It was more than that and you know it." He hissed through his teeth. "You won't trust me, but you're willing to move to some remote part of the world and put your livelihood in the hands of a drug-using director and producer?"

"No. I'm not." The truth was, I was scared. I didn't have to socialize with Yasiv and Leo outside of work. There'd be other people from the show to hang out with in Portland. But this incident had certainly been an eye-opener. I'd just have to be more careful. "My faith is in the studio, the writers, and the entire team that goes around making a show. Not just two people. I'm following my dreams. I don't need you to do that."

"You did." Steel set in his tone. "That's why you went out with me in the first place, right?"

"Yes. You played your part." *Damn.* It hurt just saying that.

"That's all I was to you?" Spite dripped from his tongue. "A part in your play?"

"Yes." *No, you were so much more. You were everything.* But I couldn't let him know that. I could feel my heart cracking.

"No." He stepped to the end of the bed and clutched the railing. "You don't throw away something like we have. Trust it. Trust the way you feel. If it is anything like I feel for you, we'll survive."

I wouldn't survive him breaking my heart. I cared for him too much. "Please. Just stop."

"No." He shook his head. "I always thought you were smart. I loved how you cared when you didn't have to. Loved that you helped me to find music again. I loved that you never gave up. But that is what you're doing now." He straightened. "You've done that since a few days ago, when I assume you started talking to this crowd about *Hollow Cove*. You didn't have the guts to talk to me about it." The distress in his voice pressed heavily against my sore ribs, making every breath cause me to ache. "You don't have the guts to stand up and fight for what you want. Which is me, not your stupid show. Stop being afraid to love me."

"Me? Afraid?" That riled a nerve. "You're such a hypocrite. All you are is afraid. You were afraid to leave your house. You were afraid to face life without Phil. You're afraid of people getting hurt or in trouble for making mistakes. You think you're doing the right thing and taking the blame for them when you shouldn't." Once the words rolled off my tongue, I couldn't stop. "You're controlling. You don't let people live and learn. You've got a bad reputation at the sake of others." The blows just kept coming. "You think *I'm* lying? You're the one not being honest. That's why your parents won't talk to you. They *do* blame you for Phil's death. Why don't you tell them the truth?"

Oh, shit! Where had that come from? I'd never vented before I'd met Flint. I went along with what everyone wanted to keep the peace and make everyone happy. Well . . . not anymore. I wanted to fight for what I wanted. Deep down, I'd meant every word I'd said. He wanted to air our issues? . . . Bring it.

Flint staggered back a step. The color drained from his face. "That's . . . different."

"How so?" I pinned him with my gaze. "Do you think it's noble to cover someone else's ass?"

"No. He was my brother." Flint slapped his hand against his chest. "I loved him. I wanted to protect him. *I* protected him."

"The guy just wanted to live his own fucking life. Get into trouble. Cause some havoc. But you took all his bad, stupid, dangerous antics away." I flicked my hand at Flint, ignoring the pain in my side. "You made him a saint when he seemed to be nothing but a dick most of the time." I hadn't known the guy, but from what I'd heard . . .

Flint's face contorted in pain. "He'd be in jail if it wasn't for me. Or rehab. Or . . . or . . ."

Dead?

"Yep." My tone still held bite. "Maybe. But that would've been the consequences of his mistakes. His choices. For him to learn from. But you covered everything up, smoothed everything over with your sweet talk, charm, and publicist on speed dial. Sometimes people take risks, fuck up, and pay the price. Like last night—it was my choice to go with Yasiv. Not yours."

"You could've been killed."

"Yep. Luckily, I wasn't." Thank God, I wasn't on the stairway to Heaven. I had so much I wanted to do and see. I was too young to die. "But look where I am? I hurt. All over." Even my toes ached when I wriggled them. I splayed my hand over my heart, dialed down my tone. "Flint, I love how protective you are, how passionate you are, how willing you were to do anything to move on after Phil. You've done that. I like to think I played a small part in helping. I care about you. So much. But it's Cole and Slip you need to thank—not me. They're the ones who gave you an ultimatum. They have stood by you and waited for you to get better. Now you're in a good place. Don't throw it away. Go. Play music. Write amazing songs. Get back on stage. Be the star you're meant to be."

He took a small step toward me. "Not without you."

"You don't need me anymore."

"It's not a need—it's a want." He shot forward, sat beside me, and seized my hand. "Why won't you let me love you? Why won't you let me in?"

"Because . . ." I tugged my hand free and set my heart on ice. I had to give him the performance of my life. "People who love you hurt you. The only person I can trust is me. I don't need you or anyone else to run my life."

"I'm not your father. I'm not a cheating asshole like Beau. I don't want to run your life; I want to be in it. Be part of it. Share it with you. Every up, down, high, low, and everything between."

Tears welled in my eyes. I wanted that too. But not from the other side of the country. I couldn't do that again. We weren't meant to be.

"Flint, enough." I sank into the pillow. "I'm tired. There is nothing you can say to change my mind. I'm moving to Maine. I want to remember the amazing time we had together—our first kiss, you running lines with me, eating home-delivered Italian, drinking vodka, and singing with you on stage. I want each and every one of those memories to stay special. Don't ruin them, please."

"Too late." Bitterness slid off his tongue. "You're just like my brother. You're afraid to tell me how you feel to my face. I know you love me. Yes, that's gonna have consequences. And raise issues we'd have to deal with. And bring up compromises we'd have to make. I'm willing to give you my all to make it work. But you won't even consider it. That's what hurts."

I stared at the window. "I never meant to hurt you."

"But you have." He rose to his feet and glared at me with too much pain in his eyes. Pain I'd caused. "I admired you for your strength and confidence and ambition to follow your dreams. But it's all just bullshit to hide how scared you are. All you've wanted is to be loved, noticed, and appreciated. That's what this publicity was all about, right? But no matter how many headlines you hit, or photos you have taken, or how many followers you have, none of that adoration is real. They don't know you." He stabbed his finger against the mattress. "Here I am, wanting the chance to love you, and you won't take it."

"I'm being realistic." I closed my eyes and took a deep breath. *Stay strong.* But my old wounds reopened. "We'll be on opposite sides of the country. We won't survive because there will always be some Rici, or a Georgia, or some girl you're photographed with that will make me question your integrity and then question myself. With no trust, there is no foundation to build on."

"When have I ever given you a reason not to trust me?" He clutched his hands against his head. "You can ask Slip or Cole or Blake, any of our crew, my damn publicist, my ex-girlfriends. Not one of them will be able to say I've cheated."

"Once burned, scarred for life."

"You're unbelievable. You're afraid to commit. Just like my exes were." His shoulders slouched. "You want to shut out love from your life? Fine. I'm done." He wiped his hand down his face and blinked the tears from his eyes. "I lost my way after losing Phil. But I'm better now, thanks to you and my friends. I don't want to shut myself off from the world. I love music too much. I love my band too much." He placed a tentative hand on my thigh. "I didn't want to fall in love during this publicity process. But I did. I fell in love with a girl who was fun, adventurous, and supportive. Kind and caring. She was always a touch nervous and anxious but willing to experience new things. Gorgeous and beautiful, inside and out." But then he drew his hand away. His eyes turned to solid ice and the temperature in the room plummeted. "But I guess she doesn't exist. It was all a lie to get what you wanted, right? An act? You're selfish, ruthless, and cold-hearted. Just like your friend Georgia."

I gaped. The virtual slap to my face stung. *Ouch.*

His lips twitched. "But lying to me, to my face, is worse. For that, you're just like your father."

What? A tear caught my cheek. The breath shot from my lungs as he plunged an arrow through my heart. "I am not."

"Save it. I'm glad you're okay after the accident. I feared the worst. But if you aren't willing to give us a chance and honestly don't love me, there's no point in me being here." He swiped his jacket and bow tie off the chair and charged for the door. "So fuck you. Have a nice life. Goodbye, Sutton."

I trembled all over. "Flint? Wait."

He didn't stop. He didn't look back.

Shit. Shit. Shit.

Tears streamed down my face. *No. Stop.*

No matter how much I wanted to pull him into my arms, kiss him, love him, I couldn't. Not from Maine.

I had to let him go.

I had to.

I couldn't put my faith in someone and let them take care of me. I had to learn to stand on my own. I couldn't do that if he was with me.

This was for the best.

So why did it hurt so bad?

Chapter 31

FLINT

Floating on a giant blow-up flip-flop, I drifted around my pool. I put the vodka to my lips and took a swig. The cool liquid slid down my throat, burning me from the inside out. Cole and Slip floated next to me, downing beer. For the past two and a half days, they'd crashed at my place to help me drink Hollywood out of booze. Judging by the quantity of empty beer and vodka bottles covering the tables and lying beside the pool, we must have come close.

It was near midnight on Monday. I pushed my dark sunglasses higher onto the bridge of my nose to block the bright blue LED lights shining beneath the pool's surface. I needed darkness. Something to match the heaviness in my chest.

Heartbreak sucked.

Since the awards show on Friday night when Sutton had stomped on my heart, spat it out, and shredded it to a pulp, the Internet had been flooded with a mix of truths and lies about the shit show that went down at the hotel and her accident. I was made out to be a psycho for throwing myself in front of Yasiv's car to stop him driving off. Sutton had been slandered with scandal that said she'd dumped me for Yasiv and had fallen further and further from grace. Yasiv was reported to have had nothing but a small unfortunate accident. Bet his fucking publicists and lawyers controlled that ton of bullshit that had been fed to the media.

But Sutton wanted to deal with her own mistakes and PR nightmare, so I let her.

I was done.

I was sure the rip in my heart would heal once I reached the bottom of this bottle. No girl was worth this amount of grief.

Slip flicked his toe in the water, splashing me with the spray. "Are you gonna call her? Or are we just gonna spend the rest of our days and nights wasted?"

I lowered my sunglasses and glared at him like he was a fucking moron. "I'm not calling her. It's over."

"It would suck having a girlfriend on the other side of the country." Cole sipped his beer. "But I was kinda looking forward to spending some time in New York, renting a shack in Maine, and getting outta LA for a while."

I'd told them that in the heat of the moment when trying to reason with Sutton, I'd said we'd move. The guys had loved the idea.

I repositioned my glasses over my sore, dry, dehydrated-from-too-much alcohol eyes. "It would've been fun. But not meant to be."

Cole rested his head back onto his inflated sloth pool toy and dragged his fingertips across the surface of the water, creating swirls and ripples. "She was the best thing that happened to you in forever, man. Next to us, of course."

"Yeah, well, shit happens." I pushed off the edge of the pool and floated across the water at a lazy pace.

"No. I mean it." Cole grabbed a fresh beer out of the cooler by the steps and cracked it open. "You two clicked. You had chemistry. A connection. A vibe that rocked. The way you looked at each other was wicked."

A muffled, high-pitched laugh escaped me. "You're fucking drunk. You always spin shit when you are."

Slip splashed Cole. "He's a sap. That's why he can't keep a girl either."

"You can talk, asshole." Cole scooped and tossed water at Slip.

All-out war broke out. They hammered each other with splashes.

I held up my hands to stop being hit in the face by the spray, although the cool droplets were welcome in the hot evening.

After they stopped dousing each other with water, Slip waved his beer at me. "So . . . before I pass out again, what do we have to do to help you get over Sutton? Set you up on another blind date? Take you out and get some other girl to suck your dick? Play 'November Rain' by the Gunners once again? For the hundredth time?"

God. I loved these guys. I didn't need a date or a blow job. But I could listen to Guns N' Roses on repeat all fucking day long. They were legends.

But for now, I was done.

"Nothing. I'm gonna crash." I placed my near-empty bottle of vodka on the side of the pool, rolled off my pool toy, and splashed into the water. I sank to the bottom. Cool water surrounded me. I didn't feel heavy. Maybe I should just stay there. It was quiet. Dark. Peaceful. But my mind raced. Lyrics and music wouldn't stop pounding my head. I hadn't slept in days. I needed to stop thinking. Feeling. Hurting. But staying here wouldn't help.

I rose to the surface. Sucking in air, I wiped the water from my face. I dragged myself over to the steps and climbed out of the pool. "You guys good? I'll catch you in the morning."

"No worries, man." Slip raised his beer. "We'll finish these drinks, then come inside."

"Get some sleep," Cole called out to me.

I just waved and headed for my room.

After showering, I slipped into bed. 12:34 a.m. blazed bright green on my bedside clock. *Sleep. Just sleep.* I closed my eyes and let the vodka lure me under.

But not for long.

My eyes shot open. 2:07 a.m. stared back at me from the clock. *Shit!* That was the longest period of sleep I'd had in days. My mind raced. Sutton. Phil. Music.

Fuck this.

I got up, grabbed my phone, and headed down the hall. Rubbing my eyes, I crashed against the wall. Oh, yeah . . . I was still wasted. I stopped outside my music room and stared at the door. I had to get the pounding inside my head out of my system.

I crashed into the studio, staggered over to the sofas, and sank onto the floor. I ran my hand over the rug where Sutton had gotten me to play. To say lyrics. Where we'd had steamy sex. My heart shuddered. I couldn't believe she was gone. Just like Lena, she'd left to follow her dreams. Dreams that never included me.

Maybe I was jinxed.

I was doomed from the start. A fool to fall for an actress.

But damn. She'd weaved her way into my heart.

Despite loving her, I'd played my part in driving her away. Just liked I'd done to Phil. I'd been overprotective. I shouldn't have jumped into damage control and released that press statement after our drunken night out at Hayley's. We should've discussed it first. I shouldn't have accused her of being like her dad and Georgia in the heat of the moment . . . because she wasn't like them at all. She'd always been upfront and honest with me about her career, intentions, and where we stood. I just hadn't listened. I hadn't wanted us to end.

I picked up the guitar I'd left beside the sofa and placed it across my lap. I closed my eyes and glided my fingers across the strings. Stretching my neck from side to side, I let the music go where it wanted to go. Lyrics formed in my head. I let my heart take the lead. The tune came out soft, slow, sad.

> *I never thought I'd end up like this,*
> *Dreaming about what could've been.*
> *I never thought you would ever leave,*
> *I always thought we were meant to be.*
> *I never thought you'd break my heart,*
> *Never thought it would hurt this much.*
> *I never ever wanted to see you cry,*
> *Seeing you walk away packed a punch.*

But then I strummed the strings harder. Angrier. Louder.

> *Now all I do is long for your touch.*
> *All I do is miss you too much.*
> *I want to hold you in my arms again,*
> *Whisper sweet things I can't contain.*
> *But instead . . .*
> *My bed grows colder. My heart grows over.*
> *Each breath hurts my chest. There is nothing of me left.*
> *But . . . if I had the chance.*
> *I'd fall for you . . . all over again.*

I played for hours. I wrote and recorded some of the lyrics on my cell phone. By 5:07 a.m., exhaustion consumed me. I crawled onto the sofa, tugged a cushion underneath my head, and closed my eyes.

My mind was a calm sea instead of a squalling ocean. Despite the new emptiness in my chest, I felt the best I had in days. The tension in my neck had eased.

I'd preserved myself in vodka since Sutton had left. That had given me time to breathe. Time to access what had happened. Time to accept that I wasn't what Sutton wanted. But . . . she had helped me. I'd found music again, and that was the one thing I could never live without. Music was what I needed most.

And sleep.

Finally, I fell under.

The door burst open, jolting me awake. Licking my parched lips, I groaned at the stench of my foul breath. Something dead had crawled into my mouth and taken up residence. *Ergh.* I needed water.

Cole and Slip staggered toward me in their T-shirts and boxer shorts, carrying cold-pressed juices and an Uber Eats bag of food. The scent of bacon hit me. *God.* These guys were saviors.

"Hey?" Cole handed me a breakfast wrap. "Lunchtime."

"Geez." I sat upright, grabbed the food in one hand, and rubbed my eyes with the other. "What time is it?" I glanced at my cell phone on the floor. *Shit!* 1:12 p.m. Now that was a decent sleep.

Slip sank onto the sofa beside me. Cole took the floor and dug into the food.

"You get some writing done?" Cole looked at me as he devoured his wrap.

"Yeah. Nothing serious." I cracked open the juice lid. "But it was therapeutic." More than I'd anticipated.

I downed half my bottle. My body sang hallelujah in thanks for the rehydration. But as I put the drink down, my gaze fell onto Phil's bass, still lying on the sofa behind Cole. Memories of Phil playing in here, at shows and events, stumbled through my fuzzy head. The ache in my chest flared, but . . . it wasn't crippling. In fact, it wasn't unbearable at all. As we ate our wraps, the tightness in my body eased.

"You wanna get out of here today?" Slip asked, licking bacon grease and ketchup from his fingers. "Hit the beach?"

"No." I finished the last mouthful of my wrap and tossed the paper in the bag. I slid back onto the sofa and stared at my notebook lying open on the coffee table. It was full of the lyrics I'd scribbled down last night. Words of heartache and loss. Things I didn't want to rule my life anymore. "But there is something I would like to do." I took a deep breath and rubbed my hands down my thighs. I checked my heart and my head to make sure it wasn't just my hangover talking. *No . . .* I was ready. "I'll need your help. Will you help me sort and pack Phil's crap in here?"

The air stilled. Solemnness set in.

Concern flickered in Slip's eyes. He ruffled his fingers through his long hair, then rubbed and wiped his face. "You mean that?"

"Yeah." I nodded. "It's time."

"I-I've never done anything like that before. I've never had to pack away someone's belongings." Cole lowered his chin and rubbed his chest. He took a deep breath and let it out slowly. "But okay. What do you want us to do?"

Phil had been a huge part of their lives. This wouldn't be easy on them either.

I'd drowned and drunken Sutton out of my heart.

Now it was time to put Phil to rest.

"Let me freshen up and we'll get started."

After showering, I dressed in ripped jeans and an old white T-shirt, and headed out into my garage. I collected half a dozen storage boxes that had been stowed behind some of our music trunks. Balancing them in my arms, I halted in front of my Ferrari. The shiny silver bonnet gleamed before me. Visions of eating Sutton out on it flickered before my eyes. I could smell her sweet skin. I could taste her on my tongue. Feel her thighs quivering around my face. *Damn.* That night had been hot. The embers in my chest threatened to ignite. But I stood on them, snuffing them out.

She was gone.

I made my way into the music room and dropped the boxes on the floor near my mic. Cole and Slip had changed into fresh cargo shorts and T-shirts. They leaned against the desk with their arms folded, waiting for my direction.

I stuffed my hands into my pockets and scanned the room. *Where do I start?* So many memories were held within these walls. I'd bought this house after our first album. I'd spent nearly every spare dime on renovating it and building this studio. I'd written most of our second album in this room. I'd spent hours in here with the guys playing, writing, and rehearsing. Now it was time to pack a piece of our history away, then move forward.

"Cole, do you want to go through the desk, find all his notebooks, and pack them into a box? Slip?" My heart shuddered. "Would you pack his guitars into their cases?"

"Sure." Slip rubbed the back of his head and ambled over to the equipment. "What are you going to do with them?"

I let out a shaky breath. I could do this. "There are three. Would you each like one? To remember him by?"

Cole pressed his fingers into his eyes and sniffled. "Yeah. That would be awesome."

I walked over to the sofa where Phil's favorite bass lay. I picked it up and ran my fingers over the strings, neck, and the body. Phil had loved this bass. It had been his pride and joy. A red custom-made Fender. The leather strap was signed by Adam Clayton from U2, his idol. We'd met Bono and his band in Vegas. Even I'd been starstruck at meeting them that night.

In my head, I could hear Phil playing his bass, low and dirty. Fast and freaky. Cruisy and cool. So much talent . . . gone too soon. "I'm claiming this one." I spun it around in my hands. The smooth, sleek surface shimmered in the light. "I'm gonna get it framed and hang it on that wall." I pointed to an empty spot beside some of our platinum album plaques. "Over there. Is that okay with you guys?"

"Sure." Slip said, wrapping and rolling up a power cord around his arm.

Cole stared at the guitar, then nodded.

"Cool. I want it to be a reminder of how far we've come, the good times we've had, and the music we've made."

I didn't want to tarnish the good memories of Phil. I wanted to remember him for his fun-loving rowdy ways. Maybe Sutton was right; I had been overprotective of him. I'd been afraid of him getting into trouble. But I loved him. There were so many things that should've been said but weren't. So many what-ifs, buts, and whys that would never be answered. He was gone but would never be forgotten. I would never regret protecting him, loving him, and having some of the best times of my life with him. His music and laugh would be embedded in my soul forever. That would be Phil's legacy—not the last couple of dark months where he'd been affected by drugs. That couldn't destroy twenty-two years of being brothers. Our love ran deeper than that.

I packed the bass away in its case, clipped it shut, and stood it against the wall behind the desk to take down to the framing shop.

As I collected Phil's items off the coffee table and placed them into a box, Cole sniffled and sobbed. He clutched Phil's hoodie that had been on the chair against his face and squatted.

Tears pooled in my eyes. I rushed over to him, pulled him to his feet, and hugged him. "Hey. It's gonna be okay."

"I miss him," Cole mumbled against my shoulder. "So fucking much."

I let the tears roll down my cheeks. "Me too."

Slip joined our hug. "Every day."

I stood there, embracing my friends, until our tears stopped. I'd survive anything with these two guys.

"Okay." Cole broke the group hug and wiped his damp cheeks. "I'm good. No more tears over Phil. This is it. He rocked. Let's move on."

"Fuck yeah." Slip slapped Cole's hand, and they pumped their fists together. The rims of his eyes blazed red from his tears. He turned to me. "You good?"

I dabbed my eyes with the sleeve of my T-shirt. I sucked in a deep breath and glanced around the room, now void of Phil's items. My heart was heavy but not down and out. "Yeah. Wanna jam for a bit?"

"Fuck yeah." Slip clapped and clasped his hands together.

But just as I reached for my guitar, the doorbell chimed.

"You expecting someone?" Cole asked, heading for his drums.

"No." I headed for the door. "I'll be back in a sec."

I meandered down the hallway, ruffling my fingers through my hair, then rubbing my sore eyes to clear them. After a three-day binge on booze and takeout, I probably looked like a demented demon.

I yanked the door open. My eyes widened. "Blake? What the fuck are you doing here?"

Chapter 32

FLINT

"Hey, Flint." Blake stepped past me and veered toward my living room.

"Come on in." Sarcasm rolled off my tongue as I shut the door behind him.

"The guys here?" Blake shrugged off his suit coat and tossed it over the back of the sofa. He undid his tie and popped open the top button of his shirt. "Their cars are outside."

"Yeah." I thumbed toward the hallway. "They're in the music room. Want me to get them?"

"Yes. Please."

From where I stood, I hollered over my shoulder, ""Boys? Blake's here."

Blake winced. "Too loud."

I just grinned.

"You got something to drink?" He scanned me up and down and looked at the clutter of empty bottles and food containers lying on nearly every surface. "Or have you drunk it all?"

"Never." I smirked. "You want a beer or something harder?"

"Beer."

As the guys came into the living room and greeted Blake, I grabbed four longnecks from the fridge. There was nothing like another alcoholic beverage to cure a hangover. I cruised over to join them on the sofas and gave everyone a drink. I cracked open my bottle, put my feet up on the coffee table, and took a sip. "So, to what do we owe the pleasure of a house call on a Tuesday afternoon? Is this prep for our meeting tomorrow?"

Blake sat on the edge of the seat. His leg jiggled. Sweat broke out on his brow. His gaze darted from me, to Cole, to Slip, and then back to me again.

My skin prickled. The hairs on the back of my neck stood on end.

"I didn't see this coming." Blake grimaced.

"See what?" Slip picked at his beer label.

"I was called into an urgent meeting this morning at WestTyme Records." Blake closed his eyes and shook his head. "I never expected, in my wildest dreams, that this gig would backfire."

"Blake?" My pulse quickened. "What's happened?"

"They're dropping you. Canceling your contract."

"What the fuck?" Cole shot forward. "They can't do that."

"They can. And they have." Blake rolled his bottle between his hands.

"On what grounds?" I asked.

"Based on you, Flint." Anguish drawled through Blake's Texan accent. "They've seen everything you've done over the past couple months as reckless, out-of-control behavior." Blake seethed. "Instead of seeing you pulling your shit together by attending high-profile events and schmoozing with Hollywood's elite, they've seen you as nothing but a drunk at after-parties, downing too much vodka in bars. They've seen pictures of girls fighting over you at night clubs, and then, the other night, you losing your shit at Yasiv. That's not the image or the kind of artist they want their company to represent."

I slammed my beer down on the table and buried my hands in my hair. "They dropped us?" I couldn't draw breath. My pulse pounded in my ears. *No. No. No.*

"They haven't seen you on stage for months—only that impromptu performance a few weeks back with Sutton. You haven't played a gig anywhere. You've been blocked, unable to write a song in months and don't have demos to turn in tomorrow. These assholes only care about how much dime they're pulling in. They've seen all this publicity we've created as you not caring about music."

"What the fuck?" I leaped to my feet and paced across the floor. "That's bullshit. That's why I did it."

My chest constricted. My gut cinched. Music was all I had left.

"I know." Blake rubbed the back of his neck. "I had our lawyers trying to find a loophole, but the clauses defining artist moral conduct and behavior gave them grounds."

Shit! I knew about the clause. Excessive drug use, alcohol abuse, breaking the law, or any destructive behavior that could insult or offend the execs were grounds for termination. That was why I'd protected Phil so much. I'd never wanted them to have reason to cut us. "So that's it." The thud in my head grew louder and louder. "No negotiation? No talking to me? No second-chance discussions? That's just it. Bang. You're out."

"They gave us a warning. That was when we had that intervention for you to get your shit together."

"I have." I flicked my hand at Blake. "Can't you see that?"

He arched one eyebrow and glanced around the room. "Really? I'm not seeing it. I'm not feeling it."

Okay. The place looked like a gazillion raccoons had had one wicked party and trashed my home. "Oh, no. This"—I waved my hand around the room—"is the result of dating Sutton."

"She left him." Slip flopped back on the sofa. "We're helping him drown his sorrows."

Cole chinked his beer against Slip's bottle. "Here's to that."

"Oh, shit." Blake dragged his hand down his face. "Flint. I'm sorry. You two are good together."

"*Were*," I snapped. "So now I can play." I counted on my fingers. "I can sing. Since Friday night, I've been writing lyrics till they're coming out of my ass. But so what? This was all for nothing?" My heart crumpled to the floor. "I have no girlfriend and no record deal. This is just fucking great." Could my life get any more fucked up?

Blake straightened. "You wrote lyrics?"

"Yes." I drilled my palms against my eyes. "I can't turn them off." The words I'd written at the awards show had been about loving Sutton and accepting Phil's death. But since then, they'd morphed into sad, depressing, angry, heart-wrenching love songs. Adele had nothing on me.

"That's great news." Blake clutched his knees.

"Can't we go back to them? I can send them some songs, raw-cut demos . . . maybe by the end of next week?"

"Flint, I'm sorry. It's too late." Blake's eyes hooded further. "And I'm sorry it didn't work out with Sutton. No one likes to be dumped."

No shit, Sherlock.

"Please believe me." Blake splayed his hand across his chest. "I tried every angle to get them to revoke their decision. But they wouldn't." He sipped his beer, then stared toward the coffee table. "I feel responsible. It was Harlow's and my idea to get you and Sutton out on the town." He glanced at the guys, then at me. "I will do everything in my power to make it up to you. I won't sleep until I find you a new deal."

I stabbed my finger at Blake. "I'm gonna hold you to that."

"No. Not just any deal," Cole snapped. "We want it to be

better than our last one. We want to tour, and not just on the festival circuit and across the States. We go global."

"I'm on it." Blake bobbed his head.

"And no more setups." I sank onto the sofa. "I'm gonna send you my cleaner's bill. Just because you fucked with my life. Our life."

"I'll be happy to pay it. It stinks in here." Blake downed his beer, then rose to his feet. "I gotta go. I have to get across town to another meeting. I'm sorry to be the bearer of bad news. But I promise I'll find you a new label."

Blake patted me on the shoulder, slapped the other guys' hands, then saw himself out.

As the front door clicked shut, reality hit me. Nausea pooled in the bottom of my gut. I'd lost my brother. My parents. Sutton. Our record deal. All because what I'd thought was right was wrong. *Fuck!* I turned to the guys sitting shell-shocked on the sofa. "I'm sorry."

"What for?" Slip jerked his chin back.

Why wasn't he mad? Why wasn't he yelling at me for fucking up? "The publicity with Sutton backfired. I lost our contract."

"Flint." He leaned forward and rested his elbows on his knees. "We were involved in setting you up with her. We went out to Dalton's and Hayley's Bar with you. We bribed and convinced Sutton to make you sing. We drank. We partied. We had fun. This isn't all on you. We contributed to the bullshit that WestTyme is using against us."

What Sutton said to me at the hospital slammed into my head. *Stop taking the blame for everything. Let people make their own mistakes. Own them. Deal with the consequences.* My heart thudded against my ribs. These guys were my life. I didn't want them to suffer because of my actions.

Dizziness swarmed in my head. Spiraled. Swirled. But I took a deep breath and let the storm squalling in my mind settle.

If my friendship with Cole and Slip was as strong as I thought it was, it was time to rely on them more. As we were a united band, I didn't have to take on every burden. It went against every grain in my body not to bear the blame, but . . . I let Slip and Cole own this. "Yeah, you fuckers. You did."

Cole chuckled and placed his empty beer on the table. "It's about time you stopped being so hard on yourself. We've all done shit over the past few years that pissed our label off. These last couple months just gave them the excuse they needed to get rid of us. Yes, it sucks bison balls. But you know what? I'd sooner have you playing, writing, and jamming with us than not. If losing our contract was the price we had to pay to get you back, I'd do it again any day."

"You're nuts. But thank you," I said. "I love you two more than anything. But next time you come up with some crazy shit to get my head out of my ass, don't involve a woman."

"Deal." Slip scratched his scruffy cheek. "So, now what?"

"Let's go jam." I slapped my hands against my thighs, then stood. "We can't fuck that up, right?"

After playing for a few hours and reheating pizza for dinner, I staggered out to the pool and sank onto one of my sun loungers. Late evening had blanketed LA in twinkling lights and darkness. Aerosmith's greatest hits played softly through my sound system. Something about Steven Tyler's raspy voice hit my soul.

Maybe it was just music.

No. It was more than that.

I rested my head against the sun lounger and breathed LA in.

Visions of being on stage filled my head—small venues like the Lodge Room; big ones like Hollywood Bowl; at festivals in places like Palm Springs; being on TV for promo; and playing in Vegas for the Billboard Awards.

I wanted to play live. I wanted the buzz from performing to ignite my veins. The hype to feed the fire in my heart. I wanted to entertain crowds overflowing with fans.

I needed to sing.

I'd lost so much but learned a great deal about myself since Phil's death. I had fallen into an abyss. But I was back. I had to thank Sutton for some of that. No . . . most of it.

Every time she crossed my mind, the center of my chest ached. I hurt. I missed her. But . . . I didn't want to reach for the vodka or crawl back into bed and lock myself away from the world anymore. She'd been good for me. But just like I'd decided to do with Phil, I would remember the good times, not the bad. *Fuck.*

Cole and Slip joined me outside and sat side by side on the sun lounger next to me.

"You okay?" Cole asked.

"Yeah." I nodded. "I am actually."

"Tomorrow . . ." Slip scratched the tip of his chin, his tone a touch tentative. "Rather than just jam, do you want to pull any of these lyrics you've been working on into something? Try to compose a song? It will be easier to shop for a new deal if we have some fresh material."

"Yeah . . . It will." But that wasn't where my head was at, right at that moment. I swung around on the seat and placed my feet on the ground. I rubbed my hands together. The embers in my belly grew hotter. I wanted to feed them. "But what would you say to getting Blake to book us some shows? Just two or three small gigs. Nothing outrageous—just to ease back into the game."

Cole straightened and sliced his fingers into his hair. His eyes widened. "Are you serious?"

"I'm sorry I didn't get to this point in time to keep our label happy. But . . . I'm ready. I want to be on stage with you. Playing.

Feeding off the crowds like we used to do." I lowered my chin and scratched the back of my head. "I'm not ready to find a permanent bassist yet. We'll just ask a friend to fill in for us or hire a session musician for now. Are you cool with that?"

"Yeah, man. Of course." Cole may have kept his voice in chill mode, but the dim lights caught the excitement jumping in his eyes. "We'll fill Phil's shoes when we're ready. But for now, let's fucking play some gigs."

"Abso-fucking-lutely." Slip hooked his arm around Cole's shoulders and shook him. "Arrrrgh! This is freaking awesome."

I caught Slip's contagious energy and grinned. "It will be." It was time to take another baby step. Again, Sutton's words, not mine. Deep down, I knew I needed to take quite a few. "But there are several other things I need to do as well."

"Like what? Can we help?" Cole asked.

"After today, I'm not drinking anymore . . . well . . . maybe not so much." My liver would thank me for that. "I need a clear head to write. I want to get out and see some more live bands. Then, I also need to eat better, get fit, and go surfing before it gets too cold."

"I'm down with that." Cole nodded. "We could all do with a detox."

Cole would probably be on my doorstep in the morning to drag me out for a run.

Slip socked Cole in the ribs. "Speak for yourself, asshole. I'm in for surfing, seeing more bands, and playing with you pricks. Nothing else."

"I can handle that." I rose to my feet. Chuckling, I waggled my finger toward the front door. "Now, get the fuck out of my house. Anyone would think you lived here."

The guys jumped to their feet and hugged me.

"We're gone." Cole slapped my shoulder. "But we'll be back here at eleven to play and call Blake."

After the guys grabbed their belongings and headed home, I cruised around cleaning up, putting bottles into the recycling garbage can, and throwing out the trash. I puffed air through my nose. All this was over a girl.

But, like always, Cole and Slip had been there for me.

And I'd always have their backs. Laughing, I shook my head. I wouldn't take the fall for them anymore. No more lying. Within reason, of course. They were my bros. But I had to thank Sutton for opening my eyes. I never wanted another Phil situation on my hands.

That left me with one huge task. To be able to move forward, I had to right a wrong. Be honest. And in doing so, I hoped I could salvage a vital relationship. Or at least, it would give me final closure.

I closed my eyes and took a deep breath.

Yep.

I needed a couple of days to pull everything together.

But then . . . I had to go see my parents.

Chapter 33

SUTTON

Sitting with my legs sprawled out in front of me on my sofa, I stared at the endless ocean. Sunlight sparkled on the surface like someone had spilled diamonds on the sheet of gray-blue satin. Seagulls darted along the shoreline. People frolicked in the water. But summer was almost over. No bright rays hit my heart. No gentle breeze whipped up my smile.

It had been five days since the accident. Five days since my world had imploded. Five days since I'd driven Flint away.

Every time I closed my eyes, the image of him that had burned into my brain—him, standing outside the hotel with the color drained from his face and the darkness swallowing his gorgeous blue eyes—made me cringe. Yep, the moment I broke his heart haunted me. I couldn't sleep, eat, or venture outside my condo.

But my frightening accident competed against Flint for real estate in my mind. Like Flint, I remembered every moment of the crash—the car connecting with the grocery cart, the blurred, spinning world, the screaming, screeching tires, the breaking glass, the airbags suffocating me. How did Flint survive being able to remember every second of his brother's death? I'd been banged up badly; so had Yasiv. But we'd both be okay.

Steven walked out of my spare room and dropped his bag on the floor. He came over and ruffled the top of my head. "Sutt, it's time for me to head off."

"Thank you for staying." I grabbed and clutched his hand against my shoulder. It had been so sweet of him to look after me for a few days after the doctor had released me from the hospital. "You got everything?"

"Yeah. You going to be okay?"

"Always."

I'd loved spending time with my brother. Hearing him rattle on about his work as a graphic interface designer for a logistics software company, took my mind off Flint. I had no idea what half the terminology he used meant and didn't really understand what he did, but he loved his job. He'd bought a house and a dog, and he was between girlfriends. My brother was cool . . . for a geek. We'd made new promises to see each other more often now our father didn't meddle in our lives.

"Catch ya, sis." Steven hugged me goodbye and headed out the door. It clicked closed. The emptiness and quiet of my condo settled around me.

I was alone.

Maddy was away filming in Vancouver. Harlow had visited me once. Other than that, no one had come by. I had no other close friends. No other family.

I had the rest of the week off work before I had to be back on set to finish filming *Brentwood*. A couple of broken ribs, bruises, and scratches wouldn't keep me down. My neck was still sore, but I could get around easily enough. Thank goodness for painkillers. I didn't miss the underlying tone in the calls and texts I'd had from fellow cast members. Everyone was pissed at me for delaying the wrap by a week. I was pissed at myself.

I just wanted it over with and to move on with my life. To pack up my belongings and move across the country to start my new role.

I needed to get away from the city that had caused me nothing but heartache.

I needed distance from Flint.

Everywhere reminded me of him—the drive to Hollywood, my favorite coffee shop, the beach. My heart hurt enough without memories being thrown at me from all directions.

I'd hated lying to him. Hating hurting him. How I felt about him wasn't a lie—only the dribble that had come out of my mouth was.

Was he right? Could we have worked long-distance?

Had I made a mistake?

Maine wasn't like New York. Portland was a bitch to get to. There were no direct flights from LA. My bones ached at the thought of the six-hour flight plus a stopover.

I didn't want him to pack up his life and move. That was insanity. His career was here in LA. We would've made the effort to see each other a few times, but then, the spark would've faded. We would've constantly been worried about each other and grown tired of traveling and scheduling our lives around each other.

But no reasoning could overrule the truth behind the melancholy in my heart. My feelings for Flint would never fade. I'd always love him. It would've been my insecurities that killed us. It would've been the fact that I couldn't stand to see online photos of him with other girls and fans at parties or when he performed or promoted his music. Deep down, it wasn't just a matter of trust. *I* was the problem. I'd be jealous that I couldn't be there with him. I'd worry I wasn't enough for him. It would eat me up inside, twist and taint what we had. Destroy us.

He didn't deserve that.

He needed to live a fabulous life and not worry about me.

I'd pushed him away to save us from further heartache.

He'd hate me now, but he'd soon realize I was right.

I'd deal with this pain now if it meant he'd be happy in the long run.

Pity my heart didn't agree with me.

My cell phone buzzed. Harlow's name lit the screen. I groaned and clutched my sore ribs as I grabbed it off the coffee table. I swiped to answer. "Hey, Harlow. What's up?"

"Hey, little lady. Are you able to come to the office? We have some business to discuss."

His tone was flat, unemotional. I couldn't tell if it was good business or bad. But . . . he should have my final offer for *Hollow Cove*. Excitement rippled beneath my skin. "Sure. I'm going stir-crazy staring at my four walls. I could be there in an hour."

"Perfect. See you then."

I hauled myself to my feet, showered, and dressed in a simple top, knee-length skirt, and killer high heels. I dabbed on a light dusting of makeup to cover the fading yellow bruises on my face, painted bright red lipstick onto my lips, then caught an Uber to Harlow's office. I wasn't supposed to drive for six weeks. *Stupid broken ribs.*

The driver dropped me off in the lot at the rear of Harlow's building on Melrose. I grabbed my purse and headed inside. Eden, the receptionist, waved me on through to Harlow's office.

I knocked on the open door.

"Sutton?" Harlow rose to his feet behind his huge, dark wooden desk. He rushed around and kissed me hello on the cheek. "How are the ribs?"

"Sore." I took a seat on his L-shaped black leather sofa. "I sneezed last night and thought I'd been shot. I dropped to the floor and cried for ten minutes, clutching my side."

"Ouch. Sounds excruciating. I wish you a speedy recovery."

He held out his palm toward me. "Can I get you something to drink? Coffee? Water? Juice?"

"No. I'm good."

"Alrighty then." He grabbed a thin manilla folder off his desk and took the adjacent seat.

I didn't like the unsettling jitter in his eyes. Had the studio refused my request for them to cover relocation costs? I didn't think that had been an unreasonable requirement.

"So?" I placed my hands on my lap. "What's the news?"

Harlow tapped the folder against his hand. *Tap. Tap. Tap.* "Do you want the good news or the bad?"

I could pay for my move if I had to. "Start with the good news. Is the final offer through for *Hollow Cove*?"

"That's the bad news." Harlow's voice nosedived as he placed the folder onto the coffee table. "There will be no offer."

"What?" My heart pummeled my splintered ribs. I couldn't draw in air. My ears rang. Had I heard him correctly? "No offer? But they gave me the role. We've been in negotiations to complete the contract. What . . . what the hell?"

"Unfortunately, the studio and Yasiv's lawyers have had to go to extremes to keep his charges and stint in rehab out of the headlines. Without Yasiv, production will be delayed. This is his show. He's sourced and secured most of the funding. They don't want a temporary director; Yasiv's too good. They're standing by him and supporting his recovery."

"Okay. How long will production be delayed? I can wait. It's not like I have plans."

"It's not just that." Harlow's dark brown eyes turned black. "Yasiv has had a change of heart after the accident and has selected an alternative candidate."

Tears pooled in my eyes. "But that's insane. Yasiv loved my audition. He was excited about me coming on-board at the award show. What happened?"

Oh . . . no. Nausea flooded my gut, bubbling and gurgling like boiling glue. *Did this have to do with the conversation in the car?*

Yep!

A tear inched down my cheek. I was quick to swipe it away. "Shit. In the car . . . before the accident . . . he said some things. Maybe I didn't get the part because I wouldn't snort cocaine? I wasn't the wild rock star party girl they'd expected me to be? I didn't *stroke* Leo's ego?" I still questioned whether Yasiv meant socially or sexually. The latter made me cringe. "I lost the job because I'm not like that?"

"Oh shit, Sutt." Concern hooded Harlow's eyes. "I would've never put you up for the part if I'd known he was like that."

The pounding in my head thudded like airplane wheels speeding down a runway. "This whole publicity stunt has caused nothing but problems. It was supposed to help me not fuck things up further."

I should sue Yasiv for . . . for what? Defamation of character? Having a clean nose? For him revoking a verbal offer? I'd be the laughingstock of Hollywood. When was I going to learn not to trust anyone in this business? That was why Harlow hadn't been able to find any dirt on Yasiv and Leo . . . Their heavyweight lawyers covered their white powder trail. There was no way I could sue. I had no grounds and after everything that went down with my father, I wanted to avoid lawyers like peak-hour traffic on the I-405. I never wanted to work with people who thought I was something that I wasn't.

Shit! Flint had been right. Dating him had helped me discover what I wanted and who I was. I wasn't a rock star's girlfriend. I wasn't a wild, reckless party animal. I wasn't willing to take drugs for a part. But I loved having a good time with my true friends. I'd grown stronger, more confident, more outspoken. I was more adventurous and bolder. I'd learned I didn't need the fancy things in life all the time. I didn't want to give people the wrong impression. I was sweet and kind and caring. *God* . . . I *was* my TV persona.

"Now I know why my colleagues said nothing." Harlow shook his head as if daunted by my revelations. "They were probably under legal gag orders and confidentiality agreements like we are. I'm so sorry."

"It's not your fault." I flicked the tear off my cheek with my fingertips. "That role was mine. I can't believe it's all turned to shit." I'd broken up with Flint for it. *Fuck.*

"Me either. It sounded perfect."

Yep. It had been too good to be true. At least they'd dumped me before I'd packed up my life and moved to Maine. I wasn't stuck in a contract, having to work with people I didn't want to be around. *Positive, right?*

"Never fear." He reached for his folder. "This is Hollywood. There are always opportunities. If you are willing to expand our search criteria and are open to taking a step sideways rather than jump up a paygrade, I'll have a lot more options to choose from."

So much for advancing and diversifying my career. "Harlow, I'm unemployed in two weeks. I've never been out of work. That makes me nervous. We were supposed to have something secured by now. Are the other roles still open?"

"HBO is still pending. *Fallow Creek* has been cast."

Damn it. Living on residuals would be hard. My lifestyle would have to change drastically. If something didn't come my way before Christmas, I'd be listing everything I owned on Craigslist to survive. *Shit.* I didn't want to have to sell my condo and move into some hovel where I wouldn't feel safe.

"Sutton. I will find you something. Please. Trust me."

They were words that didn't sit well in my gut. But I had to listen to my intuition. I'd chosen Harlow to be my agent because he was good at his job. I'd asked him to do the impossible—

finding me a new role within three months instead of six to twelve. I'd been foolish. This industry didn't operate that quickly. Castings took time. I had to give Harlow more leeway. "Okay. You're right. Do it. Expand the search. I know we've been avoiding typecast roles, but that's what might suit me best. I've liked the roles I've had, so I should play to my advantages."

"That's a smart move. I'll also scope out minor movie roles, extras on TV episodes, and some short-term gigs." He pulled out a few printed pages stapled together with his company's logo on the top.

I couldn't read what they said.

"In the interim . . ." He flicked through the four-page document. "I can talk to Izzy, my commercial agent. She can put you forward for some TV advertisements or product endorsement deals. Some can be lucrative . . . some are *meh* and don't pay much."

He handed me the printout with *"Commercial Product Endorsement Agreement"* printed in bold letters across the top and bulleted clauses covering the rest of the pages.

I sat two inches taller. Louis Vuitton, Chanel, L'Oréal, and BMW flickered through my mind. I could see myself on a billboard draped in exquisite Tiffany jewelry, or, hell, I'd been a living, breathing, walking advert for Grey Goose Vodka lately. I could do this. "I'm not sure I'm model material, but I love luxury goods."

"Oh, sweetie." Harlow chuckled and lowered his chin. Crinkles formed at the edges of his eyes. He peered at me sideways. "Those expectations of yours need to come down quite a few levels. You're not a trending A-list celebrity. Think more along the lines of low-to-midrange products—toothpaste, affordable clothing chains, food franchises."

I sank three inches and flattened the pages against my thighs. Bile billowed up my throat. I'd thought I was a somebody, but I wasn't. All this publicity had gotten me nowhere. I'd wanted to move up in the world but had failed. My ambition, hard work, and dreams had taken a cutting blow. But I wasn't down and out. Not yet anyway. I had to stop pretending to be something I wasn't. Flint had fallen for a version of me that wasn't real.

I wasn't flashy gowns and red carpets and fancy nights out.

That was all hype. All for show. Exhausting.

But I'd never acted when I was alone with him. My pretenses had disappeared after our first date. When he had panic attacks, caring for him had come from my heart. I'd had one of the best nights of my life hanging out with him, the guys, and Maddy at Hayley's Bar. I'd felt most comfortable with my hair in a bedhead mess, wearing his oversized T-shirt, curled up in his arms on his sofa. I'd been true to myself when we'd talked on the beach, when he'd run lines with me, and we'd hung out. He'd always treated me like I was his sun, his moon, his world. He'd made me feel special . . . like I *was* someone.

He'd opened my eyes and freed me from my sheltered, naïve world.

He'd changed me. Seen me. Loved me.

And I'd fucked it up with lies.

It was time I was honest with myself.

The opportunities that Harlow had dangled in front of my face would've been amazing, but I hadn't landed them for a reason. They weren't me.

I might be destined to be a B-grade actress for the rest of my days. I had to accept that. It paid the bills. It allowed me to live a great life. The paparazzi rarely harassed me. There were a lot of positives.

But was commercial work a new low? A step backward? After sixteen years on television, were advertisements all I was good for? *Fuck.* Considering my circumstances, I couldn't be too choosy.

"Harlow? You want me to do product endorsements?" I swallowed the dry lump in my throat. "Is this a wise move?"

"Absolutely." He nodded. "Sutton, millions love you for your sweet, all-American girl nature. But you've grown into a gorgeous young lady. You have this new glowing, mature, confident edge mainstream folk will connect with. We don't represent D-grade, starting out actors. Our clients are respected corporations. This might be the diversification you've been looking for."

"Can we be a little selective?" I didn't think I'd be the best choice to promote baby diapers. I was too young to play a mom. But . . . I could sell toothpaste. I had perfect teeth. A decent smile. *Shit.* I couldn't believe I'd succumbed to considering ads.

"We sure can." Harlow nodded. "It's your call."

I liked that. My decision. My choice.

Harlow sat back and rested his arm along the top of the sofa. "Are you still up for some publicity with Flint? It was obvious you two were involved. Are you talking after your fight?"

"No." I smoothed my hand over the paper resting on my leg to distract me and stop more tears from falling. Just hearing his name tore at my heart. "We're done."

"That's a shame." He softened his tone. "I'm sorry it didn't work out. You two were perfect together."

I smirked and shook my head. "There's no such thing as perfect. We weren't that." Thanks to me.

"Sutton?" His tone lifted. "I assure you, I will find you a role. I have a couple scripts and casting calls coming in over the next few weeks. One is from the agent for a new show filmed in Atlanta. One is for a series that will be based in Detroit. Until I see the details, I don't know if you're suitable. But that doesn't mean I won't stop looking elsewhere. More flexibility will give me more scope to find new opportunities."

"Okay." I folded the document and popped it into my purse.

Why were so many shows filmed outside of LA these days? *Damn cost of production!* No doubt whatever role I landed, I'd have to move.

I had made the right choice to end things with Flint.

Harlow waved his finger toward my handbag. "Read through that agreement and let me know what you think. If you have any questions, call me. If it's something you want to consider, I'll introduce you to Izzy."

"I'll let you know within the next few days. Thank you."

After my meeting with Harlow, I walked outside. Numb, upset, confused, and pissed off about not landing the *Hollow Cove* role, I went for a walk down Melrose. Cars zipped by. A warm breeze blew through the trees. People dashed back and forth along the sidewalk. They were all a blur. With every step, my heart grew heavier. My pace, slower. Wrapping my arms around myself, I trudged along with no destination in mind.

Laughter caught my ear. I stopped outside a trendy café. At the tables, friends and couples chatted over lunch, drinks, or coffees. The hole in my heart doubled in size. Flint was right. I had no one to share my life with. No one to laugh with. No one to hang out with. I'd had that with him. For a couple of crazy months, I'd had it all.

Was the chance to have fleeting moments like that worth it if I had to move away?

No. I couldn't go there. He'd never forgive me for breaking his heart. I couldn't blame him.

Dragging my feet and my tattered heart along the street, I called an Uber and headed home. I grabbed the script off my desk to read over the lines for next week. It was only lunchtime, but I changed into my pajamas and crawled into bed.

I couldn't concentrate reading.

I tossed the script aside. Shuffling underneath the quilt, I tugged the pillow beneath my head. I shuddered and shivered.

Closing my eyes, I let the tears flow.

Darkness clouded my mind. I sank deeper and deeper into the mattress and curled into a ball.

I'd lost Flint. I had no job. I had no exciting prospects.

There was nothing to look forward to.

I had no reason to get up in the morning.

Oh, God! I'd turned into Flint.

Chapter 34

FLINT

On Sunday morning, I drove to my parents' house in Pasadena. A box of Phil's belongings sat on the passenger seat beside me along with a thick file from my office. My parents should be at home. It was their Sunday tradition to walk to the local patisserie, buy croissants and pastries, then head back to have breakfast outside on the deck overlooking the garden. It was 10:32 a.m. They should have a steaming cup of coffee in hand and be reading the world news on their tablets. I hoped the six months that had passed since the accident hadn't changed their old habits.

It was time to tell them about Phil.

Sutton had made me see everything in a new light. I had been overprotective. Too caring. But not anymore. Now I didn't give a fuck about anything. My parents hadn't talked to me since February; they may never talk to me again. But at least they'd know the truth. I had nothing to lose.

I pulled into the circular driveway and parked by the steps. I killed the engine and stared at the front door of their Spanish-style two-story home. Nothing had changed. Neatly trimmed hedges. Green lawn. Same potted plant standing on the front porch. The dry, decaying remains of the flowers I'd bought for Mom's birthday had been kicked into the garden bed. *Fuck!* But the wine had gone. *Hmph.*

Here goes nothing.

I wiped my clammy palms on my jeans, grabbed the pile of Phil's stuff, then headed for the door.

I rang the bell and waited.

And waited.

And waited.

I rang it again.

I waited.

And waited.

They were there. Their cars were in the garage, plain as day through the slatted wall.

I peered up at the security camera and waved. Were they checking the app on their cell phones to see who it was? Were they arguing over letting me in? Who would answer the door? Or . . . were they pretending not to be home? It was awfully quiet.

I peered through the window toward the living room but couldn't see anyone through the sheer curtain.

I rang the bell again.

Two more minutes passed.

Fuck. I wasn't leaving until I knew for sure that they weren't there. I'd break into the fucking house if I had to.

I placed Phil's stuff on the welcome mat by the front door and walked around the side of the house. The five-foot-high solid fence loomed before me. I checked the gate. It was locked.

I jumped to steal a look at the back deck.

Oh. My. God. They were sitting at the table with pale looks on their faces.

Fuckers. They knew I was there.

"Mom? Dad?" I called to them. "Let me in. I'm not leaving until you do."

Silence.

"Please?" I jabbed one hand on my hip and rested the other one against the fence, my patience wearing thin.

Fuck this. If they weren't going to let me in, I'd just have to climb over the damn fence. I grabbed the trusty potted plant and placed it in front of the gate. I gripped onto the top rail and put one foot on top of the pot. Vaulting skyward, I hauled myself up and swung my leg over the top of the fence, crushing my balls as I lay suspended over the edge. *Ow!* I sat upright, pulled my other leg over, and hopped down onto the lawn.

I wiped my hands off on my jeans, adjusted my poor throbbing nuts, then held my hands out wide. I smiled at my parents. "Surprise."

My mother gaped.

My father shot to his feet. His wicker chair scrapped against the terracotta tiles. "What are you doing here? Get out." He pointed to the fence I'd just scaled.

Mom's eyes watered. "Oh, Flint. No."

My heart shattered. After all this time, they still didn't want to see me. Tears stung my eyes, but steely resolve set in my bones. I wasn't leaving until I'd done what I came to do. I took slow steps toward them. "It's been long enough. Don't you think?" Stopping at the bottom of the three deck steps, I placed my hand over my heart. "I miss you. I am not your flesh and blood, but I'm your son. It's not my fault Phil died. Please, talk to me."

Tears streamed down my mom's face as she shook her head.

Ice set in my father's eyes. "No. We lost him because of you. You did this. You broke our family."

I clenched my hands. My teeth. My jaw. "No. It's taken me a long time to accept that I didn't."

"You've always been the reckless one," my father spat. "The one always in trouble. The one always fooling around."

"See?" I took a breath to keep calm. Yelling and turning this into a scream-fest wouldn't help. "That's where you're wrong. You thought Phil was perfect, but he wasn't. For my entire life, I've taken the blame for all his crap."

"Stop." Mom slapped her hand on the table. "I won't have you ruining the memories of Phil. He was my baby."

I took another step forward. "And so was I."

"Please." Dad winced. "Just leave."

The back of my eyes burned. My heart didn't want to beat. It hurt too much. "I will." My chin quivered. "Once I give you something. Let me explain it, then I will be gone. Give me five minutes, tops. I beg of you. Please?"

Mom looked at Dad. I couldn't see what transpired in their eyes. It seemed like minutes passed by but in reality, it was only a few seconds before Mom nodded.

My father sighed and shook his head. He returned to his seat but didn't look at me. "Five minutes, then I call the cops."

I pointed toward the house. "It's by the front door."

"Fine." My father flicked his hand, then took a sip of his coffee.

I bolted inside, unlocked the front door, and grabbed the box of Phil's things. But as I walked back through the living room, my heart collapsed. My knees weakened. I'd been in such a rush before, I hadn't noticed the changes.

The walls used to be full of photographs of Phil and me—at school, at our first gig, and on our twenty-first birthdays. The bookshelves used to be overflowing with family holiday photos in frames. Trinkets that Phil and I had bought our parents for Christmas used to be on display in the glass cabinet. Now . . . they were all gone. Not one remained.

Holy. Shit. They erased us from their lives. *What the fuck?*

But I'd done the same with Sutton. I hadn't called her. I'd drunk myself stupid. I'd torn up and deleted the lyrics I'd written about her. But I couldn't forget her. Not ever.

A tear slid down my cheek. I smudged it into my skin with my hand. Guess I knew how this thing with my parents would go down. *So be it.*

Trembling all over, I strode outside and placed the box on the table. I didn't know where to start. My hope had been obliterated.

My mother sat still as a statue, except for the occasional sip of her coffee. Dad's cold, hard glare sent chills through my chest. Every muscle in his body was tensed, like he wanted to lunge forward and strangle me.

Gripping onto the back of the chair, I took a shaky breath and found a fragment of composure. "I was delusional too. I thought Phil was perfect. I loved him with my every breath. I never wanted him to get in trouble, so I often took the blame for what he did. I did it so much, so often, it became a habit. One night, when he was six and I was eight, you both came home from work, and Dad, you saw that your Lakers statue was broken. Phil had been dancing around with it, showing it off, and dropped it. I knew you treasured that thing. I knew he'd get a hiding for it. I didn't want you to hurt him, so I took the rap."

I hadn't been able to sit on my ass for two days after that flogging. "When I was sixteen, and we had that fight at school over Shelby . . . he started it because he liked her, and I never knew. I said I threw the first punch because I didn't want him to get suspended."

Doubt loomed in my mother's eyes. But I ignored it and kept going. "When we started playing, I often had to sneak Phil back into his room because he was too drunk to walk. Even the other guys had told him to tone it down. But he never did." I reached for the folder and took the top sheet out. I placed it on the table for them to see. "He got done for DD on a night without me and the guys." Yeah, the printout of his ugly mugshot was far from attractive. "I bailed him out, so you'd never know the truth."

My mother's hand shot over her mouth. Deep grooves furrowed into my father's brow.

"He was always picking fights, causing havoc, trashing rooms." I placed prints of photos I'd found on social media of Phil's escapades on the table—a fight, the stitches he'd gotten from being hit in the eye, and one of him with a blood lip. I added a few photos onto the pile of him swarming with groupies, his tongue down some chick's throat, and one of him dancing, spraying champagne over everyone in the middle of a dance floor. Now that . . . had been a good night. "He kept our publicist busy. We covered the trails for most of his mistakes. The ones we couldn't, I took the fall for."

"All this *is* your doing," my dad hissed. "You dragged Phil into this lifestyle, this scene, this wild behavior."

"I didn't drag him into anything. He loved music as much as I did."

"You should've been more responsible."

"I did all this because I was responsible." I slapped the folder shut. "I am no saint. But the music always came first. I've always been in control. Always been the leader. But . . . he resented me for it." I dug into the box and pulled out Phil's notebook of lyrics, the last ones he wrote. "In the last few months, he took more and more drugs."

"No." Mom shook her head. "Not our Phil."

"Come on." I straightened. "Let's be real. You saw his toxicology report after the accident. He was fucking high as a kite."

"Please. Stop." Mom closed her eyes and fidgeted with her gold necklace. "None of these things matter." A tear trickled down her cheek. "He's gone."

"I know none of this will bring him back." I placed my hands on the table and lowered my head. "But I needed to get this off my chest. I'm done protecting him. You need to know the truth." I ran my hands over the cover of the book. "Did you know Phil had problems? With me? He was jealous. Angry. Fame had gone to his head. Phil resented me being the front man."

"What?" Red blotches broke out on my dad's cheeks. A fiery rash crept up his neck. "Phil would never do that."

"It's all here." I pushed the notebook toward them. "These are the lyrics and stuff he wrote during his last few months. They're hard to absorb, but you need to read them."

"Phil loved you. He didn't do drugs."

"Yeah. He did." I pulled my cell phone out of my back pocket. "This is the last thing I want to show you and then I'll go. Again, I kept this from you so you wouldn't think less of him." I found the video on my cell phone and placed it on the table. "Don't watch it . . . just listen."

I hit play. The dark video of the dashcam footage on the night of the accident flicked across the screen. I didn't need to watch it either. It played vividly in my mind.

Phil's voice hollered from the speaker:

"I got Rici, man. I scored the hot chick. I was on fire tonight. Oh, she wanted me . . . not you. I'm the fucking rock star. Me. Not you. What's it like to lose for a change? Did you see me? On the pool table? I fucked her good. So good. I got the girl you liked. Suck on that, asshole."

"I don't care." My groggy, drunk voice came through the cell phone.

I closed my eyes. We'd just turned onto the Boulevard. Phil gunned the car faster and faster.

"Slow down. Are you fucking crazy? You'll kill us."

He'd just run a red light.

"No way, man," Phil hollered. *"That shit I got off Dave tonight*

was awesome. I'm totally buzzed. I'm wired. I'm alive. I fucking rock. I am soooo fucking sick of you telling me what to do. Do this. Don't do that. Just get out of my face. I'm the man. Not you. So get used to it, Flint. I'm not holding back anymore. I'm better with the girls. I'm better than you. Always have been. Always will be. You think you're so fucking good? Well . . . you're not. But you know what I hate most? More than anything else on this planet? Is cats. I hate fucking cats."

My gut cinched and flooded with nausea.

"Phil. No," I'd wailed. *"Not the cat."*

I hit stop before the screeching tires and the sound of breaking glass and crumpling metal played.

I wiped the tears from my eyes. My mother's cheeks were wet as she clutched her hands over her heart. The rims of my dad's eyes blazed red.

I sucked in a shaky breath. "I hate that I wasn't able to stop him driving that night. Hate that I survived and he didn't. But it wasn't my fault." I tapped the notebook. "He never told any of us how upset he was with me or the band. Not once. Cole and Slip were just as shocked as I was. Did he ever say anything to you?"

Mom shook her head.

"I miss him every fucking day. I lost my brother. We lost our record deal because I haven't been able to play since he died. I've been a fucking mess, coming to terms with the accident. Over you shutting me out. I still can't get the accident out of my head and probably never will. A girl, Sutton, helped me get better." I sniffed. "But she left me too. The guys and I will rebuild. We're not going to stop doing what we love. We're good at what we do. I'm no angel, but I'm not the total asshole you think I am. I didn't do everything I've claimed to have done."

Mom placed her hand on the notebook, opened it to the first page, and glided her fingers over Phil's handwriting. "I can't believe he's gone."

I gripped the back of the chair again. "For me to move forward, to stop blaming myself, and to let go of some of the guilt that eats me alive, I needed you to know the truth. He was no rainbow unicorn. I ate more of his shit than I should've. And it never tasted like cotton candy."

I grabbed my phone and stuffed it into my rear jeans pocket. "I miss Phil . . . every fucking day. But I miss you just as much. I lost you too that night. I hope one day you find it in your hearts to forgive me. But you know what? What's important now is that I forgive myself. To do that, I had to tell the truth. I owed that to myself and Phil, out of respect."

"Flint." Mom's voice was weak and faint. She didn't move in her chair. She didn't even look at me. "I'm not ready. It hurts too much. I'm so sorry."

Dad sat frozen in time. The only sign of life was the dampness on his lashes.

I wiped the tip of my nose with my hand. *Shit.* "Okay. What I've shown you is hard to absorb. It took me days and months to process all this new stuff about Phil. So, I'll leave you too it. If and whenever you're ready to talk, I'll be waiting."

Mom nodded and wiped her eyes.

"We can take baby steps." *Fuck.* Sutton's words *again*, not mine. I'd lost a good thing there, too. I should've fought harder for her. I missed her. But why waste my efforts if she wasn't willing to fight for us? She'd never seen past the reckless rock star. Neither had my parents. Why waste my energy on them if they weren't willing to meet me halfway? "We can do coffee. Meet for a drink. Anything. I just want you in my life." I splayed my hand over my heart. "I want my mom and dad back."

"Please. Just go." Dad waved toward the door.

My heart was so broken, there was nothing left of it to shatter.

Every artery hardened. Calcified. Solidified.

Nothing could ever touch or hurt me again.

I'd lost Phil. My family and Sutton.

But I had my guys. My music. I didn't need any more of this shit. I took a step backward toward the house and held my arms wide. "Fine. You know where I live. I'll see myself out."

Before my knees gave way, I turned and rushed out the door.

My parents may never talk to me again, but at least they knew the truth.

As I drove home, ice claimed my soul.

I wiped the tears off my cheeks. No more would fall.

Resolve hardened my heart.

Fuck lying and covering for anyone ever again.

Chapter 35

SUTTON

For four weeks, I'd been in zombie mode. I'd learned lines, gone to work, done my scenes, gone home. I'd gone to the wrap party and said farewell to the cast and crew I'd spent six years of my life with. The worst thing was, I'd probably never see most of them ever again. I'd texted Flint a few times to check in on him, but I'd had no reply.

I deserved that.

I'd hoped, after everything that had happened, we'd be able to remain friends.

No such luck.

I had a few auditions coming up for small parts in indie movies. Nothing that qualified as a lead or lead-supporting role, but they were *name-at-the-end-of-the-film* credit worthy. I'd signed the product endorsement agreement with Harlow's agency. I'd met with Izzy, and she'd been excited to put me forward to be the face of a skincare range sold through Sephora. But after having deals swiped away in the blink of an eye, I didn't want to get my hopes up until the contract was signed.

None of those opportunities overly excited me. Every day, it was a struggle to get out of bed.

Nothing could heal the hole in my heart from losing Flint.

All . . . my own stupid fault.

But Maddy was home for a few days.

She'd insisted on dragging me out for a night on the town. She wouldn't accept my broken, healing ribs as an excuse . . . and they were feeling better.

In slinky party dresses, towering high heels, and with long fake lashes adorning our faces, we lined up to enter the night club. A few people recognized us, which was always a small thrill but didn't hold the same appeal as it used to. We had photos with them. I laughed at the guys trying to hook up with Maddy, but it wasn't enough to lift my spirits.

After twenty minutes, we made it inside.

Maddy took my hand and led me into the dark depths of the venue. Music blared. Lights flashed. People jostled everywhere. "Georgia was good for some things, right?" she asked.

Bypassing lines had been nice, but I'd liked chatting with the fans. Flint had been right. Simple things could be fun. I slipped onto a stool at a table near the bar. "No. I was happy to wait."

But now the problem was, I just didn't want to be here. It was too loud, too crowded, too cramped. It was nothing like Hayley's Bar, the laid-back music venue Flint had taken us to.

"I'll grab drinks." Maddy smoothed and tugged her short skirt lower. "I'll be back in a sec."

While I waited for Maddy, I checked my emails, Instagram, and Facebook. Mainly to see if Flint had posted anything, but no. He hadn't. There'd been nothing from him for weeks. Nor the guys. It made the distance between us seem even greater. I hoped he was okay.

A few minutes later, Maddy placed a pink lychee martini in front of me. That had been Georgia's favorite drink. Not mine. I was glad I wasn't one of Georgia's sheep anymore, but I didn't want to be a wolf either. I wasn't ruthless and conniving. I just wanted to be me. Be happy. *Damn.* The last time I'd felt that had been with Flint.

I stirred my straw through the liquid and took a sip. I winced at the sickly, sweet taste. "Mads, can you be honest with me? Do you like this martini?"

"Yeah." She straightened, lifted the glass, and downed a mouthful. Screwing up her nose, she giggled. "Actually . . . no. Not really."

"God!" My shoulders slumped. "When did we let Georgia take over our lives?"

"It just happened, didn't it?" Maddy pushed her glass aside. "It was easier to play along and let her organize everything. It helped lower my anxieties. But since she's been gone, I'm happier. I don't care so much about my hair being perfect or my makeup being flawless or whether my purse matches my outfit."

"That's awesome. You look hot, but honestly . . ." I giggled and circled my finger through the air at her. "You look fucking uncomfortable in that dress."

Maddy laughed, hooking her tiny strapless dress higher over her cleavage. "It's ridiculous, isn't it?" She smoothed her hands across her tummy. "I only bought stuff like this because of Georgia. I wanted her to like me. God, I'm pathetic."

"I was too. I was so caught up in my legal cases, I didn't notice what was going on."

Maddy wriggled her shoulders and sat taller. "But she's out of our lives. We don't need to dress like this anymore."

"No, we don't." I stabbed a lychee with my straw, removed it from my drink, and wrapped it in a napkin. "We've been through so much crap over the past couple years, but we've survived. We've found our strength and are finding our way in the world. We will do it without being bullied, manipulated, or treated like shit. And . . . we will do it together." I picked up my martini and forced down a mouthful. I wasn't going to waste a drop of my twenty-dollar drink. "Here's to never being screwed over again."

Maddy raised her glass. "Cheers to that, girlfriend." She downed a mouthful, then flapped her hand in front of her mouth. "Ew! Yuck!"

I giggled. "And let's never buy this disgusting drink again."

"Excuse me?" A girl dressed in a pretty long white peasant dress and clutching her oversized Guess purse against her chest approached us. "Are you Sutton Summers?"

I straightened and smiled sweetly. "Yes."

"Hi." She waved, fluttering her fingers at me. "I'm Rici."

Ice shot through my veins. *Rici?*

Rici took a tentative step forward. "Are you still dating Flint Glover?"

Why did she want to know that? So she could pursue him now he was single? "We're—"

"Going to catch up with the guys soon," Maddy jumped in. "What's up?"

Nice save. Thanks Mads.

"Oh, good." Rici nodded. "I've been trying to contact him for months but he doesn't return my texts. I've wanted to catch up to give him something." She lowered her chin. Trouble furrowed her brow. "That night. Before the accident. I was with Phil."

"I know the story," I said with too much bluntness.

"Oh, right," Rici continued. "When Phil and I were . . . um . . . together . . . this fell out of Phil's pocket." She dove into her purse and pulled out a small velvet pouch. "I put it in my bag so he didn't lose it. I meant to give it back to him, but . . . never got the chance."

"Why don't you take it to Flint? Or mail it to him?" I asked.

"I don't know where he lives. I moved to Dallas two days after Slip's party. I forgot this was in my bag. I missed the funeral because of my long-haul roster and don't fly through LA anymore. I'm here for a friend's birthday and brought it with me, hoping to track down someone to get it to him." A touch of shyness slipped into her tone. "I don't know the guys that well. I saw them play a couple of times. I had a crush on Phil. My friend Jessie, who used to date one of their lighting techs, took us to Slip's party." She fidgeted with the pouch. "I wanted to get this to Flint via Jessie's friend, but he's taken off on the festival circuit since The Flintlocks haven't been playing."

LED lights flashed in my eyes. My head pounded with the booming drum beat from the DJ. "Wait. What? You were into Phil?"

"Yeah. He was hot." Sadness darkened her eyes. "But . . . we only had one night together."

"I'm sorry." I tried to be compassionate and considerate, but my mind spun on new revelations. I'd always considered Rici a threat, vying for Flint's attention. Flint had liked her, but the feelings weren't reciprocated. We'd both gotten it wrong. I sat straighter. "So . . . you're not interested in Flint?" I had to hear it again.

"No." Rici shook her head. "What made you think that?"

I grimaced. "I questioned your texts." *Fool. Idiot. Insecure moron.*

"Oh, no. I'm sorry. I hope I didn't cause any issues. I only wanted to give him this." She dangled the pouch. "Will you take it to him for me? I fly out early tomorrow."

"What is it?" I held out my hand and she dropped the small bag into my palm.

"Um . . . it's a bracelet." Rici said. "It was Phil's birthday present for Flint."

"Oh." I tipped the metal bracelet into my hand. Heavy chain

links clasped an ID bar. I flipped it over and read the cursive inscription:

We may not be blood, but we are brothers.
Let's rock until the end of time.
Love you, bro. Phil.

I covered my mouth with my hand. Tears stung my eyes. *Oh, Flint. Phil really did love you.*

I nodded to Rici. "I'll make sure he gets it. I promise."

"Thank you." She touched my arm. Gratefulness swung in her sweet tone. "I have to get back to my friends. It was nice to meet you, Sutton. Enjoy the rest of your night."

Rici disappeared into the crowd.

I ran my fingers over the cool metal, then slipped the bracelet back into the pouch. Now what was I going to do with it? Post it? Drop it in Flint's letterbox?

"So?" Maddy's eyes glinted in the disco lighting. "When are you going to see Flint? You have an excuse to see him now."

"Never." I stuffed the bracelet into my clutch. "I'll post it to him."

"Sutt, you miss him, don't you?"

My heart shuddered. I automatically went to deny it, but I pulled myself up short. No more lying—not even to myself. "Yep. Like crazy."

"Then call him. Try to work things out?"

My stomach sank to the floor. "I have. He hasn't responded. He doesn't want anything to do with me, Mads. It's over."

"Where's the new Sutton who fights for what she wants? The one who doesn't take shit from anyone?"

"I broke his heart."

"Yes. For being stupid about a few thousand miles and completely missing the fact that he wanted to move for you.

You just shut him out. Commuting isn't that bad. I loathe flying, but I come home once a month to see you and my mom."

"I did what was best."

"For who? You're miserable thinking you did the right thing. You were in love and wanted to end on a high. But you left when you'd only had half the glass. You haven't had the whole drink. You never gave yourselves the chance to find out if you could work. You don't have closure. You need to ride it out until you either fill up your glass, fall more in love and live happily ever after, or hit the bottom and burn each other to a cinder. Only then will you know if you were meant to be. This *I'll-never-know-if-we-could've-been-happy* zone sucks."

"He doesn't want anything to do with me. Am I supposed to go over to his place and bash down his door?"

"Yes, if that's what it takes." She clasped my hand across the table and squeezed it. Her tone softened. "Do you love him?"

"You know I do."

"Then fight for him. Make it work."

A slow song came on and couples filled the dance floor. I hated watching people being all loved up and happy. My chest grew hollower with each slow, angsty beat.

She jerked her head toward the dancing couples. "Sutt, you want that."

I sniffled and nodded. "I do, but I fucked up."

"You did. But you could fix it." Maddy's cell phone buzzed on the table. Eyeing the notification, she caught her bottom lip between her teeth. She met my gaze and smiled. "What would you do to make it right? If you had the chance, would you give him another shot?"

I wanted to but I was afraid of breaking us further. "Mads, what can I possibly offer him? I have no job. No prospects. No set plans. I hurt him."

"But he's miserable without you."

"How do you know that?"

"Um . . ." She threw me a sheepish smile. "I kinda keep in touch with Slip."

"You *what?*"

"We're not together. Just texting."

"Oh. My. God. Madison Reed. Why didn't you tell me?"

"There's nothing to tell. We're just friends. But he's worried about Flint. He says Flint acts like a robot. He's playing but has no emotion or energy. His heart is dead."

"Yeah, I killed it." I hated that he was hurting.

"Then fix it," Maddy pleaded. "You helped him get over Phil."

"That was different."

"No, it isn't. It's all heartbreak. I know you've been hurt. We all have. But don't deny yourself the chance to be happy. We're too young not to take risks. We need to be crazy. Fall in love. Make mistakes. I promise I'll be here for you if it doesn't work out."

I stared into my martini. "I wouldn't know what to say to him."

"How about . . . I'm sorry. I fucked up. I love you. Take me back."

"It wouldn't be that easy."

"Want to give it a shot?"

I glanced around the club full of people I didn't know. The noise hurt my head. This place wasn't me. I'd discovered many things about myself since meeting Flint. That I preferred bars over nightclubs. Cappuccinos over fancy lattes. And the biggest thing I knew for sure was that I loved Flint.

Was Maddy right? If I got a job elsewhere, I could commute. I loved travel. I'd done long-distance with Beau when he'd moved to New York. It had turned into a disaster because of who Beau and *I* were at the time. We'd been at different points in our lives and careers. Too young to settle down. During all the drama with my father and my paranoia over Beau's behavior, I'd been treated like shit and manipulated, and I'd lost my self-worth. I'd been too inexperienced and insecure to know any different. But now I knew I deserved better than that. Flint had never treated me like crap. He'd made me face my insecurities head on. He'd made me feel good about myself. I was not that same girl anymore, and Flint wasn't Beau.

Flint loved me. I loved him. I'd never given us the chance to be anything. *Stupid fool.*

I wanted him. There was no one else.

I would never give up my career, but with Flint, I wouldn't have to. I would be willing to do whatever it took to be with him. "I miss him so much."

"Then let's go."

"What? Now?"

"Yep. We're going via my place. Getting changed. Then going to The Velvet Vault."

The Velvet Vault? A live music venue on Sunset? "Why there?" It would be ticketed. We wouldn't get in.

"The Flintlocks are playing. Slip just sent me backstage passes. You're going to see Flint."

"Am I?"

Oh, shit.

"Yep."

Okay, I can do this. Oh, wow! I was going to see Flint.

Chapter 36

SUTTON

Backstage at The Velvet Vault, Maddy and I followed Jude, the security guard, down the corridor to the band's dressing room. With each step, my heart clambered toward my throat. I had no idea what to say to Flint. My head hurt as I juggled through different scenarios, each one more pathetic than the last. We stopped outside the door that had *The Flintlocks* printed on a yellow piece of paper and sticky-taped onto it.

Jude knocked.

I hooked the strap of my clutch higher on my shoulder. *Okay. Breathe. I can do this.*

"Come in." Slip's voice bellowed from the other side.

Jude opened the door. Holding onto the handle, he leaned into the room. "Visitors," he announced, then left.

Placing my hand on my churning gut, I let Maddy enter the dressing room first. My feet hesitated at the threshold. Steadying myself, I took a deep breath then stepped inside.

Within the span of two seconds, Slip, dressed in ripped, faded blue jeans and a black leather vest, jumped up from his seat next to Cole on the sofa and rushed over to greet Maddy.

Cole, spinning his drumsticks around in his hands, caught sight of me, gaped, and waved hello. Then my gaze went straight to the back of the room. *Holy. Smoking. Hotness.* Flint, in black leather pants and a tight T-shirt that accentuated his toned muscles, sat with his back to me on a chair in front of the mirror. Leather bracelets and cuffs with silver studs were wrapped around both his wrists.

I locked onto his kohl-lined icy gaze reflected in the mirror. My breath lodged in my throat. The eyeliner just quadrupled his level of sexiness. Every hair on my body tingled and stood to attention. Between my legs throbbed just looking at him.

He spun on his chair and leaped to his feet. "What are you doing here?"

The anguish in his voice punched me in the chest.

Wiping my clammy palms on the white T-shirt and floaty short skirt I'd borrowed from Maddy, I took a tiny step forward. "I was hoping we could talk."

He growled, low and gravelly, and gnashed his teeth. "No. We go on stage in ten minutes. We need to prep."

"Please." I inched forward but was met with a daggered glare that stopped me in my tracks. "Just for a minute."

He closed his eyes. His brows pinched together. Tension radiated off him, rippling through every taut muscle on his face, in his arms, and in his clenched hands. I'd done this to him, to us. The weight of my mistake crushed me.

I couldn't breathe. Each nanosecond he didn't move was excruciating.

Slip sighed and slapped Flint on the shoulder. "For fuck's sake, just hear her out. Look on the bright side. I doubt if she can make things worse." He placed his hands on Maddy's waist, spun her toward the door, and shuffled her forward. "We'll give you five minutes. That's it."

But Cole draped his arm over the back of the sofa and sank

deeper into the seat. "Oh. I'm not going anywhere. I want to see this shit go down."

"No, you don't." Slip grabbed Cole underneath his elbow, dragged him to his feet, and shoved him out of the room. The door banged shut behind the three of them.

Flint ruffled his fingers through his hair, enhancing his already tousled, messy hairdo. It didn't help with my concentration.

"What do you want, Sutton?"

My head spun with a thousand things to say. I struggled to see through all the clutter in my mind to make sense. "To talk. I miss you. I messed up on so many levels. I'm sorry."

Shaking his head, he stepped backward. The second his ass connected with the counter, he lowered onto it. "It doesn't matter."

"Yes, it does." I took a tiny step toward him. "What I did . . . how I treated you, the things I said . . . I was stupid. I was wrong about us and want the chance to make it right."

His shoulders stayed tight, his face void of emotion. He was shutting me out. That was what he did when he was hurting. I know that now.

"There's nothing to make right." The blunt coldness in his voice made me shiver. "Ever since we met, you've had a wall up. You always had one foot out the door, ready to run. It never mattered to you how good we were together. You could never see past the bullshit. But I did. I saw how amazing you were." He rose to his feet and turned to face the mirror, but he closed his eyes. "I fell for you. But I'm over it."

"Clearly." I quirked my head sideways. "How's that going for you?"

"Sutton. I don't have time for this. Please. Just leave."

"No." I glued my feet to the floor. "Don't shut me out like you've done with so many things in your life. You locked yourself away from the world when Phil died to avoid dealing with the hurt and grief. You let your parents think you're an asshole when you should tell them the truth about Phil. Now, you're pushing me away when I'm apologizing and want to fix things."

He spun, lunged forward, and got up in my face. "You broke my heart."

The crippling pain in his voice ripped open my chest all over again.

His eyes darkened. "Now you're here, wanting me to face things I don't want to face. That I'm not ready to deal with. Just like you did to me with Phil, my music, and writing. I confronted my parents. They still won't talk to me. You dared me to have hope and believe I was better. I fell in love with you, but it meant nothing."

"It did mean something." Tears dampened my lashes. "I was afraid to love you."

"You think I wasn't afraid? Everything about you makes me question my sanity."

"Me too. You're nothing like I expected. You're stereotyped in the media just like I was." I took a quick breath, steeling my resolve. *No more lies.* "I was so anxious around you when we first met. You intimidated the crap out of me. But I got to know the real you. The one who is kind, protective and passionate. Talented and inspiring. Not to mention fucking amazing in bed. You saw the real me and you still wanted me. You taught me to be strong and brave." Tears escaped, slipping down my cheeks. "How could I not fall in love with you?"

He stumbled backward and sank onto the counter. "You're finally admitting it?"

"I've known for a long time. But I was scared and couldn't let go of my past. Almost everyone I've cared about has left or burned me. They killed my trust and faith in love. They stripped away what I thought was good in the world. But then you came along. You pushed me out of my comfort zone at every opportunity. You pressed my buttons and made *me* face things I'd never dreamed of. Being with you has been confronting and challenging. Life-changing. You are . . . without a doubt . . . the best thing that has ever happened to me. You taught me how to stand up for myself, showed me more good times in the past few months than I've had in my entire life, and made me feel more loved and adored than ever before."

His shoulders slumped. "Then why did you leave?"

"I made a mistake." I tossed my clutch onto the sofa and eased toward him. "I wanted to avoid getting hurt but failed."

"Too fucking right."

"I'm so sorry. I cut us off before we had the chance to see if what we had was something amazing or was meant to die a slow, painful death. I want the chance to find out. Fully. Completely. All in."

"Why?" He closed his eyes. "We're already dead."

"Do you honestly believe that? Is that what you want?" My heart drummed in my chest, praying, begging, pleading for him to say no. But I got nothing. If he was done with me, I'd have to accept that. I'd done this to us, not him. But I wasn't giving up without a fight. I had nothing to lose now if I had already lost him.

I dashed forward and clutched his hand against his thigh. "Flint, I'm crazy about you. Head over heels in love with you. I don't want to be afraid anymore. I've had time to assess my life since the accident. You helped me discover who I am and what I want. I'm not an innocent sweetheart. I'm not an A-list diva or a total wreck or a party animal. I'm just an average hardworking girl who loves you." No matter what happened, I'd always be grateful for learning more about myself. I was sure that road was far from over.

He lowered his chin but squeezed my hand. There was life in him after all.

"Flint, I was so worried about finding work, I forgot to slow down and appreciate everything I have achieved. I can survive and have learned to appreciate the simpler things in life, like cappuccinos and vodka. I'm not going to and will never give up acting. I love it too much. But I'm not in a rush or hell-bent on landing another role. Until something comes my way, I'm doing one-off appearances on some TV episodes. I've been a fill-in on a movie set. I've signed up to do TV commercials and product endorsements. I'm working. I'm paying my bills and being true to myself. I have you to thank for that."

He tugged his hand free. "So if you land a role, you could still move?"

"Yes." I forced my way between his legs and caught his face in my hands. He didn't pull away. Closing my eyes, I rested my forehead against his and breathed him into every one of my cells. "But I will do whatever it takes to make us work. I will fly, drive, or hightail it on a train to see you, wherever you are. Even when you're on tour. If I only get to see you once a month, it's better than not at all."

"You said you'd never trust me."

I combed my fingers through his hair, then clutched onto a fistful of it softly at the back of his head. "It's hard for me to trust people. But I trust you. You've never lied to me. Never given me reason to doubt you. I'm sorry it took me so long to realize that. So please give us another chance. My heart is yours."

He tilted his head back and met my gaze. He swallowed hard. "You played me once, Sutton. How am I supposed to believe you?"

"What does your heart tell you?"

"You kinda destroyed that."

"Then trust your gut." I cupped his cheek. I missed touching him so much, my fingers trembled. "What does it tell you?"

"Run." He smirked.

Anguish buckled my knees. "Please don't."

"Sutton." His voice dropped so low I struggled to hear him. He caught my hand and lowered it to my side. "Stop."

"No." I shook my head, fighting the sting in my eyes. "If you still love me, don't give up on us."

Pain rippled across his face.

What could I do to get through to him? This couldn't be the end.

"I made a mistake. I'm sorry. But it doesn't mean I don't love you. Sometimes, no matter how much it hurts and terrifies you, you have to take risks." I swiped a tear off my cheek. "Just like at the club tonight when I saw Rici. I didn't want to talk to her, but my gut said *listen.*"

"Rici?" He grimaced.

"Yes." I sucked in a deep breath and sniffled. "To cut a long story short, I found out why she'd being calling you. She wanted to give you this." I slipped over to the sofa, dug into my clutch, and pulled out Phil's bracelet. I placed it in his hand.

He rolled the velvet between his fingers. "What is it?"

"Rici ended up with this on the night she was with Phil. She moved interstate and has been trying to contact you to give it to you."

He tipped the jewelry into his hand.

"It was your birthday present from Phil."

He turned the ID bar over and read the inscription.

> *We may not be blood, but we are brothers.*
> *Let's rock until the end of time.*
> *Love you, bro. Phil.*

Tears welled in his eyes.

"Flint, you know in your heart Phil loved you. I've seen how much you loved him and the lengths you went to in order to protect him. He had issues, like we all do. It's tragic that you never got to sort them out. I don't want that to happen to us." I fanned my hands over my chest. "I love you. With all my heart."

He just sat there, clutching the bracelet in his fist.

Exhaustion seeped into my bones. My head hurt as much as my heart. I couldn't think of anything else to say. He knew how I felt. I'd apologized, but I was too late. I was a fool for not being honest. Lesson learned. One that would haunt me for the rest of my days. But at least I'd tried and given him my all.

I flicked a tear from my cheek and sniffled. "Okay. I've said what I wanted to say and have given you the bracelet. So, that's it. Thank you for hearing me out." With my heart bleeding across the floor, I took a few steps back, the small distance already making me miss him. I grabbed my clutch and headed for the door. Halfway across the room, I paused and spoke over my shoulder. "I'm sorry. I fucked up. I love you, Flint. Always will . . . Good luck with the show."

"Sutton." His voice rasped like gravel.

I spun so fast, I stumbled on my feet. "Yes?"

Pain darkened his eyes. "I never wanted to lose you."

"I know."

He clutched the front of his T-shirt and tugged on it. "I'm in this zone, this void, where music is in me, but I can't feel it. I can write, play, and sing, but it doesn't touch my soul. I want the walls to break, but I can't push through them."

My heart cried for him. I whispered, "You're forgetting to take baby steps."

"How?"

"May I?" I held out my hand toward him.

He closed his eyes and nodded.

I stepped over to him, grasped his hand, and held it against his heart. "Close your eyes. Breathe. All you have to do is remember. When was the last time you played, sang, and felt music in here? When did it make you feel alive, swirl through your veins, and touch your heart?"

He shuddered and winced. "When I was with you. On stage. At Hayley's Bar."

Tears pricked my eyes. That had been one of the best nights of my life. "What was so good about it?"

"You believed in me. Gave me the push I needed. Made me feel again."

"Then let me do that once more." I spoke over my tears. "I promise. No more lies. Let me love you."

He shook his head slowly. "Not if you plan on fucking leaving."

"I won't." I cupped his cheek. "Unless the world wills it."

"Not even then."

"Okay. I promise." I nodded. "I just want to be yours."

"Do you have to be so impossible to resist?" His hand shot up and clasped the back of my head. He crushed his lips against my mouth. Relief flooded through me in rolling rapids. My heart thundered in my chest as our tongues lashed out to taste each other. He bit, licked, and sucked my lips, bruising them and driving me crazy with each brush of his mouth. Knotting my fingers into his hair, I tugged him closer. Heat ignited my body. He spun me around and shuffled me backward until my butt connected with the counter. As he lifted me onto the surface, he edged between my legs. He drove his hardness against my crotch, teasing my core. My insides clenched with an aching hunger.

"I've missed you. So fucking much," he murmured over our kisses. "I can't stop loving you. I can't switch it off."

"Then don't. I don't want you to."

"We need a new deal."

I tilted my head to the side to give him access to my neck. "What are the conditions?"

"No more bullshit. No lies. And do whatever it takes to be together. Forever."

"I like those terms."

"One more thing."

"What's that?"

"Take off your panties."

"But you have a show?"

"It can't go on without me. It will kill me if I don't have you."

I injected a touch of sauciness into my soft voice. "Are you going to fuck me here in the dressing room like a groupie?"

He caught my chin between his fingers and tipped my head back. "You will never be a groupie. You are mine. And mine only."

"Can you lock the door?"

"If you take off those panties."

"Okay, deal."

He rushed to the door and flicked the latch. I slipped my hands underneath my skirt and eased off my tiny pale-blue lacy panties. This was crazy hot. The hungry, animalistic fire that blazed in his eyes ignited my want for him. I was so turned on, so overwhelmed that he wanted me, my head spun with dizziness. I raked my gaze over his gorgeous face, chest, and legs. *So hot* "You look so fucking hot in leather pants."

He stopped three feet in front of me. He arched an eyebrow, licked his lips, and swallowed hard. "And I love you in short skirts. Now . . . spread your knees."

Oh, my hotness. I eased up my skirt and widened the distance between my thighs. My breath quickened. As I sat exposed in front of him, my vulnerability quaked but my core clenched in anticipation.

A low growl rumbled deep in his throat. "That . . . is mine."

Dropping to his knees, he claimed me with his mouth.

I gasped and fell back against the cool glass. His hot tongue, torturous touch, and the smell of his cologne had me in a sensory overload. I wrapped my leg around his back. My hips bucked and pulsed against his onslaught. He worked me so hard and fast, licking, and sucking and fucking me with his tongue, my vision blurred. All the pent-up tension, my love for him, and relief he was in my arms exploded beneath his fiery lashings. I came in less than thirty seconds. "Oh yes. That's so good." But before I could catch my breath, he rose to his feet, unzipped his pants, and thrust his throbbing cock inside me.

Shivers darted up my spine, tingled my scalp, and rippled across my skin. He drove into me again and again, unrelenting and quick. With my orgasm still spiraling through my body, electric shocks of pleasure charged through my veins. I kissed up the side of his neck, rushing my breath across his skin. "I've never had sex in a dressing room before."

Grunting, he crushed his lips to mine. He pummeled me and panted; there was nothing sweet and gentle about him taking me. I fucking loved it. I wanted more. I'd take anything he'd give me.

His searing breath brushed across my lips. "How can you not have had sex in a dressing room?"

"I was waiting for the best."

"God, I love you . . . Fuck, I've missed you."

With a sharp drive of his hips, he spilled into me. Convulsing and shuddering, he wrapped his arms around my shoulders. His lips found the small of my neck and kissed my sensitive skin. "That's just a taste of what is in store for later tonight. You okay with that?"

"Oh, yeah."

He withdrew and tucked himself back into his pants. He grabbed me the box of tissues on the other side of the counter to clean up. But when I reached for my panties, he grabbed them and tucked them in his pocket. "No. They're mine. You won't be needing them. You'll have to get into my pants after the show if you want them back. To do that, you'll be coming home with me. If you think we've had wild sex before, you are delusional. I'll make sure I ruin you for anyone else."

"You've already done that." I slid my hands over his chest, loving his hard pecs beneath the soft fabric. "There will never be anyone else. I only want you."

"Good answer." He swept my hair off my face and kissed me.

There was a loud knock on the door. "Flint? It's time."

Cole.

"Okay," Flint hollered. "One sec."

He gazed into my eyes and stole my heart all over again. "There is something about you, Sutton, that has infused into my soul. I never want to lose you again."

A fresh tear fell onto my cheek. "Me either. I love you."

He brushed his thumb down my damp cheek, erasing my tear. "No more of them, all right?"

"Deal," I whispered.

"Flint?" Cole slapped his hand against the door. "Let's go."

Flint dashed over and opened the lock.

Cole stumbled into the room. His gaze jumped back and forth between Flint and me. "You two make up?"

"Yeah." Flint nodded. "Just needed a good ass-kicking."

"About time." Cole pumped his fist in the air.

Flint caressed the side of my head. "I have to go. But we'll continue this right after the show."

"I'll be waiting."

He brushed his lips against mine, stealing my breath. "You gonna watch us bring the house down?"

"I wouldn't miss it. Show me the way."

Chapter 37

FLINT

I took to the stage. My head still spun from what had just gone down with Sutton. She was here, watching me from the wings with Maddy. Hope returned to my chest with a vengeance. The love I'd been trying to stomp out of my heart simmered back to life. Hell, who was I kidding? When it came to Sutton, I just wanted to leap off the highest mountaintop and let the wind take me wherever it desired. I may fly or fall, but for now ... we were together. I'd learned to treasure every precious moment and face my fears. With Sutton by my side, I could do anything. And best of all ... I could do what I loved. *Sing.*

The crowd hollered and screamed as I grabbed my electric guitar off the stand and hooked the strap over my shoulders. Striking the strings, I listened for any feedback in my ear monitors. Soundcheck seemed like a lifetime ago, not hours.

I gave a thumbs up to Gena, our sound tech, sitting at the control panel. Having our crew—lighting, sound, and equipment—back together again warmed my chest. I'd missed them. Missed this energy and excitement.

As I stepped up to my mic, my heart pounded. Nerves

jittered in my belly. It had been way too long since our last gig. But this was where I belonged. On stage. With my best friends. I took a deep breath and cleared my mind. "Evening, folks. How is everyone at The Velvet Vault doing tonight?"

The partygoers clapped and cheered and waved their hands above their head.

"It's good to be back. It's been a while." I scanned the room. "Sorry I've been AWOL for a few months, dealing with the loss of my brother. But thanks to these two guys, Slip and Cole, and a very special lady, the gorgeous Miss Sutton Summers, for kicking my ass, The Flintlocks are back and are here to stay."

I glanced to my left, where Phil used to stand. Evan, the bassist from Duke's band, filled the space. He'd offered to help us out for a few gigs. My chest ached, missing Phil, but I was okay. His bracelet jingled around my wrist. I closed my eyes for half a second and said a silent prayer.

I miss you, bro. You will rock with me forever.

I turned to the crowd. "Are you all ready for some music?"

"Yes!" "Woohoo!" and "Yeah!" sounded muffled through my ear monitors.

"Let's do it then."

Cole tapped his sticks together. "One. Two. Three."

He slammed them against his drum kit and led us into our first song, "No Way Home." We followed it with our hits, a medley, and then a few of the songs off our albums that only the true fans would know. I loved that quite a few were here. Squinting beneath the blazing stage lights, I could just make out the first couple of rows of people singing along to my lyrics.

That hit me in the chest, hard and heartfelt.

When one person, let alone a whole room full of people, knew our songs, it made this all worthwhile. My words touched listeners. Affected them. That was freaking awesome.

At the end of each hit, the weight that had been pressing

down on my shoulders lifted. The beat coursing through my veins renewed my energy, my zing, and my love of music. Most of it was thanks to Sutton.

Crazy woman. And yeah, she was mine.

Near the end of our set, on cue, our lighting technician dimmed the lights. I wiped the sweat from my face on my shoulder, handed my electric to Joel, our stagehand, and grabbed my acoustic. I pulled up a stool in front of the mic. Slip joined me.

I adjusted my mic. "Hey, folks. Time for a new song." A roar erupted from the crowd. I placed my fingers on the strings and plucked the notes. I swayed to the melody, waited for the fans to settle. "This one's for Sutt."

> *There is one thing you always said to me,*
> *Don't care how much it hurts, just be honest with me.*
> *Tell me the truth, even if it breaks my heart,*
> *Falling in love with you was a risk from the start.*
> *Didn't think the blow would hit me so hard,*
> *Didn't think when I said I loved you we'd ever part.*
> *'Cause when you were gone, I missed . . .*
> *I missed your touch. Missed your kisses. Missed you in my bed.*
> *Must have been a fool 'cause you messed with my head.*
> *But no matter how much I tried to forget,*
> *I can't stop recalling . . .*
>
> *How you turned the night into day,*
> *Blew the gray clouds away.*
> *Made the sun want to stay,*
> *Got me on my knees to pray.*
> *And say . . .*
> *I love you, babe.*

Time to ad-lib and change the next verse since the night had taken an unexpected turn. Taking a deep breath, I eased into the lyrics that filled my head.

> *There is one thing you always said to me,*
> *Take it slow and remember to breathe.*
> *Couldn't do that without you in my arms,*
> *'Cause girl, you're the one who holds my heart.*
> *I wanted the chance to make things right.*
> *Praying must've worked, 'cause you're here by my side.*
> *I love your touch. Love your kisses. Love you in my bed.*
> *Must be true love, because it's like you never left.*
> *But no matter what our future holds,*
> *I just want you to know . . .*

> *You turn the night into day,*
> *Blow the gray clouds away.*
> *Make the sun want to stay,*
> *Got me on my knees to pray.*
> *And say . . .*
> *I love you, babe.*

I played the last note, leaped from my stool, and rushed over to Sutton on the side of the stage. I cradled the back of her head and drew her lips to mine. Despite sweat trickling down my face, my hair clinging to my skin, and perspiration coating my lips, I kissed her hard and hot. She was my girl. I was never going to let her go.

"I love you," I whispered.

"Love you too."

Her hot breath on my face gave me shivers and weaved its way around my heart. I was hers. Only hers. Forever.

She ran her hand over my soaked T-shirt and tapped my chest. "Now get back out there and finish up so we can be together."

"On it."

We played out our last three songs, ending our show to a sea of applause and cheers. On an adrenaline-fueled high, we bowed and waved farewell. I rushed off stage, flung my arms around Sutton, picked her up, and twirled her around. "I can't believe you're here."

She squeaked, grabbing hold of the bottom of her skirt. *Oops, no panties. I'd nearly forgotten about that. Not!*

"You were awesome." Letting go of her skirt, she wrapped her arms around my neck. There was nothing sweeter than her body against mine, the taste of her lips, and her soft voice in my ear. "I loved my song."

"*Mmm.* Better get used to it. The next album might be all about you."

"That makes me nervous."

"You should be."

Cole play-punched me in the bicep. "So glad you two made up."

"Yeah." I tucked Sutton underneath my arm and kissed her head. "I needed my girl back."

"Thank fuck." Slip wiped sweat from his face with a towel.

"Evan." I shook his hand, then slapped him on the back. "You were awesome. Thanks."

"Anytime." He dipped his head. "Great crowd tonight."

"They were, weren't they." The high still surged through my veins. "God, it felt good to be back on stage. Let's clean up and celebrate."

"We'll meet you at the bar." Sutton kissed me on the lips then took Maddy's hand and dragged her toward the front of the venue.

I didn't miss Slip's longing glance at Maddy. They'd been texting ever since they'd met. That was how I'd found out about Sutton's role falling through and her new work. I might have to bend the dibs rule for them. I'd just have to live with the consequences if it all turned to shit.

After a shower and changing into fresh clothes, the guys

and I ventured out to the bar area. The obligation to mingle with fans and partygoers following our show was sweet torture. I loved meeting the ticketholders, signing shirts, and smiling for photos. But my balls begged me to get Sutton home. Every glance she gave me didn't help—the sexy glint in her eyes, the hunger burning in their depths, the wickedness in her winks, and the subtle way she played with the hem of her skirt—and drove my temperature higher and higher. I nearly blew my load when she sat on a stool, made sure no one else was looking, then flashed her pantie-less crotch at me. The little bite of her lip had me close to coming undone. No way would the Sutton I'd first met boldly flash me in public. She really had changed. So much. I adored her even more. The zipper on my jeans had nearly snapped when she'd hugged me tight and crushed her groin against my throbbing dick. I burned from the inside out. After forty minutes, I couldn't take it anymore.

I slapped Slip on the shoulder. "The rest of the night is yours. I'm outta here."

"Pussy power, huh?"

"You bet. Make sure Maddy gets home safe."

"Me? Why me?"

"'Cause you're into her. It's as obvious as the dick on your forehead."

"We're . . . just friends."

"Yeah. Right. We're outta here."

Slip's mouth hit the floor. "But . . . but . . . we're just friends."

Chuckling, I downed the last of my beer and placed the empty glass on a table. "But you want to be more."

"I won't break the dibs rule, man. What if it didn't work out? Sutton and Maddy are best friends. It'd cause problems."

"True. But what if it worked?"

"Get out of here." He pushed me on the shoulder. "I've seen love fuck up too many people. Especially you. So, I'll pass, thanks. I'll stick to groupies and one-night stands."

I wasn't so sure about that. But I'd let him be.

I said goodnight to Cole and Maddy, then grabbed Sutton by the hand. "Let's go."

She didn't falter as I veered via the dressing room to collect my gear and headed outside to the parking lot. "Are you okay with my place? It's closer."

"Won't the long drive to my place and delaying gratification be worth it?"

After tossing my gear in the trunk, I caught her by the hips and pinned her against the side of my Ferrari. "I have waited long enough. I don't want to cause an accident. And what I want to do to you should be done in private. It's forty minutes to your place. Ten to mine."

Her chest swelled. Her heartbeat raced. "Yours is good."

I drove home in record time.

Just inside the hallway, I grabbed Sutton around the waist and pressed her against the wall. I rained kisses down her face and over her lips, and fire coiled through my veins. She was here. *Mine.*

She tugged at my T-shirt, yanked it off my head and tossed it on the ground. "I know we've only just made up and have things to work out, but can we talk after more makeup sex? I'll go as fast or as slow as you want. We'll go at your pace."

I ripped off her shirt. It joined mine on the floor. "Is fast okay with you?"

"I'd like that."

I cupped her breast and raked my thumb over the pale blue lace of her bra. It matched the lacy panties I'd kept before the show. "This is a bit sexy."

"I bought the set because they were the same color as your eyes. I'd wear them to remind me of you."

"You missed me that bad?" I eased her bra off and dropped

it on the floor.

"Every day." She curled her hands around my shoulders. "It was like an enormous piece of my heart was missing." So much sorrow and regret swirled in her eyes.

We'd both made mistakes. It was time to put the past behind us and move forward. "Two broken pieces can make a whole, right?"

"Yeah. I think that's what we are."

She grabbed my belt and unzipped my jeans. I quickly discarded them and my briefs, along with her skirt. Pressing my naked body flush against hers, I gazed into her gorgeous brown eyes. Our breaths entwined, hot and heavy. She was my everything. My new reason for living.

Rocking my hips forward, I rubbed my cock against her bare pussy. "Hmm. I've missed you. Let's make up for lost time."

"Live like there's no tomorrow?"

"Absolutely."

Gripping her thighs, I lifted her up and wrapped her legs around my waist. As she linked her hands around my neck, I carried her to my room. I yanked off the bedcovers and laid her gently down on my mattress. Her lips sizzled against mine. Her touch burned my flesh. I wanted her so badly. My brain screamed at me to hurry. But no . . . Now I was here, I wanted to take it slow. Adore every inch of her body. Worship her. Thank her for saving me.

Trailing kisses from her lips down her neck, I meandered toward her breasts. The sweet perfume of her skin ignited my senses. I tasted her body like it was an elixir sent from heaven. Catching her smile, and hearing her laugh, her moan, and her wanting mewls as I made her come embedded into my heart. The gaping hole that had been there for so long was filled, creating a new home that belonged to her.

She kissed up the length of my chest scar and made her way

to my lips. "I love all of you. Every scar. Every wound. Every piece of you."

"Sutt." I cupped her soft cheek. "I'm not gonna lie. We have a long way to go. But I want you here. With me. I don't ever want you to leave. You are my new muse."

"Oh . . . your muse?" One fine eyebrow arched skyward. "I've never been one of those before."

"No acting required. Just be you."

"I like the sound of that."

Flipping Sutton onto her back, I hovered over her. My shoulder was much better thanks to physical therapy and working out. I glided my hand over her silky-smooth skin, down her chest. Cupping her breast, I teased her nipple between my fingertips. Her eyes fluttered closed as she arched toward me. Pleasuring her would be my new favorite pastime.

I wanted to rush, go slow. Savor every second, race to the finish line. But we had all night. We had tomorrow off. I had no plans to leave my bed until she was beyond sated and satisfied.

As I glided my fingers lower, heading between her legs, my pulse quickened. I worked my index finger between her folds then dipped into her arousal. My breath hitched. My dick jolted. Her warm wetness tempted me to eat her out again. "I love touching you. Watching you tense, wanting me to be inside you."

"Yes. That would be good."

I smiled against her lips. It seemed like a lifetime since I'd smiled and felt it in my heart. "Patience," I whispered, playing with her clit. Once her hips bucked against my touch, I delved one finger, then two, inside her.

She moaned. Arching her back, she dug her nails into my shoulders. I flinched but loved the pleasurable pain. She tugged me closer. "Stop torturing me."

"Me?" I kissed up the length of her throat. "Why, Sutton?

What do you want?"

She hooked her leg over my hip and drew me down on top of her. Wriggling beneath me, she eased my cock toward her opening. "Exactly what you want."

"I want you. That's all."

Taking a deep breath, I pushed inside her. Just the tip. Then withdrew. Then pushed all the way into her depths. I closed my eyes. My heart pounded. I took a split second to thank every god in the known universe that I got to be with her again. That we'd found our way back to each other. That our stupidity hadn't destroyed us.

Her hands swirled across my back, tingling and electrifying my every nerve ending.

Within a heartbeat, I drove into her again. Rocking my hips, I found rhythm, penetrating and thrusting into her. Harder.

Our bodies were made for each other.

Panting and pulsing, I slid my hand down her thigh, raised her knee, and drove into her deeper. Sweat slicked our skin. Good thing I had stamina; I didn't want to stop. But my dick had a mind of its own. It throbbed, searching for that spot inside her to hit and find release. With a deep drive of my hips, she tensed. We connected with just the right friction that drove me wild. Fire burned in my core. My muscles tensed. Her insides clenched around me. *Shit! Hold on.*

"Flint." Her lips parted. "Oh. Wow. There."

I clutched onto the sheet, nearly ripping it off the mattress. I drove deeper. Deeper. Deeper.

Her fingers raked across my back. Her breath came in short, sharp breaths.

"Sutt?" I hissed, not able to form any other coherent sound.

"Oh, babe. Yes." Her body convulsed and quivered beneath me. The most gorgeous smile curled across her lips as she laughed.

I let go and spilled into her. "I'm with you." *Thank God!* I couldn't have held out another second. Coming had never felt so good. Hot rushes coiled through my veins, shuddered through my bones, and wrapped around my heart. I closed my eyes, and my head fell back. Even my toes tingled. "Wow. That was good . . . for round one."

I collapsed beside her on the pillow and draped my arm over her hip, every inch of our bodies aligned perfectly.

Her heart pounded against mine. "I like makeup sex."

"Good. Because in a minute or five, there will be more."

"I'm down with that. But promise me after tonight, we never have to have makeup sex again."

"I pray we never do." I caressed her face and kissed her lips. "Sutt, I want us to work. I want to do this right. While I'd love you here by my side every night, I think we need to take things slow. We need to rebuild trust. I want to date you. Take you out to dinner. Hang out. Write songs about you. I don't want to ever feel like you're going to walk out on me again."

"You won't. I'm not going anywhere. I want to wake up next to you on Sunday mornings. Run lines with you. Spend every holiday, like Halloween, Thanksgiving, and Christmas, with you."

"On one condition."

"What's that?"

"We start now."

"Deal."

Rolling on top of her, I kissed her until I saw stars swirling before my eyes. I buried myself inside her again, making love to her until she shuddered and screamed my name.

I'd never felt this loved. Never had a connection this strong. She wasn't the baby step I needed. She was my forever.

Chapter 38

SUTTON

By the end of October, six weeks after Flint and I had gotten back together, my daily routine revolved around scouring the Internet casting call sites and having Harlow send my portfolios and show reels to opportunities that caught my eye. Over the past few weeks, I'd done several stand-ins on movie sets and had been to more auditions. Nothing had come to fruition yet. But I was actually enjoying it. There was no pressure or long hours spent in the studio. And although I missed the atmosphere and stability of working on a show, the change of pace was nice. I met with Izzy and Harlow every two weeks to discuss potential roles and commercials. Earlier in the month, I'd had coffee with Shona, my old producer. She was in line to work on a new show and had recommended me to the casting agent. Harlow had sent them my online audition and I'd had a face-to-face callback two weeks ago, but I hadn't heard anything since. That was a sure sign it was dead.

But something good had come out of working with Izzy. I was now the face of the GerberaNaturals skincare range. I loved being pampered on set for photoshoots. It still weirded me out that by Thanksgiving, my legs, smile, and hands would be plastered on billboards, grace the pages in magazines, and fill shop windows promoting beauty products. I never in a million years would've thought I'd end up modeling in any shape or form. I was no Gigi Hadid or Adriana Lim. No Georgia. But I didn't have to be, or want to be, anymore. I was done with trying to be someone I wasn't. My all-American charm appealed to the company's "young natural woman" approach for their campaign. The dollars were too good to refuse, the products felt and smelled divine, and the studio shoots were fun.

After a long day of pouting and posing for the cameras, I couldn't wait to take the heavy makeup off my face, soak in a hot bath, and chill out with a glass of wine before Flint and I headed to a party at one of his friend's houses.

I opened my front door and staggered into my condo. The aroma of Thai food filled the air. *Hmm.* Flint had arrived with takeout. *Awesome.* My belly grumbled loudly. I hadn't eaten anything since lunch. But as I stepped around the entrance into my open-plan living room, the bottle of champagne on ice and a dozen yellow roses sitting on the kitchen counter were not what I'd expected to see. Nor did I expect to see him, resting his arms on my balcony railing, with a beer in his hand . . . talking to Harlow.

I dumped my purse on the counter and stepped outside. "Hi guys. What's going on?" Suspicion and surprise simmered in my voice. "Why the flowers and champagne?"

"They're from your new admirer." Harlow slipped his tie through his fingers. "Me."

"Aww." I batted my eyelashes at him, then slapped Flint's arm. "I didn't think you were the flower type."

"Hey." Flint rubbed his arm, then kissed my cheek. "I know you're more of a shoe, lingerie, jewelry, and vodka type of girl."

Hmmm. Okay. He did know me.

"I come bearing good news. Shall we sit inside?" Harlow waved his beer toward the sofas inside.

"No." My heart beat too quickly. "Tell me now."

"Alrighty then." Harlow chuckled and pulled out a folded piece of paper from his jacket pocket. He handed it to me. "We have an offer. Shona came through for us."

"Shona?" My hands trembled as I read the printed email.

Dear Harlow,

TK Ryder Productions would like to offer Miss Sutton Summers the lead role of Sienna Weston in the pilot production of "Angels in LA". Preproduction, writing room discussions, script rehearsals, and readings will commence from January 23rd. Filming will commence at Warner Bros. Studio, Burbank, and various sites around Hollywood from February 12th. We will hold an initial meet and greet with fellow cast and crew on January 7th. We will provide further details on this event once contracts are signed.

We can't thank Shona Wylde enough for recommending Sutton for the role. She will be an asset to our team.

All contracts abide by industry and union standards. All salary, benefits, and insurances are detailed in the appendix of the attached contract. If the pilot is approved, we will proceed with two seasons of production, with the option to add additional seasons at the end of season one.

If you would like to accept the offer or have any questions, please contact Masie Kilpatrick, TKRP Casting

Director, by November 7th.

Yours sincerely
Terry Kirkley-Ryder
Owner/Director
TK Ryder Productions

My hand shot over my mouth, and I screamed. I jumped up and down. I pumped my fists in the air and spun around. *"Oh. My. God.* I got a role. I got a role. I got a role."

Trembling all over, I threw my arms around Flint's neck and kissed his lips. Then I flung my arms around Harlow's middle and bear-hugged him. My feet wouldn't stand still. "This is so incredible."

"Yes, it is." Harlow rubbed my arm. "Shona worked her magic. God, I love that little lady."

"I'll love her forever."

"She'll be producing the show as well."

"Argh. That is even more incredible." My heart raced too fast. My head spun. I'd have to call her and thank her. It would be so much fun to work with her again.

"I'll grab the champagne." Flint disappeared inside. I heard the cork pop and moments later, he returned with two glasses, one for me and Harlow. He had a fresh beer for himself.

"To Sutton." Harlow raised his glass. "Persistence and patience have paid off. You certainly are one of my most interesting clients. I love working with you. The bonus is that you two ended up together. That's a first for me. Most other setups I've done haven't lasted."

I nudged Flint's arm. "We almost didn't. But thanks to you, Harlow, I have a new career and . . . I don't have to move cities."

"I do like that." Flint kissed the side of my head. "Babe, you've been to so many auditions, I've lost track. What is this show about?"

"It's like *Sex and the City*. It's about four women who are building their careers, dealing with relationships, and surviving in LA."

Flint wiggled his eyebrows. "Are you playing *Samantha* so we can practice all the sex scenes before your shoot?"

"Ha. No. I'll be playing a junior executive at a firm who has a thing for her boss. We'll be the sexual tension in the show. He secretly likes her too, but they never get together. It will be such a fun role to play." I clapped my hands. "I can't wait to meet the other girls. I have no idea who they are."

"I do." Harlow pulled out his phone and scrolled through the screen. "They are . . . Peyton White, Mia Avery, and Tia Tanner. They've all had some experience on smaller shows. I can see the four of you hitting it off."

"Wait." Flint shook his head. "Did you say Tia Tanner?"

"Yes."

"Um . . ." Flint gave me a strange look. "That's Cole's sister. I didn't know she was leaving her show. Cole hasn't mentioned anything."

"Not to me, either. I can't wait to meet her. This is so exciting. I got a role." I jumped up and down again. Twirled around. But before I broke my balcony, I stopped dancing. I took a deep breath in, then let it out slowly. "Okay. I'm good. Harlow, I'll have my lawyers review the contract tomorrow and send it to you. I won't get too excited until I have signatures on the page."

It might have been a bit late to contain my excitement. It had already invaded every pore on my skin.

"Excellent." Harlow sipped his champagne. "I've already had my lawyers review the offer. It looks clean. They're paying above award. It's all legit, with no hidden fees or scrupulous payments."

"Yay!" That was what I wanted to hear. But I would read

every damn line of the fine print. Even after my lawyers had reviewed it. No more mistakes. *Ever.*

"Okay, lovebirds." Harlow downed his last mouthful of champagne and placed the flute on my small outdoor table. "I'll leave you to it. I have to head to Malibu to some gig that Izzy roped me into attending."

"You love it." I followed him inside to see him out.

"It's a tough job, having to go out to lunches and dinners and drink expensive wine just to network and find potential new clients." He chuckled, grabbing his jacket off my dining room chair. "But I'm happy to sacrifice myself for the cause."

I opened the front door for him. "Someone's got to do it, right?"

"Absolutely." He swooped in and gave me a farewell kiss on the cheek. "Congrats, Sutt. I'll talk to you tomorrow."

"Thanks, Harlow. Bye."

I closed the door and locked it.

A hot buzz rushed through my blood. I rushed to the balcony, grabbed Flint by the hand, and dragged him into my bedroom. I pushed him onto my bed and straddled his lap. My heart raced as I ripped off my shirt and tossed it aside. Before he could draw a breath, I wriggled off his jeans and Calvins.

"Sutt? You don't have to rush. We have plenty of time before the party."

"I know." I unhooked my bra and flicked it aside. "But this is celebration sex. Hot. Quick and crazy."

"I can do that." He drew my lips to his and kissed me. "God, I love you."

"And I love you. My new show will be awesome. We'll be together. No moving. No long-distance. No leaving."

"I'd still follow you across the globe if you had to move. But thank fuck you don't have to."

Could it be that life had finally fallen into place? Flint was writing. I was acting. We were happy. All we had to do was let love in.

What could possibly be better than that?

Chapter 39

FLINT

Thanksgiving was a time to make new traditions. Starting with waking up and burying myself inside Sutton. Especially from behind. I closed my eyes, drowning in the scent of floral-perfumed skin. I caught her earlobe between my teeth and gently tugged on it. A small smile curled across her lips as I sucked her lobe into my mouth, massaged her breast, and tickled her soft flesh.

Over the past few weeks, we'd become inseparable. She'd spent more and more time at my place. Our initial three-nights-a-week sleepovers had slowly crept to four, and we were now at five or six. I'd emptied three drawers for her in my walk-in closet, cleared a rack for her to hang up her work clothes, and made space in the master en suite cabinet for her toiletries, makeup, and toothbrush. We'd talked about moving in together but agreed it was too soon. Technically, we'd only been back together for one and a half months, despite knowing each other for nearly half the year. We were content, happy, and enjoying spending time together. Dating. Being boyfriend and girlfriend.

But I was convinced that by the time she started shooting

her show in February, she'd be here permanently.

After making love, we emerged from my room and ate breakfast, and I put the turkey in the oven. Our new holiday tradition would bring together our friends, Sutton's brother, and a few other important people in our lives who had no family around to spend the holiday with. I'd reached out to my parents and invited them to come, but I still had no response. Their loss. I'd finally moved on and accepted how things were between us.

Thanks to Sutton, my house looked like a Thanksgiving festival. She'd set the dining table with a centerpiece of candles, miniature pumpkins, sprigs of wheat and greenery. Fairy lights were draped around the room and a banner hung over the mantle above my gas fireplace. More candles and decorations filled my coffee table in the living room. It certainly suited the occasion. The entire house smelled divine. The burning cinnamon-scented candles and the baking turkey and pies made my mouth water.

With everything ready two hours before visitors were due to arrive—Sutton liked to be organized—we'd had a cup of coffee and were settling into cuddling on the sofa when the doorbell rang.

"Who is it?" I hollered.

The door swung open and in charged Cole, Slip, and Blake.

"What the fuck?" I sat upright. Sutton stayed lying down, resting her head against my lap. I rubbed my eyes and scratched the back of my head. I wasn't even dressed for visitors yet. I was still in my pajama boxer shorts and T-shirt. "Why are you so early? I said midday, not ten a.m."

"Don't you ever answer your phone?" Cole shoved his dessert into the fridge, then took a seat on the adjacent sofa. His leg jiggled. He searched the room. His eyes were wild and lit.

Shit. What had happened?

"Rarely before noon. Why?"

Oh, crap! Was this another intervention? Surely not. Maybe they were concerned I'd become a sex addict and wanted to send me to rehab for that? No freaking way. I could never get enough of Sutton. She was one addiction I was happy to live with.

"Where is it? Your phone?" Slip scanned every surface, spotted it on the kitchen counter, and rushed over to grab it. He handed it to me.

Sutton lifted her head from my lap. Concern etched her features. "What is it? What's going on?" she asked no one in particular.

Notifications filled the screen. Three missed calls from Hunter. One from Blake. Two from Cole and seven from Slip.

Fuck! My heart stilled. My brain jumped to the worst conclusion. What was so urgent? Was someone hurt? Had someone . . . died?

My phone trembled in my hands.

"Call Hunter. Now," Slip ordered.

Without question, I unlocked my screen, found his number, and hit Call. It would be almost one p.m. in New York. I hit my cell phone onto speaker. As it dialed, I pleaded to Blake and the guys. "Just tell me what the fuck is going on?"

"You'll see." Blake had placed several bottles of wine on the dining table and returned to sit beside Cole. He rested his elbows on his knees and rubbed his hands together. But there was an edgy glint in his eyes I hadn't noticed before.

Sutton shimmied closer to me on the sofa, placing her hand on my knee.

None of this settled my stomach.

The call connected.

"Flint? Buddy." Hunter's husky voice filled the air. Cheers

and hollers vibrated through my phone. "Yo, dude." . . . *Kyle.* "Flint, baby." . . . *Gemma.* "Miss you." . . . *Kara.* "Fucking get your ass to New York." . . . *Hayden.* "Shh . . . Hi Flint." . . . *Lexi.*

"About time you returned my call. Well, our call." Hunter's voice drowned out the others.

"Sorry. I've been busy."

"Fucking Sutton is no excuse."

"Yeah. It is." I stroked my fingers through her soft hair and winked at her.

"Okay." Hunter chuckled. "You got me on that one."

"What's so urgent?" My gut wouldn't settle.

Kyle butted in. "We are now the proud owners of EH4 Records."

I sat taller. "That's awesome. You did it?"

"Yep," Kyle said. "We bought the production company that made our last album, started our own label, and have signed an agreement with Ashlem Entertainment to handle distribution, marketing, promo, and tours."

Holy shit! Ashlem was huge. They were one of the biggest independent artist entertainment management groups that chomped on the heels of Warner Music Group, Sony Music Entertainment, and Universal Music Group.

"That's wicked." I was thrilled for my friends. My pulse pumped faster. They loved producing, wrote all their own material, and now had even more control over their future direction. But this news shouldn't have caused a meltdown on my cell phone or for my friends and manager to barge into my home.

Slip bent down, rested his hands on the coffee table, and wriggled his brows. His hyper energy had doubled. "But that's not the best of it. Wait for it."

My heartbeat drummed erratically. *Wait for what?*

"We want to sign you," Gemma hollered. "We want to

produce your next album and help you guys go next level."

"What?" I shot forward to the edge of my seat. Excitement and shock ping-ponged through my brain. "Are you fucking serious?"

Okay, now I understood why I had a gazillion messages on my cell. This was freaking insane. Sutton clutched my knee. Her eyes sparkled like the LED twinkling lights around my room.

"Yes." Hunter slipped into the conversation again. "We want you to be the first band we sign. We love your music and know you're in the market for a new home. We want you. That means we'd love you to come here, work with us, our team, and churn out your new album when you're ready."

"We're . . . we're ready." I glanced at Cole and Slip for confirmation. They both nodded. "I've written a ton of songs. We've been pulling them together. We're happy with where they're going."

"Well, get your asses on a plane and come to New York." Kyle joked, but his voice resonated with an undercurrent of seriousness.

"Wait. Wait." My head spun in circles at one hundred miles an hour. "What's the actual deal?"

"We've sent the contract via email." Gemma's tone simmered with excitement. "It's mostly an industry standard, but you're our buddies, so we're giving you special treatment. High royalties, retention of all music rights, full creative control, the opportunity to use another promo company if you don't want to use Ashlem . . . and the option to fuck off if you hate working with us. We want our friendship to come first, so we've made sure that business won't ever get in the way."

My heart pounded against my ribs. A fevered rush charged through my blood. This was incredible. Everhide had been through so much to reach their heights of success and had a wealth of industry experience we'd benefit from. We could do no wrong signing with them. They'd supported us from the beginning.

Tears pricked my eyes. I was overwhelmed that they had faith in us and wanted to play a part in our future. *Wow!* "I . . . I don't know what to say."

"Say yes," Hayden roared.

Cole nodded like a madman. Slip gave me the thumbs up and a big cheesy grin. Blake dipped his chin, leaving the final decision up to me. I didn't hesitate. "Yes. Fuck. Yes."

"All right." Cole shot to his feet.

"Fuck yeah." Slip joined him.

I leaped up, hurdled the coffee table, and flung my arms around Cole and Slip. We jumped around in a circle, laughing, crying, cheering.

"We're so excited to have you on board." Hunter's voice boomed over our celebrations. "Our guys will talk to your guys. Let's make this happen as soon as possible."

"You bet. We'll talk tomorrow."

"Make it after the weekend," Hunter added. "It's Thanksgiving, and we don't want to fucking work."

"Deal. Chat then." I ended the call. I hauled Blake to his feet and bear-hugged him. "This is going to be awesome." Blake had stuck by us through some crazy hard times, especially during the past several months. He deserved to share in our success. We wouldn't be here without him.

"And a freaking lot of work." He laughed, but already had dollar signs in his eyes.

At lightning speed, I dashed around to Sutton, dragged her to stand, and kissed her. "We've got a new label."

"I'm so happy for you."

Holding her against my chest, I breathed her in. I wouldn't be here without her help. I was in a good place. I had music, my best friends, and her. "Let's celebrate."

I grabbed beer for the guys and a champagne for Sutton. Over a drink, we read through the contract and talked to our lawyer. The offer was better than we'd imagined. We'd sign for sure.

After a hellish year, finally everything had fallen into place.

From midday on, people streamed into my house. Maddy, Steven, Harlow, and Izzy arrived first, followed by some of our tech crew. It had turned into more of a party than a dinner. But we had every reason to celebrate.

We had a few drinks, caught up with everyone, and sat down to a delicious meal. I'd just finished my loaded plate of food when my doorbell rang.

"Are you expecting someone else?" I asked Sutton, sitting beside me.

"No." She glanced around our full table. "Everyone is here."

"Okay." I kissed her on the cheek, then stood. "I better see who it is. Back in a sec."

I opened the door, and the breath shot from my lungs. My knees buckled. "Mom? Dad?"

What the flying fuck?

Mom held out a pecan pie, her hands trembled. "Happy Thanksgiving."

Her quiet voice boomed in my ears. Tears prickled my eyes as I swayed on my feet.

"Son." My dad dipped his chin. *Son.*

"I hope you don't mind us dropping by." Tears pooled on the rims of Mom's eyes. "We're sorry. We understand if you don't want us here. We just wanted to let you know we're willing to try and make amends. If you'd be willing to give us a chance. You're right. It has been long enough."

Avoiding the pie, I flung my arms around my mom. I crushed her against my chest and sobbed. "I missed you. Not having you around made losing Phil so much harder."

"We know." Dad sniffled, placing his hand on my arm.

I drew him into our embrace and clung onto the back of his shirt, never wanting to let go.

"We're sorry." His voice cracked. "Losing Phil broke us. He was our little miracle. And we lost him. But you were our miracle too. Sent to us via an angel. We never loved you any less. You are our son, and I'm sorry if we made you feel like you weren't."

My heart ached. Tears streamed down my face and soaked into my mom's hair. "Then why did you cut me off?"

"You reminded us of what we'd lost." Mom shuddered. "I couldn't bear to see you without him. We wanted everything, every memory, to stay perfect. We didn't know of the things you'd done to protect him or that he'd struggled in the past few months. The accident wasn't your fault."

"I miss him every day."

"We do too," Dad croaked. "And we miss you too."

"A lot has changed." I broke out of our embrace and wiped away my tears with my palms. "But you're here. If you're willing to take baby steps, so am I. You want to come in? We're about to have dessert."

Mom nodded. "Good thing I bought pie."

I kissed my mom on the head and led my parents into my house. "Everyone," I called out above the chatter. "This is my mom and dad. So move your asses and make room at the table."

Sutton's face lit with a warm smile, and her hand shot over her chest.

Cole and Slip rushed over to say hello. Hugs went all around. These guys had grown up with me. They'd missed my folks, too.

I waved Sutton over. She came to my side and slipped her arm around my waist. "Mom? Dad? This is Sutton. My girlfriend."

"Nice to meet you." She shook their hands. "I look forward to getting to know you."

"Like wise." Dad nodded. "Anyone who's tamed this one must be someone special."

"She sure is." I kissed Sutton on the temple.

Returning to the table, we shared dessert around. Laughter and cheer filled my house. It had been way too long since those sounds had shaken these walls. I was truly blessed to have amazing people in my life. They needed to know that.

I tapped my spoon against my beer and rose to my feet. *Speech time.*

All eyes were on me. Good thing I didn't get nervous in front of a crowd.

"Folks. Thank you all for coming. We certainly are a mob of misfits. But I am honored to call you my friends, my family. It has been a fucked-up year, but also one of the best. We lost Phil—may he rest in peace and rock on in our hearts forever. But we gained Harlow, Izzy, the magnificent Maddy, and Joel, our new stagehand—you're a crazy motherfucker, and I love you. But for me, the best thing came in the form of Sutton. Harlow and Blake, Cole and Slip, I will never be able to thank you enough for setting us up. She came in like a wrecking ball, knocked down my walls, and put me back together." I placed my hand over my heart and gazed down at her. "Sutt, I love you. Thanks for kicking my ass, loving me, and just being you."

"Love you," she mouthed, her eyes a little wet as they shone back at me.

I raised my glass to everyone at the table. "To health and happiness."

"Cheers," everyone hollered.

But I didn't sit down. "There's one more thing. We're ninety-nine-point-nine percent sure we've just secured a new record deal. That means a new album is on its way. But even better than that is we'll be playing more. New gigs, big shows, rocking promo, and touring."

"Woohoo." Everyone clapped, whistled, and cheered.

My pulse quickened. "But that means we're missing one vital piece of the pie. I hope, but I'm sure, Cole and Slip agree with me."

We'd had conversations that skirted around the topic, but they'd left it up to me to decide when I was ready. Now . . . I was.

"We're on the same wavelength." Cole grinned.

Slip's eyes lit. "You mean it?"

I sure did.

I felt it in my gut.

My soul. In my heart.

"Yep." My heart pounded. Light filled my soul. Zing zipped through my veins. I filled my lungs, then let my breath out slowly. I checked my head and heart one last time. *All good.* This would be great. This was what we needed.

I clutched onto Sutton to steady myself. I wouldn't be doing this if it wasn't for her. "Put the word out, folks. It's time. It's time for us to find a new bass player."

And they'd better be something special because they had some pretty big shoes to fill.

Thank you for reading SCARRED STRINGS, the first book in
The Flintlocks Rockstar Romance Series.
Would you like to find out who joins The Flintlocks?
Continue the series with Book 2: BROKEN BRIDGES.
The details and information about my other titles are on the
following pages.

Receive a BONUS BOOK, if you sign up to my newsletter.

P.S. If you loved Scarred Strings, would you kindly take a
moment and leave a quick review.
They are music for an author's soul.
Visit this title on Amazon to leave a Customer Product Review.
Thank you.

NEXT IN SERIES

BROKEN BRIDGES
The Flintlocks Rockstar Romance Series - Book 2

NEWSLETTER

Sign-up to my newsletter (approx. monthly) to stay informed about new releases, giveaways, special features and more.
Receive a BONUS EBOOK of
ROCKED - The Price of Dreams.
This is the prequel to the Everhide Rockstar Series.
Subscribe at: https://taniajoyce.com/subscribe

***

FOLLOW ME

You can find me on the following social media platforms.

Amazon: https://amazon.com/author/taniajoyce
BookBub: https://www.bookbub.com/authors/tania-joyce
Facebook: https://www.facebook.com/taniajoycebooks
Goodreads: https://www.goodreads.com/taniajoyce
Instagram: https://www.instagram.com/taniajoycebooks/
Pinterest: https://www.pinterest.com/taniajoycebooks
TikTok: https://www.tiktok.com/@taniajoyce
Web: http://taniajoyce.com

BOOKS BY TANIA JOYCE

For eBooks visit Amazon.
Paperbacks available at all good online book retailers.

The Flintlocks Series

The Everhide Series

Billionaires and College Romance

www.ingramcontent.com/pod-product-compliance
Lightning Source LLC
Chambersburg PA
CBHW020247120726
47904CB00001B/114